# A TIME TO LIVE

## BOOK THREE OF THE TURNING POINT

Mark Wandrey

Blood Moon Press
Virginia Beach, VA

Chris Kennedy/Blood Moon Press
2052 Bierce Dr.
Virginia Beach, VA 23454
http://chriskennedypublishing.com/



Cover Design by Konstantin Kiselyov.

Ordering Information:
Quantity sales. Special discounts are available on quantity purchases by corporations, associations, and others. For details, contact the "Special Sales Department" at the address above.

A Time to Live/Mark Wandrey -- 1st ed.
ISBN: 978-1648550164

*This book is dedicated to the most welcoming person in fandom I knew, the creator of LibertyCon, Timothy Bolgeo, or as we affectionately knew him, Uncle Timmy. Thank you for all you did, and God Speed.*

# Prologue

"Wake her up."

"I don't think that's a good idea, considering the severity of her burns." Dr. Meeker looked at the patient with some concern.

"Do what I said."

Meeker looked from his patient to Michael and back again. After a moment, he went to the wheeled medical cart, removed a hypodermic, and slid the needle into the IV port to inject the drug. In less than ten seconds, the patient's eyes were fluttering.

"You might only get a few minutes," Meeker explained. Michael nodded. "And this could kill her."

"Then she dies." The doctor's jaw dropped. "Get out." He hesitated. "Now." He fled.

Michael walked over to the edge of the bed. The woman was uncovered, exposing most of her naked body. He wasn't interested in her in any way other than clinically. Moist bandages covered the vast burns where her flesh was all but gone. Her face was ruined, and all her hair that hadn't been burned away had been shaved off. He wished he could have let her drown, but he had questions that needed answering.

"You awake yet?" he asked. When there was no response, he reached for one of the moist bandages and laid a hand firmly on the wound underneath. Her eyes shot open, and she screamed. "Ah, there you are."

She looked from side to side in the darkened medical bay, from the beeping bio-sign monitor next to the bed to the IV dripping into her arm, then up at him. "W-who are you?" she stammered.

"You may call me Michael," he said. "And you are LTJG Pearl Grange, acting commander of the USCGC Boutwell. You took command when your captain succumbed to Strain Delta. Afterward, you began assisting in SAR off San Diego." Grange watched him for a moment, her mind hazy from drugs and pain. He was a big man, physically powerful and clean shaven, with ultra-short, black hair. Despite it being dim to the point of darkness in the room, he was wearing sunglasses.

"Are you the one who sank my ship?" He didn't comment. "Are any of my crew alive?" The sunglasses didn't waver. "What do you want, damn you?"

"I want to know if you are who I described."

"Grange, Pearl, USCG," she said through clenched teeth, then added her ID number. Inconceivable pain made her jaw muscles quiver.

He grunted. "Good. Now, tell me what you were doing in the Columbia River a week ago."

"A week?" her voice croaked. "It's been a week? What about my crew?"

"Answer the question, Lieutenant."

Grange's mind was still buzzing, but more of her memory was returning. The fight at the lighthouse. The trip up the river. The attack by the gunships, and the missile exploding. Shock, shattering glass, screaming men and women, then fire and agony. So much agony. Then she had felt the slap of water, and darkness had followed. Until now.

"Where…is…my…crew?" She spoke slowly and deliberately, as if she were talking to a child.

"What were you doing in the Columbia River? Whose orders were you following? Who's in command of this Flotilla?" She felt herself slipping into darkness, her vision like a tunnel.

"Go to hell," she said, the last word a whisper. She drifted into darkness again.

Michael sighed, looking from the unconscious form to the life signs monitor. Her pulse was elevated but slowing. She'd survived the brief questioning, but the stimulants the good doctor had administered had worn off. Michael walked to the door and pulled it open. Dr. Meeker spun on him, eyes wide in surprise. "Your patient is still alive," he said. The doctor nodded. "I'm going to need to question her some more. CVR."

"I'll need your authorization for the supplies."

"You'll have it." He walked out and turned down the hall.

"What then?" Dr. Meeker asked. "I said, what then?" he yelled after Michael's retreating back.

Michael passed through three security doors, all guarded, then rode down in an elevator, getting off at the bottom. Two guards waited there. Both checked his identification, even though nobody on the ship would fail to identify him. Cleared, he walked down the short corridor, turning at the biohazard sign into a room. The space was filled from top to bottom with computers and monitors.

"Good afternoon, Michael," the only person in the room, a woman, said. She had three large screens arrayed in front of her covered in raw data and symbols. She was quite old, with nearly waist-length, white hair held in a single tie at the back of her head. Despite her advanced age, her eyes were bright blue and spoke of extreme intelligence. Like all the non-combat personnel on the ship, she wore a simple, blue coverall. However, she, Michael, and five others had a simple, seven-sided symbol on the right sleeve of their coveralls.

"How are things proceeding, Jophiel?"

"Slowly," she said, shaking her head. "Oh, so slowly."

"Let me see," he said, and he pointed to the only wall not covered in monitors or computer hardware. Jophiel shrugged and touched a control. The wall became a window. On the other side was a cell the same size as the observation room. Its sole occupant reclined in a small, self-supporting hammock in one corner, apparently asleep. As if it knew the wall had become transparent, its tiny, black eyes popped open. It turned its pointy, snouted head slightly to look at him in a strange, uncanny way.

"How do we know it can't understand us?" Michael asked.

"Because aliens only understand English in bad science fiction films. I'm a linguist; it isn't easy to fool me. He's had numerous opportunities to respond and gain some benefits or give away some truths. Never once has he taken the chance."

"Why do eggheads always think aliens aren't smart enough to fool them?" Michael responded. He regarded the alien through the thick plexiglass. The bio seal was perfect, or at least as perfect as mankind was capable of manufacturing, even with the advanced technology they had. "Why should we trust it?"

"Him."

"Huh?"

"Him," Jophiel said and gestured toward the alien who seemed to be watching them through the mirrored window. "He is a male."

"Well," Michael said, "we're running out of time, and we need answers." The alien hopped gracefully from the hammock and padded over to the window. With his stooped posture, reversed knees, bushy tail, and pointed, reddish snout, he really did look like a terrestrial fox. He was half Michael's size. He looked up into his face, which he must have been able to see though the glass somehow. "The Heptagon will meet in a few hours and then we'll have to decide what to do about the Flotilla. If LTJG Grange doesn't give us answers, we'll have to find them somewhere else."

From the other side of the glass, the alien fox stared at him. The two regarded each other, calculating and considering what came next.

*****

# Chapter One

**Morning, Thursday, May 2**

**The Flotilla**

**150 Nautical Miles West of San Diego, CA**

Lieutenant General Leon Rose, former commander of US Army III Corps, stood on the bridge of his ship and looked through binoculars. "I'm on a fucking ship," he growled.

"Yes, sir," one of the bridge personnel said.

Rose took the glasses from his eyes and turned toward the man. "How the fuck does an army general end up living on a fucking ship?" The formerly helpful man shrugged in reply. Rose shook his head and returned to his binoculars.

The USS *Ronald Reagan*, CVN 76, was less than a mile away. Rose might not have known shit about nuclear powered aircraft carriers, but he knew they weren't supposed to be tilting 20 degrees or so and pouring flames from the side. "How in the hell did things gone so sideways?"

"I don't have any details yet," Captain Mays, Rose's assistant said. The man had been with Rose for three years, the longest he'd ever had an aide. Now that general command and his III Corps were no more, the record would never be broken. "The Marines were about to go aboard when a huge explosion blew out the hangar deck."

"You sure it wasn't the fucking Marines who caused the explosion?"

"Pretty sure," Mays said, trying hard to hide his grin. "Captain Rutledge is now in command of the *Essex*. He reports having just over two companies available. One was in those inflatable boats—"

"RHIBs," Rose said, lowering the binoculars. "They call them RHIBs."

"Sure," Mays nodded. "They were in RHIBs, about to climb aboard, when it blew. Rutledge said his men were armed only with small arms, not even grenades."

Rose grunted again and put the binoculars back to his eyes. Whatever was on fire was *really* burning. Jet fuel, maybe? A titanic explosion sent sections of steel cartwheeling through the morning sky. The RHIBs accelerated farther away from the stricken ship. One of the big elevators leaned, then collapsed. The ship slipped further into the water.

"There goes a few billion dollars," Rose said as the ship's nose slipped below the waves.

"What about the reactor?" Mays wondered.

"Least of our concerns," Rose replied.

"Navy reactors are designed to keep from melting down," the still helpful bridge crewman said.

"See," Rose said. "Not our concern."

"You're the ranking military officer," Mays said.

"And the fucking president is dead," Rose said. He didn't sound upset. An undertone of *good fucking riddance* was easily discernable. "Anyone ever figure out what happened?"

"We're a little short on navy personnel just now," Mays said.

Rose nodded. The navy had lost most of their pilots in the fiasco that had allowed Coronado to receive the president. Why hadn't the silly bitch just bailed out, like any sensible person would have? Any other sensible *president* would have.

Rose hadn't met the pilot who had crashed into the president's plane. He only knew the man was at the right place, at the right time. He'd provided vital CAS, close air support, dropping ordnance on exact targets, multiple times, to save lives. Then he'd blown the Coronado bridge—against orders. It had helped, too, because thousands of infected had been flowing across the span, drawn by the battle. Then he went back to helping the Marines, as if he'd never disobeyed orders.

In the end, he'd rammed the president's plane when it was on final approach. Fucking hell, what had gone through the man's head? *Probably the dashboard*, Rose chuckled at his own gallows humor. So now, they had no president. He shrugged. So what? Until she had shown up a day ago, they hadn't had one.

It had only been a few weeks since the plague struck. The scientists called it Strain Delta. Naming the thing had been the end of their usefulness. Eggheads had struggled for weeks to understand the basics of how the disease worked. The only one who had a clue was Dr. Lisha Breda on her oil platform converted to a mad scientist's lab. The eggheads at the CDC were probably eating each other, but Dr. Breda was working on the nightmarish thing.

"Any word from the young lieutenant we sent north?" he asked Mays.

"No, General. Last comm we got was two days ago."

"Another lost soul we'll never hear from again." Rose turned his glasses to look at the oil platform where Dr. Breda lived and worked.

It sat in the sea, stolid, angular, timeless. He dearly hoped she figured out a way to stop the disease, though he doubted it was possible. He turned back to the *Reagan*; it was more than halfway below the waves.

"You see the comms from the Marines coming through the Panama Canal?"

"More shit about aliens?" Rose asked, then shook his head. "We'll see if they get here." He continued watching until the ship was no more.

* * *

**HAARP Research Facility**
**150 Miles West of San Diego**

"One of their carriers just sank."

Dr. Lisha Breda looked up from her coffee and muffin in confusion. "What?"

"A carrier sank."

Lisha could see her assistant, Edith Unger, or Beth as she preferred, was excited and a little scared. "You mean an aircraft carrier?" Beth nodded. "Dear, there's nothing here that can sink a carrier."

"A Strain Delta outbreak on the ship," Beth explained. "Then something exploded."

"Show me," Lisha said, and Beth led her out to the observation deck.

At first, Lisha thought it was just a fishing boat on its side. Then, slowly, her mind put the shape together into a recognizable form. The fantail of a huge carrier was slipping below the waves, flames pouring from it as the great ship sank.

"Oh, that's not good." Hundreds of ships and boats were moving away from the sinking carrier as if it were an infectious person in their midst. Maybe such an analogy wasn't too far from the truth. "Any idea how there was an outbreak?"

"None," Beth said. "Their admiral was on the boat."

"Hopscotch or Hoskins?" She couldn't remember which was right.

"Yes, ma'am."

"Shit," she said and went back inside. They didn't have much to fear more than 100 miles from shore. The converted oil platform served as a base of operations for a research project deemed illegal by most governments.

HAARP, the Human Advancement and Adaptive Research Project, was a cute acronym for an endeavor which had the potential to change humanity's destiny. Through complete mapping of the human genome and comparison against other animals already sequenced on the planet, all possible 'problems' with the species' genetics could be identified and removed. Further, possible improvements could be introduced. Some called it eugenics, others God's work. For Dr. Lisha Breda, HAARP was her life's calling. Then, along came Strain Delta.

Back in her lab, she looked at the computer terminal and sighed. Petabytes of data on HAARP were stored there, and she hadn't done anything with them for weeks. Everything had been backed up in nine locations around the planet. Quietly duplicated, though only a few knew where. Shortly after the catastrophe went worldwide, she'd verified that all the backup locations were offline, possibly destroyed. They were an island in the midst of the storm.

"I need to get this data packed up and mobile," she told Beth, who nodded. "Get Oz on it when he wakes up."

"Yes, ma'am."

The military was coming apart without leadership; that much was obvious. The sinking carrier spoke volumes about the disintegrating situation. More military was coming soon, but would they bring cohesion and control, or chaos and death?

She used her computer to access the rig's various cameras. Thanks to the camera placement, they provided almost 360-degree coverage. Most of the boats and ships were moving away from her rig. One wasn't. It appeared to be adrift only a short distance away. Further out was the distinct and unusual shape of a ship modified to launch rockets. It was obviously under control. Her eyes narrowed as she looked at it, and the beginnings of a plan formed in her mind.

* * *

**County Courthouse**
**Junction, TX**

The howls and barking calls of the infected never stopped, day or night. Colonel Cobb Pendleton woke and stretched, ignoring the dozens of minor aches and pains. They reminded him he was alive and not a snack for the crazies, like the ones below.

"Morning, Colonel."

Ann Benedict was standing outside the office Cobb had chosen to bunk in. She held two steaming cups as she observed him. Her long, dark hair was tied back in a ponytail, and she looked tired, just like the rest of them.

"Good Lord, is that coffee?" he asked.

"Indeed, it is," she said and held out a cup. He climbed off the less-than-comfortable Ikea couch and reached for the cup.

"Hot and black, just the way I love it. What?"

Ann was chuckling. "That's what all you military guys say."

Cobb shrugged. "A lot of my men in the 'Stan preferred energy drinks. I'm one of the old-school types. The kids gave me a lot of shit over it." He blew on the brew and took a sip. Tasted like Starbucks. Eh, better than nothing. "How are the others?"

"Tim and Vance are downstairs, checking on the barricade. Belinda is changing Harry's bandages. He's got a low-level infection. Nicole is doing inventory."

"You guys have been through the shit," Cobb said. "You didn't have a Stryker, either."

"No, we didn't have an armored car. Might have been nice." She took a sip of her coffee. "We wanted to let you get some sleep, then maybe talk about our situation."

"Sounds great. Any chow to be had?"

"MREs?"

"Yum," he said. The look on his face made her laugh. Cobb could see why Vance liked her; she was a straight-up kind of gal. Vance Cartwright was their leader, which he hadn't quite figured out. While the man wasn't a slouch with a gun or basic leadership, Harry Ross was a former Marine, and you'd expect him to be in charge. Weird situation.

"We're one floor down in an old courtroom, and we have hot water ready for MREs."

"Be there in a few minutes," he said. She nodded and left. Cobb walked out into the hall and over two rooms. This space, like several others, was pretty fucked up—a 12-ton armored personnel carrier was wedged in the wall. He'd jumped it over from the adjacent parking garage. A desperate and stupid maneuver. The four survivalists holed up in the courthouse had thrown a rope across to him, but he hadn't seen it.

In the office next to his former APC, half the wall was collapsed. The hole gave him a good view of the neighbors—at least a couple thousand screaming, insatiable infected. As soon as he came into view, they began to cry out, growling and gnashing their teeth at him. Hundreds were on the parking garage he'd jumped his Stryker from. Dozens fought for the privilege of leaping toward him through a hole in the concrete retaining wall, only to fall three stories to the ground. Many were injured when they landed on other infected. They were set upon and, often, devoured.

"It's like something out of Dante," he said aloud. He moved to the edge and looked down. It was like a mosh pit at Hell's gates. They were hundreds deep, surrounding the courthouse on all sides. Some tried to climb on top of others, but they didn't seem to be cooperating. Such attempts ended in bites and, sometimes, gruesome dismemberments. *Damned good thing they don't get along.*

"Hey, Colonel," Harry Ross called out as he entered. Cobb turned around. When he saw the other man, he could see Ross' restrained temptation to salute.

"Just Cobb is fine," he told the man. "I suspect you got your DD-214 some time ago." *Of course, I got my release form some time ago as well. Yet here I am.*

"Just over ten years, sir."

Cobb admired the man's build—he was still thick necked and relatively fit. You could usually spot the leathernecks who'd done more than a term or two. They never quite let go of the lifestyle. Harry looked like he'd gone to seed a little, but who didn't when they passed 40? He had almost ten years on the Marine, and his stomach wasn't flat anymore.

Harry's wife, Belinda, was just finishing with his bandages and helping him back into his shirt. The man looked like someone had taken razors to his abdomen. He saw Cobb looking.

"Infected," he explained. "Fingers, not teeth. Good thing, too. I suspect getting bitten might be a problem."

Over to one side, Nicole Price, Tim Price's wife, was going through packs and bags. Cobb had learned, after they'd been cornered by the mob downstairs, that the survivalists had been forced to abandon their vehicles, taking only what they could carry. He had to admire their survivalist mentality; they'd grabbed quite a bit. Nicole waved him over.

"Can I help, ma'am?"

"I was hoping you would let us salvage what we can from your tank," she said.

"APC," he corrected immediately. "Sure, help yourself."

"I was hoping you'd say that," she said and pointed to a pile by the door. Standard military ammo cans were stacked neatly, by caliber, next to other ordnance and his three surviving M4 carbines. "I'm afraid those automatics will come in handy."

"Trouble?"

"You looked outside lately?" she asked.

"Yeah," he said and half grinned at the memory of relieving himself. She narrowed her eyes at his expression, no doubt wondering if the army guy was all there.

The door to the courtroom opened, and Vance Cartwright and Tim Price entered. Tim was tall and muscular, with thick shoulders, whereas Vance was more of the stereotypical accountant type. The two moved together with a sort of familiarity that spoke of long-time friends. Both had AR10s, the .308 caliber version of the AR platform, cradled in their arms. The ARs had a lot more stopping power but were heavier and sported smaller magazines.

"Morning, Colonel," Vance said. Tim just nodded.

"Cobb is fine," Cobb replied. "We're all in this shit together."

"That's true," Tim said.

"We're good for a bit, so let's get some chow. Afterward, I'd like Cobb's input on our situation."

"You bet," Cobb said. They took seats at the long counselors' table below the judge's bench, and Nicole brought in a pan of boiling water. Belinda retrieved seven MRE breakfast packets, and soon they were all tearing plastic and pouring water. In no time, the courtroom was filled with the smell of military maple sausage and French vanilla cappuccino.

"I kinda miss the old veggie omelet," Harry mumbled.

"I always thought you Marines were crazy," Cobb said. "Now, I know it." There was general laughter as they ate.

"I like eggs," Tim admitted. "But that veggie omelet wasn't what I'd call eggs." Cobb nodded and Harry shrugged. "We have two cases of Mountain House eggs with bacon in my truck."

"You feel like going to get them?" Vance asked. Tim shook his head. The group was quiet for a time as they ate.

Cobb noted that two women gave Ann their toaster pastries, which she quickly devoured. He wondered if they were a favorite of hers. She didn't offer them anything in return. He filed the information away for later.

"Okay," Vance said when he was done eating. "Give me a hand?" he asked Cobb.

"Sure, let me grab my gun." He'd left his rifle by the door when he'd come into the courtroom. He still had his personal M9 in its holster. He had no intention of ever being more than arm's length from a gun again. He checked the condition of his M4 and followed Vance down the stairs.

"We checked your APC while you were sleeping," Vance said as he descended. "Thought maybe we could get it into the action somehow."

"It wouldn't survive the fall," Cobb said.

"Yeah, we came to the same conclusion. Tim is a fair mechanic. We're also afraid it would act as a ramp for the infected. We've seen them do some crazy things."

"Crazy how?" Cobb asked.

"Olympic athlete crazy. Sometimes more." They reached the bottom of the stairs. The double-wide staircase was somewhat ornamental with a carved, wooden banister and polished steps. It was entirely blocked between the second and first floors by a dozen benches from the courtroom arranged in an ingenious interlocking pattern. Growls and pounding came from below. "I've also seen them…change."

"Huh?"

Vance grabbed the closest bench and gave it an experimental pull to make sure it was still lodged in place, then turned to face Cobb. "When we were trapped in my bunker—"

"You had a bunker?"

"Sure, don't you? Anyway, the bunker had a three-inch-thick, wooden door. I wish I'd had the metal one put in, but three inches of wood was pretty damned good. Well, the infected were pounding on it to get through. They'd figured out we were inside. Just when we started using the escape tunnel because they were getting through, I noticed that several had beaten all the flesh off their hands."

Cobb shuddered. He'd seen the horrible injuries some of the infected had, sure. But the thought of a human being continuing to pound on a door when their hands had been beaten to bony messes made him swallow hard.

"But there's more." Vance seemed to consider how to explain. "It was almost as if the bones in their hands had reformed into chisels."

"What? That's crazy."

"Yes, it is. Doesn't change what I saw. I'm the only one who saw it, so I don't know what to think." He looked at the barricade. "I've been checking the barricade every hour on the hour, waiting and hoping I was imagining things. So far, so good." He looked at the barricade and gave a little shudder. "Anyway, you got any ideas to improve it?"

"Did I see metal grates on the courtroom's exterior windows? We could put those under a layer of these benches."

"Damn, that's a good idea."

"Thanks," Cobb said. "Even if they can…*mutate.*" He tried to wrap his mouth around the word but didn't do a good job. "Even if they can mutate their hands to chop through wood, metal is stronger than any bone."

"Right you are," Vance said. "Next, I was thinking we could dismount the radio from your APC and see if we can get it going."

"They're tricky to work with," Cobb cautioned.

"We've got some experience with military surplus," Vance said and winked.

"I bet you do," Cobb said and winked back. Yeah, he liked these people. Besides, you fought your battles with what you had, not what you wanted. The two turned to head upstairs but only made it two steps when they heard a splintering sound from the barricade.

Both men turned around, staring first at the barricade, then at each other. Another crunching sound came, only this time it was followed by deep growling noises.

"What the fuck is that?" Vance wondered.

"I have no clue," Cobb said. "But we'd better expedite the metal grating. I fear our barricade won't survive whatever that thing is." The two men ran up the stairs, the sounds of splintering hardwood and growling echoing in their ears.

* * *

**Joint Combined Evacuation Fleet**
**Panama Bay**

"Dr. Bennitti, please report to conference room #3. Dr. Bennitti, please report to conference room #3."

The blaring PA system shut down, and Theodore Alphonse Bennitti, III, shook his head. The military didn't do anything quietly. He saved his work on the computer and got up, stretching and listening to his bones creak. At 62, he wasn't a spring chicken anymore. Getting up and down decks on the 25-year-old USS *Bataan* wasn't easy.

Outside his suite of offices, through the watertight door, a pair of young Marines waited. As soon as they saw him, both came to rigid attention. Al could almost see their desire to salute him, to salute anything. He walked past, and they fell in without comment. "You don't have to follow me everywhere," he said over his shoulder. Neither replied, so he kept walking.

Learning your way around a *Wasp*-class amphibious assault ship was challenging enough without two gung-ho Marines following you everywhere. As a senior director at NASA, he wasn't used to asking simple questions such as 'where is the bathroom.' He learned such things for himself. The trouble was, he didn't have time for trivialities.

He went down a deck, moving slowly and carefully along the nearly vertical ladders topped by a big steel hatch. Al understood the need for watertight doors, but every single damned door?

"Are you okay, sir?" one of the Marines asked.

"Fine," Al grumbled as he hobbled away from the stairs.

"Sir?"

"What is it?" He turned around, and the Marine was pointing the opposite way down the corridor. "Oh." He found conference room #3 a short distance farther down the hall. Two Marines were guarding the conference room door, and the pair who'd followed him stayed. *Maybe they can all play cards or something.* He entered the room.

"Dr. Bennitti, about goddamned time!"

"Admiral Kent," Al said as he examined the other people in the room. Dr. David Curie, Chief Immunologist at the CDC, and his boss, Dr. Theodor Gallatin, Director of Immunology. Off to the side, as if she were afraid of the brighter light in the center of the conference room, was Dr. Wilma Gnox. She had a paper notebook in her lap and was mumbling as she wrote.

"Get lost again?" Dr. Curie asked.

"Piss off," Al replied and took a seat. "I was working. Why did you call me?"

"Because we've entered the Bay of Panama," Admiral Kent said.

"And that means what to me?"

"The USS *Stout*, one of our *Arleigh Burke*-class destroyers, was the first to leave the canal yesterday. They detected two deep-moving contacts. We've got helicopters following up."

"I'm still confused about what this has to do with me and what it means?"

"Submarines," Admiral Kent said. "Two submarines in the bay. They're not ours; we don't have any. Even if we did, we can't talk to them because your people haven't been able to break the jamming signal."

"Admiral," Al said. "We had 11,000 people working for NASA before this alien plague hit. You managed to rescue 591 of our personnel from a surprising cross section of our specialties from Kennedy Space Center. However, only nine are the kind of computer experts who would have a chance in Hell of cracking the bug which has infected your global communications network. I have two of them working on it."

"What about the other seven?" the admiral demanded.

"They're on another project."

"What other project?" he demanded.

Al glanced pointedly at Dr. Gnox, then back at the admiral.

"Shit," Admiral Kent cursed.

"Why are you worried about a couple of submarines?"

"Because, if you find two, it means there are a lot more. Think of it as shaking a haystack and three needles falling out."

"Aren't you being paranoid?" Al wondered.

"My job is to be paranoid. How do you think things worked out when we passed through Gamboa?"

Al hadn't been on deck or anywhere he could watch when the two supposed yachts suddenly attacked a frigate which was scouting ahead of the fleet. He'd seen footage of the aftermath, including the burning yachts and the damaged frigate. The admiral had ordered all ships to implement combat conditions from the moment they'd entered the canal.

"Can we get back to why the subs are a problem? You do have all kinds of...anti-sub stuff?"

"We have substantial ASW capabilities, yes," Admiral Kent agreed. "However, employing them to sweep for subs is going to slow us down quite a bit."

"Another day, one way or another, to reach this Flotilla shouldn't be a problem," Al said. "Once there, when we have the president on board—"

"That won't happen," the admiral said. "The president is dead; her plane collided with a navy fighter and went down."

"There were multiple outbreaks on some other naval and civilian ships," Dr. Gallatin added.

"At least one carrier is believed to have sunk, taking with it the senior admiral on site, Admiral Hoskins," Kent finished.

"Which makes you senior?" Al asked.

The admiral nodded. "But not if you can help us get the goddamned GCCS up," he said, referring to the US Military's Global Command and Control System, an interconnected data system linking all the armed forces in all the theaters of operations and DC. It was supposed to be uninterruptable, even by a nuclear war. So much for that idea. "And, the favorable atmospheric conditions allowing us to talk with the Flotilla have become less favorable. So, we're cut off by radio too."

"Even if we could communicate, it doesn't mean there's anyone else out there," Dr. Curie pointed out. "Based on our most conservative model, Strain Delta reached 100% worldwide exposure 92 hours ago."

Admiral Kent's jaw muscles clenched, and the grinding of his teeth was audible over the constant thrumming of the assault carrier's steam-driven turbines. "Look, people, we left Miami with three fleet oilers. We emptied one just after we made it through Aquas Clara. Now, we have two. Every goddamned ship we have is drinking bunker fuel at a frightening rate, and these skulking subs are not making things go any faster. If we don't make it to the San Diego area in 70 hours, we'll be leaving ships behind." He looked at Al. "Have you made progress with the alien stuff?"

"Not much," he admitted. Admiral Kent looked ready to pop. Al raised a hand. "This isn't like the movies, where you can conveniently grab a part off a shelf and have it instantly interface with the aliens' tech. These things use superconducting properties we don't understand. They transmit anti-gravity fields through ferrous metal. *Any* ferrous metal. Do you want a carrier to accidentally float a hundred feet up, then come crashing down?"

"That would be sub-optimal," Kent said.

"Slightly more than sub-optimal if you're on the boat," Gnox said, the first indication she'd been listening to the conversation.

"Maybe your 'Star Fox' can help out?"

"I've only just figured out how to say hello," Gnox said.

"How damned hard can it be?"

"Very hard," she said, finally looking up. "Their syntax changes depending on context, as does the morphology. I didn't realize we were missing a dozen phonemes, because they were on the borderline ultrasonic range. Lastly, every word, besides having seemingly random phonemes tagged to them, may have as many as six morphemes."

"What in the fuck is all of that supposed to mean?" Kent demanded.

"She means it's a very complicated, very *alien* language," Al said.

Gnox looked at him and nodded appreciatively.

"Can you understand it, or not?"

"Yes," Gnox said. "Given time," she qualified. "I dearly wish we had an expert in Pirahã. The Star Fox's reluctance to use recursions suggests certain elemental familiarities." She glanced at Admiral Kent who was staring at her in annoyance. "I am fluent in 42 languages, conversational in another 11, and have a spattering knowledge of 20 more. Like most polyglots, I pick them up like some people collect fridge magnets. However, linguistics isn't my specialty. I'm a biologist by profession."

Kent continued to examine her. She had a vaguely Asian appearance with a hint of epicanthic folds on her eyelids and straight black hair which she wore in a short, pageboy cut. She might have been 20 or 30 pounds overweight, though probably from poor personal habits rather than a genetic predisposition. She also seemed to be always smacking chewing gum which, for a career naval officer, was highly frustrating. She went back to her notebook.

"Do all your scientists dabble in multiple fields?" he asked Al.

"Specialization is for insects," Gnox answered for him.

"They're not really my scientists," Al reminded him. "The director of NASA was eaten, remember? I was only the director of the colonization program. We had less than 100 employees."

"Yes, you've reminded me every time we've had a meeting. However, since your boss is a pile of shit and bones in DC, you are the head honcho." Gnox gave a tiny laugh, obviously finding the image he created amusing in some way.

"Right," Al said. "Which is why I came to you with information about the alien ship and what it is capable of."

"Theoretically capable," Kent corrected.

"It's more than theoretical," Al insisted. "We've had three successful tests."

"You call putting a seven-ton skiff into orbit fast enough to nearly capsize the *John Finn* a success? Jumping Jesus, man, the shockwave tore one of the .50 caliber gun mounts off her deck! It's a miracle nobody was lost."

*A damned good thing we decided to run the test remotely at the last second, too.* "You need to understand, there are risks with trying to reverse engineer something like this."

"A half-mile high waterspout from a seven-ton boat going from zero to Mach 10 is more than a slight risk."

"I agree," Al barked, getting tired of walking on eggshells around the admiral. "Damnit, you can't do research like this on military ships! We need somewhere with better equipment and people suited to direct innovations. NASA doesn't just invent stuff, we set it in motion and shepherd the development."

"NASA doesn't invent stuff," Admiral Kent said and snorted. "You convinced me to pull into Cape Canaveral and rescue your people before you told me you had an alien and its ship. You convinced me, because you said it would lead to a cure and probably advance our space program a couple hundred years. So far, I have one alien who won't talk and the coolest water park attraction in history."

Gnox snorted with laughter and shook her head as she wrote. "Star Fox can talk, just not any human language we recognize. And, as I said, we're making progress."

"What's with its name, Star Fox?" Admiral Kent asked. "People laugh when they hear it."

"Long story," Gnox said.

"Suppose you tell it."

"Do you really want a lecture on the origin of a video game?"

Admiral Kent narrowed his eyes as he tried to stare down the scientist. She didn't look up, which made the game more difficult. "Never mind," he grumbled under his breath. Al could see the barest of a smirk on Gnox's face from where he was sitting.

"We've made progress on their biology, at least," she said. "We are sure their amino acids are not the same as ours, which is why she won't eat the food we give her."

"Can't we just sprinkle something on it?" This time she laughed out loud. "What's so goddamn funny?'

"Having a different amino acid chain isn't something you can sprinkle new seasoning on. The alien's biochemistry is completely…well…alien. It can't eat our food; it could be toxic. Same if you tried to eat the alien's food. It might taste just fine. But it would either do nothing for you or cause a chemical reaction which could kill you. Sort of like anaphylactic shock on steroids."

"How much of its alien food do we have?"

"Enough for another month. She's been rationing herself, probably because she knows she can't eat our food. I have the only other biochemist on our team working with samples to try and synthesize some basics. Think of it as watery soup." She shrugged. "It's a start."

"You keep calling it a her," Dr. Curie said. "Why?"

"Because she said she was a female," Gnox said. "I told you we had our first breakthrough. We have a couple of words we're sure of, and now we are beginning to develop a lexicon of simple terms."

"Okay," Admiral Kent said and turned to Dr. Gallatin. "What can you tell me about the disease?"

"We've managed to pull together some data we got from HAARP and the other three nations that shared data before the world's communications went down."

"Sorry, HAARP?"

"The Human Advancement and Adaptive Research Project, led by an old colleague of mine, Dr. Lisha Breda."

"Wait, isn't that those nutjobs who were chased out of California for trying to make superman or something?"

"Their research was rather non-standard," Dr. Gallatin said. "They weren't doing eugenics. They were trying to unlock sequences within DNA which would make us effectively immortal, as well as immune to all diseases and cancer."

"Sounds like they're the ones who created this zombie plague," the admiral said.

"Hardly," Dr. Curie said. "You don't accidentally make zombie plagues like they do in the movies."

"Dr. Curie is right, of course," Dr. Gallatin said. "Besides, if Dr. Breda is correct, this plague isn't a lifeform."

"Sorry, are you saying it's not alive? Then what the hell is it?"

"Closest thing would be a nano virus," Dr. Gallatin said. Admiral Kent blinked, so he elaborated. "Think of it as a super-small machine."

"Like them nanites I've heard about?"

"Yes!" Dr. Gallatin said, obviously relieved he wouldn't have to school the admiral on the subject. "Only, these are smaller than the best we've managed by several orders of magnitude. So small, their programming may be embedded in their construct at the atomic level. In other words, it's not from around here."

"No way it came from Earth," Al agreed. "If a country could have produced something as complex and elegant as this, they would have revolutionized the entire biochem industry ages ago." Dr. Gallatin nodded in agreement.

"Okay," Admiral Kent said. "You know what it is; how do we stop it?"

"We can't," Dr. Gallatin said.

"Why not?"

"Because it's everywhere," Dr. Curie said. He took a glass of water from the table. "It's in this water." He gestured around the room. "It's in the air we're breathing." Then he patted his chest. "And it's in us, Admiral. We can stop it with airtight seals, but it's already in the air. We know it automatically mutates to different forms when various versions of it come into contact with each other, though we don't know why."

"I stand by the theory that it's a form of vector," Dr. Gallatin said. "A bioweapon."

"My God," Admiral Kent said. "Did the foxes give it to us on purpose?"

"That's one of the questions I'm going to ask," Gnox said. "Once we get past 'see Dick run,' of course."

"What about surviving it?" Admiral Kent asked.

"The only way to survive it might be to hide from it," Gallatin said. "Get away from uncontrolled groups of people. Have proper food production set up. We know very high temperature breaks it down, so we can start with that. With time, we can hopefully find ways to mitigate it." He looked the admiral in the eye. "But frankly, there is no way to stop it."

* * *

**Pacific Northwest**

**Classified Task Force**

"You're wasting your time with her."

Gabriel was the last one he expected to speak up about the Coastie. "Somebody sent her," Michael said.

"Probably the same person who's trying to break my satellite kill switch," Gabriel said.

"So, you're saying it might be worth getting info out of her?" Michael asked. She shrugged in reply. Michael gestured over the conference table they were seated around, and satellite imagery popped up. "We weren't tracking the south because we were monitoring the west in preparation for leaving the Columbia River." The images displayed various surface contacts identified by markers; friendly in green, unknown in blue, hostile in red.

"The Russians are still out there." Chamuel was staring at the red marker.

"Yes," Michael said. "Even after you said they would move on."

"Something's changed," Chamuel said. "Before you ask, I don't know what." Her dark skin was shining with sweat as she slouched in her mobility chair. "But something is influencing the Russian's actions."

Michael looked at the projected map and narrowed his eyes in thought. Chamuel was the tactical genius. A savant. She could manage dozens of simultaneous situations on a global scale. Her gifted mind was not affected by the infirmities which plagued her body. "You need to find the exact position of the sub. What orders should I give our ASW?"

"Nothing, for now," Chamuel said.

Michael nodded. "Ariel, report?"

The man code named Ariel looked up into the video pickup. He was of average build and appeared indiscriminately Asian. Most who met him guessed he was Japanese, but he insisted otherwise. There was no way to tell from his accent because he was mute. He wasn't present at the table as he was too busy with his analysis, but he typed an answer into his computer which was spoken for him by his voder.

"We've made real progress on the amino acids issue. We're testing synthetics on cell samples from the alien classified as Vulpes. So far, so good. We'll know more in a few days. Their biology isn't dissimilar from ours in most ways. They have chromosomes, though a lot more than we do. They breath oxygen and exhale CO2. They eat and shit."

"That's good to know," Jophiel said and laughed. Most of the seven around the table laughed or nodded.

Ariel typed another line of text. "The Vulpes' food supply is in excess of 4 months. The ship had large stores. I'm not concerned—we'll have the issue licked long before our visitor's chow runs out."

"You want to go next, Jophiel?" Michael asked.

"Sure," the linguist replied. Despite being the oldest among them, her eyes were sharp, and she was as spry as a woman half her age. Her hair was pure white and looked like it hadn't been cut during her lifetime. She kept it pinned up in an intricate knot. "Their language has elements we've never seen before, or rarely, at least. It has more in common with Pirahã than any other terrestrial language. I've just nailed down how he uses phonemes, and there are five or six morphemes."

"How far are we in developing the Rosetta stone for their language?"

"I'd say 55%. We're still running into a lot of ambiguities because of those damned phonemes."

"We'd like to have the first questioning session before we arrive at base," Michael said.

"I think we'll be close," Jophiel said.

"Good. Raphael?" Like Ariel, Raphael wasn't present. While he worked, no other humans except his team had been in physical contact. He looked up from his lab equipment, and Michael wondered if he'd been listening. "Do you have a progress report?"

"This alien nanovirus is a stone-cold bitch," Raphael said. "I know I've reported how bad it is, but the more I study it, the worse it gets. The damned thing is hard to kill, and it reproduces using dozens of energy sources from sunlight to thermal and even some sorts of radiation."

"Did you just say it reproduces using radiation?" Ariel asked.

"That's what I said."

"How is it doing that?"

"We don't know," Raphael admitted. "The more we take this thing apart, the more I think we should have a robotics expert on the team instead of an immunologist."

"I'm the closest thing you've got to a roboticist," Michael reminded him. "I've read your report. It might be a machine; however, it responds more like a virus." Raphael shrugged. "Do you want to alter your conclusions in regard to Strain Delta?"

"No," Raphael said. "It cannot be contained or stopped with any technology we have."

"What about your position on our visitor and the virus?"

"The Vulpes didn't intentionally bring it."

"But the alien did bring it," Chamuel said. "Recently, not decades ago?"

"Yes," Raphael said. "Given the rate at which this thing replicates, there's no way in Hell it's been here since the '50s and only started reproducing now."

"So, one of the first questions we need to ask is *why* they brought us a world-ending, zombie plague?" Michael asked.

"I'll be sure to ask him as soon as he understands the question," Jophiel replied.

"Azrael, anything to add?"

"Not at this time," the man replied.

Michael had always found Azrael's pale, white skin and pink eyes disconcerting. His mannerisms, which were somewhere between Jeff Goldblum's and Captain Jack Sparrow's, didn't help. "According to my information, you got the crates from archive before everything went to shit, and we shut down worldwide GCCS. Correct?"

"Yes," Azrael confirmed. "I've been going through the crates, but it's going to take a lot of time. The air force didn't label things well in the '50s." Michael gave him the stink eye. "If I do this too quickly, I could ruin some very fragile, glass sample slides. I'm a damned archeologist, not an investigative journalist." Michael nodded slowly. "Vulpes is the same species—it explains why the government dropped everything in a hole and shoveled dirt over it."

"Our charter was to keep this sort of thing from happening," Michael reminded them, casting his gaze around the seven-sided table. "We failed."

"The Heptagon was created before anyone had a clue what was coming," Chamuel said. "With as little funding as we've gotten over the years, is it any surprise what happened?" Nobody could argue her point. "The powers that be had decided it was more important to guard the tech than to prepare for a possible botched contact scenario."

"Very well," Michael said. "Everyone, keep up the good work. We'll arrive at base in two days."

*****

# Chapter Two

**Afternoon, Thursday, May 2**
**County Courthouse**
**Junction, TX**

Cobb peeked over the heavy railing and down to the first floor. The sound of crunching, splintering, and snapping wood reminded him of a woodchipper, without the motor. It was accompanied by growls the likes of which he'd never heard before. It didn't sound like the infected, it was much, much deeper.

"What the fuck is it?" Vance hissed from behind him.

"I wish I knew," Cobb said. He lifted his M4 and set it on the railing. Judging by the sounds of tearing wood, he'd see soon enough. A big chunk of bench went flying. "I think we're about to find out, though. Better get some more guns down—"

He was cut off by three, massive benches exploding away from the barred doorway. They revealed a massive, furry, brown shape which triggered an old, old memory.

"It's a bear!" Vance yelled. A big head tilted to look at them. Blood dripped off a massive muzzle with half its skin torn off. Cobb saw a splinter at least a foot long embedded in the bear's face. It locked its tiny, black, beetle eyes on him, and Cobb felt his bowels turn to ice water.

Cobb welded his cheek to his M4 and found the bear's head through the ACOG scope. He flicked the safety off. *Bang!* The bullet took an alarmingly small divot out of the bear's head. The effect was nil. The bear snarled, grabbed another of the barricade benches in its massive paws, and tore it free.

"Oh shit," Vance hissed and swung his riffle off his shoulder.

"Is that a 5.56mm?" Cobb asked.

"Yeah."

"Not good enough. Got a hunting rifle?"

"Harry has an AR-10."

"Better than these," Cobb said and patted the M4.

Vance looked at him for a second, then turned and ran.

Cobb looked back at the bear. Its whole upper body was through the doors. One of the benches was stuck, but the bear had the wood in its jaws, furiously shaking it from side to side. *It's a damn grizzly. Where did a grizzly bear come from in Texas?!* He started pumping rounds into the beast. Half his rounds missed the wildly swinging head. Others hit and tore away fur, flesh, and some bone. Blood poured from its head, but it took no notice.

"Fuck, fuck, fuck!" he yelled. The bolt on his M4 locked back.

"That's a goddamned grizzly bear," Harry said as he came up to Cobb.

"No shit," Cobb said as he dropped the empty magazine and pulled another from his web gear.

"Where'd a damn grizzly bear come from?"

Cobb sighed and let the bolt fly forward on his gun, charging the chamber.

"There are a bunch of wildlife parks around here," Ann said from the doorway. She looked like she didn't want to see the monstrosity downstairs.

"It's behaving like the infected," Cobb said.

"Strain Delta is in every organism," Belinda said.

Cobb looked back at her. He knew she was a nurse. She understood the damned zombie plague better than anyone he knew.

"We've heard some other animals were affected; we saw it with our dogs." She gestured toward the raging animal sounds. "It only makes sense."

"Sick fucking sense," Vance said, his eyes wide.

"Cap the damn thing," Cobb said, looking at Harry.

"Uh, yeah," Harry said and looked over the railing. The bear had just about torn the carefully constructed barricade to pieces. "Mother fuck," he hissed and raised his battle rifle. The roar of the AR-10's 7.62mm round was considerably more powerful than the lighter 5.56mm's.

Cobb saw the bullet tear a big chunk out of the grizzly's neck. The bear roared and attacked the last barricade.

"What are you doing?" Cobb yelled. "Put it down!"

"Shit," Harry said and pumped rounds into the bear. He worked the rounds from the head down the bear's back. Its roar was cut off mid scream, and it crashed twitching to the floor. Harry popped the empty 20-round magazine. "Sorry," he said. "Don't have a lot of ammo."

"There are times to conserve ammo, and this wasn't one of them," Cobb said. He evaluated the situation. Infected were already clambering over the dead bulk of the grizzly. There were benches clogging the stairs, but they'd get over those. He turned and ran.

"What should we do?" Harry yelled.

"Slow them down!" Cobb replied.

He raced up to the Stryker, set his M4 down, and crawled in through the open crew hatch. With the APC wedged into the side of the courthouse, it wasn't easy. He could only get his torso in, but it was enough. He located the metal box he wanted and grabbed it, dropped back out, snatched his rifle, and ran. The sound of rapid small arms fire urged him onward despite the pounding in his head from when he crashed the Stryker into the building.

Cobb came up behind the survivalists. All six of them were leaning their weapons over the railing and firing in rapid, semi-automatic volleys. Vance glanced back when Cobb came though the double doors, and Cobb could see the relief in his eyes.

Cobb slung his rifle and set the case, labeled M85, on the floor. Popping the release and opening the lid, he revealed four olive drab blocks and some electronics.

"Is that…" Harry started.

"Yeah," Cobb said. "Hold them for a second." He pulled out one of the four controllers and started wiring it. The six survivalists glanced back intermittently to watch, their eyes wide in alarm. Cobb knew he was making a mess of what he was doing, but the system was robust and forgiving. He set the timer, armed it, and slammed the lid closed. "Make a hole," he said.

The two men closest to the top of the stairway, Vance and Tim, ceased fire and moved as Cobb carried the case past them. He looked down the stairs, picked his target, and heaved the case. It crashed into a bench and nearly flew over the side of the stairway. Cobb gasped. It hit the railing and flipped back into the middle, lodging pretty much where he'd wanted it.

"Better run," Harry said, grabbing his wife's arm and beating a hasty retreat through the double doors. Cobb pushed the rest to follow.

"How far?" Vance asked.

"As far as we can get," Cobb said.

"You had to use the whole can of explosives?" Harry asked.

They ran into the courtroom, now nearly empty of benches, and out the back where Cobb's Stryker was lodged in the wall. They split up on either side of the door and dropped to the floor.

"How long?" Vance asked. No sooner were the words out of mouth than everything exploded.

* * *

**Afternoon, Thursday, May 2**

**The Flotilla**

**150 Nautical Miles West of San Diego, CA**

Jeremiah Osborne yawned and rolled over. Sunlight streaming through the window suggested it was either early morning or late afternoon. He coughed and ran his tongue over the roof of his mouth. It was rather…sticky. He glanced at the bedside table where a bottle of Pappy Van Winkle rested on its side, a tiny bit of amber liquid still in the bottom. *That explains the goo.*

He sat up slowly as his head threatened to explode and stretched. The bed was dry. *One step at a time.* Naked, he walked more-or-less straight to the head and relieved himself. Now less 'full,' he walked back and sat down. He took the bottle and emptied the last few drops. "Hair of the dog," he said as Kentucky bourbon sizzled down his throat. It was a thousand-bucks-a-bottle smooth.

"Now, if I could just remember why I was guzzling a bottle of the good stuff," he said. "Might be good if I found my pants too." He walked to the small dresser, bent over, and looked inside. No clean clothes. Standing back up, he looked out the window and saw a navy ship burning. Then it all came back to him. "Oh, zombie apocalypse. Right."

He dug through the pile of dirty clothes, found the cleanest, and put them on. While he dressed, he went over the previous night's events.

After they'd stripped down the latest alien ship, his tech team had taken him up to the ship's deck and showed him what they'd discovered. The alien power supply, when coupled with the drive modules, produced a much more energetic response than when coupled with a terrestrial power source. They were able to surround the entire ship with a forcefield which cut it off from the outside world. Before, all they'd been able to do was make it fly. In fact, his original prototype orbital ship, *Azanti*, had taken a crew millions of miles into space. Not on purpose, though.

Dressed, Jeremiah exited his cabin and walked down to the small executive dining room. He'd lost a fair amount of staff, so there wasn't anyone to make him food. To his surprise, a plate of sandwiches was waiting for him. Someone had even put a note on the plate letting him know the sandwiches were made from frozen and preserved food that predated the plague.

"Good to know," he said as he took a sandwich. They were all turkey and cheese. No complaint. It tasted fine. He walked to the cooler as he ate. It was stocked with soda and beer. He almost grabbed a beer, then decided that wasn't the best idea and took a

Coke instead. *Look, I adulted today.* The sandwich wasn't bad; maybe the day wouldn't be bad either.

Alex West and Patty Mize came walking in, laughing at some unknown joke. They stopped when they saw Jeremiah sitting at a table eating.

"Afternoon, Boss," Alex said and nodded.

"Afternoon," Patty added, and they both walked over to the table. Patty picked up the note and showed it to Alex, who grunted. They both took sandwiches and got a beer.

Jeremiah looked at the beer darkly and drank his Coke. "What fun have you two been having?"

"Merino fit one of the drives and the power supply onto the Huey," Alex explained. "We took it for a little spin."

"Jesus Christ," Jeremiah cursed. "If the military finds out..."

"They won't," Patty said. "The assault on Coronado went to shit. One of the navy pilots rammed the president's plane; they both crashed."

"Oh," Jeremiah said, then he went and got a beer.

"Yeah," Alex said. "Besides, we ran the engine, so if anyone saw us, they'd think it was a regular helicopter."

"Only had to run the helo on idle, though," Alex said and winked at Patty. The two chuckled. "The hard part was finding some ferrous metal to hook the drive to."

Now Jeremiah got the joke. If anyone had been close enough, they wouldn't have heard a thing, either. The forcefield, when the drive was used with a power supply, made anything inside virtually indestructible and cut off all sound. He decided to change the subject. "What's with the burning navy ship?"

"One of their carriers went down," Alex said. "They had an outbreak, then something exploded."

"The smaller ships?"

"Not sure. I think maybe evacuees from Coronado. Some might have been infected."

"None came here, did they?" Jeremiah asked, casting a worried glance between the two. Both shook their heads.

"The captain played stupid, so the evacuees went elsewhere," Patty explained.

Jeremiah finished his sandwich, popped his beer, and drained half of it. *I wonder how much more of this we have on board?* "The military babysitters still in the labs?"

"No," Alex said. "They took off shortly after the shit hit the fan."

"Well, there's that at least," Jeremiah said. He raised his beer as did the others, and they all drained their drinks.

"There you are."

Jeremiah turned and saw Jack Coldwell, his head physicist. He'd been heading up the project to figure out how the alien tech worked. "What's up, Jack?"

"You know the military guys who were watching us?"

"Yeah. Alex and Patty just told me they vamoosed when the carrier blew up." He got up to head for the fridge. Another beer sounded good.

"Yeah," Jack said. "I'm curious why they both left so quickly."

"Everything was going to shit on their ships," Alex said. "Probably hurrying back to help shoot infected."

"They were both techs," Jack said. "One was an engineering grad student."

"So?" Jeremiah asked as he selected a beer. "They're gone, aren't they?"

"Yes, they are," Jack said. "And they took one of the backup hard drives with all our data on the alien tech with them."

"Motherfucker," Jeremiah spat. Suddenly, he didn't feel like another beer, he felt like a bottle of Pappy Van Winkle.

* * *

Wade Watts scanned the code one more time before loading it into a data packet. The navy woman assigned to help him, a PO3 (Petty Officer 3rd class) named Sanchez, was also going through the data, albeit considerably slower than he was. "I'm ready to send it," he said.

"Wait," she said. Sanchez, who was no more than 25, was a CTM—Cryptologic Technician, Maintenance. Wade had looked it up, and the job description said she was in charge of computer networking and software installation. In the civilian world, she'd be a network administrator. The military was weird.

"Your captain said he wanted the ship back on the GCCF network," Wade said, tapping his foot.

"GCCS," Sanchez corrected. "Global Command and Control System."

"Right," he said and glanced at a screen, using it as an excuse to eye PO3 Sanchez's chest again. He'd been trying to get up the courage to hit on her for two days. "So, we need to get this done."

"Yeah, no shit," she retorted. "But, if I let you upload something dangerous to a DoD satellite and it makes things worse, I might as well find some fresh fish and have sushi." Eating any fresh meat was a death sentence. "Looks good, go ahead."

"About time," he mumbled. She frowned, and he wished he'd kept his mouth shut. She was hot, and he'd been hoping he'd get to know her better. Putting his libido aside, Wade entered the command code he'd been given, and the *Ford's* computer linked with a military satellite thousands of miles above them.

As before, the satellite accepted the login. He transmitted the command string, a packet of orders telling the satellite to override whatever had shut it down and resume comms. And like before, nothing happened.

"Son of a bitch," he cursed.

Sanchez laughed. "I told you," she said.

"Doesn't make sense," he complained.

"What doesn't make sense? It's jacked up. Bet the satellite is fucked."

"Not a chance," he replied.

"Why do you say that?"

"It took the commands." He pointed at the screen. A little icon indicated the satellite had accepted the input, but it hadn't executed the orders. She frowned. "Let me see the flowchart again." Sanchez handed him the 2-inch-thick notebook. The mil-sat, or military satellite, command flowchart was 210 pages long and covered everything from sending a message to inquiring about gyro status. Most of the commands were off limits to field units, even supercarriers like the *Ford.* Wade suspected an admiral would have relevant codes, but he also suspected the admirals had tried to fix the problem shortly after it occurred.

Everything about the way the overly complicated government communications system was working spoke of a hack. The fact that all the satellite links through MILSATCOM (military satellite communications), commercial satellites, and even Iridium were down basically pointed to one conclusion—they were down because someone hacked the satellites. *Did a world-class job of fucking it up, too.*

They hadn't wrecked it, just ruined any connectivity. He went through the notebook for an hour or so while Sanchez did some other stuff. In the back of the book was a section on legacy systems. "What's WWMCCS?"

"That's an old system. Dates back to the Cold War," she said.

He looked at her. Her face was screwed up in concentration. She looked so *cute*. If she'd been wearing glasses…

She snapped her fingers. "Worldwide Military Command and Control System. Predecessor to GCCS. Well, kind of a stepfather. GCCS was pre-internet."

Wade looked up the ways GCCS communicated and saw that it used various regular internet connections when not back-boning on MILSATCOM. "Jesus, you guys like acronyms," he moaned. "Nipper? Sipper?"

"Nipper, NIPR, Non-classified Internet Protocol Router Network. Sipper, SIPR, Secret Internet Protocol Router Network. There's also JWICS, Joint Worldwide Intelligence Communications System, but we can't use it for the kinds of comms we want."

"Why not?" he asked, only half listening as he followed flowchart connections.

"It's more for sending drone data and intel from assets. Spook shit. We don't have the proper reception gear, if I recall."

He grunted and read on. He was still in the legacy section of the book. The diagram was old-style. He was pretty sure several of the flowchart icons were for mainframes and tape storage. But there, off to one side, in a system symbol surrounded by a dotted line, was GCCS.

"You said WWMCCS was Cold War era?"

"Uh huh."

"Why would there be charts about it in a manual about GCCS?"

Sanchez gave him a knowing smile. "Because this is the US Military." He stared at her blankly. "Did you know that a lot of ships still use Windows?"

"What's unusual about that?"

"Windows XP?"

"Oh, holy shit!" he exclaimed. She laughed. He looked at the book's instructions, then at the screen. He leaned forward and typed.

"What are you doing?"

"Trying a hunch."

He typed. A series of dots appeared on the screen. A second later, the unmistakable intro screen to an old-school mainframe server came up. WWMCCS had been built from big chunks of graphic elements which were clearly made to be displayed on a monochromatic monitor.

"Holy shit," Sanchez said.

"Yup. Any chance there's some documentation on this beast?"

"Would you look at that!"

Wade glanced over his shoulder. Chief Kuntzelman, Sanchez's boss, was standing behind him. Wade thought he was a warrant officer but had no idea why they called him chief.

"I haven't seen that screen in a month of Sundays. Maybe more!"

"You've used this before?" Wade asked. He examined the man. He was at least 50, so it wasn't out of the question.

"Yeah, last time I worked on it was aboard the *Forrestal* in 1992. The old girl was retired the next year. She wasn't a nuke, so we had the old crap a lot longer. They weren't using it, but in typical navy fashion, I trained on it."

Wade smiled widely and flipped pages. "Can you log us into the NIPRnet?" He gestured at the screen.

"Nipper post-dates WIMEX." Wade blinked. "The nickname for WWMCCS."

"Ah. Well, you know what? I have a hunch."

Kuntzelman shrugged and pulled up a chair. He tried a few keystrokes, then grunted. An error message flashed, so he tried again.

"Not working?" Sanchez asked.

"Hold on," the chief said. "This is like trying to speak in a language you haven't used in 20 years. WIMEX ran on the old Honeywell 6000 series. It used a language called GCOS."

"They still use that," Wade said, remembering his programming school days.

"Yeah, GCOS 7 or 8. This was the original. The new versions are for legacy code. The damned machines are still being used in places." He typed and got a menu. "You know, this is far too fast. It has to be an emulator."

"If the military dumped it a decade ago, why keep an emulator up and running?" Wade asked.

Sanchez and Kuntzelman exchanged the same knowing look. "Because it's the US Military," the older chief said. "Worse, the US Navy. But this is extreme, even for us. I know for a fact that this contract was canceled before I learned how to use it. The last machine was probably sold for scrap in 1995 at the latest. Or it's in a warehouse somewhere, next to the Ark of the Covenant."

All three chuckled at the last joke. Another menu came up labeled "Linked Systems."

1. Offline storage
2. Base status
3. Archives-physical
4. Archives-virtual
5. Archives-media
6. MILSATCOM link
7. Heptagon personnel
8. Project Genesis

"Woah," Wade said, staring at the simple menu.

"What the fuck is this?" Chief Kuntzelman asked.

"Take option 6," Wade said. The chief entered 6, and various satellite communications protocols appeared. After exploring for a bit, Kuntzelman found an active link via Sipper using, of all things, the Iridium Satellite Telephone Network.

The chief continued, entering access codes and establishing a data connection with the ship's systems. When he was done, he had opened a single channel of communication though the military SIPRnet. The formerly dead screens came alive, albeit slowly, with status readouts.

"Well, look at that," Kuntzelman said and pointed. One of the monitors showed a ready icon. "Just one channel?"

"I was hoping for more," Wade admitted. "But now that one works, I can see about others."

"No, don't fuck with it. Sanchez, inform the XO we have comms back."

"Yes, Chief."

"Mr. Watts, please come with me. I have another job for you."

Wade made a face, remembering the screen with all the cryptic options. Heptagon? Project Genesis? He desperately wanted to go back in. Kuntzelman was standing by the watertight door, waiting impatiently. Sanchez was busy typing in commands related to the ship's status reports through the newly established network. She didn't notice him slip a notebook into his pocket as he got to his feet.

Out in the hall, Wade had to ask the chief a question. "Did you tell me to go ahead because you thought it would work, or because you wanted me for the other project?"

The older man looked at him, and Wade could have sworn he saw the man give the barest of winks. "You did us a favor; that's good enough for now."

They went down several decks, then though several more compartments. In his time aboard the *Ford*, he'd largely kept to a few areas. Nobody seemed to care where he went as they were too busy doing navy shit. However, he got lost the first couple of times he started exploring, so he quit venturing out.

Following Kuntzelman, Wade quickly left the familiar areas behind. He thought he was in one of the hangar deck work areas, though he wasn't certain. The walk only took five minutes, and then they passed through a pressure-tight door into a workshop full of electronics. A pair of navy techs in coveralls were leaning over something on a workbench, deep in conversation.

"Gentlemen," Kuntzelman said, clearing his throat. Both men turned to look at him.

"Yes, Chief?" one of them answered.

"I've brought someone to help you. This is Mr. Watts."

They both examined Wade, quickly taking in his coveralls without any insignia, patches, or name tab, as well as the way his girth stretched the 'XL' to its limit.

"Civilian?" the other asked.

"That's right, Seaman. He's officially a contractor."

"Am I getting paid at some point?" Wade asked. He'd meant it as a joke.

"You get fed and have a bunk," Kuntzelman said. "If you're smart, you'll call it even." He left him with the two navy techs. Wade gawked.

"Don't let Chief Kuntzelman get under your skin," the first one said.

"When they make you a chief petty officer, they remove your sense of humor," the other said. "I'm Seaman Bond, this is Seaman Apprentice Dodd. Watts okay?"

"Just Wade is fine."

"Wade Watts?" Dodd asked. "Like in the movie?"

"Please don't go there," Wade said and walked between the two. They were no more than 20 or so years old, around 10 years his junior. They looked at each other and exchanged grins. "What can I do to help?"

"We've got this key drive," Bond said and held it up.

"Encrypted?" Wade asked.

"Yup," Dodd agreed.

Wade took the drive and looked at it. Other than the letters OOE printed on it in gold, it was a nondescript key drive. It didn't even have the storage size printed on it.

"Can you get into it?" Bond asked.

"Well," Wade said, "it doesn't look like an IronKey. So, unless they've got some crazy floating-point encryption, sure." Both men grinned. "I need my laptop." Wade glanced back at the hatch, frowning as he tried to remember the route Chief Kuntzelman had led him on. "Uhm…" he said.

Dodd laughed. "Tell me where your billet is, and I'll go get it." He pointed to a section of workbench. "You can set up there."

True to his word, Dodd was back before Wade finished organizing his section of workbench. Sitting between Dodd and Bond was a partially disassembled machine. Wade didn't think it was military. His biggest clue was the Nintendo controller wired into it.

"Here you go," Dodd said as he handed Wade the computer bag.

Wade removed his laptop and equipment pouch. He took out his discreet logic analyzer and hooked it up via USB before booting up the PC.

"Aren't you just going to plug the drive into the computer?" Bond asked.

"No," Wade said. He looked up at them. "I thought you two were computer experts."

"Experts?" Dodd said and laughed.

"Give him a break," Bond said, "he's a civie." Dodd grunted.

"This device isolates the USB from the laptop."

"Why?" Dodd asked.

"Virus, stupid," Bond said.

Wade snorted and nodded. "USB key drives are awesome, but they're like a conduit to your computer's brain. Load the wrong drive…" He mimed an explosion. They both gawked. "It won't literally explode; that's movie bullshit." He patted his computer. "This is custom built. I'm not burning it up for your secret porn files."

"It's not porn," Bond said, a grin on his face.

Wade wasn't convinced.

He used his equipment to examine the drive. It was encrypted, like they had said. However, it wasn't encrypted at the directory level, just the files. He checked one of the files, then blinked. "It's encrypted with BitLocker?"

"Is that bad?" Bond asked.

Wade snorted and grinned at him. "Only if you're in the military."

"What's that supposed to mean?" Dodd asked.

"Nothing," Wade said, "chill out." He ran the first file through his decryption tool. The computer turned its considerable power toward a brute force assault on the file. It cracked in 12 seconds. "Got the first file," he said. The two men leaned in to look at his screen. "It's a text file, some notes on a…drive cluster?"

"So, you can get the rest?" Dodd asked.

"Sure." Wade fed the other files into a buffer and set his computer to work. Quite a few were image files. The encryption on the image files was broken in seconds as they were easier; the rest took just under an hour.

While they waited, the pair of sailors left and returned with food. Rice flavored with soup and some canned chicken. Wade was sure it was all packaged before the outbreak, or they wouldn't be serving it. The three ate while his computer tore the data apart and put it back together.

They piled the empty plastic plates on the bench with the computer once all the files had been decrypted.

Wade transferred the data onto an SD card from his bag and gave it to the men then examined the files. They took the SD card over to their own computer as he looked at the files. Quite a few were text and audio files—notes on research. Others were schematics and diagrams and, he thought, theoretical physics. Then, one of the images suddenly clicked.

"OOE," Wade said. "Oceanic Orbital Enterprises." The other two men weren't looking at him. "This is the spaceship they were going to fly, but never did." Wade looked at more schematics. "This drive, though?" He tapped the screen. "It's an add on. New. All this data centers around it. Where did it come from?"

"Aliens," Dodd said.

"Bullshit," Wade said.

"Remember the floating C-17?" Bond asked.

"Yeah, but..." Wade let the thought taper off. Kathy Clifford had been mumbling stuff about aliens yesterday after the president's plane went down. The fucking virus, like nothing on Earth. While they were looking over the files, he slid his chair down and looked at the weird machine with its Nintendo controller. He took the top off and saw a glowing, blue, crystalline cylinder. It looked like a sci-fi prop, surrounded by electrical components and obviously improvised wiring.

"Is this what flew the C-17?"

"Yup," Dodd said.

"So, why did you need all this data?" Wade asked.

"They cobbled together the controller," Bond explained.

"Who?"

Wade listened as the two men explained how the OOE people, after their helicopter crashed on the *Ford*, finally explained what they had with them—an alien ship—then used parts of it to MacGyver a drive and get the C-17 off the ship. Afterward, the drive was removed and given to the two seamen to figure out.

"We couldn't quite figure out what they'd done," Dodd admitted. "We finally got it working. At least the machine comes on and the lights glow. But we hooked it to a fighter, and nothing."

"So, we asked for copies of their work," Bond said, gesturing at the drive still in Wade's computer.

"They gave you an encrypted drive?"

"We didn't say they gave it," Dodd pointed out.

*They stole it,* Wade realized. Then he shrugged; it was no skin off his back. "You said it doesn't work?" They nodded. "Have you connected it to ferrous metal?"

"What difference does the type of metal make?" Dodd asked.

"I don't know, but the documents mention ferrous." The two stared at him in amazement. "The docs also mention that you can increase sensitivity by coupling a signal booster with a potentiometer." Wade pointed to the contact points on the breadboard. The techs grabbed some components and started wiring them in.

"How did you find the info so fast?" Dodd asked as they worked.

"I learned speed reading techniques years ago," Wade explained. "They really help in computer game competitions."

"The table over there is ferrous metal," Dodd said, pointing.

Wade glanced over and nodded. It was an older style, heavy, steel table, probably meant for holding batteries or other heavy gear. "That should work," he said and picked up the module.

"We're not sure about the interface," Bond said, stepping over. "It wasn't calibrated right when they moved the C-17. Took them all day to get it back onto the deck."

Wade walked over to the other components. There were star-shaped, blueish, metal pieces. He grabbed two of those and a hexagonal black module. Stopping to read a section of the documents, he returned to the machine. "This is the power module," he said, holding up the black hexagon. Then indicated the star-shaped items. "These are the interfaces. With these we don't need the cobbled power supply to operate the drive."

"How much of the documents did you read?" Dodd asked.

Wade ignored him. "We'll float the table," he said. "Worst case, it hits the roof, or something." He wired in a Bluetooth adapter. "Now, we don't have to be near it." He looked at the two navy men. "Okay?"

They stared at each other for a second, then looked back at him and shrugged. "You're the expert," Bond said.

"Right," Dodd agreed.

"Okay." Wade grinned. "Let's make something fly." He attached the drive to the table with a single sheet metal screw, then taped the power module and controller on. Finished, he examined his handiwork. "Should be fine," he said half under his breath. "But let's stand in the doorway, just in case."

The navy men retreated quickly, but Wade simply backed up. He looked above the—only some light fixtures and bare metal. No worries there. Behind the table was bare bulkhead, and under it was the painted deck. *Nothing vital if this goes sideways.* He turned on the controller.

The blue, alien drive module's glow became a deep azure, and the star-shaped interface seemed to shimmer like hot concrete on a summer day. He moved the controller up. The table moved backward and clanged into the wall. It didn't hit hard or fast, but the sound seemed to resound though the ship. "Oops." Both men looked alarmed. "Must have the controls mixed up. I'll try again."

"Yes," Dodd said in an affected Jewish accent. "This time without the oops?"

Wade examined the control pad. If the one he'd pressed was sideways instead of up, then the one below it must be down. So, he pressed the other. Nothing happened. He pressed it again. Each press should have yielded a foot of measured movement. Nothing.

"Calibration must be off," he said and popped open the cover, examining the potentiometers.

"We didn't build it," Dodd pointed out.

"The guys from OOE set it up," Bond added. "It worked fine on the C-17."

"Maybe it was bumped?" Wade wondered. The sound of running feet outside made them look up. A pair of seamen rushed past. The three looked at each other. Wade shrugged and used a precision screwdriver to increase the control calibration increment a step. "Okay," he said, "let's see if this works." He pressed up this time. Nothing. He pressed it several times, the last one in frustration. "What the fuck is wrong with this?" He looked at the alien components, wondering if they were hooked up properly. Just as he reached for one, an alarm blared.

"General quarters! General quarters!"

"We better shut it down if something is happening," Dodd said. Bond nodded.

"Okay," Wade agreed and reached for the off switch.

"STOP!"

Wade jumped and spun around. Chief Kuntzleman was standing in the hatchway, a look of mixed horror and rage on his face. "What—" he started to ask.

"Don't touch it." Kuntzleman growled. Both the seamen straightened up and looked alarmed.

"Why?"

"Come with me," Kuntzleman said, making a stilted 'come here' gesture with his index finger.

Wade got up and followed without comment. Dodd and Bond fell in behind.

It was slow going. The alarm continued to blare, and crewmen were running around like crazy. Many looked panicked. Wade was getting a sinking sensation in the pit of his stomach.

"I told you to help them," Kuntzleman said. "I didn't say fuck with the blasted thing."

They reached a bigger hatch, and the chief moved through and to the side. It was one of the carrier's hangar decks. Dozens of seamen were standing around, their duties forgotten as they stared. Wade blinked, uncertain what was going on.

"What's your explanation for this?" Kuntzleman demanded and pointed.

Wade looked in the direction the chief was pointing, toward one of the big elevator openings. Only, instead of a view of the Pacific Ocean, there was an unmistakable view of the Earth…from orbit.

"Oops."

* * *

"Jeremiah!"

He ran out of the office where they'd been assessing the missing data when Alex West yelled from just outside. Jeremiah cleared the door and came up against the ship's rail. It didn't look like anything was different. Lots of civilian ships, a few military ships, some of both burning. It looked like the Flotilla was coming apart at the seams.

"What am I looking at?" he asked as other crewmen ran out behind him.

"The carrier," West said, pointing.

Jeremiah spotted it at least a mile away, maybe two. He thought it might be the *Gerald R. Ford*, the one he'd landed on after retrieving the second alien ship. They'd dumped his damned helicopter over the side. He noticed a wave washing away from the carrier. A big one, at least 20 feet tall. He looked around—the surrounding waters only had low whitecaps.

"I don't understand," he said.

West explained. "I was standing here, watching the carrier. They've been shuttling helos between ships, fighting outbreaks. Seemed like a losing battle. Then, suddenly, the *Ford* kind of jerked sideways."

"Huh?" Jeremiah asked.

"Yeah, I know, but that's what happened."

Jeremiah opened his mouth to comment when the carrier jumped *up*. He tried to guess how far—maybe 20 or 30 feet? A considerable number of his people were gathered nearby, and many gasped in surprise. The water around the carrier was sucked inward, then exploded out again.

"I think we know where the stolen data went," Maria Merino, his rocket propulsion specialist, said.

"They hooked the damn thing to the *carrier*?" Jack Coldwell asked. "Are they crazy?"

"If they mess with the calibration..." Alison McDill warned.

Jeremiah nodded, and a second later the USS *Gerald R. Ford* shot straight up so quickly it became a blur. He tried to track it, but by the time he lifted his head, the 1,100-foot long supercarrier was a retreating dot. The shockwave, however, was still there.

"Cover your ears!" West yelled as he crouched and jammed his hands over his ears.

Jeremiah did the same thing. He could see the shock wave distortion—a rapidly advancing white line tearing over the water—moving toward them, just like the ones in those old nuclear bomb tests. He had a fleeting image of the obliteration of a small sailing ship, its mast ripped free and the sail flying like a leaf caught in the wind. Then the shockwave hit his ship.

The wind was like a hammer blow, causing the ship to list at least 10 degrees. It was a seconds-long hurricane. Then, as quickly as it started, it was over. "Is everyone okay?" West asked. They weren't. Two of the techs who'd come out to watch were down. One was unconscious.

"Idiots!" Jeremiah yelled. His ears were ringing, despite his having covered them.

"What was that blast?" someone asked.

"Air rushing in to fill the void created by a supercarrier going from zero to multiples of Mach in a fraction of a second," Patty Mize explained.

Jeremiah saw West nodding in agreement. "Like a thunderclap," West added.

"Where do you think the carrier is?" Jeremiah asked.

"Mars?" McDill asked.

West shook his head. "No, if it went faster than light, we'd all be dead."

"Yes, I agree," Coldwell said, nodding. "It wouldn't have been a blast of wind; it would have been a nuclear blast—a damned big one."

"This was bad enough," Jeremiah said and looked at Maria. "Why do you think this means they got the notes? They had the drive we made to move the C-17. Couldn't this be from the same one?"

"Yes, it could," Maria said. "However, the acceleration we witnessed would probably have turned the carrier into a burning meteor."

"Unless they had it hooked to a drive module," West agreed, snapping his fingers. Jeremiah shook his head, not following. "The forcefield when a drive module is connected, remember?"

"Oh, yeah," Jeremiah said, finally understanding. "But I still don't understand why they hooked it to the carrier and not a boat or a plane."

"Who knows?" West asked and craned his head to look up. There was no sign of the massive carrier. "But I sure hope it doesn't come down at the same speed!"

* * * * *

# Chapter Three

**Evening, Thursday, May 2**
**County Courthouse**
**Junction, TX**

Vance Cartwright tried clearing his ears for the dozenth time, with the same results. They were all blast-deaf, to one degree or another. Cobb's improvisation with high explosives had fulfilled its intended purpose—the stairs were gone. The infected had no way to reach them. Of course, there was now a massive hole in the side of the courthouse—almost one entire side was gone.

Mercifully, the fire caused by the explosion had gone out. However, the structure was significantly weakened. It seemed the double whammy of having a huge armored combat vehicle slam into the side and then a pile of C4 explosives detonate inside had been too much. Vance wondered how long they had before the building collapsed in on itself.

The problem now facing them was how to get out of the building before it decided to collapse or the infected mounted a better assault. Because they hadn't given up, not by a long shot.

"The blast killed at least 200," Cobb said, glancing over the ruins of the once ornate county courthouse balcony. He moved back and shrugged. "Maybe more."

"That was a lot of high explosives," Ann Benedict said. She stood nearby, an arm protectively across her stomach where her and

Vance's child grew. Of them all, she'd been the least enthusiastic about Cobb's solution to the waves of infected.

"He didn't have time to plan better," Harry said. From the look on the former Marine's face, he rather appreciated Cobb's response to the infected grizzly and the swarm of infected humans.

"How many down there?" Vance asked Cobb, trying to change the subject.

"Maybe 50 or so," the army colonel replied.

"What are they doing?" Nicole Price asked.

"Do you really want to know?" The sounds of snarls and ripping flesh echoed around the ruined lower floors.

"Good Lord," Tim Price intoned. They all nodded.

Vance left the sounds of inhuman carnage behind and walked around the half-destroyed atrium and through the courtroom which was their center of operations. All their guns, ammo, food, and other meager supplies were cached there. They'd been barricading the main door as best they could. A lot of the benches were already gone, though, used to try and stop the infected from getting up the stairwell. It wasn't an ideal place to make a last stand.

At the other end of the courtroom was the judge's office. It overlooked the street below. The sun was down and the moon up. It was a beautiful night, and there were fewer infected. Down from a thousand to maybe half. So, only about 100 to 1 odds now. They had enough ammo, if they didn't miss many shots. He was no combat vet, but they'd been in a few fights since the world went to hell. He knew better than to assume things would go well if they tried to shoot their way out. He looked out again. Not good odds.

He noted that a couple of cars were burning on the far side of the street. He guessed they'd caught shrapnel from the detonation. Neither was fully involved. A small fired burned in the upholstery of one, and the other appeared to have a tire burning. The latter could well turn into a raging inferno. Two infected stood watching the fires, heads cocked curiously.

Something caught his eye, and he looked up. A light was moving across the sky from north to south. Before the world fell apart, such a sight hadn't been unusual. He hadn't seen or heard a plane in the sky for days. He thought the lights were from a plane at high altitude, only they didn't look right. Too bright, too big. It was close. And he couldn't hear anything. How could something fly so silently?

A growl snapped him out of his reverie. A hand reached up and grabbed him by the throat. A dark shape crawled over the balcony, jumped, and bore him to the floor. Vance tried to yell as strong fingers closed around his neck and squeezed with mind-numbing force. Nothing came out of his mouth as he fell back, the infected on his chest. Red stained teeth reflected the moonlight as they descended toward his face.

* * *

**Evening, Thursday, May 2**
**USS *Gerald R. Ford***
**Approximately 400 miles above San Diego, CA**

Kathy Clifford stood on the flight deck for a time, simply taking in the view. How often did a washed-up reporter get the chance to look at Earth from orbit? Especially while standing on the deck of a nuclear aircraft carrier. It seemed half the crew was doing the same. She glanced up at the tall structure they called the island. A walkway on top surrounded the bridge, and she could see several officers standing there, also taking in the inconceivable image of a carrier in space.

She carefully made sure the tiny camera was still clipped to her vest pocket. Nobody would know what it was, she was sure. She used it to record constantly, then she archived the footage to her laptop. She had hundreds of hours of footage, including quite a bit from her ill-fated trip to Mexico where she had gone to investigate the plague before it had turned into a global catastrophe.

Now, weeks later, she didn't know why she was still recording. She had two hard drives full of video. Hundreds of hours. She hadn't had time to look at most of it. Maybe she never would. She didn't know, and hundreds of miles up in space on an aircraft carrier, she didn't care.

"What the fuck happened?" one of the flight deck crew asked. He wasn't more than 20 years old, black, and from the sound of his voice, probably from a big city. Kathy thought he sounded on the edge of panic. He wore a red uniform which, she'd learned, meant he handled bombs.

"You tell me, man, I just work here." The other crewman was slightly older, white, and sounded like he was from Alabama or Arkansas. His uniform was purple, so he handled fuel. Only in the service would you see people from vastly different backgrounds working together.

She spent time wandering around. The uniform (minus insignia) they'd given her and the job of creating news reports for the Flotilla allowed Kathy to move quietly through most of the common areas of the ship. The crew, and those who were temporarily on the ship, took no real notice of her. The general feeling was one of panic. Section chiefs were keeping everyone they could away from the flight deck and hangars to reduce the panic; it left fewer ways to see their situation. It wasn't working. Everyone knew they were somehow, incredibly, in space.

Kathy was passing one of the mess halls when she overheard a snatch of conversation.

"...Watts fucked around with some confiscated tech."

"That fat computer geek?"

"Yeah, him."

She came to a sudden stop in the hallway, causing a pair of rushing crewmen to nearly crash into her. Each mess hall had two crew entrances; she went in through the second one. The normally overflowing buffet steamer tables now carried little fare. Overcooked fish stew was nearly ubiquitous, with potatoes and onions mixed in more often than not. Huge trays of bread were common, along with margarine and jams. Sometimes there was canned pasta and sauce, though that was getting rare.

She moved sideways, bypassing the food line and approaching the other door where she'd heard the conversation. When she was close enough, she listened.

"…idea what he was doing?"

"Supposedly, yes. But he started screwing around, and now we're in fuckin' outer space."

"What did they do with him?"

"The old man had him thrown in the brig."

Kathy took a piece of buttered bread and left, heading down the nearest gangway for three decks. She'd never been to the area herself, so she relied on her memory. Being a reporter required a good memory. She came within view of her destination only a minute after overhearing the conversation.

"Hi, Kathy," Chris Brown said.

"They put you in charge of watching him?" Kathy asked.

Chris had come in with Wade Watts, Andrew Tobins, and her. Chris, Wade, and Andrew had used an old gunship to rescue her and Cobb Pendleton from a farmhouse in South Texas just as they were about to be overrun with infected. They'd all ended up at Fort Hood. There, General Rose had reactivated Cobb, and he'd helped the three C-17s escape as the fort fell.

Kathy had fallen for Cobb when the man saved her from infected by following her all the way to Mexico. She wasn't the kind for casual flings. Their bond had developed quickly, as it sometimes did in life or death situations. When Cobb was left behind after the evacuation of Fort Hood, she'd been devastated. She hoped he was out there, somewhere, still trying to reach the coast.

"Yeah," Chris replied, shrugging. "They're pretty short staffed."

She knew very little about Chris, except that he was a good shot and had been drafted into service on the carrier as part of the security staff. Lacking anything else useful to do, he'd taken the job. She couldn't help thinking that whoever had him guarding Wade didn't realize they'd come in together.

"Can I talk to him?" Kathy asked.

Chris screwed up his face as he considered the request. Like her, he wore a uniform of navy-blue camo. Unlike her, he had a black band with SP in white wrapped around his upper arm. They'd never been ashore, of course. Still the shore patrol band gave him the authority he needed to help with security. At least, she figured that was the reason he wore it.

"Well," Chris finally said, "I don't know."

"It isn't an interview," she said. "I just want to talk to him."

Chris looked up and down the companionway outside the *Ford's* nominal brig. It was just a line of four small rooms with locks on the outside. Crewmen were moving about, but none took any notice of the occupied brig cell or the two people standing outside it.

"Okay," he said. "Only ten minutes, though. If the chief comes by, I'll probably get thrown overboard."

"Thanks, Chris," she said. He unlocked the door and opened it for her.

Inside the little room were a bench, a table, and a sink/toilet, like she'd seen in prisons. Wade was sitting on the bench, looking annoyed. "Hi, Kathy."

"What happened?" she asked, not wasting any time.

"One of the navy chiefs I was working with got me from the comms project."

"So, they gave up?"

"No," he said, grinning.

"You licked it?"

"Yup." His grin got even bigger, then it slowly died. "Well, sort of." Wade explained how he had found an ancient system that should have been shut down decades earlier and used it to work around the virus that was shutting down the military. He babbled on about the weird menu options in the system. He showed her the notebook and flipped through the pages of data. Kathy made sure her angle was perfect, so everything was recorded in 4k. He was like an excited school child. "Something huge is inside that old legacy system."

"Amazing," Kathy said. "But it doesn't explain why we're in space."

"After I got them back online, Chief Kuntzleman hustled me out of the room before I could do any more exploring, and he took me to the electronics repair section where two specialists were messing with the alien drive used to move the C-17."

Kathy sat on the closed toilet, as it was the only other seat she could find in the small cell. At the mention of the alien drive, she leaned closer. "You saw it?"

"Sure, it wasn't exactly hidden. It turns out someone also stole a key drive full of OOE data on the alien technology. The specialists couldn't break the encryption. So, I did it for them. There was a lot of data, and it explained how the alien tech worked, including some stuff that wasn't incorporated into the version built to move the C-17."

"What was different?" she asked.

"Have you looked outside?"

"Oh, right," she said. "Then they threw you in jail?"

"Pretty much."

"But, if you're in here, how are we going to get down?"

He scowled. "I think they're going to try to do it themselves."

"Do you think they can?"

"The data in the key drive contained a lot of hard math and calibration data. I screwed up; I understand that now." He shook his head and looked at the deck. "The alien effect travels through metal. The test table was electrically insulated on its feet to avoid making a circuit with the floor, but not the wall. I warned them not to turn the drive off or pull the table away from the wall. But I don't know if they listened to me."

"I think I understand," Kathy said and got up. She walked to the door where Chris had been listening curiously to the conversation.

"Where are you going?" Wade asked.

"To talk to Captain Gilchrist."

"Make sure they don't turn the drive off!" Wade yelled after her. Chris watched her leave in amazement.

* * *

**The Flotilla**

**150 Nautical Miles West of San Diego, CA**

"Got it!"

Jeremiah threw back the rest of his beer and ran out onto the balcony. A pair of OOE personnel familiar with astronomy had set up a telescope and had been working for hours, trying to find the aircraft carrier, without luck. Then Alex West took over. He'd only been at it for a few minutes before his sharp, pilot-trained eyes found what they were looking for.

"Where is it?" Jeremiah asked.

"Almost directly above us," Alex said, not taking his eye away from the eyepiece. "It's got a ball of water around it, just like this ship did."

"Must have used the data to connect a power module," Jack Coldwell said from a few feet away. He was smoking a cigarette and obviously savoring it. Jeremiah knew the physicist didn't have many left, and as he was one of the few smokers on the ship, he wasn't likely to get more.

"Then they're all still alive," Jeremiah said. He looked at his people, and they all nodded.

"At least until one of them unplugs the drive," Coldwell said.

"Boom!" Alex said, miming an explosion with his hands. "Wanna see?" he asked.

"Sure," Jeremiah said and moved over to the telescope. The telescope wasn't overly powerful, but the aircraft carrier filled up about a quarter of the view. The image shimmered because Jeremiah was seeing the ship through the water it 'floated' in. "How far up is it?"

"I'd estimate 500 miles or less." Alex gestured at the telescope. "Hard to be sure with that piece of junk."

"How about using radar?" Maria Merino suggested.

"The radar on the ship isn't powerful enough," Jeremiah said, shaking his head. "We only use the ship for low altitude observations. We rented orbital radar capacities from various sources and NASA." Jeremiah considered. "How long will their air last?"

"They've already been up there three hours," Alex said. "The interior volume of the forcefield bubble is pretty big. Maybe a day?

Probably less, if they're running any motors; carbon monoxide is a concern."

"Why haven't they tried to fly back down?" Alison McDill asked. She'd mostly designed the control interface that allowed them to use the alien drive.

"Afraid to try?" Alex asked. "I mean, they are in orbit. If I were a sailor, I'd be a little freaked out."

"Only a little?" Jeremiah asked. Alex shrugged. "We need to help them," Jeremiah said.

"What?" Patty said, her voice filled with surprise. "Why the fuck should we care?"

"They're up there because of us," Jeremiah said. Patty blanched, but Alex held up a hand.

"No, he's right."

"They *stole* the data," Maria Merino reminded them.

"Doesn't matter," Jeremiah said. He looked around at the group of scientists, pilots, and engineers. None of them looked excited at the prospect of rescuing the carrier. Not at all. He didn't care. "Get the *Azanti* ready to fly."

"The rear airlock is still dismounted," one of the mechanical engineers reminded him.

"So, weld a damn plate over it!"

* * *

Alex followed Alison through the hatch. He paused to look at the welds. It looked like a junior high school shop class had done the work. But the hatch was airtight, more or less.

"It'll hold up fine, Mr. West."

Alex turned a skeptical eye on the man. The welder was a big, beefy guy with hundreds of little burn scars on his arms and skin which was permanently tanned so dark he could pass for native American.

Patty nudged Alex forward and smacked the bulkhead. It rang dully. "Looks stout," she said.

"It should," Alex replied. "They cut it off a corridor in the ship and welded it on."

"As long as the forcefield holds up, we won't need it," Alison said. She was already in the flight engineers' seat, running a systems test.

"I'm more concerned about flying in a ship without any visible means of propulsion," Patty said. She was examining the controls—the pair of joysticks that replaced the single stick—the empty holes in the control panel, and most importantly, the glowing alien drive components. Maria Merino had added a power supply and a controller earlier, upgrading the tiny spaceship so it would have a forcefield.

"We have propulsion," Alex said as he took the pilot's seat and buckled in.

The problem was the metal-on-metal contact. The *Azanti* didn't have wheels, it had metallic landing struts. Normally, they'd act as skids on a runway with rubber pads. Those pads had never arrived. Thus it sat, metal legs on metal landing deck.

"We could have lifted it with a crane and set it on plastic drums." Alex set the controls to prepare for liftoff. "It would have taken too long to rig the heavy lift crane, though. This was quicker."

Patty shrugged and put on her headset. "This is the *Azanti*, we have a green board. Clear out, we're going to blast off." Alex gave her side-eye, and she laughed. "Or something."

Outside, the ground crew moved away quickly. Alex could see Jeremiah Osborne standing on his office balcony, high above the flight deck. The brilliant brain behind Oceanic Orbital Enterprises gave a thumbs up. Alex flipped a salute and verified nobody was near the ship.

"You're clear," came over the radio. Alex stroked the power controls, and the ship's dozen hydrazine-powered maneuvering jets roared. Fire ripped at the ship's deck and smoke billowed as the jets strained against the 90-ton mass of the spaceship. The jets weren't designed to lift the ship; they were designed to move it around in orbit.

Alex watched the fuel readout as the engines roared toward 100%. If the ship didn't move before the readout reached 50%, he'd have to abandon the effort. "Come on," he said under his breath. "Lift, you fat bitch!" The fuel level was dropping below 60% when he felt the first shudder. He pushed the throttle hard against the stop. *Maybe there's a little more?* The nose rocked up, and the computer compensated. All three contact lights went from green to red.

"Yes!" Patty yelled.

"We're up," Alex said.

"Gear up," Patty said.

"Engage the drive," Alex ordered.

Alison powered the drive, and Alex cut the rockets. They stayed perfectly level, and didn't move a millimeter.

"This is crazy," Patty laughed.

"You have no idea," Alison said.

"Here we go," Alex warned, and they accelerated upward slowly so they wouldn't suck the OOE ship into orbit with them. Once they were over a mile high, Alex slid the alien drive control throttle a couple notches forward, and the ocean fell away quickly.

* * *

**Classified Task Force**

Lieutenant JG Pearl Grange opened her eyes and looked around in confusion. *How did I end up in bed?* The room looked like a ship's infirmary, only not like anything on the *Boutwell.* Then it all came flooding back in one terrible wave of anguish. The ship, her ship, was gone, as was all her crew. Destroyed by a missile attack by an unknown enemy while she was trying to scout a place to set up a base in the Pacific Northwest.

"Glad to see you're awake," a man said.

Grange followed the voice and found herself looking at a man in some kind of spacesuit. He held a clipboard and was examining her with a sharp eye. "Who are you? What is this place?" She remembered someone questioning her. A tall man with sunglasses?

"I'm Dr. Meeker," the man said.

"Where am I?"

The man gave a small smile. "As for where you are, I cannot easily describe it. Suffice it to say you've been saved for a reason."

"Reason? What reason?"

"Not my place to say," he said. "I was ordered to heal you, and I have." He tapped on his tablet. "You are completely healthy."

"How?" she wondered. "Wasn't I blown up?"

He didn't answer; instead, he turned and left. She yelled after Dr. Meeker, but he didn't respond. She was alone in the perfectly white medical room.

Grange half expected to find herself strapped or handcuffed to the hospital bed, and she was surprised to find out that wasn't so. In fact, she didn't have an IV or any of those little sensors they used in hospitals to monitor your heart and stuff. The bed didn't have side rails or controls she could see. She sat up and turned, putting her feet over the side. She pulled down the bed covers and saw that she was wearing a gown just as white as the room and its fixtures. She was naked underneath, but strangely, she still wore her Coast Guard dog tags.

Feeling vulnerable and confused, she lowered her bare feet to the white tiled floor. It wasn't cold to the touch as she'd expected. She felt, for lack of a better word, perfect. It was as if she'd just woken up from a particularly satisfying nap. She got up and walked around the room, examining its contents.

Aside from the control-less bed, there was a nightstand with a lamp on it. She looked but found no control there either. She opened a drawer in the nightstand and found nothing inside. A dresser at the end of her bed had three drawers, also equally empty. Light came from a defused source set around the edges of the room, which looked to be about 15 feet on a side. Two doors exited the room—one the doctor had left through; the other was a mystery.

Upon finishing her circuit of the room, she suddenly figured out why it was giving her such a case of the creeps. It looked a lot like the room at the end of *2001: A Space Odyssey*—the room Frank Boorman seemed to live his whole life in, right down to the ubiquitous white hospital bed. She looked up, half expecting a big, black monolith to appear. It didn't, and she noted there was no chandelier either. The resemblance was still uncanny.

Grange tried the door Dr. Meeker had exited and found it locked. *No surprise there.* She went to the other door and found it opened into a small, fully equipped bathroom. Like the main room, it was almost completely white except for the fixtures on the sink and toilet, and the toilet paper holder, which were all chrome. Everything looked as though it had never been used—there wasn't a speck of dust anywhere or a scratch on the floor.

Realizing she needed to go, Grange used the toilet. All the while, she cast her eyes about suspiciously, wondering how many devices were watching her every move. Since she had just hiked up her hospital gown, they hadn't seen much. Of course, they'd taken her clothes off at some point, so being prudish seemed like a waste of effort.

She flushed the toilet and returned to the main room, where she found a woman waiting for her. She squeaked in surprise, taking a step back. The woman was old, very old. At least 80 was Grange's guess. She had a head of strikingly white, waist-length hair worn in several gold-threaded braids. She marveled at how long it must have taken to comb out and braid the hair. At Grange's exclamation, the woman turned ice-blue eyes toward her. Despite the woman's age, her eyes were filled with almost otherworldly intelligence.

"Pearl Grange, it is good to meet you." The woman took a step closer and held out an almost skeletal hand. "I am Jophiel."

"Are you really?" Grange asked. "Does everyone here have weird names?" She took the hand, which was quite cold but had a firm grip.

"Oh, without a doubt." She gestured toward a pair of chairs which Grange was certain had not been there before. They were placed against the wall to the left of the bed, opposite the bathroom. "Please, sit."

"Only if you tell me why I'm here."

"I can only promise to tell you what I am allowed to tell you." She crossed and sat gracefully in one of the two chairs. She didn't seem to be affected by her advanced age. Grange's eyes narrowed as she glanced at the other chair. "Please?" Jophiel inclined her head toward the chair. "I am old and tired; it hurts my neck to stare up at you."

*I doubt it,* Grange mused, yet she moved to sit in the chair.

"Drink?" A bottle of water was on the table between them. It, like the table and chairs, hadn't been there before. She gawked openly at it, and Jophiel gave her a knowing smile.

"Is this a dream or am I dead?"

"Yes, of a sort, and no."

It's a dream, and I'm not dead. Well, that's something at least.

"I will allow you two questions, which I will answer if possible. Then, you will answer two of mine. If you do not, we are done. Quid quo pro, Ms. Grange."

"Lieutenant JG," Grange corrected her.

The barest of smiles crossed Jophiel's thin, bloodless lips. She gestured for Grange to speak.

"Where is my crew?"

"You are the only survivor."

Grange cursed. Despite not being navy, Coasties were still sailors. An advanced skillset in curses was considered a resume builder. "Why did you attack the *Boutwell*?"

Jophiel stared at her for so long, Grange wondered if she'd heard the question. Then she spoke. "You trespassed on a classified operation and fired on federal agents who were performing their duties."

"They fired on us first!" Grange snapped. "If we were *trespassing*," she snarled the word, "why didn't someone call us on the radio to warn us? We were in the damned Columbia River, after all."

"You've had your two questions," Jophiel said without answering. Grange cursed again, and her interrogator's eyes twinkled. "Why were you in the Columbia River basin?"

"Orders," Grange replied.

"Who's orders?"

"Nobody you would know."

"Come, come, Lieutenant JG Grange. Your duty station is California. I'm sure there were plenty of people in need of rescuing off the California coast. Since I doubt *your* mission was classified, you won't be breaking orders by telling me."

Grange frowned. She had her there. "Okay, fine. We were tasked to look for an island to use as a safe harbor."

"By whom?"

"General Rose."

Jophiel stared into space for a second. "General Leon Rose, commander of III Corps?"

"Now, now," Grange said with her own grin. "You've had your two questions. Quid pro quo, Agent Starling."

Jophiel's smile grew big this time. "Very well. In answer to your earlier, third question, we were operating under strict radio silence. The sniper attack was an attempt to divert you without employing overwhelming lethal force. Sadly, you didn't take the hint. Next question, Hannibal."

*I wondered if she got the reference.* "I won't ask what's going on here, because I'm sure you won't answer. Instead, how have you avoided the plague?"

"We took precautions early on," Jophiel said simply.

Grange opened her mouth to follow up, then remembered she'd asked her second question. Instead, she picked up the water bottle and took a drink while she waited for Jophiel to speak. The water tasted…perfect.

"Is General Rose in command of the Flotilla?"

"No," Grange replied and set the water bottle down. "It's under naval control. Someone who was in Pearl."

"Is your Flotilla coming this way?"

"I don't think so," Grange said. "I never found a suitable location. I'm sure when I never returned, they didn't come after me." The last was a lie, she wasn't sure. However, General Rose only had a single ship and a few hundred soldiers. She doubted he'd risk them on one lost Coast Guard cutter.

"Very well," Jophiel said and got up. She gracefully headed toward the door.

"Wait, I have more questions."

"I have no doubt, but I don't need any more answers right now. Your questions will have to wait."

"Just one more?"

Jophiel stopped and turned back. She crossed her thin arms over her chest and waited. Grange took that as tacit approval to continue.

"You said this was sort of a dream. Is any of this real? Are we actually talking?"

"Two questions," Jophiel said. Grange spat. "However, the answer to your first question is no, and the second is yes. We'll talk again."

Grange moved to follow her, planning to grab the woman and make her answer more questions. She couldn't weigh more than 90 pounds, fully dressed. Grange had slung wet coils of rope weighing more than 100 pounds in her career. But as she reached out for Jophiel, the other woman dissipated like fog. An instant later, so did the room. Grange fell back into slumber.

* * *

::Cognitive VR Session Terminated::

Jophiel took the headset off and handed it to a waiting technician. Now unencumbered, she slowly and painfully got to her feet. Her back made a popping sound as she straightened. Sitting in the damned chair was like sitting on concrete and steel.

"Well?" Michael asked.

"As you thought, the navy is in charge. However, there's an army general, Leon Rose of III Corps, on the scene, too."

"The one who shot up our recon mission in Truth or Consequences, New Mexico," Michael said, his expression unreadable. "One mystery answered, at least. And the Flotilla, is it coming north?"

"I don't believe so," Jophiel said. "Looks like Rose sent her to look for an island base. Probably other scouts out too, but she doesn't know about them."

Michael turned to the CVR tech. "Confidence on those answers?"

"High," the man replied. "She seemed to realize early on the environment wasn't real, but her vitals indicated she was telling the truth, based on her neurological response to the news of her dead crew."

"Good," Michael said. "We'll do this again tomorrow."

"Isn't four times enough?" Jophiel moaned.

"Not to be certain she isn't concealing something, no," Michael said. "And before you go pissing and moaning about why you, you know full well you have the best, friendliest VR avatar in the group. The harmless, old librarian type."

Jophiel stared daggers at him, to the usual effect. Nothing. "I'm a linguist, not an interrogation expert."

"You are what Genesis needs you to be," he said darkly. "Just like the rest of us. Since you can't seem to break the alien's language, you might as well be useful."

"Fuck you, Michael," she spat and left the lab.

Michael gave a single snorting laugh most would have mistaken for a cough and walked over to the one-way glass. Grange was on the other side in her hospital bed, being carefully kept alive with drugs and medical devices. She'd been burned over 70% of her body. Despite the grievous injuries, the medical technology at Project Genesis' disposal could keep her alive indefinitely. They could have healed her, if they'd wanted. He shook his head. After they drained her of useful intel, they'd shut off the machines and toss her overboard. No loose ends.

The body on the other side of the glass twitched slightly. Another few days, a week at most, and he'd be able to stop worrying about this Flotilla. The satellite recon run an hour ago showed a general fragmenting of the ships. The group was slowly breaking up as they suffered outbreaks. In addition, the *Gerald R. Ford* was gone. It wasn't visible within the 100-mile-wide camera run. It must have sunk between passes of the spy satellite. Time was on their side.

The earpiece beeped, and he touched the control. "Michael."

"It's Chamuel," the voice came back.

"What do you have?"

"The techs have worked out the alien control interface for their space drive."

"It's about goddamned time," Michael said, excited despite the tone of his voice. "And the other systems?"

"This breakthrough should lead to others."

"Good. That it?"

"No."

Michael could see her in his mind's eye, body crippled by birth defects, mind as powerful as any of theirs. Her personality was as annoying as she was smart. "Well?"

"The Russians are moving against some of the surviving US assets."

"Who cares?" Michael replied. "They don't matter in the long term."

"We're some of those assets."

Michael pursed his lips, brought up short. "I thought they didn't know about us?"

"I calculate an 11% probability a Russian spy sat spotted our missile exchange with the USS *Boutwell.* That would have drawn attention to our squadron."

"We're in open water now," Michael said, recalling the afternoon briefing. "We left the Columbia River delta over five hours ago, and we are over 70 miles off the coast."

"There were nuclear attack subs stationed in this region. This was a high priority monitoring area for the Russians, both before and after the fall of the Soviet Union."

"Why the fuck didn't you say something before?"

"I was unaware you planned to have a naval battle in the river. Maybe if you had consulted me beforehand, when I warned you the sniper attack only had a 29% probability of succeeding, I could have warned you about the outcome."

"Yeah, whatever." Michael said under his breath. "Take whatever actions you deem appropriate to ensure we are not a target of the rogue Russian survivors."

"As you wish," she said and cut the line.

Michael contemplated the bigger picture for a minute, then left the medical section and walked up to the deck. The Pacific Ocean extended from horizon to dark horizon. A million, million stars lit the heavens. He desperately wanted to know which one of them spawned the alien and its society. Genesis was created to manage just such a first contact, only things had gone drastically wrong.

"We can still manage the situation," he said with conviction. A shooting star streaked across the sky and died.

***

**County Courthouse**
**Junction, TX**

Vance slammed a forearm into the infected's throat and pushed back as hard as he could. The former human being was incredibly strong, his face lean, and tendons stood out on his neck. He had all the hallmarks of someone who'd worked hard for a living or was an athlete. Regardless, he was now a flesh-eating, infected zombie, and he was trying to tear Vance's face off.

The fingers around his throat dug into his flesh, and he felt his skin tear. In a near panic, he brought his knee up into the infected's groin with all his might. A surprised grunt was all he got for his effort. The animal tried to lower his chin and bite Vance's hand. Vance felt a sinking sensation in his stomach.

The infected's head shattered in a blast, part of the energy from the impact rocking the creature off to the side. Vance closed his eyes and mouth to keep the blood out and rolled in the opposite direction.

"Vance, you okay?" Tim yelled as he ran over, his Mossberg shotgun still against his shoulder, the barrel smoking.

"I think so," he said as he got shakily to his feet. He pulled a cleaning rag from a pocket on his pants and ran it over his face. There was no blood on the rag. His breath was coming in shuddering gasps. "Fucker came out of nowhere." He pointed at the edge of the balcony.

Tim moved over and slowly looked over the side. "Holy shit," he said. *Boom, boom, boom.* "They're climbing up the damned brickwork!"

"How?" Vance asked. He drew his Glock and went over to look. One female infected was dangling from her fingertips only a few feet below them. He shot her in the top of the head, and she fell into the eager arms of a hundred hungry zombies below.

"I think they're wedging their fingers into the spaces between the bricks," Tim said. The other five in their group ran in, demanding to know what had just happened. Tim and Vance explained. Ann and Belinda instantly examined his face for signs of blood, Ann with concern and fear in her eyes, Belinda with the expert eye of a trained trauma nurse.

"I didn't get any on my face," he said.

"You've got blood all over the rest of you," Ann said. "You didn't get bit or cut?"

"No," he said and felt his neck. It was painful. Belinda checked it too, confirming the skin wasn't torn enough to bleed. "Dodged a bullet," he said.

Cobb, Harry, and Nicole were firing over the side, picking off the ones who were trying to climb. "Their hands look deformed," Harry noted.

"They're fuckin' mutating," Cobb said, then noticed how they were all looking at him. "Or something, man. Look at their hands, they're not human!" The sound of breaking glass from the other side of the building made many of them spin around, weapons at the ready.

"They're coming in the other side of the building," Cobb snapped and ran toward the sound.

"Help him check the barricade in the courtroom," Vance said.

"We're cornered," Ann said, her voice a low moan.

"We've been cornered since we retreated here," Vance reminded her.

"Now we're *really* cornered," Tim said.

Those left on the balcony took turns leaning over and picking off the infected with carefully placed head shots, so ammo wasn't wasted. Another problem was looming. The bodies were piling higher, giving the rest a grisly meat ramp with which to speed their attempted assault on the trapped humans above.

"Got it shored up as best we can," Cobb said when he returned.

"It's not going to hold long," Harry observed as something banged on the barricaded door.

"No," Vance said. "No it won't."

"Hey!" a voice yelled from above.

They all looked up and their mouths fell open.

"I must have died," Vance said after a second.

"Then I died too," Tim agreed, "because that's a flying houseboat." It was perfectly steady and quiet, maybe twenty feet above them. It illuminated the area in all directions, probably from lights on the deck. Its hull was hard to discern because it was dark and covered in dirt. Vance could just see a gleam from the craft's motionless propeller.

"You dumbasses going to just stand there gawking?" a voice boomed from above them. Vance looked to one side of the houseboat and saw a big, round, red-cheeked face with a bald head looking down at him.

"Bisdorf?" Vance gasped.

"No, I'm the goddamned Easter Bunny! No shit, it's Bisdorf. You all gonna grab the rope or not?"

The only one with the wherewithal to grab the dangling rope was Cobb. Vance guessed the army man had probably seen crazier things in his wanderings after the plague. Or maybe he was beyond the point where he could be struck dumb. Either way, he took the rope.

"Good. Now climb your asses up here before you get made into zombie goulash."

"We can't just leave our shit," Vance said.

"You got supplies? How much?"

Vance gave him a brief list of the guns and ammo they had, but he didn't mention the precious little food that remained. "There's a lot more in the pickups in front of the courthouse," Tim added.

"They're three deep under zombies," Bisdorf said. "Here, hold on." A second later, ropes started dropping over the side. "Start tying shit up, real fast like."

"What do we do?" Harry asked.

"You know this guy?" Cobb asked.

"Yeah," Vance said. Tim nodded. "He's Paul Bisdorf, one of the preppers from my network. Man's a legend in the ham radio community. Last I heard from him, we'd all agreed it was a Code-B."

"B for bugout," Tim added for Cobb's sake. "Means we believed society was toast, and the government couldn't stop the collapse."

"Yeah," Vance agreed. "It means use deadly force to protect your property. Kinda stuff you don't do when the law could show up. SHTF, shit hit the fan."

Cobb nodded in a way that indicated he didn't understand preppers.

"Time's a wastin'!" Bisdorf yelled from above.

"It's a floating boat!" Ann said incredulously to Vance, one hand resting protectively on her stomach. "You can't honestly expect us to climb up there?"

The sound of splintering wood in the courtroom made them all look nervously in that direction. "You have a better idea?" Vance asked.

"Fuck it," Cobb snarled and ran back into the courtroom. A second later, he came running back out, staggering under the weight of four huge ammo cans salvaged from his Stryker. When he headed back for his second load, the others joined in.

As they worked, Bisdorf continued to throw ropes over the side instead of hauling up the ones with secured loads. Vance didn't take time to question the tactic. It took them five minutes of breakneck work to get the majority of their gear tied onto the ropes, by which time the big, heavy, oak, courtroom doors had a crack wide enough to allow them to see ravenous flesh eaters on the other side, tearing their hands to bloody shreds trying to get through.

"Time to go, I think," Vance said, far calmer than he felt. Then he looked at the rope and the improbably hovering houseboat around 20 feet above. He swallowed. The best description of his size would be rotund. He could do a few pushups and jog a half mile without giving himself a coronary. However, it had been many years since he could do a pullup.

Cobb, Harry, Belinda, Tim, and Nicole all grabbed ropes and climbed. Vance looked at Ann who looked back in growing panic.

"No way I'm going to be able to climb," she admitted to him and patted her growing tummy.

"Me neither," he agreed and patted his grown tummy. He was trying to come up with a solution and checking his AR-15 when the courtroom door cracked down the middle and failed.

Out of time to consider, Vance grabbed one of the remaining ropes and looped it over Ann's back and under her arms. He tied a quick overhand knot.

"Vance…" she started to complain.

He looked over his shoulder. At least a dozen infected were falling over themselves to be the first into the courtroom and the feeding frenzy which awaited them. Time moved in slow motion as the first broke free and sprinted toward them. Vance looked at Ann, smiled, and nodded. "I love you," he said and yelled up. "If you can, lift!" Then he turned his rifle toward the rushing monsters and fired as quickly as he could.

"Vance!" Ann screamed as the floating houseboat rose. The dozen odd ropes lifted their attached gear like a bunch of lures from the water as the boat ascended. Ann tried to get a hand under the rope around her chest but failed as it tightened, and she was pulled off her feet. "Vance, no!"

"I got this," he said. The magazine in his AR locked empty. He ejected it, found another in his belt pouch and rammed it home. A pair of rushing female infected were only a yard away when he closed the bolt and fired at hip height. Both sprawled on the dusty, brass scattered floor. More infected were right behind them.

Everything was rising now. He glanced up and saw Cobb reach the gunwale of the boat and scramble over the side. Harry wasn't far behind, and the others were making progress. None were looking at the drama below. The courtroom doors were torn off their hinges, and a wave of infected came at him, looking like army ants.

The last rope swung over and hit him in the left shoulder. Vance coiled his left arm around the rope and locked a hand on it. Instantly, it went taut, and his shoulder ached as his bulk was lifted. He wanted to drop his rifle and grab the rope with his other hand. Wanted it with all his being. Only the wave was approaching, and the weapon was all he had. He fired methodically, a small part of his mind counting down from 30.

The pain in his shoulder quadrupled and something grabbed his right leg and pulled. Vance looked down and saw one of the two female infected he'd shot. Blood was jetting like a fountain from her torn carotid artery. It was a lethal wound, but she took no notice of it.

Automatic weapons fire from above tore into the advancing infected, ripping great chunks from flesh and bone. Vance was dimly aware of dozens being cut down. Confused by the sudden attack, the wave faltered as Vance was borne aloft.

Pain consumed him as he lowered his weapon and tried to aim. The sights blurred as he lined up the weapon's muzzle. *I can't aim*, he realized. But then the infected saw the barrel and grabbed it with one hand, thinking she could use it as leverage to reach higher up Vance's body. He let her pull the weapon downward as far as his arm would allow, then squeezed the trigger. The 5.56mm round blew the top of her head off, and she fell away.

The rope he was holding moved, then moved again. Vance managed to get the AR's sling over his shoulder and grab the rope with his other hand. A short time later, he was being pulled over the gunwale of the houseboat by many hands and lowered to the deck.

Bisdorf's round, ruddy face looked down at him. "Welcome aboard, my friend."

"Thanks," Vance gasped as he gingerly moved his shoulder. He looked down, sighed, and quit checking his shoulder. It didn't matter.

"Vance!" Ann cried and pushed through to him. "Baby, are you okay?" The look on his face made hers turn white. "What's wrong?"

Belinda was kneeling next to him, examining his right leg. Blood was pooling on the deck. She produced a pair of medical sheers and cut away the BDU fabric to expose his flesh. It was torn in the half circle pattern of a bite.

"No," Ann moaned.

"Yeah," Vance said.

"You should have pulled him up first!" she screamed at the others. None of them would meet her rage-filled gaze.

"No, they shouldn't have," Vance said sternly. "You're pregnant."

"It doesn't matter," Ann cried. "It doesn't matter."

"It does to me," Vance said. The other men began pulling up the gear dangling below the floating houseboat. Now that he was on it, Vance realized it was indeed Bisdorf's old houseboat that he kept on the Ninnescah River river just outside Wichita. "How?" he asked

Bisdorf. Belinda was bandaging his wound. He didn't have the heart to tell her to stop. Ann was sitting on the deck, crying into her hands.

"It's a long story. Can you walk?"

Belinda had finished applying the bandage, so he held out a hand. Bisdorf took it with one of his big, beefy paws and easily pulled Vance to his feet. The leg hurt like a son of a bitch, but it supported him. He nodded, and Bisdorf led him to the cabin. Ann got up and followed mechanically. Cobb fell in, watching him closely.

He heard Tim asking Cobb if there was a chance nothing would happen.

"I don't know," Cobb replied. "One of my men was bit on the hand. He turned in hours."

Vance pretended he hadn't heard, but he could hear Ann sobbing louder. He'd known as soon as he was bit that he was a dead man. The virus was far too communicable. It hadn't hurt as badly as he'd thought it would. If he hadn't been trying to keep his arm from being dislocated, it probably would have been worse.

Bisdorf led him into the cabin and showed Vance the hatch opening into the engine section. There was a weird crystal taped to the framework, and what looked like a cobbled together electronics module with wires leading away.

"What is it?" Vance asked.

"I found…well," Bisdorf looked uncomfortable.

"Spill it," Vance said.

Bisdorf responded by taking out a smartphone and calling up an image before handing it to Vance. It displayed a picture of a silvery thing, pointy at one end, wider at the other. "It's a damned space-ship, Vance."

"Bullshit," Cobb said. Bisdorf reached over and swiped the phone's screen, showing more images. Tim and Cobb leaned in to watch. The pictures showed the object opened up with several glowing rods like the one before them inside.

"I intercepted some shortwave traffic," he explained. "It was encrypted, but not very well." Bisdorf grinned. "It was a bunch of locations and instructions on how to use ultrasonic frequencies to open up the ships. Well, one of those locations wasn't a mile off the Ninnescah River, so I tied up at an old fishing pier and checked it out."

He moved further forward, into the hallways leading to the houseboat's various cabins. In one was the thing he claimed was a spaceship. A pair of openings showed panels he'd removed, and one still had a blue, glowing crystal inside. "Still think it's bullshit?" Vance shook his head in amazement.

"Along with the other data were some details on how to wire this and make it work. Didn't say what it did," Bisdorf said, then laughed. "Imagine my surprise when Hubba Tubba here took to the skies."

"I'd have shit myself," Tim said.

"How long can it just…float?" Vance asked.

"Don't know," Bisdorf admitted and shrugged. "I haven't set it down since I turned it on—goin' on three days now. I been looking for survivors. Found quite a few. When I locate them, I take them to a safe place."

"Where?" Tim asked.

"Right now, up by Amarillo."

Vance coughed and staggered. Tim and Bisdorf looked at him in concern. "I don't feel well," Vance said.

"Come up on deck," Tim said and took his old friend by the hand.

Vance was having trouble concentrating. He blandly allowed himself to be led. The rest of his group was on deck, their faces wearing looks ranging from fear to mourning. Ann stood in front of him, despair etched on her features. "Ann," he said. His words were slurred. She ran over and took him in her arms. "Ann…I…I…" he couldn't make the words form.

"I know," she sobbed in his ear. She moved to kiss him.

"Ann, no," Cobb said.

"He's my husband!" she sobbed.

"You are going to throw away everything he sacrificed for you. You're pregnant. Think about the baby."

"It's not fair," she cried.

The words didn't make sense anymore. Another voice was speaking in the back of his mind, its sound becoming louder and clearer. *Bite, chew, rend!* A little snarl escaped his lips, and suddenly, Ann was pulled from his arms. His teeth snapped closed, just missing her fingertips.

Tim and Harry held him from behind. He struggled wildly, the voices driving him to attack. He felt them remove his gear belt and pull him toward the side of the boat. He fought as hard as he could, harder than he thought he could. *The flesh. Share the flesh!*

"Belinda, Nicole, for the love of God, get Ann below," Tim yelled. Bisdorf stood aside, his eyes wide, unable to do more than watch. Cobb was near him, waiting, in case they needed help.

"We can't just throw him over the side," Harry said. Ann screamed as she was taken below.

"No, he deserves better," Tim said.

Very little of Vance Cartwright's mind remained his own. He did everything he could to pull his arms free from where they were pinned behind him. He heard a safety click without understanding what it was. He never heard the boom of the gun firing.

* * *

**USS *Gerald R. Ford***

**Approximately 400 miles above San Diego, CA**

"Miss Clifford, I would have to be insane to let the man anywhere near the alien drive." Captain Gilchrist was surrounded by a dozen officers begging for his attention. Kathy had managed to get to the door of the CIC by saying she had vital information. The powerful ship's captain had been less than impressed when she only appealed to let Wade try again.

"Have your people been able to do anything?" she asked.

"Not yet," he said.

Despite his seeming confidence, Kathy could see the faces of the men around him and knew they had no clue.

"Then what do you have to lose?"

"A carrier, Ms. Clifford, and the thousands of lives aboard her."

"Come on, Captain, see logic—"

"Madam, I won't be lectured. We'll figure this out without Mr. Watts' none-too-gentle help. An idea has been proposed, and we're making plans around it."

"I hope it doesn't involve cutting the power to the alien drive."

Gilchrist blinked and shot a look at one of the men behind him. The other man swallowed. "And why is that?"

"Because Mr. Watts says doing so would probably kill everyone on board."

His mouth became a thin line, and he nodded. "Okay, I'll take it under advisement. Now, you must excuse me."

She tried to stop him, but the burly Marine guarding the door strongly, but gently, moved her back as it closed. That was that. Well, she'd given it her best. She turned and headed back toward her compartment. A little smile played across her face. At the least, she'd gotten several minutes of video from inside the CIC on her concealed camera!

*****

# Chapter Four

**Early Morning, Friday, May 3**

**Private Spaceship Azanti**

**Approximately 400 miles above San Diego, CA**

Alex had hoped that with the addition of more advanced alien components, the *Azanti* would be more controllable. It wasn't. It was still like trying to fly an F-18 with oven mitts on his hands and beer goggles over his eyes. Clearly, the alien drive was designed to be operated with a considerable amount of automation. The last thing he wanted was to accidentally end up going faster than light again, so he played the controls as lightly as he could.

Once they reached orbit, it took hours to find the supercarrier. He'd thought it would be easy, but he'd made the rookie mistake of not following the bearings he'd gotten from the ground. By the time he realized his mistake, they were hundreds of kilometers up and had to resort to Mark 1 Eyeball reconnaissance. The radar didn't work through the damn forcefield. He made a note for the engineers.

The first spotting turned out to be a false alarm—a big old satellite they'd almost plowed right into. After that he took the time to really look at a target before heading toward it. By the time they actually located the ship, sunlight had covered the coast of California far below.

He overshot his first approach and had to circle back, slower this time. When he finally got the *Azanti* within a kilometer of the *Ford*, the ship's clock said they'd been in the vessel for seven hours. He took his hands from the controls and sighed, rubbing his eyes and massaging the bridge of his nose.

"Tired?" Patty asked.

"You know it," he replied.

"Shoulda gotten sleep before we went up," Alison suggested.

"The longer we waited, the more likely someone on the *Ford* would have pulled the plug to see what would happen," Alex replied.

Patty took the little telescope Jeremiah Osborne had loaned them from his swank office and focused it on the floating aircraft carrier. She snorted and shook her head. "It's like something out of a Japanese cartoon."

"Anime," Alison corrected. Patty glared at her. "Japanese animated shows are called anime."

"Whatever," Patty mumbled as she focused again. "It's just hovering there, in the water," she said. "Like a ship in a bottle."

"Any signs of life?" Alex asked her.

She moved the telescope back and forth with tiny movements as she examined the ship. "I don't think so…wait, yes, I can see colors moving around."

"Deck crew," Alex said. "They haven't tried turning the drive off and on or anything."

"Wouldn't the water be gone if they had, even for a second?" Alison asked.

"How am I supposed to know? This alien shit makes no sense to me."

"Woah!" Patty suddenly said.

"What?" Alex asked.

"Something exploded right next to the carrier."

"Inside with it?" Alison asked.

"No," Patty said. "Outside."

"Maybe a satellite," Alex said. "Any signs of damage to the carrier?" Patty said no. "Then we can't worry about it right now." He took a breath and resumed the controls. "Okay," he said. "Here we go." He mumbled curses under his breath as he moved the joystick ever so gently, pushing the forward velocity control upward. As they zoomed toward the carrier, it grew at an alarming rate.

"Shit!" Patty cried.

Alex moved the control to neutral, and they instantly stopped. He guessed they were less than a hundred meters away. "Okay," he said. "Now that we're closer, Alison, can you fix the stupid sensitivity?"

"It was fine until they hooked the drive module to the cluster," Alison said and opened the little metallic box that housed the flight control systems. "We need a more sensitive potentiometer. I'll turn this one all the way down."

"Keep an eye on the systems while I see if I can raise anyone," Alex told Patty. She nodded and settled into the task. Alex put on his headset and keyed in the common fleet frequency. They'd tried contacting them just before taking off, but they received terse warnings from other US warships about not using the frequency.

"USS *Gerald R. Ford*, this is private spacecraft *Azanti* calling in the open. Do you read? Over."

"Private spacecraft?" Patty asked, laughing.

"What the fuck would you call us?"

"Alien technological kludge," Alison replied.

"Doesn't have the same ring to it," Alex said under his breath, then repeated the call. On the third try, he got a reply.

"USS *Gerald R. Ford*, who is this?"

"We're a privately owned spacecraft, operated by OOE. You know, the ones you stole the key drive full of data from? The key drive which let you fucking idiots accidentally stick an aircraft carrier in orbit? Get me the captain, and we might be able to get you back on the water in one piece."

He must have struck pay dirt, because the radio was silent for over five minutes. Finally, a stern sounding, confident man, not the younger person he'd spoken to before, came on the radio.

"This is Commander Tobias, XO on the *Ford*. Who am I speaking to?"

"This is Captain Alex West, on the *Azanti*."

"I don't recognize the ship's name, but I do recognize yours. You were with the group who brought the artifacts aboard."

"If you mean the alien spaceships, you are correct."

"What else did you do while you were here?"

"I flew the C-17 off the deck using one of the alien drive modules. Probably the one you foolishly hooked to the ship's superstructure which turned the carrier into a spaceship."

"I wish I could say you were mistaken. Sadly, I cannot. Captain Gilchrist sends his regards, but he is unavailable at this time."

"If he can't talk, we've got a problem. It would behoove you to be frank with me, Commander."

The line was silent for a time, then Tobias came back. "We're having reactor problems. Bad ones. We are afraid it's linked to the alien drive."

"Don't turn it off!" Alex said loudly.

"We've been warned," Tobias said, his voice sounding sour. "It's a long story, but we threw the idiot who did this in the brig after he screwed around with the thing without talking to anyone."

"What a moron," Alicia said.

Alex glanced back and noticed her working on the control panel, while it was live, and shook his head. *What would some alien think if they could see you now?*

"How can we help you?" Alex asked. "You've been up here a long time, so we guessed you're at a loss."

"We are. Since we borrowed *your* notes, can you help us better understand how to operate the interface?"

"Borrowed," Alison growled.

Alex waved her off and replied. "We have remote video capabilities. Hold on, our electronics engineer, Alison McDill, will provide the video connection details."

"Looks like we have another eight hours of life support," Patty said. "Hope you guys can figure things out by then."

"I'm not sure we have that long," Alex said and pointed. Inside the invisible globe where the *Ford* floated, the water next to the hull was boiling. Clearly, something was desperately wrong with the warship. Time was running out.

* * *

**Morning, Friday, May 3**

**Somewhere Over North Texas**

Ann Benedict had stopped crying sometime in the last hour and finally fell into a slumber in Nicole Price's arms. The survivors of the group who had saved

Vance looked devastated. He had been their leader, the one who'd kept them alive through a combination of ingenuity and resourcefulness Cobb had seldom seen. The man would have made a wonderful army officer. He commanded respect and loyalty, which he rewarded by sacrificing himself at a critical moment.

Cobb had shot the former leader when Strain Delta took him. He could see the crushing burden on the faces of the other survivalists, so he lifted it from their shoulders. After all, Cobb hadn't known the man more than a few days. It had been long enough for him to learn to respect Vance, and it was with that respect that he pulled the trigger and watched the body drop into the night.

The sun lit the big Texas sky for them. A few clouds drifted by lazily, not far above them. Cobb wasn't a pilot, but he guessed the ship's height was around 5,000 feet—high enough that it was cooler, on the verge of chilly. It felt like the time he'd taken a hot air balloon ride with his late wife.

*Damn it.* He wished he hadn't thought about Jen. He hadn't thought about her in days. Lately he'd thought more about Kathy than his late wife, and it bothered him. Jen had only been gone some two years. The memory of her wasting away from late stage breast cancer was one of the most painful in his life. Seeing Kathy fly away on a C-17 while he sat on the ground in a Stryker armored combat vehicle battled for supremacy with his other painful memories.

His time with Jen had been measured in decades, his time with Kathy in days. Still, his feelings for both were strong. The reporter had found her way into his heart far faster than he'd thought possible. Not a single woman had interested him after Jen passed, until Kathy. She'd hit him like a lightning bolt out of the blue. Now, she was probably dead.

Flying to the west coast had been a desperation move. Shortly after the armada of planes left, he'd tried repeatedly to reach another unit with his army radio. Any unit. It was like they'd all disappeared. So, he'd driven his Stryker west with the silly idea of reaching her. He made it all of 150 of the 1,700 miles before everything had gone to shit.

"I knew Vance for almost 20 years."

Cobb looked up from his ruminations at Bisdorf who was standing next to him. "Don't you have to fly this thing?"

Bisdorf looked confused, then shook his head. "Naw, you just set the direction and the speed. We have a couple of electronics whiz kids who McGuyvered up some modifications to the plans we intercepted." The big man shrugged, then grinned an infectious smile. "It's pretty damned amazing, especially since they figured out the forcefield."

"I'm sorry, the what?"

"Forcefield," Bisdorf repeated. "Like *Star Trek*. Light and radio waves go right through it, but bullets and bombs don't." He got a queer look on his face. "No air, either…isn't that strange?"

"Strange doesn't explain it," Cobb said. "Why don't you explain it to me?"

Bisdorf relayed a story about how they'd intercepted the radio transmission about the alien ships, where they were located, and how to take them apart. Cobb had heard some of it before Vance succumbed to the plague. Hearing it again put things in context. Then Bisdorf dropped a bomb.

"We've recovered six of the alien ships so far, and we found a dead alien on one of them. When we hooked up with someone who'd been doing work for the CDC, he said they think the plague came from an alien on one of those ships."

"No shit," Cobb said. "An alien zombie plague?"

"Yup," Bisdorf said. He tried to look serious, but he was grinning.

Crazy bastard thought it was cool. "You can't make this stuff up." Bisdorf shook his head. "So, what kind of safe place do you have? Must be hard to keep the infected away."

"Not as hard as you'd think," the other man said and pointed. "There it is. We call it Shangri-La."

Cobb followed the other man's arm and saw what he thought was an optical illusion. A strange shimmer on the northern horizon. Over the next minute, his eyes adjusted to the light, and he realized it wasn't an optical illusion; something was hovering over the Texas sky. The sun, still low in the east, was reflecting off multiple surfaces, making it hard to focus.

"What is it?" he asked.

"You might call it a junkyard. Except, junkyards don't fly."

Cobb grunted and continued to watch. "Can't we go faster?"

"We've had a hard time controlling the speed. Almost ended up in space once, so now we keep it under 200 mph."

"We're going 200 miles per hour?"

"Yeah," he said. "Remember the forcefield I mentioned? I can turn it on and off." Birdorf showed Cobb the controls, which appeared to be using an Xbox controller and a video game throttle body. The forcefield sounded like sci-fi, except Cobb could see the ground whizzing by a couple thousand feet below, and he felt absolutely no air flow.

"How can we breathe? Does air go through it?"

"No," Bisdorf replied. "I have to shut the shield off every hour." He showed Cobb his watch with a timer running down. "Of course, I have to slow down first. Almost tore the damned pilot cabin off the other day!"

"This isn't real."

"My best friend is dead," Tim Price, who'd come up during the discussion, said. "It's pretty damned real to me."

Cobb had forgotten the group who'd rescued him were long-time friends. Vance might not have been a soldier, but he'd inspired his friends to follow him. He'd managed to keep them alive in the middle of a fucking zombie plague. Cobb had lost his whole Stryker crew, and they'd all been experienced combat vets.

In the time they'd been talking, Shangri-La had come much closer. It had more shape and definition. In particular, Cobb could see that it was primarily constructed from Conex cargo containers. Hundreds, no, thousands of them. They formed the base of the structure. On top was a fleet of mobile homes and trailers, both bumper-pull and big fifth wheels. There were buses, cars, trucks with campers, semi-trailer style bunkhouses, and a big paddle wheel boat.

"That's got to be the craziest assortment of vehicles I've ever seen," Harry Ross said. The big former Marine had joined them in the cockpit to observe the approaching spectacle.

"How many of those…" Cobb struggled to say it. "…those alien drives does it take to keep it in the air?"

"One," Bisdorf said. Cobb gawked at him, and Bisdorf nodded. "I know, right? Yeah, just one. Since we don't have to worry about zombies, we don't bother with a shield. Just a drive, and it's run by a solar panel and a lithium ion battery."

"Take a lot of voltage?" Tim asked.

"I think 12 volts, less than an amp."

By now, they were less than a mile away, and their host was slowing his flying houseboat. It was obvious Shangri-La was bigger than an aircraft carrier. Longer, wider, and thicker. Cobb guessed two or three times bigger, in fact. He thought it was floating about 500 feet above the countryside and was slowly moving north. A series of five cranes had been mounted around the perimeter of the roughly wedge-shaped craft.

"What are the cranes for?" Tim asked, voicing Cobb's question while he struggled with what he was seeing.

"Salvage, of course." Bisdorf pointed. They could see a lot of people now. "We have over 2,000 people to feed, after all."

"Who's in charge?" Cobb asked.

"Ann Taylor," Bisdorf said.

"You mean…"

"Yeah, the Lieutenant Governor of Texas. We picked her up a few days ago from the top of a building in Austin. She had some staff and a bunch of state patrol officers with her."

"Tough broad," Cobb said. "I voted for her."

"Vance didn't like the way she kept pushing for an income tax," Tim said. "But she was firm on guns." He chuckled and shrugged. "With Vance it was always all or nothing."

They were only a few hundred yards away, so Bisdorf slowed to a crawl. Cobb could see everything now, and the dizzying variety of construction made him speechless. The base was five containers thick, and some of the top was built from tankers. They were situated in groups with tubes connecting them and running off to huge generators, which were also mounted on Conex bases. "Whoever put the thing together was a damned genius."

"A lot of containers," Tim said.

"Metric shit ton," Harry agreed. "All empty, I presume?"

"Oh no," Bisdorf said. "Most are full. We loaded up in Houston after we had the basic structure, which came from a container yard in San Antonio. One of our people worked for customs; he had files on almost every container in the south—where it was and what was in it. We've been working non-stop to fill all the containers with canned or preserved food which was manufactured more than two months ago. I think we have a billion packages of ramen noodles!"

"I like ramen," Tim said.

"You won't in a couple weeks," Bisdorf said and winked at him. "We have a couple dozen refrigerated containers with beef, pork, and chicken." The other three men looked at him in alarm. "It's from China, and we checked the date. All butchered months ago. But we have someone from the CDC office in Corpus Christi who developed a test for the virus."

"Wow, amazing," Cobb said. "Never heard about it in the military."

"You wouldn't have; they only worked it out a few days ago."

"I think I need to talk to the governor," Cobb said.

"Why?" Bisdorf asked.

"I'm a US Army colonel, reactivated, and I know where a whole lot of soldiers were heading."

Bisdorf stared at him for a second, then nodded. "Okay. Let's land, and I'll take you to her."

***

**Private Spaceship *Azanti***

**Approximately 400 miles above San Diego, CA**

"Well, that was a bad idea," Alison said, holding a bandage to her bleeding forehead.

"Certainly a surprise," Patty agreed.

"Can we keep the seat belts locked from now on?" Alex asked.

Alison nodded. "The stupid fake gravity was rock solid for half a light year away and back, why did it choose to go ape shit when I wasn't buckled in?"

"We hit the carrier's field," Alex said. "At least I think we did."

After talking with the *Ford* for a time they were unable to walk the sailor in charge through the process of fixing the *Ford's* alien drive. Chief Kuntzleman was knowledgeable, as were the two sailors helping him, Seaman Bond and Seaman Apprentice Dodd, however they couldn't figure out what was wrong.

The module was the same as the one that had been cobbled together by Alice so the navy could get their C-17 off the deck. Alex should have known, as he and Alison were the ones who flew the plane. It still sat on the deck, right where they'd left it. The carrier looked like a ship in a bottle, complete with water under her keel. Only ships in a bottle weren't surrounded by steaming water from a wonky reactor.

"Mr. West," Kuntzleman said suddenly, "Captain Gilchrist wants to talk to you."

"Oh?" Alex asked. "Sure."

"West? You in command of that spaceship?"

"Yes, sir. I was a test pilot for NASA a long time ago."

"Look's like you upgraded. I understand you're trying to get this thing back into the damned ocean?"

"We've been trying, sir."

"What happened a few minutes ago? The entire ship jerked."

"We tried to pass through your forcefield. Proved to be a bad decision. The fields are interacting in some strange way."

"We noticed. It's also doing something to our reactor. The techs can't get it to scram, or shutdown. It keeps making more power, and the cooling water is overheating."

"We saw. The ocean, or rather the water in there with you, is starting to boil."

"Yeah, getting hot in here too. West, you gotta help us get outta here, or I'm going to have a couple thousand dead sailors."

"We're doing what we can. Kuntzleman said someone modified your drive module. Can you get him to work on it again?"

"Mr. West, I'm not so inclined. Mr. Watts is in the brig for taking liberties which got us into this."

"He might be the only one who can get you out of it."

"I'd rather you unscrewed this."

"Stubborn," Patty whispered.

"Comes with the eagle," Alex said. "You don't get a carrier by letting others tell you how to do things."

"He ain't gonna have a carrier much longer if he can't get it out of space," Patty said.

"I heard that last part," Gilchrist said. "As much as I'd like to be annoyed, I agree with you."

Alex thought for a second, then pointed at the carrier only a hundred meters away. "You know, there might be a way to solve both problems."

"I'm listening."

"Your ship is watertight, isn't it?"

"Wouldn't be much of a ship if it weren't."

"Okay," Alex said. "This is going to sound crazy, so if you'd rather let Mr. Watts get back to work on the controller…"

"I wouldn't."

"Fine, then listen. You don't have a lot of time."

A minute later Captain Gilchrist spoke. "You're right, that's crazy."

"It might be your only choice, Captain. What's it going to be?"

The alarm claxon sounded over and over making Kathy Clifford look up from her computer in alarm. She'd been cutting and splicing video footage she'd obtained during her clandestine wanderings and other events on the *Gerald R. Ford.* It might be the end of the world, and she might be aboard an aircraft carrier in orbit, but she was still a reporter. *Maybe it will make a great book someday.*

She got up and looked out into the corridor just as a voice blared over the big speaker they called a squawk box.

"Now hear this, now hear this. All stations secure for NBC attack. All stations, secure for NBC attack. This is not a drill!"

A dozen sailors had been within sight of where she stood. At the first mention of NBC, they leaped into motion, running in every direction. *What does a TV network have to do with a carrier?*

"Clear the corridor!" one sailor yelled. Kathy barely pulled back in time to avoid being flattened by the man.

"What's going on?" she yelled after him. He didn't reply.

A sailor in an adjoining compartment came out and ran to her. "Ma'am, step back please?" He framed it like a question, but she knew he didn't mean it as one. She stepped back.

Before she had time to ask what was going on, he slammed the big metal door on the video room she'd been assigned shut. It closed with a rusty squeal of protest, and she saw the steel locking bars move as he spun the wheel. She didn't know much about the workings of a ship, but she did know enough to realize she'd just been locked in. *What the fuck is going on?*

Kathy tried the big handle in the middle of the door. It didn't budge. The goddamned claxon kept blaring. She was below the waterline, so she didn't have a window or porthole. What she did have was access to all the camera feeds.

She sat at the metal desk where her equipment was set up and clicked through the camera feeds. They'd only given her access to a few. One was of the hangar deck and the few planes and helicopters on it. Another pair of cameras showed the flight deck, one looking forward, one aft. Sailors were scrambling around, checking the planes to be sure they were tied down. The hangar looked the same, only they were closing some weird-looking doors which she'd never seen closed before. They were dividing the hangar deck into sections. Everyone was moving like Satan was on their asses.

"How can we be under attack? We're in space," she said to the empty room. It was then that she remembered her little handheld radio. Chris Brown had one, and they'd used them occasionally to keep in contact, because they were forbidden to use the ship's intercoms. It took her a second to find it. "Hey, Chris, you there?"

He answered almost immediately. "Yeah, Kathy, you in your quarters?"

"No, some damned sailor just locked me in the video room. I can't open the door."

"Okay, good. I'm secured in the brig with Wade. Don't try to leave."

"Why? What's an NBC?"

"It stands for Nuclear, Biological, and Chemical."

"Oh…shit."

"Yeah. The Marines down here are taking it seriously."

"But we're in *space*, Chris. How can we get nuked?"

"The Marines think the reactor might be leaking."

Kathy swallowed. She'd done some correspondence work around nuclear power plants. She'd even looked in the pool they stored fuel in and saw the ghostly blue glow. None of that made her nervous. She had visited Fukushima and done a report from the exclusion zone. The dosimeter she wore recorded that she had absorbed the equivalent of a dozen chest x-rays worth of radiation in less than a day. She hadn't felt a thing, yet her skin still crawled, and she was nervous about every ache and pain for weeks afterwards.

"Radiation," she whispered.

"Yeah," Chris repeated. "Look, some of the Marines want me to secure in place. So, I gotta go; bye!"

"Chris, wait!" He didn't reply, and Kathy frowned. She didn't like being locked up and not told what was going on. It was the investigative journalist in her; she liked answers.

About 15 minutes passed before another announcement came over the PA.

"Attention all hands, secure for rough sea and possible collision." Like before, the message repeated another time.

"Rough seas? Collision?" She tried to imagine what the message could mean as she looked at the views the monitors afforded. It was then that she noticed the flight deck was abandoned. As was the hangar deck. *What's going on?* Then, everything exploded, and she flew across the compartment.

* * *

"I'd like to go on record as saying this is insane," Patty said.

"Yeah," Alison said. "I'm gonna have to go with Patty on this one. Nuts."

"Your objection is duly noted. Their reactor is losing its mind, and the captain trusts Mr. Watts even less than this plan. So stand by, here we go."

"Oh shit," Alison said and tugged on her straps to make sure they were tight.

"*Ford*, this is the *Azanti*, you may proceed when ready."

"You sure about this, Mr. West?"

"Yes, Captain Gilchrist. We've got more than a little experience with these devices."

"We've never done this in *space*," Alison hissed.

Alex made a shushing gesture, and she glared back at him and flipped him the finger.

"Very well. Standby, handing you back over to Chief Kuntzleman."

"Ready on this end," the navy chief said after a few seconds.

"Ready out here," Alex replied.

"Roger. In three…two…one…"

From a short distance away, the view was spectacular. The slight shimmering of the atmosphere inside the forcefield was there one moment, gone the next. The water which sat under the huge super-carrier's keel seemed to explode away from the hull in every direction. Alex thought it looked like a snow globe which had been shaken for several minutes.

Alex could see innumerable small, unidentified objects, metal racks, a couple of plane tugs, and the venerable C-17 he'd rescued float away. Apparently, there hadn't been time to tie it down properly. Too late to worry about it.

"Here we go," he said and carefully nudged the controls forward. He hadn't had much experience flying the *Azanti* like an airplane. He lined it up with his target as best he could by eyeballing it, so when the *Ford* turned off their alien drive, he shot forward.

"Easy, *Jesus!*" Patty cried as they raced toward the huge carrier like a bullet.

Alex nodded but didn't slow. They rocketed toward and into the side entrance to the carrier's cavernous hangar deck. He zeroed the forward momentum control, and just like it had before, the ship came to an instant stop.

"Holy shit, holy shit, holy shit," Alison said repeatedly.

"Crazy mother fucker," Patty agreed.

"Smooth as a baby's ass," Alex said. He moved them forward a couple meters and stopped. "Kill the drive," he ordered.

"I hope they welded the door on well," Alison said.

"Me too," Alex agreed. Alison turned off the drive power.

*BOOM!* The atmosphere around the *Azanti* vented in a split second. The spaceship's hull groaned, and they could hear hissing from the temporary hatch the OOE techs had welded on the back. Alex didn't waste any time; he switched to the ship's OMS, orbital maneuvering system, the same one they'd used to get it off the ground. He pulsed it downward, pushing the ship onto the hangar deck with a *gong* which reverberated through the *Azanti's* hull.

"Now!" he yelled, and Alison turned the drive back on.

With metal-to-metal contact against the *Ford,* the effect of the alien drive on the *Azanti* was miraculously extended from the 50-ton space craft to the 100,000-ton aircraft carrier, reestablishing the forcefield and gravity around both. The hissing of escaping air continued, and the 'pressure loss' alarm blared for attention.

"*Ford,* this is the *Azanti.* We have established contact. We also have pressure loss, can you please open the doors?"

"We're working on it, *Azanti,*" Kuntzleman replied.

"What do you mean by working on it?" Alex asked, his two crewmen exchanging nervous glances.

"The doors are reluctant to move with all the interior pressure against them."

"Oh boy," Patty said.

"One of them is moving," Alison said and pointed out the cockpit window.

Sure enough, the big, wide door they'd flown through a minute ago was grinding slowly closed. It finished with what Alex was sure would have been an impressive *boom* worthy of an action film, but they didn't hear anything since they were still in vacuum.

"Halfway there," Alex said.

They sat and waited, pressure bleeding slowly off their ship, replaced by oxygen from internal tanks. Alex glanced at the displays. They could continue for another 30 minutes before the oxygen tanks were exhausted, at which point the cabin pressure would begin to fall. Once that happened, another 5 minutes, and they'd be sucking vacuum. Luckily, they didn't have to worry about it.

The big door on the other side moved with a sudden jerk. Slowly, it ground closed, and the hissing lessened.

"We're pumping air to the hangar from the rest of the ship," Kuntzleman said. "The chief engineer says we can pressurize your bay and only lose about 2 PSI on the rest of the ship."

"That's not too bad; we appreciate it." He looked at the displays and saw that the outside pressure was already up to 5 PSI and climbing steadily. "In the meantime, want to go home?"

"Mr. West," Gilchrist cut in, "we'd very much appreciate being back in the water. However, don't you have to come down to our drive module?"

"Not at all, Captain. When we connected to your hull, our ship's drive took over. If you can send me as many external camera feeds as you have, we'll be happy to take us down to Earth. I'm blind in here, and need eyes outside."

"I'd appreciate it."

Alex grinned. The man sounded more than skeptical. That was fine; he was about to learn. "Let's head down, shall we?" Alex asked.

"Sounds good," Alison said.

"For sure," Patty agreed.

Their monitors displayed the somewhat grainy views of the carrier's fore and aft. It looked like the view came from the bridge. Alex took the controls and moved the Z axis slowly down. On the camera feed, the horizon moved upward; the *Gerald R. Ford* was going back to Earth.

* * *

When the drive was cut off, aboard the *Ford* it was anarchy given birth. There wasn't time to explain to the thousands aboard that they were about to experience freefall. Most didn't fully understand that they were in space.

The human body, in the simple act of standing, exerts enough force against the ground to keep itself upright. When gravity simply disappeared, anyone standing basically performed an unintended vertical leap straight up. Absent gravity, there was nothing to arrest the leap, so countless crewmen crashed into the roofs of the compartments they were in.

In a second, hundreds were spinning around hangar decks, rec rooms, galleys, engine spaces, and everywhere else imaginable. People screamed and yelled. Some collided with metal roofs and supports with enough force to crack skulls.

Kathy Clifford was lucky enough to not be standing. She still floated off the deck and squeaked in alarm, her hands shooting out to grab hold of something. She managed to catch the counter as one of her computers sailed past; however, all she succeeded in doing was changing her upward flight into an arc which caused her to collide with the wall and rebound.

"What the hell?!" she screamed as she spun like a pinwheel. Her left arm slapped painfully against a steel beam running across the roof. She cried out, but still managed to grab the beam and stop her spin. She spent a minute looking at the room full of bouncing, spinning, rebounding electronics gear. It was like the movie *Gravity*, only there was air.

"Is the air about to go away?" she wondered, suddenly worried.

One of her laptops floated by, and she nabbed it with her sore left arm. The laptop showed the visual feed of the hangar deck, so she watched as the *Azanti* shot in and came to an instant stop.

Despite her insane situation, she watched in amazement as the ship drifted down into contact with the deck and seemed to latch on, like a magnet. Suddenly, gravity returned. The deck came up and smashed her into unconsciousness.

* * *

"Kathy, you okay?"

She opened her eyes and moaned. Her head felt like it had been used for a football by several exuberant punters. "No," she said, recognizing Chris's voice.

"Should I call a corpsman?"

"No," she said and opened her eyes. She moved her limbs. Her left arm hurt, but nothing seemed broken. Her compartment looked like a bomb had gone off. There was scattered equipment everywhere and tons of broken stuff. It was a mess. "Would have been nice if they'd warned us."

"Probably didn't have time," Chris said. "The Marines had me hang onto something when it happened. They weren't expecting *Star Wars* either, but they're gung-ho about being ready for anything. I think I was in the only place nobody got hurt. I hear a few people might have died."

"Holy shit," Kathy said as she sat up. Her head was throbbing. "Where are we now?"

"Back in the water," he said.

"What? How long was I out?"

"Maybe 10 minutes. Apparently, a spaceship from OOE flew aboard and took us down to the ocean. Don't look at me, I have no idea how."

Kathy started digging through the scattered and busted electronics, looking for her laptop. She found it and checked it out. Not only was the machine not broken, the camera over the bow had recorded *everything!*

"Well, at least you're smiling," Chris said.

"Oh, yeah," she agreed. This was going to make a hell of a movie. Chris shook his head and left her to her fun.

* * *

**Joint Combined Evacuation Fleet**
**Just off Gulf of Nicoya, Costa Rica**

Theodore Alphonse Bennitti, III, had never been invited to the CIC on the USS *Bataan.* He and his scientists were aboard as a means to an end, not because they were considered essential. The Marines and the navy had a rather novel view of scientists on their ships. In short, they were treated more like cargo than passengers.

"Don't touch anything," a young, navy sailor said as he held the door for Theodore.

Theodore's eyes narrowed in annoyance, though he kept his peace. As if he, a NASA director, needed to be told not to push random buttons. He stepped over the door lip, which the sailors called a knee knocker, into the CIC. It wasn't like it was in the movies except it was kinda dark and had lots of computers. Admiral Jayne Kent saw him and waved toward a big, glass board with grease pencil marks on it.

"Thanks for coming," the gray-haired officer said.

"Not sure what I can do for you," Theodore replied.

"We have four Russian subs bracketing the fleet," Kent explained. "They're locked and loaded."

"Oh, wow," Theodore said. "That's bad?"

"To say we're in a tight space is an understatement."

"What do they want?"

"Our asses?" the *Bataan* captain suggested.

Theodore shot him a surly look. More obviousness, navy style.

"There are two reasons we aren't dogpaddling right now," Kent said. "One, we've deployed the squadron's modest ASW capabilities." He saw Theodore's eyebrow go up. "Anti-submarine warfare. The other is that the top dog in the subs is willing to talk."

"Really? I thought Russians weren't chatty when they want to fight."

"It's a unique situation," Kent said. "Russians and Americans haven't exchanged direct hostilities in a very long time. Anyway, his name is Captain Chugunkin."

"This is fascinating," Theodore said, "but why does it concern me?"

"Chugunkin is here because he thinks we created Strain Delta."

"Absurd," Theodore said. "The virus is light years ahead of any technology on Earth."

"Convince him of that."

Theodore laughed out loud, shaking his head. It took him a second to realize Kent wasn't laughing. "You're not kidding."

"I'm deadly serious."

"Admiral, how is this Chugunkin going to be convinced by me?"

"Because I know the man, at least by reputation. He is not your average sailor. If you've ever read *The Hunt for Red October*, he's a lot like Ramius."

"In the book, Ramius was considerably less rash," Theodore mused.

"Yes, if you can imagine a real captain acting like the movie? However, our real-life Russian is convinced we started this even in the face of logic. Will you talk to him?"

"Sure," Theodore said. "How?"

Kent gestured toward a console where a microphone on a stand waited. A chair had been placed in front of the console for Theodore to sit in.

Theodore nodded and moved to the console and sat down. He closed his eyes for a second and took a calming breath. He was a scientist, an astronaut who'd never been in space. But he wasn't cut from the same mold as Neil Armstrong or Jim Lovell. He wasn't a former test pilot. He might have had the right stuff, but not that kind of right stuff. But he could at least try.

"Doctor, we're perched on the edge of hostilities. I know you aren't comfortable with this…"

"I'll try," Theodore said. "It would help if Dr. Gallatin and Dr. Curie were here."

"They're on their way. We don't want to wait, though." Kent nodded toward a technician and spoke. "Captain Chugunkin."

"I am waiting," a strong voice responded.

Theodore was surprised by how little Russian accent the man had. He was quite understandable, which made Theodore wonder more about him. Maybe Kent would elaborate later.

"Sir, I have with me Dr. Theodore Bennitti."

"The name is familiar."

"Captain Chugunkin, I am…or rather was…the Director of Space Colonization at NASA. You know what NASA is?"

"I am aware. Why are you now speaking to me?"

"Captain, you must surely understand that the United States has nothing to do with Strain Delta?"

"Your CDC was the first to name it. And, here, I find a large squadron of warships underway with a purpose. Admiral Kent is unwilling to share your mission. The conclusion is difficult to doubt."

Theodore narrowed his eyes. The man spoke as if the conclusion had been presented to him, not as though he'd come up with it himself. While he was considering this, his friend, Dr. Albert Gallatin, was escorted into the CIC. The heavy man looked out of breath and was staring around with the same amazed look Theodore must have had on his face a short time ago. He waved to get Albert's attention. Albert was alone.

"Captain Chugunkin, I'd like to try and help you understand what has happened and what we, as a species, are facing."

"I am listening."

"A moment please?" he asked.

"I do not have all day…" the distant Russian replied.

A sailor moved another chair over, and Albert ponderously and gratefully lowered himself into it. Theodore leaned over and gave him a quick crib notes version of what was going on. Albert's face got even redder as he listened.

"Where is Curie?" Theodore asked.

"He…couldn't…come…" Albert said between huffs.

Theodore nodded and spoke into the mic. "Captain Chugunkin, another scientist has joined me." Theodore gestured at the mic, and Albert spoke.

"Captain, I am Dr. Albert Gallatin. Do you recognize my name?" He struggled to control his breathing as he spoke.

The line was quiet for a long moment before an answer came. "You were the president of America's CDC?"

"Director, yes, sir."

Albert was still trying to even out his breathing and having a difficult time. Theodore examined him and felt concern growing. Albert was not a young man, and his excessive weight wasn't helping.

"The fact that you are with a military task force does not help dissuade me of the belief your government created this plague. Why exactly are you both there?"

"The same as you, sir, and the same as everyone today: surviving." Albert was not breathing as hard and was able to concentrate better. "Tens of millions, maybe hundreds of millions, are dead in the United States alone. The idea we created this thing on purpose is simply ludicrous."

"Do you deny your government has created virus to kill?" Chugunkin demanded in righteous anger.

"No more than you can deny your government has done the same," Albert countered immediately. "The CDC has never been involved in this. In fact, we have advised against it at every turn as it represents not only a risk to foreign armies, but to the world at large.

"Captain, do you understand the nature of Strain Delta, which is what we call the virus?"

"I am neither a scientist nor a virologist."

"Under whose definition of this virus are you operating?" The captain did not immediately reply.

Theodore spoke up. "Captain, we all operate under the control of government at one level or another. NASA answered to both congress and the president. The CDC is under the Department of Health and Human Services, so it is also controlled by congress. Who is controlling you, sir?"

Theodore purposely left out the fact that there was no congress or president anymore. He didn't think the information would help the situation. He had a theory about what was going on with the Russians, though.

"The Russian Republic Navy answers to the chief of staff, and through him, to the president."

Theodore looked at Admiral Kent and frowned. Kent gestured to the radio operator who pressed a button, then said aloud, "Muted."

"What are you thinking?" the admiral asked.

"There is no Russian government. I think he's running on autopilot."

"You might be right, but how does that help us? He's in charge of a lot of firepower and, probably, nuclear weapons. His boat is likely the *Severodvinsk*, their newest nuclear fast attack ship. Our ASW believes the others are an *Akula* and two *Victors*. But one operator is pretty sure his returns matched a Delta IV, a nuclear missile boat."

"I think we tell him we're leaderless."

Kent's eyes narrowed. "This is high stakes poker, doctor. You're suggesting we show our hole card."

"I'm suggesting we all recognize the rules we're playing under."

Kent's jaw muscles bunched, and his mouth became a thin line. "Okay, I don't see our situation getting any worse. We either start shooting, or we don't. Play your hand." He gestured to the radio operator who opened the channel again.

"Captain Chugunkin, this is Bennitti again."

"I continue to listen but am, so far, unmoved."

"Sir, you should know we are likely in the same boat. There is no functioning US government we are aware of. The last known president died two days ago in a plane crash off San Diego, California."

"Your frankness is appreciated," Chugunkin replied.

"We'd appreciate the same in reply."

The pause was even longer this time. Theodore wondered if the Russian was discussing it with his fellow officers or if it was an internal argument. Maybe a representative of his surviving government was on board, giving orders?

"We are indeed in the same boat, Mr. Bennitti. There is no more functioning Russian government. Shortly after this plague was identified, all naval assets already at sea were ordered to remain at sea. Those in port were ordered to leave, but not many made it, so we are mostly submarines.

"Before our government completely ceased to function, it was decided you Americans must have released the plague. No logical reason for this was given, as it was apparent you were suffering as greatly as anyone else. I know, for a fact, the plague appeared all over the planet at roughly the same time. Still, we were ordered to find surviving assets of the United States and destroy them."

"Are there nuclear missile submarines involved?" Albert asked.

"I cannot say," the captain replied. Admiral Kent's mouth became even thinner, something Theodore would have thought impossible.

"Captain," Albert spoke again, "do you believe we did this?"

"How am I to know such things?"

"We know quite a bit about Strain Delta," Albert continued. "We know more than we did before our government fell. After we were picked up by this squadron of ships, we continued to put the pieces together. I began to quickly believe the virus was not of terrestrial origin."

"Are you saying it's from Mars?"

"No, but not from Earth."

"How can you prove such a thing?"

"First, based on its makeup. The virus isn't one virus, it's a series of them which mutate when they come in contact with each other. Further, it's not alive as we know it. It is actually a microscopic machine; a nanovirus. Infinitely small, infinitely complex, and just as infinitely mutable."

"Doctor, this is so fanciful, I do not know how I can believe it."

"I have one other piece of evidence. We have an alien and its ship. We believe they are responsible for Strain Delta."

"Bozhe moi!"

"God had nothing to do with this," Theodore said.

"Admiral Kent, do you believe this?"

"Faced with a live alien and its ship, I see little choice," Kent said. "So, Captain, in light of these facts, I believe your orders to engage us are based on flawed data. I see two courses of action going forward. You go ahead and attack, at which point my ASW assets will probably destroy you, though not before you sink several of my ships. Or, you come aboard, we show you our evidence, and we see about charting a course to save humanity instead of killing more of it for no reason."

The radio was quiet for only a second. "Please inform your stealthy, anti-submarine aircraft to not fire on us. I am surfacing. We should talk more."

Kent turned to Theodore and slapped him on the shoulder. "Mr. Bennitti, remind me never to play cards with you."

Theodore finally took a breath.

* * *

**Afternoon, Friday, May 3**
**HAARP Research Facility**
**150 Miles West of San Diego**

Dr. Lisha Breda leaned over the railing to watch her crew carry equipment down the small dock attached to the rig's leg and onto the ship. She turned and walked back into the rig, her home for so many years, and sighed.

"You okay, ma'am?"

She turned and saw Jon Osborne, whom everyone called Oz. He'd been responsible for keeping HAARP's supercomputers operating. He'd also assisted in programming them to decode and understand the alien virus. Strain Delta was talking, only they couldn't understand what it was saying.

"Yeah," she said. "You packed up yet?"

"I have all the data archived on SSD arrays, in pelican cases. Joseph and his logistics people are taking care of them."

"What about the computers? They should be on board by now."

Oz looked sheepish. "We need those computers; they might be the last supercomputers in the world."

"The last slides of brain material are being scanned," he said and grinned. "The geeks in the electronics shop cobbled up a multi-frequency emitter and receiver. Maybe Strain Delta is communicating on a wavelength we haven't checked."

"You've got a few more hours before the ship is ready," Lisha reminded him. "Robert Boyer says he'll need some time to change out the filters on the ship's generator."

"I'm surprised the old tub still floats," Oz said.

Lisha smiled. "It's a small port freighter. One that's delivered a lot of our equipment. Has its own cranes and stuff. Designed to operate in places where the big container ships can't or there's no infrastructure."

"If you say so, ma'am." He gestured toward the ocean. "What about the name? *Helix*?"

It was Lisha's turn to look sheepish. "I kinda like it."

"I wonder about you," Oz said and headed for a ladder down to the computers.

Lisha walked down to the floor where all her principle research had taken place. Most of the equipment was gone, crated and loaded. The time to leave her home had come. They needed mobility in this brave, new world. Sitting still made them easy targets.

Her three heavily armed lunatics, the Zombie Squad as they called themselves, agreed with her. She'd been horrified to find out that Oz, Robert, and Joseph had a small arsenal of guns stashed away on the rig. But they used them for hunting and skeet shooting when not working. There was no strict rule against it. Maybe it was an oversight on her part. Considering what had happened, maybe not. The three had used their guns to clear the ship they were using as a new home.

The military had forbidden 'ship hopping.' Lisha was sure they meant taking an occupied ship, not an empty one. There hadn't been anyone still in possession of independent thought on the ship they took, only a dozen zombies. At least, that's what Oz had told her.

*They wouldn't have killed non-infected, would they?* Her face screwed up as she considered. Ultimately, Lisha decided it wasn't worth worrying about. She'd never know either way. She'd done her own share of ethically questionable things.

A dull thumping sound made her sigh. She slowly turned her head to look at the locked door. Not all of her research had been loaded. Lisha walked to the door, her footfalls echoing strangely in the nearly empty room. She suddenly remembered coming onto the decommissioned drill rig. It looked a lot like it did now, maybe oilier. It smelled like sweat and grease then. Now it smelled like death.

She unlocked the door with her code and pulled it open. *Thud, thud, thud.* The same rhythm and timing, always. On the far side of the ancillary lab was a section that was walled off with an inch of plexiglass. There weren't bloody smears on it anymore, but the glass was showing deformities.

"How's the mutating coming?" she asked. Grant Porter had once been a brilliant biologist. Then Strain Delta had come to HAARP via some freshly caught fish. Sushi was a favorite among her crew, but once Strain Delta went global, the Japanese delicacy had become a death penalty. They all carried the airborne variation of the nanovirus. There was also a waterborne one and one that was carried in the bodies of the infected. If you drank the water, the airborne one mutated into the active version. Or, if you got bitten by someone who was infected, you joined them.

Grant was the only 'survivor' among those initially infected. Most of Lisha's personnel had succumbed and had to be dumped into the ocean. She'd have learned a lot more about the virus if the better part of her team hadn't turned into zombies and had to be dispatched. Grant had been subdued, and she'd used him for experiments to analyze the virus. Then she'd gone much further.

At one point, she'd removed half his brain for samples. That should have been the end of Grant Porter, even as a zombie. But they'd stitched his head up anyway, just out of curiosity. His virus-controlled brain had rebooted itself, and he'd been on his feet in hours. With half a brain.

Lisha walked closer. Grant stopped pounding on the glass and looked at her. His eyes conveyed a profound desire to reach her. He held up his hands toward her. Or rather, what used to be hands. They had no flesh on them. Instead, they were hardened bone and closely resembled sledgehammers.

"Amazing," she said, shaking her head. "Simply amazing."

Grant snarled and lunged, his face smashing into the plexiglass, pulping his nose and spraying blood. She took an unconscious step back in surprise. Grant lowered his head and rammed harder. The plexiglass, weakened by hours on end of pounding, split with a *crack* like a gunshot.

Even with half a brain, the creature formerly known as Grant seemed to grasp the meaning of the crack. He raised both hands over his head and brought them down against the plexiglass with devastating force. The bones in his hands cracked, and the plexiglass sheared along the break.

"Oh, crap!" Lisha cried and turned to run. She made it two steps before she tripped over a bundle of cables which had been attached to a mass spectrometer. Lisha crashed to the deck, crying out in pain, as her face smashed in to the metal grating of the floor. Doing her best to ignore the pain, she rolled over. Grant was forcing himself through the huge crack in his supposedly impenetrable cage.

He'd been naked since the brain surgery. After all, there was no need to clothe a zombie. As he squeezed through, the sharp edge of the glass took his skin off like a razor. Blood spurted and his skin curled away to reveal the yellowish fat and muscle underneath. Lisha shook her head in disbelief. She'd seen the infected incur incredible injuries with no reaction, but somehow, this was different.

She pushed herself up with her hands and moved backward, crab walking as fast as she could. Grant fell through the broken glass in a pile of mangled skin, fat, muscle, and blood. In an instant, he was on his feet, slipping in his own bloody mess. *You're not going to make it*, she realized. Lisha rolled over and tried to get up and run at the same time, not really succeeding at either. She ended up falling face-first through the door into her former laboratory.

This time she didn't drag her face across the metal decking. She turned and executed a messy shoulder roll. She landed on her back and had a great view as Grant ran in great, loping strides toward her. *I'm dead.*

A booming shot took half of Grant's head off in an explosion of bloody fluid. He fell to his knees, and his bony hammer-hands slammed against the metal decking. He shook his head, blood spraying, then struggled back to his feet.

Lisha craned her neck and saw Oz standing there, a big revolver in his left hand, blinking in confusion when he saw that Grant wasn't down. "I took part of his brain out!" she screamed.

"I shot him in the fucking head!" Oz said incredulously.

"Shoot him *again!*" she screamed.

Oz blinked, then leveled the gun. *Boom!* A bullet punched through Grant's shoulder with no effect. *Boom!* A bullet tore a great chunk from Grant's neck. Blood sprayed like a fountain. Grant strode onward, his eyes never leaving Lisha.

"Fucking die," Oz yelled, grasping the gun with two hands and squeezing the trigger. The other half of Grant's head, the one with intact brain matter, exploded. Grant dropped and smacked the deck like a sack of potatoes.

Lisha realized she was gasping for breath. A hand fell on her shoulder. She screamed and rolled away.

"Doctor, it's Oz. Take it easy."

She focused on his face, his visual and audio cues finally penetrating her terror-strewn consciousness. "My God, he got through the plexiglass."

"Never thought your little science experiment was a good idea," Oz said. He held out his hand and she took it. He easily pulled her to her feet.

"I guess this answers the question about what to do with him," she said.

"You want me to get someone to dump him overboard?" he asked.

"No, don't worry about it. We're leaving anyway. It's kind of fitting he remains behind." Oz nodded. The intercom buzzed. She went over and pressed the button to activate it.

"Is someone shooting up there?"

It sounded like one of Oz's techs. "No, no problem here," she lied, keeping her voice even. "That all you need?"

"No, ma'am. Is Oz there?"

"Right here, Weasel. What's up?"

Weasel? Do any of these people have normal names?

"You wanted the results of those last scans? The material Dr. Breda gave you?"

"Yeah, is the data ready?"

"No, something's wrong with it."

"Shit," Oz said. He opened his revolver, dumped the empty brass and reloaded. "I'll be right there."

"I'm coming with you," Lisha said, her eyes straying to the twitching corpse of her former research assistant. "I don't want to be alone."

"No problem," Oz said. "But we need to find a first aid kit and clean up your face."

She reached up and felt her face, then yanked her hand away and hissed in pain. From what she could tell, she was missing some skin. "Later. Come on, let's go."

She followed Oz down the ladders to the deck where the supercomputers and other IT assets were stored. She hadn't been down there since the celebration marking the supercomputer's acquisition and its first operational day. A lot of the equipment was already gone, a disturbing amount wasn't. Dozens of big, padded cases stood open along the walls, waiting to be loaded with supercomputer parts for safe keeping.

Only one person was there, a balding, middle-aged man with thick glasses and a scraggly beard. Lisha thought he'd look more at home in an online gaming parlor than a computer room. "Weasel?" she asked.

"Dr. Breda, good to meet you at last. Sorry it's under these circumstances," Weasel said with an infectious smile. "You can call me Paul, if you'd rather."

"If you like Weasel, Weasel it is."

"What happened to your face?"

"Long story," she said. In a flash, he produced a first aid kit and handed her some gauze and antibiotic ointment. "Thanks," she said and made a quick bandage. Weasel grinned.

"What's up, buddy?" Oz asked.

Weasel pointed to a series of monitors. "Test results."

Oz walked over and fell into a chair with the kind of casual comfort that spoke of many hours spent there. Weasel joined him, and they talked in their own tech speak. Lisha passed the time by examining the room. Gaming posters, some questionable pics of women, a bunch of gun advertisements, and a no-shit, neon Heineken bar sign hung on the walls.

"Are you completely sure the sensor is working?"

Lisha turned back to Oz and Weasel. "What's up?"

"The results of the scan. You know I've been isolating the electrical impulses from samples of the former Mr. Grant's brain?"

"Former?" Weasel asked.

"I blew out what brains he had left; he tried to eat Dr. Breda."

"Oh, that was the shooting. Tell me about it." Weasel had a gleam in his eye, and Lisha moved in.

"Later, Oz, continue."

"Oh, sure. Anyway, even the biopsies were remaining alive a *long* time. I was able to get signals from them for hours. If we kept them in the nutrient fluid your lab guys gave me, they stayed alive as long as we wanted."

"Right, it's supposed to do that."

"Okay, so Weasel set up a radar signal system. Transmit/receive."

"Why?" she asked. "Radar?"

"I was spitballing," Weasel admitted. "I thought we might be able to get something on the radar frequency? You know, alien nanobots talking to each other?"

"You guys have seen too much sci-fi," Lisha said.

"Maybe," Weasel admitted, "but I did it anyway. I was getting a little something. I'm not sure what. The gear was having a hard time reading it. So, I pulsed the sample, a wide range shot from 20 centimeters down to 1 millimeter."

"Microwave range?" Oz asked.

Weasel shrugged. "I cobbled the unit out of junk from the old oil rig trash pile. It wasn't very delicate. The point is, no results."

"No improved signals?" Lisha asked.

"No. No nothing."

"I don't understand." She leaned forward and looked over the data. Radiation wasn't her thing. They'd tested Strain Delta to see if microwaving food would kill it, with no result. By the time it was gone, they'd turned anything except water into desiccated, inedible trash. Only extreme heat, about 400 degrees, did the trick. "Did you roast it?"

"Just a five-millisecond pulse."

Lisha stared at the screen. The sample number was there along with an electromagnetic reading of 2.46 hertz, the same as Grant's pounding rate on the wall. It was the processing speed of the nanovirus. Afterward, there was no electric stimulus.

"Do you have more samples?" she asked. Weasel pulled out a box and put it on the table. A dozen petri dishes with slices of Grant Porter's brain were inside. "Run another."

"But…"

"Just do it, please?"

Weasel looked at Oz, who shrugged. So, he selected a petri dish and entered the data from the label into his computer. Then he opened his test rig. It looked like it had started life as a microwave oven. Now, it was missing its metallic cover and wires went everywhere.

"How do you know how to do this?"

"I have an undergrad degree in nuclear physics from IUPUI," Weasel said.

"I thought you were just a tech."

Weasel shrugged as he worked.

"Weasel doesn't play well with others," Oz explained.

Maybe the name has a deeper meaning, Lisha thought.

"Ready," Weasel said, closing the door.

Lisha eyed the rig suspiciously. "I don't want my brain to get microwaved."

"You won't," he said. "The magnetron is modified, and I changed out the capacitor. It can only fire a pulse every millisecond, and the frequency oscillates."

Her level of confidence wasn't any greater because he'd been to school. Maybe he had gotten tossed out for cooking his professor's brains. Still, she'd come this far. She nodded, and he gave a thumbs up.

"Wait," she said, "can you set it up so we can see what happens while you bombard it?"

Weasel stared at the rig for a second, snapped his fingers, and started digging out parts. "I like her," he said.

"He enjoys being challenged," Oz whispered to her.

"Remind me to keep him away from my lab."

Within five minutes, Weasel had modified the rig and was again ready to go. More wires came out of it, and an additional window on the computer display showed the familiar 2.46 hertz. "Confirmed it's still alive," Weasel said. "Ready to fire. Three…two…one…"

Lisha tried not to cringe as the transformer came on and the 'test machine' made a sound somewhere between that of a traditional microwave and an old-style camera strobe charging. Instead, she watched the monitor. She heard a snapping sound, and the electrical readings from the brain tissue sample were gone.

"See, just like before."

"Oh, my God," Lisha said, putting a hand to her mouth.

"What?" Weasel said, looking around.

She turned to Oz. "Get Joseph to pack all this up. *Carefully*. Have Weasel stay with it. I want this in my new lab on the ship ASAP."

"Okay, sure," Oz said, pulling his Zombie Squad two-way radio from his belt. "Why?"

"Weasel just found a way to kill Strain Delta without cooking it to a crisp."

"I did?"

"You did."

"Oh, cool."

A few minutes later, she was on the dock watching a couple of Joseph's big, burly, logistics guys carrying crates marked "Weasel" to the ship. She knew she might be able to duplicate what the mad scientist had done, but why start from scratch? His crazy science project had narrowed down the target. She'd never considered trying anything as simple as radar waves.

A microwave was a sort of radar. They used to call microwaves Radar Ranges, until they learned to isolate the frequencies at a much higher range. Cooked better. Anyway, military radars were still dangerous. You could get seriously injured standing in front of one when it was operating. The power levels Weasel was working with were tiny, and the results were instantaneous. Damn it, he had stumbled upon something big.

It was now infinitely more important that they get away from the old HAARP facility before something went drastically wrong. This needed to get out. Weasel might well have saved the world.

The rear half of the huge ship floated against the dock, gangway in place to provide access to the men carrying gear. The ship was too big to safely back under the platform. The name on the stern in weather-worn, white paint was *Helix*, Falkland. How a ship like that had gotten from the Falklands to San Diego was anybody's guess. Lisha thought the name was perfect.

Something caught her eye, and she looked up. "That's something you don't see every day," she said. A carrier was slowly descending from the heavens like a gift from God. She'd only heard anecdotal accounts of the carrier exploding upward into space, though she'd heard and felt the shockwave in her laboratory while she was packing. Despite weirdness heaped on top of weirdness, the ship's ascent wasn't the strangest thing she'd experienced in the last few weeks. Though seeing the ship 'flying' back to the ocean might have been.

It settled onto the water, an invisible dome under it, like a forcefield, holding the ocean back. Then there was a massive *BOOOM!* and the dome disappeared. The water flew inward, breaking against the carrier in a wave. The entire bulk of the ship dropped a short distance and smacked into the water, sending a wave several meters tall racing away from it. "Huh," she said. Meanwhile, the loading continued.

***

**USS *Pacific Adventurer***

**150 Nautical Miles West of San Diego, CA**

Lt. General Leon Rose had commanded the US Army III Corps after a long and distinguished career dating back to just after Vietnam. He'd been too young for that conflict and thought he'd missed his chance to command troops in wartime. Then along came Saddam Hussein, and he had gotten his chance.

He'd earned his first star during the buildup to and subsequent Desert Storm. He'd earned his second for Iraqi Freedom. Finally, he'd earned his third and command of III Corps after several years in Afghanistan. Thousands of soldiers had made careers working under his command, and he was widely considered one of the best commanding officers in the service. A fourth star and a stint on the Joint Chiefs would have been a great end to his career. Alas, it would never be.

"Is this how my time as a soldier ends?" Rose asked. The ocean spread out before him. The ocean and ships. A yacht, once worth millions, burned a short distance away. "I hate the ocean."

Behind him, his assistant, Captain Mays, remained quiet. Rose knew the younger man wasn't happy on the water, either. Yet, what was to be done?

He'd picked the bridge wing, which extended out past the hull, because it gave him a better view and because it was away from that smug, little shit, Sampson. Rather, *Captain* Sampson. Rose snorted. *Captain, right. Trumped up O-2, little better than a butter bar.*

The door to the bridge slid open, and the captain spoke. "General, the *John Paul Jones* reports there's activity on the oil platform those scientists are using."

"Thanks," Rose said and lifted the binoculars he was using to his eyes.

"Two o'clock, General," Sampson said.

Rose grunted an annoyed thank you and turned to focus. The little shit could be less useful, it would make it easier to hate him. The former oil platform was easy to spot; it was much taller than the supercarriers. There were usually a lot of ships around the oil platform's four, huge legs. Like chicks hiding under a mother goose, they hung around for the security it suggested. However, few docked with the platform, and the navy had been providing security for the scientists there.

Now, a not-so-small ship was docked there. It looked like a civilian version of the transports the navy used to move tanks ashore. A RORO, roll on, roll off. It also had cranes and a big mid-deck for cargo.

"Captain Sampson, do you know what ship that is?"

"It's a private merchant vessel named *Helix*. Logistics on the *John Paul Jones* states it arrived 36 hours ago, and the crew transferred to one of the temporary housing cruise ships, the *Fun on the Sea.* There were infected aboard, though no report on how many."

"Looks like Dr. Breda got tired of her oil rig," Captain Mays said.

"So it would seem." He turned to his ship's captain. "What does the *John Paul Jones* want me to do?"

"In the absence of a naval flag officer, you are the highest-ranking military presence, sir. Since you've met with the HAARP staff, they'd like you to find out what's going on."

"So, I'm a detective now?" The young captain shrugged. "Okay, why not. Mays, get an RHIB over there, will you?"

"Right away, sir."

Rose raised the glasses and looked again. Yeah, they were transferring gear to the *Helix*. Lots of it. Did the quirky scientist know something he didn't?

"Holy shit!" someone on the bridge yelled loudly enough for Rose to hear.

He turned and looked. The three sailors inside the bridge were all looking out the wide glass windows and up. He followed their gaze and saw a 'flying' aircraft carrier.

"Well, that's not something you see every day," Mays said behind him.

One of the sailors happened to be recording on his phone when *Gerald R. Ford* blasted into the sky the previous evening. Rose had been in the officer's mess drinking coffee and talking to his senior officers. He'd been working contingencies when Grange and the *Boutwell* didn't return, forcing him to begin considering other options for a land base. When the Mach shockwave rolled over *Pacific Adventurer*, then the wave of water, he'd been quite surprised. Everyone had watched the cell phone video afterwards.

He squinted at the carrier as it slowly descended. *It's not falling*, he realized. *That's good, at least.* Maybe someone from the ship could tell him what the fuck was going on. Flying aircraft carriers? What was this, a Marvel movie?

The *Ford* settled into the water on an invisible forcefield, which shut off with a huge explosion that let water rush in. Rose grunted at the spectacle. *Might be nice to have some tanks with those kinds of defenses.* He walked over and rapped on the bridge window. Everyone jerked and looked at him.

"Can you find out what *that* is all about while I'm gone?" He hooked a thumb in the direction of the now settled *Ford.* Sampson nodded. For a change, he was at a loss for words. Rose nodded in reply and turned to Mays. "Come on, lets go see Dr. Breda before things get even more complicated."

It only took a few minutes for them to get a boat. The navy had been nice enough to loan him and his ship full of grunts a trio so they could move about and help as needed, though the Marines seldom asked. Now that there were a whole lot less Marines, he wondered if they'd be tapped for more jobs.

The three junior sailors who operated the boats were talking when Rose and Mays appeared on the boat deck. None of the three immediately noticed them.

"What's going on?" Rose asked in his command voice. All three sailors, two young men and a young woman, almost jumped out of their skins.

They immediately came to their senses and attention. But when they saw him in camo instead of navcam, they seemed uncertain what to do. Eventually, they saw the stars sewn on his epaulets and saluted. He returned it. "So?"

"Sir," the woman answered. "There's so much going on—the *Ford* flying, ships sinking, and missing RHIBs."

"Missing?" he asked.

"Yeah," one of the men answered. "Uhm, yeah, sir!"

"At ease, son."

"Sorry, sir. It was off the *Dewey*, which was my ship. The scuttlebutt is it was attacked by a sea monster."

"A sea monster?" Rose asked in his perfect officer's dead pan, 'are you fucking serious,' tone. "Like a sea monster from a movie?"

Mays leaned a little closer. "Flying aircraft carriers, zombies…"

"Stow it," Rose growled back. "I need a ride to the oil platform." He scanned the young faces and pointed at the female. "You were quick to answer, can you drive one of those?"

"Yes, sir, no problem." She almost tripped over the mooring line when she jumped in.

Rose didn't seem to take any notice. He was pushing 60 and carrying extra tonnage, so he was no ballerina getting on board, either. Mays, being in his early thirties, leaped in like a pro.

"Show off," Rose said. Mays grinned.

The boat's dual outboards roared. One of the sailors who wasn't going untied the boat from its cleat and tossed the line onto the RHIB's bow, then they were off in flash. Luckily for Rose, this RHIB had seats. Not all of them did. In some, you had to sit on the big, inflated side or stand by the control console and hold on for dear life.

"What do you think happened to the RHIB they're talking about?" Mays whispered/yelled in Rose's ear.

"No clue. The RHIB crew could have become a zombie, run off, or the boat just sunk." *I think we can rule out sea monsters, though.* As the

RHIB cut through the water, he glanced over the side. Nothing but white foam and blue water. He looked away with a snort.

The boat reached the platform and slowed. The ship that was tied up to the rig was big, no doubt about it. It was more than 400 feet long, which put it around 100 feet longer than his new command ship, the *Pacific Adventurer.* He wished he'd known about this ship; it would have made a better base of operations. He had almost a thousand dependents on a cruise ship with a broken engine.

As the RHIB began to idle and the young seaman expertly used the last of its velocity to bump it up against the dock, a bunch of the men and women moving gear looked over curiously. Rose noted two men standing by the ship, both armed with AK-47s, keeping an eye on everything. They weren't in uniform despite the assurance with which they wielded their weapons.

"Can I help you?" a man asked. He was a big bear of a guy with a shaved head and full beard. He had a Glock in a holster and four magazines in holders on the opposite hip.

"Yeah, I'm General Rose. I'd like to talk with Dr. Breda about this ship."

"I've heard of you," the man said. "She talked to you before. I'm Joseph Capdepon, Chief of Logistics for HAARP."

"Lots of logistics people carry guns around here?" Mays asked.

Joseph's eye flicked down to his weapon, and he grinned. "We're also Dr. Breda's Zombie Squad." He saw Rose's confused look. "My friends and I are gun bunnies, you see? When you live offshore, you tend to take all your favorite toys with you. It's easier than storing them in the People's Republic of Commiefornia. So, when the shit hit the fan, we were ready."

"Bunch of red-blooded republicans?" Rose asked, a smirk on his face.

"It's not that simple," Joseph replied. "A few of us, yeah, but not all."

"Hello there, General."

Rose looked up. Dr. Breda was leaning over the railing of the *Helix,* staring down at him.

"Dr. Breda, how are you?"

"Fine. What do you need?"

"Got a minute to talk?" She nodded. "Good. Captain, why don't you and Mr. Capdepon discuss politics or beer or something. I'll be back in a few minutes." He left the two looking at each other distrustfully and climbed the boarding ramp to the *Helix*. Lisha was waiting for him. "Where can we talk?"

She led him into one of several cabins behind the bridge. It was not luxurious, but it did have enough room for a couple of people. The cabins on the *Pacific Adventurer* weren't nearly as roomy, but more luxurious.

"We didn't take the ship," Dr. Breda said immediately.

"You certainly did," General Rose corrected. "It wasn't yours yesterday."

"Okay, point. We didn't take it from anyone like a pirate would."

"Will the crew aboard the *Fun on the Sea* agree with your assessment?"

"I didn't ask them," she admitted.

The woman was more than a few years his junior. Still, she was obviously used to getting her way. While not a leader of combat men and women, she was a leader. He couldn't imagine the level of intelligence and training it took to do what she did. All he knew about genes was that they all had them.

"Why did you take it?" he asked.

She motioned him over to a chair next to the desk. A coffee pot with steaming coffee in it was sitting on the desk. "Care for a cup?"

"I'd love one."

She put out a couple of Styrofoam cups and poured. She did it with no obvious haste. In fact, he guessed she was using the time to consider what she was going to say. He gave her the time she needed and waited patiently. Once the coffee was poured, she placed a container with sweetener and creamer in front of him.

"You haven't dealt with soldiers much," he said. It wasn't a question. He sipped the bitter black beverage and sighed. "Only the navy uses cream and sugar. Army takes it black."

She grinned, nodded, and took a sip of her own. "Army and scientists," she said, smacking her lips.

*I like this woman*, he decided. "Now that we're both caffeinated, you gonna give me a reason?"

"I already said we can't beat this thing."

"I know; I was at the meeting with the late Admiral Hoskins."

"Does his death put you in charge?"

"The military is complicated. You can't order around a member from another service just because you outrank them."

"Last time I looked, we're short a president."

"Yeah, she's spread all over Coronado. We're looking for someone to succeed her. We can't find anyone from the line of succession. They're supposed to ensure someone remains available. Still, you have a point. Just now, they're nominally listening to me. We have a rear admiral on the way."

"The fleet from the east coast?" He nodded. "With their alien?"

Rose laughed and shook his head. "Man, rumors *are* faster than radio. Still…"

"Yes, yes." She sighed and took another sip of coffee.

He wondered why she was so hesitant. She didn't appear guilty or seem to feel bad about helping herself to a multi-million-dollar ship. Quite the contrary, actually. There was something more.

"One of my people may have accidentally found a counter for Strain Delta."

"A cure?!" he said, almost spilling hot coffee on himself.

"No," she said, holding up her hands. "Don't get carried away. It might be possible to clean it out of someone. However, removing the virus won't stop the infected from becoming blood thirsty killers. Strain Delta rewrites the brain, reforms it entirely. Without the nanovirus, it can't continue to mutate their brains."

"Mutate? What?"

"I'm getting in too deep. The countering process, if it proves out, can't make you human again. It will allow us to purify food and water, though."

"We can do that already."

"Sure, by cooking it until it's leather. What we've found is an astoundingly low-energy solution involving radar or, perhaps, low powered microwaves."

"You don't know?"

"It's too soon," she said. "Weasel just did it."

"Weasel? Is that a computer or something?"

"Close enough," she mumbled. "We acquired the ship before we had the breakthrough. I'd decided we needed to protect the data we have. Staying on the oil platform wasn't a good long-term solution. We were sitting ducks."

"You have security provided by the military."

"General Rose, having watched this situation develop and the fiasco at Coronado, I have come to the conclusion that the military can't even protect itself."

Rose scowled, and Lisha took a drink of her coffee. She had a point. Dozens of ships had left over the last day and a half. As the *Reagan* went down, so had the confidence of the Flotilla's civilian elements. Sure, most had stayed. Still, the number of departures were discouraging. He'd even done a brief interview with the reporter on the *Ford*, Kathy Clifford. When the damned carrier shot into orbit, dozens more ships lit out for parts unknown. Shit was coming apart at the seams, and the east coast fleet was still a couple days out. But they hadn't checked in since morning, a fact which was not public knowledge, for obvious reasons.

Who knew if they really had an alien? A few days ago, he would have laughed at the idea. Now, he'd seen an aircraft carrier fly to space and back, so he kept his opinions to himself.

"Okay, you might have a point. Where are you going?"

"Nowhere, yet. The guys are going to get us fueled up and provisioned first."

"Where are those provisions coming from?"

"Somewhere legitimate, I assure you. Also, I plan to ensure we preserve all my data."

"Including the illegal genetic research?"

Dr. Breda's smile remained, but it left her eyes.

"Yes. I've done some research in our database. The military keeps a lot of data offline, and just before the *Ford* took its trip to outer space, they found a workaround for the military network connectivity issue. It was some kind of virus, but they figured it out."

He took a sip of coffee. "You were being investigated by our nation and Interpol. Your research has been called borderline eugenics, and you were out here because your supporters were afraid you were going to get raided."

"There's a lot more to what we are doing than so called eugenics."

"Such as?"

"Have you studied genetics, General Rose?"

"Not since high school, no."

"Then I probably can't explain all of it. Regardless, you must realize I'm just about the only authority when it comes to Strain Delta. I'm all you've got. So, what do you plan to do?"

Rose nodded and finished his coffee. It wasn't too bad or too hot. "If you leave, let me know."

"Why?"

"Because I want to go with you."

"I thought you were in it for the big win?"

"When we came here from Texas, I thought what we had here was a lot more than it was. Enough forces to take back the land and save as many people as possible. A lot of effort was spent trying to save the president, on her orders." He spread his hands wide. "I'm the ranking US Army officer present, so until they dredge up a presidential successor, I'll do what I want. I agree with you and your data. It might be our only chance to save humanity. So, Dr. Breda, I'm your protection going forward."

The smile returned to her eyes. "Some more coffee, General Rose?"

"Don't mind if I do. And, please, call me Leon."

* * *

**USS *Gerald R. Ford***

**150 Nautical Miles West of San Diego, CA**

Jeremiah Osborne wasn't thrilled to find himself back in the same conference room he'd been in a few days ago. He was afraid then that he'd regret letting the navy have one of the alien drive devices; now, he was having to deal with the aftermath of the decision.

"Mr. Osborne," Captain Gilchrist said, "you were not very forthcoming about the capabilities of the alien device you found."

"So you had one of your sailors steal a drive off my ship."

"It was part of an investigation," the navy captain said without missing a beat. "The contents of the drive prove you knew far more about the alien technology than you led us to believe."

"We were still learning about it," Alison McDill said. "Most of what we learned was from trial and error."

"At least we weren't stupid enough to slap it on a 100,000-ton aircraft carrier to see what would happen," Alex West said.

Commander Tobias, Gilchrist's XO, looked mad enough to chew steel and spit nails. "It was him," he said, pointing at Wade Watts.

Wade shrugged and took a drink of his Coke.

"Computers or electronics?" Alison asked him.

"Mostly computers, but some electronics to learn more about computers."

"What happened?" she asked him.

"Accidentally grounded a cart with the drive on it against a bulkhead." He shrugged again. "Not used to everything being made of metal."

"Why didn't you let him bring you back down?" Jeremiah asked.

"We had him arrested," Tobias said immediately.

"Did he break in and mess with it?"

"They asked me to work on it," Wade said.

"Nobody told you to put us in orbit," Captain Gilchrist said.

"Chief Kuntzleman said to help get it working. I did."

Gilchrist looked like he was about to lose his temper, so Jeremiah figured he needed to be the adult in the room. "Captain, since my people got you down, maybe we should consider the matter closed?"

"I have 73 injured crewmen," Gilchrist said. "And nine of them are in critical condition."

Jeremiah sighed. "I doubt you have the necessary facilities to keep him in jail."

"We have a brig," Tobias said.

"The point remains. You don't want to have to deal with him. I'll take him off your hands."

Wade looked at Jeremiah in surprise. "Why would I want to go with you?"

"You want them to keelhaul you?"

"We don't do that anymore," Gilchrist said.

"Exceptions can be made," Tobias mumbled. He looked at his captain who nodded. "Fine, he's your problem now."

"Is your ship okay?" Alex asked.

"Minor damage," Gilchrist said. "Our speed was already screwed from pushing the drives too far. Doubt we can do 20 knots. We're as slow as our escorts, now."

"Glad nothing other than a few crew members was hurt too bad," Jeremiah said.

"I'd like to know what you intend to do with the technology."

Jeremiah gave the captain an appraising glance. The man appeared to be an archetypical military leader on the surface. Hidden under the salutes, crisp uniform, and sharp looks, though, was a keen intellect. He'd never been in the military and only dealt with them for contracts. Maybe this sort of man was more common for a ship's captain or a naval officer. Jeremiah had had few chances to meet navy personnel, even when doing government contracts.

"To tell you the truth, Captain, there wasn't time to form a plan. As I explained, we found the first drive before Strain Delta was a thing. At least, before anyone knew about it. While I waited to hear from my contact at NASA, my people started working out the technology. After everything went to shit, what else was there to do? We had no idea the alien ships and Strain Delta were linked."

"You found a dead alien with the first ship?" Gilchrist asked.

"Yes, we still have it in a freezer. We weren't even sure it was an alien for a long time."

"You always thought it was," Alex said in a low voice. Jeremiah nodded.

Gilchrist steepled his fingers and looked Jeremiah in the eye. "I know you're a businessman, Mr. Osborne. However, you must realize our nation, our very species, is at risk. You found the spaceship you had with you nearby. I'll ask you again, in light of what's happening and appealing to your humanity, how did you find it?"

Jeremiah looked at Alex West, then at Alison McDill.

"It was always your call," Alex said. Alison nodded.

"My people figured out how to use several of the systems on the alien ship. Among those systems was the radio. We studied it and realized each of the alien ships had a sort of transponder. You see, they're not really ships, they're lifeboats."

"How do you know?" Gilchrist asked.

Jeremiah spent some time running the captain through the logical arguments his people had used—ships not meant for long-term use (no facilities), redundant drives, and redundant communication systems.

"They do sound like lifeboats on civilian ships," Tobias agreed.

"How many?" Gilchrist asked.

"We found signals for 25 alien craft. The one we had with us brings it to 26."

"All right around here?"

"No, all over the planet. The alien transmitter seems to work right through the planet."

"So does VLF," Tobias said, referring to the navy's very long frequency radio system used to talk with submarines.

"Yes, but VLF takes an hour to give a weather report," Alison said. "This system sends quite a bit of data, quickly."

"I've been thinking about the potential uses for those drives," Jeremiah said. "Think of it, being able to hover over a site and rescue people, assess infected levels, provide support, and find stuff."

The navy people were looking at each other and nodding. It would be impossible for someone to miss the potential benefits of a flying craft, with no danger of crashing, that could hover over a spot for days, weeks, or even months.

"What about power requirements?" Gilchrist asked.

"We've done some evaluations," Alison said. "The basic drive requires only milliamps of power to operate, and it doesn't appear to matter whether you're hovering a dingy or an aircraft carrier. Admittedly though, the biggest thing we've tried it on was our ship."

"And now, ours," Tobias said. Wade Watts snorted with laughter, and Tobias speared him with a death stare.

"We didn't have time to evaluate power usage on the carrier, but there are a bunch of abandoned ships we can try it on," Alison added. "The problem is that the power modules are needed to create the forcefield which keep the air in while you are in space. It might *appear* that the power modules have infinite energy, but that's impossible."

"Why?" Gilchrist asked.

"Physics," Jeremiah deadpanned.

Gilchrist nodded, then cocked his head. "Isn't it against the rules of physics to go faster than light *and* to violate gravity?"

"Man's got a good point," Watts said.

"Okay, Mr. Osborne, what do you want out of this?"

"Survival is a good motivator," Jeremiah said. "Sure, being rich is nice, but I suspect money is worthless. There might still be some benefit to being at the center of this. Tell you what, our people will get this figured out. You protect us, keep us fed, make sure me and mine are included in any benefits, and let people know we figured it all out."

"Not asking for much, is he?" Tobias asked.

"He's offering a lot more than he's charging," Gilchrist replied. "I can agree to all of those except letting people know what you're doing. We have to keep this classified for now."

"Who are we hiding it from, the Russians?" Alex asked.

"Exactly. We cannot assume all the global players folded up their chairs and went quietly into the good night. Tell me, Mr. Osborne, do you think this forcefield can stop a nuke?"

"I'd rather not try to find out," Jeremiah admitted.

"So, we keep the details quiet. At least, as quiet as you can after a *Ford*-class aircraft carrier flies to space and back."

"Tobias will see to your transport back to your ship. I'll brief the other captains about what's going on, assign security for your ship, and see if we can get some Marines for on-site security."

"As long as they don't steal anymore stuff."

"Guaranteed," Gilchrist said.

A few minutes later, they were on the hangar deck where the *Azanti* sat. Several sailors were curiously walking around, looking and pointing. Wade Watts looked suspiciously at the craft after the others had already boarded. Patty Mize had stayed on board to keep an eye on things, just in case.

Alex looked back at the overweight man checking the improvised welds with a dubious expression on his face. "Safer than a helicopter," he said.

"Says you," Wade replied. "I've been on helicopters before."

"You know what a helicopter is?" Patty asked. "It's a million parts, rotating rapidly around an oil leak, waiting for metal fatigue to set in. Who is round boy there?" she asked Alex.

"The guy who put the *Ford* into orbit."

"We going to dump him in the ocean for Gilchrist?"

Wade had been halfway through the door, but he froze upon hearing Patty's words.

"No," Jeremiah said. "He works for us now."

Wade finished boarding. Alex had to squeeze by the 2XL man to reach the hatch and pull it closed. "Speaking of that," Wade said. "How am I getting paid?"

"Same as we are," Jeremiah said. "Food and safety."

"Not much of a deal," Wade said.

"Half a helicopter ride is still an option," Patty said.

"Where do I sit?" Wade whined.

"It's a two-minute flight. Just stand," Alex told him, squeezing past him again to get into the pilot's seat. "They get us off the deck?" he asked Patty.

"Yeah, they used a crane to set us on wooden blocks."

Alex nodded. "Should work. Powering up." He heard a gasp from Wade and grinned to himself.

"Good field," Alison confirmed.

Alex translated up a tiny amount and moved them toward the open hangar doors. Alison laughed at something.

"What?" Alex asked.

"Check the aft camera. They should have lifted us a little higher."

On the screen, they could see the sailors staring in amazement at a perfectly shaped ice-cream scoop of metal missing from the hangar deck and no doubt riding inside their forcefield.

"Huh," Alex said, "I wondered about that." The *Azanti* flew out of the hangar and out over the water.

* * *

**Shangri-La**
**Over Amarillo, TX**

Cobb had to admit it; he was impressed. The floating conglomeration of metal dubbed Shangri-La was organized on every level. After Bisdorf landed his craft in a designated landing spot (one of three Cobb spotted), a crew came to check it for offload and to take care of basic maintenance—replenish the water, fill it with fuel, and dump the waste tanks. The process reminded him of a gas station in the 1950s. *Check the oil for you?*

There appeared to be a lot of survivors in Shangri-La's population. There was also a sizeable number of professionals. Many were big, burly guys who moved about with a purpose. *Roughnecks?* They certainly had the look and demeanor. They were people who weren't afraid of getting dirty and wanted to see a job through until it was done.

The top of the structure, despite being made mostly of steel Conex containers, was shockingly level. A short distance away, a crew was using arc welders to cover the tops with steel plates, all cut to shape with a plasma cutter. They were even covering the locking points on the corners so you could move about safely without fear of tripping. They reached a point where the plates were much thicker. Cobb was about to ask why when a golf cart, one of the big ones with room for a dozen people, rolled up. *It's a roadway!*

"How big is this place?" he asked Bisdorf.

"When I left it was 40 containers wide, by 60 containers long."

"2,400 containers!" Tim Price exclaimed.

"I think we're up to 3,000." Cobb turned at the voice. A man at least twice the size of Harry Ross, who Cobb thought was huge, was standing next to one of the big cranes. His skin was like rich, dark chocolate, and he seemed like the kind of guy who was always ready with a smile.

"Hey, Clark. Six hundred more since I left?"

"Yeah, we're almost out. Gonna have to hit another container yard."

"How's the alien field holding up?"

"Every 200 or so containers, Hans runs a test. Great so far. Who're the newbies?"

"I rescued them in Kendal; they were stuck in a court house, surrounded by zombies."

The man named Clark looked at the group, and his gaze settled on Cobb. "Army?"

"Yes sir, Colonel Cobb Pendleton, reactivated."

"Colonel, you say? I know someone who'll be glad to meet you."

"What about my friends? The woman over there lost her husband as we were being rescued." Cobb looked at the group and sighed. "They've been through a lot."

"Haven't we all?" He pointed at a group of men and women who were approaching. "They're from a group called the Angels. They take in new people and help them deal with what they've been through."

"Talking about us, Clark?" a woman in the group asked.

"Colonel Cobb, this is Amelia. She's the Angels' leader."

"If you can call me a leader," the woman said. She was an elderly woman with American Indian heritage, unless he missed his guess. Her eyes and face showed frown lines, which spoke of a tough life. "We do help get people adjusted to life here, but we also enforce a quarantine."

"Have you had problems?" Cobb asked.

"In short, yes. We're lucky it hasn't gone beyond a few instances with new arrivals. The infection hasn't spread here, and we've had no casualties. To be safe, everyone spends 24 hours under observation."

"What about me?"

"I'm going to take him to the sergeants, then to Ann," Bisdorf said. "The sergeants will take care of him."

Sergeants, plural. Interesting.

Amelia narrowed her eyes as she examined Cobb, and he wondered if she had x-ray vision. He felt like he was under a microscope. "Fine," she said and turned to her people who were helping Vance's group of survivors. Two young women, no more than girls themselves, were supporting Ann Benedict. She still seemed to be in shock.

"Amelia?" Cobb called to her. The older woman looked back at him. "Were you ever a Catholic nun?"

She laughed out loud and left to help load the others into the big golf cart. Then they drove off.

Cobb fell in behind Bisdorf and Clark as they led him along the surreal landscape of Shangri-La. It reminded him a little of an aircraft carrier, a Hollywood set, and a temporary army FOB, or forward operating base. There were tank farms, long lines of brand-new mobile homes and bunk houses, actual military mobile field kitchens, and what looked like an honest-to-God control tower in the center of the construct.

They passed within a short distance of the control tower—close enough for Cobb to see that it was mounted on a huge truck bed. "Is that a portable control tower?"

"Yep," Bisdorf said. "Liberated it."

"From a military base?"

The other man looked nonplused and didn't answer.

"Would you agree survival is the name of the game?" Clark asked.

"At the cost of others not surviving?"

"I can guarantee you, nobody was harmed or deprived of anything by our taking these assets."

"How can you be sure?" Cobb asked. He really wasn't worried; he'd done some traveling through the landscape, seen tens of thousands of infected, and knew how few uninfected likely remained. He was merely trying to get a feel for this group of survivors and where he'd stand with them. He found it interesting that nobody had said anything about the M-16 over his shoulder or the pistol on his hip.

"We'll have to show you later," Bisdorf said and gestured. They'd come to a series of standard, portable military bunkhouses. They were more evidence the group had raided at least one military base. They were set up on steel legs which were welded to the metal container base of Shangri-La. Outside the nearest one, a dozen soldiers in army and marine camo were sitting on metal barrels, working on weapons.

As Cobb and his two escorts approached, one looked up and did a double take when he spotted the eagle on Cobb's epaulet. "Shit," he cursed and jumped to his feet. The other 11 men saw, quickly figured out what was happening, and jumped to attention as well.

"At ease, guys. I'm new here."

"Sir!" the first one who had come to attention, a specialist, said.

"Sergeants inside?" Bisdorf asked.

"Yes," another soldier, a PFC, replied.

Cobb and the others walked to the trailer steps. “Calm down, guys, I’m not wearing stars,” Cobb said as he passed. A couple of them chuckled as the door opened, and he went inside.

The interior was laid out in a command trailer configuration, with a large conference room at one end. It also included one large office and four small ones. A trio of NCOs, two men and a woman, were sitting at the conference table, pouring over a large Texas/Oklahoma/New Mexico map covered in Legos. The oldest among them, a sergeant major, looked up and blinked when he saw Cobb.

“Who do you have here?” he asked Bisdorf and Clark.

“Says he’s an army colonel, Sergeant.”

“We’ve heard that one before,” the female NCO, a staff sergeant named Groves, said. The other man, a buck sergeant, watched the proceedings through narrowed eyes.

“Colonel,” the master sergeant said as he approached. “Can I see some identification?”

Cobb nodded and fished out his well-worn wallet. He opened it, took out two cards, and handed them to the master sergeant. The name on the master sergeant’s BDUs was “Schardt.” *Oh, I bet he got a lot of grief over his name.*

Schardt took the cards and looked them over. “DD 2765,” he said. “Retired. Says here Lieutenant Colonel.” His eyes flashed to the subdued eagle sewn on Cobb’s epaulets. Then he looked at the other card, a freshly minted CAC, or common access card. It didn’t have a picture, but it did have his service number, name, and rank of Colonel. Schardt grunted. “Looks legit, but it’s a bit confusing. Can you elaborate?”

"I was reactivated at Hood when I brought in a group of survivors, including a zoomie."

"A fighter pilot, huh?" the buck sergeant, Zimmerman, asked. "Who was in command at Hood?"

"Lieutenant General Rose, III Corps."

"Something anyone could know," Staff Sergeant Groves mumbled.

Schardt glanced at her, then at Cobb. "What would you say if I said I'd served under Leo Rose?"

"I'd say you were lying; he goes by Leon. Doesn't like being called Leo to his face."

Schardt nodded and handed back the cards. He came to attention and saluted. The other two sergeants did as well, though Groves was slower than Zimmerman. "My apologies, Colonel. You understand, with the situation…"

"No apologies necessary, Sergeant Major." Cobb put the cards away. "Can you bring me up to speed?"

Schardt nodded and gave a quick report. The soldiers present were survivors of a dozen different commands, and more than half were reservists, national guard, or retirees. In total, there were 82 men and women—35 army, 22 Marines, 15 air force, 9 navy, and one coast guard. In a strange twist of fate, the only officers were a navy ensign fresh out of the academy and an army WO1, warrant officer rank 1.

"The navy kid straight up refuses to use his status as an officer," Schardt explained.

"Thank God," Groves said. Schardt gave her some side eye.

"He did take command of our only armed sky-barge."

"What's a sky-barge?" Cobb asked.

"I'll show you later, sir."

Schardt continued to explain that they'd started with him and five men from their command, part of a supply unit trying to get back to Hood after the SHTF. They'd been picked up by the flying city early on and had continued to add more soldiers since then.

"A few refused to come aboard," Zimmerman explained. "I think they thought we were a hallucination."

"Can you blame them?" Cobb asked. For the first time, Groves grinned slightly.

"Gentlemen and ladies," Clark spoke up. "I'm going to leave you with the colonel. There is a small rail yard we'll be passing over in a few minutes, and I want to be in the gondola."

"Gonna need security?" Schardt asked.

Clark looked between the sergeants and Cobb, licking his lips. "I'll let you know once you get everything sorted out. Talk to you later." He left without another word.

"He's nervous," Bisdorf explained. "The military makes a lot of them nervous."

"They're afraid we're going to take over," Schardt explained.

"Would that be such a bad thing?" Groves asked.

"Yes, it would," Schardt replied, staring at her. "We've been over this."

"Not to my satisfaction."

Groves turned her steely blue eyes on Cobb. "What's your intention, *sir*?"

It was clear to Cobb, or anyone with functioning hearing, that Groves didn't like officers. That seemed to often be the case with staff sergeants. She looked to be between 30 and 35 and had probably had her career sidetracked by a bad fitness report whether she'd deserved it or not. Bad officers were as common as bad NCOs. Now, however, she was his problem.

"Well, it looks like I'm in command." Groves rolled her eyes. "Staff Sergeant, are we going to have a problem?"

"Just because there's an eagle on your shoulder doesn't mean you're qualified to lead us," she said, her eyes as sharp as her tongue.

"The chain of command disagrees. I'm no operator, but I've been shot at. A lot more than most staff sergeants." She bristled, and he pushed on. "I wore the uniform for 29 years, Sergeant, and when General Rose asked me to put it back on, I damned well did." He looked at all three. "Fate put me here. The lack of officers around here seems to suggest it was for a reason. So, whether you like it or not, I'm in command until relieved." He looked at a laptop on a nearby desk.

"Unless I miss my guess, you have a TOE already done up. This Shangri-La looks pretty squared away. Let's take a look at it so I know what I'm dealing with."

Schardt and Zimmerman nodded and went to the computer. Cobb followed to watch them work.

"I have to use the bathroom," Groves said and left without waiting for approval.

"Gonna read me in?" he asked Schardt.

Zimmerman sighed and spoke. "One, doesn't like officers. Two, doesn't like men. Three, she liked being one of the big dogs."

"She's a competent NCO," Schardt added. "But what Zim said is accurate. She was with six men we picked up outside Austin. They're guard. The bunch didn't talk much about how they got picked up, or what they were doing. Had a couple trucks chocked full of gear, though. A lot of it wasn't military. Said they'd been picking up stuff along the way."

"But not people?" Cobb asked.

"Claimed they helped some civvies, but none came along."

Cobb grunted and looked at the computer as Zimmerman explained how the tabs on the spreadsheet were set up with age, service, and MOS, military occupational speciality. Throughout the discussion, his mind kept wandering to Staff Sergeant Groves and her story. When she returned, she stayed at the back and watched without comment. Cobb could feel her eyes on his back like bugs crawling. He decided to keep a close eye on her.

* * *

**USS *Pacific Adventurer***

**150 Nautical Miles West of San Diego, CA**

General Rose watched from the bridge as the oceangoing tugboat he'd 'acquired' in the same way Dr. Breda had acquired the *Helix* finished tying up to the derelict cruise ship *Ocean Vista.* Most of the dependents he'd brought from Fort Hood were aboard, along with some of his injured and a few older retired servicemen to help guard the dependents. Behind it was an oceangoing barge holding all their air assets—four V-22 Osprey and four AH-64 Apache gunships. A single UH-60 Blackhawk rested on the *Pacific Adventurer's* helicopter pad.

The pilot was nervous about the helipad on his ship; he said it wasn't rated for the load. But it hadn't collapsed yet, so Rose wasn't too worried. He had more important things to worry about than the helicopter pad.

Rose was very concerned about food. They were down to a few days' worth of usable, fresh food for the roughly 1,100 people. Dr. Breda promised a fix, only she wouldn't say how long it would take to get it ready. He wasn't positive she could deliver. He was thinking the best way to give her time to work was to get clear of the Flotilla. Some deep part of his combat infantry officer's instincts was screaming a warning; get out of this area of operations. The AO was not one he was used to dealing with. Deep water was anathema to an army officer.

A storm was moving across the Flotilla. Captain Sampson called it a squall. Rose could see both sides of it and the streaks of rain pouring into the ocean just to the south of his position. A few drops splattered against the bridge window, which was why he'd elected to stay inside with the annoying Sampson. Army got wet, a lot. Not surprisingly, Rose had had enough of being soaked.

"We're just waiting on the fuel," Sampson said.

Rose nodded and looked at the nearby ships. There were fewer than there were this morning. Little doubt remained; between sinking and flying carriers, the civilians were losing their confidence in any implied security. The *Ford* was a mile off with a couple frigates nearby, or maybe they were destroyers. He couldn't tell.

In all likelihood, a lot of people had reached their capacity for absorbing weirdness. He felt close, himself. When he'd gotten back to his ship, Sampson hadn't been able to give him any more information about the carrier—how it flew, why it flew, or what the fuck was going on. In the end, it only reinforced his idea that it was time to have an exit strategy.

Fuel was also going to be an issue. Dr. Breda was working on a solution to the food situation. Maybe they could grow more? There were also stores with billions of MREs in different places around the country. The packaging process guaranteed they'd be good. Fuel, however. Fuel took more than a place to store it.

Over time, fuel went bad. Diesel stored better in a motor because gasoline usually had alcohol added, and alcohol damaged components. Aviation fuel aged somewhere between the two. As soon as he'd decided on his course of action, he'd sent some of his men, in small boats, to the dozens of abandoned ships and those infested with infected. They'd found a surprising number of fuel sources, one of which really stood out.

"They'll be here soon," he said, then glanced at Mays who nodded in the affirmative. Rose took his binoculars and scanned the horizon through the storm. There were so many small ships scattered around, he didn't know how he'd recognize what he was looking for if he spotted it.

"*Ocean Vista* to *Occluded*, we show a good tie-off."

Rose listened to the radio chatter between the powerless cruise ship and the tugboat.

"*Occluded*, roger that. We're bringing in the sea anchor, then we'll be ready to come under tow."

"*Helix* here, we've finished loading and are casting off. Where do you want us?"

Rose recognized the voice of Joseph Capdepon from Dr. Breda's Zombie Squad. During his logistics jobs, he'd also done some time as a merchant marine, so he'd taken nominal command of the *Helix*. Luckily, it had full fuel bunkers. After days of floating around, the fuel on the *Pacific Adventurer* was down to half, and the tug, *Occluded,* had less than a quarter remaining. If his men didn't deliver, they wouldn't be going anywhere.

"We're not asking the navy for gas," Rose told Mays when they'd decided to be prepared to cut out with Dr. Breda. "I don't want to answer any questions."

"I think those are your boys," Captain Sampson said and pointed.

Rose followed the man's arm and, after a second, he saw them. Two of their boats were tied up to a dingy, rusty, old tub chugging toward them. He didn't know what kind of ship it was, but there were trucks on the rear deck. Fuel trucks.

"Bingo," he said.

A few minutes later, the rusty, old ship tied up next to the *Pacific Adventurer*. They'd found the ship a mile away with a group of infected on the deck. After dealing with them, they'd searched the ship and found it was some group of survivalists idea of preparing for the apocalypse.

"Their loss, our win," Mays said. "So, what do we do now?"

"Get the men to help offload those fuel trucks. Fill up our ship and put the rest on the *Helix*."

"Our navy crew is going to have to help," Mays said.

Rose grunted in ascent. Resupplying on the water was tough. The navy called it unrep, underway replenishment, even if you weren't moving. Craning shit from one ship to another was tricky, he'd seen as much. "Just get it done. I want to be able to move ASAP."

"Right away, General." Mays left the bridge to find the senior lieutenant and get the crews working. Alone on the bridge with Sampson and his people, Rose looked out as rain lashed the ocean and the waves swelled to a few feet high. *God, I hate the ocean.*

A dark shadow seemed to pass under the ship. He tried to focus, wondering what it might be. But it was gone as soon as he noticed it. *Sea monsters.* He quietly chuckled.

*****

# Chapter Five

**Dusk, Friday, May 3**
**Joint Combined Evacuation Fleet**
**100 miles West of Corinto, Nicaragua**

"They'd court martial me if the CNO ever saw this," Admiral Kent mumbled as he watched the RHIB pick up its passengers. They were steaming north at a slightly reduced speed because of the *Yasen*-class Russian nuclear submarine pacing them 200 yards off his starboard. The shape of the sub's mast immediately marked it as foreign, as if the Russian naval officers in their gawdy, gold-bangled black uniforms weren't enough. He was in his dress uniform as well, waiting on the *Bataan's* bridge wing.

Their RHIB grounded on the Russian sub, the *Severodvinsk*, just like he'd suspected, and a door opened on the sail to allow two men to exit. They quickly and expertly boarded the RHIB, which was pushed clear by a pair of white-uniformed Russian submariners, and the RHIB spun about and headed back toward the *Bataan.* With the sun setting over the Russian sub, Kent wasn't sure what kind of message God was sending him. He frowned as he exited the bridge and headed down toward the well deck.

A few minutes later, he was standing at a railing over the well deck. The aft door was down, and the RHIB rode up inside. The boatswain piloted the craft well, and he brought it up onto the ramp where an LCAC would have been. They didn't have any of the Marine hovercraft aboard. Instead, the *Bataan* had a very different cargo.

The older Russian looked around curiously, eventually glancing up and seeing Admiral Kent standing at the railing. He saluted Kent and yelled up in his slight accent, "Permission to come aboard, sir?"

"Granted," Kent said, and he walked down the stairs to join him. "Captain Chugunkin, welcome aboard the USS *Bataan*."

"Thank you, Admiral. This is my XO, Captain Lieutenant Svetan."

The much younger man with very blond hair, blue eyes, and dimples saluted crisply. There was no hint of a smile on the man's face.

Kent returned the salute. "I am sorry I cannot offer you visiting captain's honors. We don't have a band aboard."

"Understandable," Chugunkin said, nodding. "Pardon my misunderstanding, but I did not know a flag officer of the US Navy would command an…what do you call them, Amphibian Assault Ship?"

Kent smiled and shook his head. "Amphibious Assault Carrier," he corrected.

"Ah, yes, sorry."

"Your English is excellent; I am surprised you missed that one."

"You will forgive my ignorance. We are trained to sink your supercarriers and nuclear missile submarines. Targets this…" he looked around, "…small are not of any serious concern."

Kent's eyes narrowed at the dig. He resisted replying. At one point, the US Navy had functional carriers. Instead, he gestured at the huge tarp hanging over the forward section of the well deck. "Would you like to meet Dr. Gallatin?"

"I would."

Kent escorted the two men to the tarp where a sort of door had been mounted. A pair of Marines stood with M4 carbines shouldered. They both saluted the admiral and gave Chugunkin and his XO dubious looks.

"At ease, men," Kent said, returning the salute. He pulled the fabric door open and motioned the two Russian officers inside.

Behind the barrier was the *Bataan's* principle cargo. Dozens of mobile office modules and trailers. Some were marked with the NASA logo, euphemistically called the "meatball". Others bore the blue CDC logo with white rays running through it, and still others said FEMA in red. Chugunkin's eyes took it all in.

"Not the cargo I was expecting," the captain said.

"As I explained," Kent replied, "we left most of our war assets behind at Norfolk when we evacuated. My carrier, the *Eisenhower*, was in for repairs and unable to put to sea, so I borrowed the *Bataan*."

Dr. Gallatin came out onto the steps of the nearest trailer with a NASA logo on it, saw the three officers, and waved. "Captain Chugunkin," he said. "Welcome."

"Thank you, Doctor," the Russian said. Theodore gestured, and they walked up the short metal steps and into the trailer.

The interior was set up like a conference room with a half-circular table against one wall and a dozen chairs arrayed around it. Each chair had a notepad, a pen, and a glass of water on the table in front of it. Arrayed on the far side of the table were Alphonse Bennitti, Dr. David Curie, Dr. Albert Gallatin, and Dr. Wilma Gnox. Kent realized he had far too many doctors on his boat.

"Gentlemen and Lady," Kent said. "This is Captain Chugunkin and his XO, Captain Lieutenant Svetan." He saw most of them squint at the XO's rank. He couldn't fault them; Russian ranks were strange. They all spoke greetings to which Chugunkin merely nodded. "Would you care to sit?" Kent asked the Russian.

Chugunkin and his XO examined the room for another moment, the younger officer waiting to follow his senior's lead. Eventually, the senior captain took the chair in the middle of the table, the one closest to the door. Kent had noted neither were armed when they came aboard. Regardless, a squad of armed Marines were only a couple seconds away, if he needed them.

He doubted the Russians would start anything. Should the Americans cause problems, most of their ships would be sunk in retaliation. It would be a slaughter, probably on both sides, though he wasn't certain of his ability to inflict serious casualties. He didn't have a proper task force and was severely light on ASW assets. He dearly wished he had comms with some of his submarine assets. Sadly, they were probably lost to Strain Delta.

"I await details of your interesting story," Captain Chugunkin said. Neither of the Russians did more than glance at the water and notepads provided.

"Since I've been nominally placed in charge of our efforts," Bennitti said, "let me introduce you around." Chugunkin's eyes narrowed. Bennitti noticed and cleared his throat before continuing. "Quickly, of course.

"First, myself, Alphonse Bennitti, NASA. Dr. David Curie, Chief Immunologist at the CDC, and his boss, Dr. Albert Gallatin, director of same."

"Captain," Gallatin said. Curie remained silent.

Chugunkin gave the barest of nods. Kent was sure his level of trust regarding the entire situation wasn't helped by the presence of the CDC people. *The Russians probably think the CDC was used to develop biological weapons. Sure, the US had people who did. However, if even half of what the CDC men said was true, there was no way Strain Delta came from Earth.* Bennitti continued.

"And over there is Dr. Wilma Gnox. She's not with any of the agencies mentioned."

"Then why is she here?" Svetan asked, the first time he'd spoken.

"She's an expert NASA employed as an independent contractor."

"My specialties are biology and paleontology, but I'm considered a bit of an expert in xenobiology."

"The study of alien biology?" Chugunkin asked.

"Precisely. It's more of a hobby, though, as there weren't any aliens to study. We liked to play around with what might be possible. During one get together, we tried to figure out if a silicon lifeform could exist. Between science and beer, we had—"

"I don't think the captain needs details about your conference exploits," Kent intervened.

Gnox gave him an aggrieved look but shrugged. "What I've mostly been doing has to do with linguistics—learning to talk to our guest."

"This is all fascinating," Chugunkin said. "But I fail to see any proof."

Bennitti looked at Kent. He knew what they wanted and dearly wished there was some kind of command authority left. God only knew how many national security acts he was violating. Of course, a Russian submarine commander was sitting in a NASA trailer on a navy boat. In for a penny, in for a pound. He nodded to Bennitti.

"You can hear it from the fox's mouth," Bennitti said.

"I thought it was horse's?" Chugunkin asked.

"Not in this case," Kent replied.

Bennitti pressed a control in his hand, and the wall against the flat part of their table hummed as a shield moved away. It revealed a glass wall and a room on the other side. The room was simple with white walls of a soft-looking plastic. The lighting was more subdued than you would find elsewhere. A pallet against the back held a blanket and something furry. As the shield moved aside, the furry object raised a small, delicately pointed face and opened black-on-black eyes.

Chugunkin gawked at the alien sitting a few feet away. He got up and moved closer to the window, coming within inches. Kent could see him carefully examining every detail. The alien was doing the same to him. "What is this?" the Russian asked. "You dress up an animal and tell me this is some kind of alien?" He'd turned toward Kent, so he didn't see the alien pick up the microphone and speak.

"I am not animal."

Chugunkin spun, his jaw falling open in shock. "Did you speak to me?"

"Obviously," the alien said. The words were English with a certain quality that was hard to put your finger on. Kent thought it was because the alien didn't have movable lips. Her voice was slightly higher-pitched than an adult man's or woman's and had something of a nasal tone to it.

"As I said," Gnox spoke up, "linguistics is also my thing, though more of a hobby. Nikki, there, proved better than I was and more-or-less mastered basic, conversational English. Now that we can talk, Nikki's helping us master her language."

Chugunkin was spluttering and staring, his mouth wide open. His XO crossed himself and muttered something in Russian.

"As the humans explained," the alien said, "we are, unfortunately, responsible for the plague." She gave an almost human shrug. "We are sorry."

"You called it Nikki?" Chugunkin finally managed to speak. "What is it?"

"She's a female," Gnox said haughtily, "not an it. And yes, she chose the name after reading some books."

"Nikki is from Gliese 436, a star about 32 light years from Earth," Bennitti said, his face beaming. "We named her species Stellae Vulpes." Chugunkin's head spun to stare at him. "Star Fox."

He turned back to look at Nikki.

"What do you want to know?" Nikki asked.

"`Tchyo za ga`lima?"

"Sorry?" Nikki asked.

Gnox, knowing Russian, smiled and laughed.

* * *

**Shangri-La**

**Over Amarillo, TX**

Cobb took a long drink of the scalding hot, real-as-shit, coffee. It was in a Yeti mug, which kept it super-hot. The creamer was fake, of course. He didn't care; it still tasted great. The view out of the office was spectacular. The area of Texas Shangri-La was flying over was pretty flat. At over 1,000 feet above ground level, he could see for almost a hundred miles. The view from the military camp was clear to the west where the sky was turning bright red.

"So," he said, "it looks like you've got plenty of ammo, around 20,000 rounds, but you are short on small arms. You've got fifty M4s and a few older M-16s, five M-240s and a pair of Ma-deuces."

"Spot on," Schardt said and nodded.

"It looks like they raided at least one military installation," Cobb added. "Why didn't they pick up anything heavier?"

"It was all locked up," Zimmerman said. Groves had left at one point and still hadn't returned. "Everything we have, we brought with us when we got picked up."

Cobb glanced at the heavy machine gun ammo. Just six boxes of ball, 600 rounds. An M2 machinegun could chew through 600 rounds in a few minutes.

"If we could get access codes to some of the armories, Governor Taylor would be agreeable to going for it," Schardt explained.

"She wouldn't have access as a lieutenant governor," Cobb said under his breath. Both the sergeants grunted in agreement. He was wondering where Groves had gotten to when the door opened.

"Where's this new officer?" asked a deep, feminine voice with a decidedly obvious Texas accent.

Cobb stood and turned around, coming to attention. "That would be me, ma'am. Colonel Cobb Pendleton, US Army."

"Well, good to meet ya," Governor Taylor said. TV didn't do her justice. She was nearly 6 feet tall. On the large side of what you'd courteously call chunky, she had short cut auburn hair, a permanent, somewhat disingenuous, smile, and eyes which spoke of a dangerous, barely hidden rage. "I thought Bisdorf was gonna bring ya by to meet me?" She looked around the room, quickly taking in the situation and the two sergeants, including how they were letting him do the talking. She had a pair of uniformed state patrol officers with her who wore looks of calm determination. They were both examining Cobb curiously. "I assume you are in command now?"

"You are correct, ma'am."

"Some of these boys and girls aren't army or guard."

"In the absence of a proper chain of command, the highest ranked officer can assume command of any available military units in order to maintain a semblance of cohesion and defense of self and US assets." He shrugged. "Paraphrased."

Taylor nodded, and the smile manifested again. "Fair enough. Has Master Sergeant Schardt brought you up to speed on the situation?"

"I've mostly spent my time getting up to speed on our personnel and equipment situation. We were going to get to the physical situation next."

Taylor nodded again and gestured toward the door. "It might be simpler to show you." She looked at Schardt. "The recovery operation has a problem."

Schardt quickly stood up, alarm on his face. "Bad?"

"Not yet."

"I'll get a squad."

"Make it two squads," she said and headed for the door. She stopped when Schardt didn't move. The master sergeant was looking at Cobb for approval. She examined the situation critically, her eyes narrowing.

"Have them meet me…" Cobb looked at Governor Taylor for details.

"The gondola," she said, her voice icy.

"Got it," Schardt said.

"Make sure the men are informed of my arrival and assumption of command."

"Yes, Colonel."

Cobb walked over to Taylor. "Ma'am, lead the way."

Outside, a small, four-seated electric cart waited. A young man in immaculate khakis sat in the driver's seat. When he saw Cobb, he looked surprised and confused. Cobb started to sit in the front, next to the driver.

"Why don't ya sit back here with me," Governor Taylor said, the same smile on her face. She gestured toward the other rear seat.

"As the governor wishes," he said and sat.

"Now, you don't have to be like that," she said. Once they were both seated, the driver started the car and moved slowly on the improvised steel-plate road, careful to avoid the ever-present foot traffic. "Don't get me wrong, I'm glad to see some military leadership arrive."

"You seem a little put off, Governor Taylor."

"Call me Ann," she said.

"I think it's best to keep it on a professional level."

"Should I call you Colonel Pendleton, then?"

"That is my rank and name."

For the first time, her smile faltered. *Good.*

"Something bothering you, Colonel?"

"I'm concerned," Cobb said.

"About what, may I ask?"

"A casual observer would think you were using military personnel and assets for your own purposes, outside military leadership's counsel."

"We're just trying to survive, Colonel Pendleton. This place was put together by some very smart men and women. When they picked me up, I said I'd do my best to help...*guide* their efforts."

"This guidance include ordering military personnel around?"

"I'm sorry if it looks as though I'm giving orders," she said, inclining her head slightly. "The situation precludes any sense of propriety. You must understand, I was unsure if you were who I was told you were."

"And what do you think now?"

"Why, ah thank there's a new sheriff in town," Taylor said, making her Texas accent extra thick on purpose.

Cobb did his best to imitate her cool smile. "Rest assured, I will endeavor to give you whatever support you need, if we're able to provide it." She didn't respond. Instead, she watched her driver navigate the many obstacles.

They arrived outside a building that was manufactured out of scrap metal. Many welds and cans of Rust-Oleum had obviously gone into its manufacture. It was surrounded by quick and dirty container modification jobs with clear weld marks and standard single-wide mobile homes and office modules. He was immediately curious about the purpose.

"Follow me, please," Governor Taylor said coldly.

"Where are we going?" Cobb asked as he got out and followed.

"To the center of the empire, as it were."

Inside the building were several rooms filled with people operating computers and large monitors showing images of the ground below them. In the center was a surprisingly ornate, wrought iron, circular staircase that descended to the area below. The governor headed down immediately, so Cobb followed. Nobody took notice of them.

As he went around in circles, Cobb wondered where they'd gotten a stairway like the one he walked on. Had someone made it on the spot? He hadn't seen a metal shop, and he didn't think they would have had time to create one. He thought it would be dangerous to have a metal shop on an aircraft, then he remembered the aircraft he rode on was anything but conventional.

They reached the bottom of the stairs and entered a large, open space. He realized, though, as his eyes adjusted, it wasn't really open. It was like a skybox in a professional sports stadium with 360-degree views. When his booted feet touched the floor, he saw he was below the hull of Shangri-La.

The hull spread out in all directions for hundreds of feet. He caught himself gawking at the sheer size of what they'd created. *It's a gondola*, he realized. The room was hanging under the craft like the gondola on a blimp. Fitting. He went over and put a hand on the glass, which was slanted from the top of the ceiling inward to the floor. Each pane was at least nine feet tall, creating a spectacular view of the ground below, which he noticed was closer. They'd been descending.

"The glass feels substantial," he said.

"It should," a man said. Cobb turned toward the speaker and saw a middle-aged, balding man with dark hair, thick glasses, and a rather advanced paunch. "It's armored glass we found in Houston." His accent was…German?

"It was going on the new federal building there."

Cobb recognized Clark's rich voice. He was standing on the other side of the gondola with a pair of field glasses pressed to his eyes, looking almost straight down.

"It was just there, shame not to use it," the first man said.

Something clicked, and Cobb snapped his fingers. "You must be Hans Daimler, mad scientist?"

"I thought of changing my name to ze Frankenstein, but it seemed too much, ya? You are ze soldier zat Clark tolt us about? Bisdorf found you in a building?"

"Surrounded by zombies," Cobb added.

Hans nodded knowingly. "I think most of us have been there at one point or another, yes?"

About 20 people occupied the spacious deck of the gondola. Most were typing on laptops, using their own vision gear. Some were talking over headsets. It was an impressive operation. A loud *Spang!* sounded under his feet, and Cobb unconsciously jumped a little.

"Un zat is vy we have armored glass and titanium floors," Hans Daimler said. Several people around the room nodded.

"Good Lord! Who's shooting at us?" Cobb asked.

"Every idiot redneck with a gun," someone said in what sounded like a Boston accent.

"Hey, I resemble that remark," someone else said in a thick Louisiana accent. Several people laughed, including the Bostonian.

"It's some of my former constituents," Governor Taylor said. "I doubt they voted for me."

"Why?" Cobb persisted.

"If you saw what looked like a bad sci-fi movie spaceship floating over you, what would you do?"

"I wouldn't shoot the fucking thing," Cobb mumbled.

"Now say you saw this bad sci-fi movie spaceship during a zombie apocalypse?" she added.

"Okay, you have a point, Governor."

She grunted and went to Clark. "Any more developments?"

"They found the cats," Clark replied, not moving his glasses. "Only the zombies seem interested as well."

"Mind bringing me up to speed?" Cobb asked.

"The soldiers are answering to him now," Taylor explained.

"Not really a surprise," Clark said. "You ain't planin' to leave, are you?"

"And do what, play Mad Max down there? Been there, done that, got the T-shirt."

It was Clark's turn to laugh. "You have to understand, we have a lot of guys and girls with guns and stuff. Not many who really know how to fight. The men you've taken command of are all survivors of this shit storm below us. We need them."

"Tell him vat we are doing," Daimler suggested.

"Right," Clark said. "So, we explained we've been harvesting containers everywhere we find them and rescuing people?" Cobb nodded. "Well, we're kinda on a treadmill now. We have so many people, we have to continually get more stuff. Water filtration, waste management, food, food, food."

"I see. And you use those cranes to hoist up whatever you find?"

"Pretty much," Clark said. "Courtney Raines is our divining rod." He gestured to a very petite brunette who was standing to one side, holding a large tablet. "She used to work for US Customs and Border Patrol."

"CBP keeps an eye on every container that comes into the country," Courtney said. Her speech was smooth and businesslike. "I was in charge of mid-American waypoints, but when the shit hit the fan I mirrored the bureau's national database as best I could and got the fuck out of dodge."

"How did you know the shit was hitting the fan, as you said?" Cobb asked.

"Colonel, please. Anyone in government knew it was bad. We'd just been ordered to keep our mouths shut. My daddy didn't raise no fools. I read the writing on the wall. My boyfriend, a dozen others, and I ran for it. I was the only one who survived. These guys spotted me on a roof in Austin." She gestured around. "Here I am."

"What do you think the government would do if they found out you were giving out the data?"

"Colonel, there is no functional government."

"We've been getting some atmospheric skip traffic from the ham radio," Clark explained. "A naval flotilla is near San Diego. The president was trying to hook up with them, and her plane crashed."

"Wait, San Diego?" Cobb asked, suddenly excited. "Do you know if any of the army unit I was with made it there?"

"We heard some crazy shit about a C-17 landing on an aircraft carrier," Taylor said. "Figured it was bullshit."

Cobb smiled hugely. General Rose had evacuated with a dozen helicopters and more than a few Osprey from Fort Hood. He'd also taken three C-17 transport jets. Cobb helped rescue one of the pilots. On board one of those planes was his recent girlfriend, Kathy Clifford. It was the first time, in days, he'd dared to think she could still be alive.

"So, the story might naht be bullshit?" Governor Taylor asked.

"Maybe not," he replied. He took a minute to explain the evacuation of Fort Hood.

"I hope they're still alive," she said.

"Heading there would be the smartest move," Cobb said. Most of the eyes in the gondola turned toward him. "They'll have resources we don't have. Plus, this technology, wherever its from, could save a lot of lives."

"We're already saving a lot of lives right here," Taylor said. "My citizens' lives."

"You just said there was no government."

"No *federal* government," Taylor corrected.

"The distinction is tenuous at best," Cobb countered.

"Maybe we can save the civics debate for later?" Clark suggested. "Right now, we have three teams on the ground, and they're having a hell of a time trying to meet their objectives."

"What are their objectives?" Cobb asked, moving over to the big roughneck.

"Look down," Clark said.

Cobb searched around and found another pair of field glasses. There were dozens hanging on pegs all around the inside of the gondola. Another round bounced off the armored plates under his feet. He only twitched the second time. Using the glasses, he followed Clark's gaze and focused down into the growing gloom.

"A rail yard?" he asked.

"Yes," Clark confirmed. "A BNSF transfer yard. They take apart trains and put them back together. This one isn't particularly big, but it has something we want. Several somethings."

"What?"

Clark took the glasses from his eyes and pointed. "See those bright orange cables running down from the edge of Shangri-La over there?" He pointed.

Cobb found them and nodded. "Why orange?"

"Visibility."

Cobb nodded; it made sense. He followed them with his eyes down toward the ground, then switched back to his glasses.

"On one of the trains, you'll see several bright yellow things."

Cobb searched for a moment, following the orange cables until he found the yellow, cube-shaped things. "Got 'em." He could immediately see hundreds of infected around them. He also saw that the cables ended at a square platform and men were standing on it a short distance above the yellow cube. The platform was swaying back and forth. "What are they?"

"Those are three big, beautiful Caterpillar C175-20 generator sets."

"Generators?" Cobb asked. "Why are they so important?"

"We have over 2,000 men, women, and children," Taylor explained. "Refrigerated food containers, air conditioning (y'all might notice Texas starts getting hot in late April), not to mention lights, stoves, and many other things."

"Bisdorf said you have generators."

"We do," Clark said. "About two dozen of them, the biggest being 40 kilowatts. Those down there are 4,000 kilowatts. Each!"

Cobb whistled. Four megawatts was a lot of juice. "What about fuel, do they use a lot?"

"At peak output, over 1,000 liters an hour," Daimler said, then looked at Cobb. "Zats about 300 gallons for your yankees."

"I keep telling you, southerners ain't yankees," the man with the Louisiana accent said.

"You all sound ze same to me," Daimler retorted.

"Fuel not a concern?" Cobb asked, getting back to the matter at hand.

"A lot easier to get than generators," Clark said.

"You can't just hook up the generators and lift it?"

"No," Clark said. "We have light shipping cranes we took from Houston. They can handle the load, no problem, even with 500 feet of cable. Problem is, we're so high, the connection cradle is waving like a tree in high winds. If there weren't any fucking zombies, my team would just jump off and use cables to control the cradle."

Cobb again focused on the generator and saw that the infected were not only swarming around it, but also on it. He guessed there were a few hundred, at least.

"We always operate in early morning or at dusk," Clark said. "Tends to draw less of them. Of course, it greatly shortens our operating window."

"Can't you go lower?"

"Too risky," Taylor explained. "The gondola is only lightly armored. We almost lost a window once when we got really low to try and get a whole string of diesel railroad tankers."

Cobb looked around the gondola and spotted a window with a nasty impact spot. The glass was white and spiderwebbed badly. "Must have been a .50 caliber."

"We don't stay anywhere more than a night," Clark remarked. "I had a friend with a 20mm WWII anti-tank rifle. We used to take it to Kentucky and shoot it every year at the Knob Creek shoot. Anyway, I bet there are others out there. A 20mm would go right through this glass or the floor."

"And just rattle around in here," Cobb agreed. "Okay, what can we do?"

"We need to figure out how to give my crew time to get the generators. One would be okay, but I want them all. We don't need four megawatts right now, but at the rate we're growing, we'll need more soon, and a backup would be priceless."

"Where do all the infected come from?"

"The zombies?" Taylor asked, then gave a dry mirthless chuckle. "Amarillo used to have 200,000 people."

"Not anymore," Clark said, the glasses welded to his eyes again. "Jumping Jesus!"

Cobb lifted his own glasses and saw what the other man was cursing about. The infected were piled so high on the generator closest to the suspended cradle and the men on it, Cobb couldn't see the generator at all. And they were starting to pile on top of each other! *This is crazy.*

He used his own glasses to scan the rail yard. There weren't many good places to set a force down. He could see several big cranes, but it would be difficult to provide stable fire from another crane. And if random yokels were popping shots at the big, floating city, a group of dangling soldiers would be at even more risk.

"Have salvage crews been fired upon?" he asked.

Clark looked away from his glasses to Governor Taylor who looked back at him. "Yes," he said. "We lost three men yesterday."

"Thanks for being honest." He looked through the field glasses again. "Do I have comms with my men?" Someone handed him a small VHF radio of the kind you could buy at any store. He examined it and shrugged. "This is Colonel Pendleton."

"Sergeant Zimmerman here," came the immediate reply.

"We need to assist a salvage operation. Have two squads stand by. I'll be there in a minute." Turning back to Clark, he said, "Can someone show me back to the military trailers so I can get some gear?"

"You going down yourself?" Clark asked, the surprise on his face obvious.

"You don't tell a soldier to do something you won't do yourself." Something about the way Clark looked at him struck Cobb as peculiar. But when he looked at the other man, Clark looked away.

* * *

Cobb climbed onto the platform they'd use to descend below Shangri-La. It was spacious, even with 20 men on it. He glanced around at his new command. Two nine-man squads, one Marine and one army. The Marine contingent was led by a corporal they called Tango. The army had Sergeant Zimmerman, who preferred to go by Zim. When Cobb had drawn gear, he'd met the warrant officer they mentioned, WO1 Boca. The young, Asian man was an armorer and seemed to spend all his time tending to the military weapons in a secure trailer. He barely seemed to notice Cobb, who wondered what was going on.

He'd elected to draw an M4, just like every other man under his new command, so they were all using the same ammo and magazines. He'd added new body armor but kept his BDUs, despite how well-worn they were. They fit, while new ones often didn't.

The men were selected using a rotational spreadsheet created by Master Sergeant Schardt. They were drawn from all the combat-trained personnel, with an eye toward hours on duty and specialty. It also seemed to consider who was with what unit, and this made Cobb wonder how it was generated.

The Marines all knew each other. Most of the Devil Dogs had arrived in intact squads. The army folks were much more scattered. Cobb hadn't seen two of the same unit patch. One man had an Arkansas National Guard patch on his shoulder. The man looked surly at the idea of being on this mission.

"This thing safe?" Cobb asked the men who were checking their mags and verifying that their gear was in place. He'd met them while gearing up and noted the huge amount of ammo and knives they carried. Considering what he'd experienced since everything went south, he did the same. His web gear was stuffed full of mags, and he had picked up a pair of extra knives.

"Fairly," Tango said and winked. "You army guys get nervous when you're more than a hundred feet off the ground."

"More than twenty," Zim said. Everyone chuckled, even the Marines. The Arkansas guardsman flipped Zim the bird behind his back, and Cobb's eyes narrowed.

"You funny boys ready?" the crane operator asked, leaning out of the glass-enclosed cab, a cigarette in the corner of his mouth.

"Sure thing," Cobb said and grabbed one of the railings. There were metal plates on all four sides of the framework, like railings, and more on the floor. The welds looked fresh. He also thought he saw some residual blood spots in one corner. "Lower us down."

The operator nodded and worked the controls. The platform jerked, lifting off the deck, then slowly swung out over the side. Cobb swallowed as the distance below them loomed. Almost instantly, a round bounced off the side armor.

"Goddamn civvies!" the guardsman snarled as everyone kneeled.

Cobb took note of the side hit as well as their orientation to the ground. The shot had come from the same direction as the previous fire. He bristled as he considered having the tall, thin Marine to his right use the accurized M4 he was carrying to return fire. *We're supposed to help civilians, not kill them.* Only, weren't the civilians the ones trying to kill *them*?

Instead of worrying about it, Cobb leaned over the small hole in the center of the platform's floor to look down and gauge how far they had to go. The sun was touching the horizon and would be down in just a few minutes. They needed to act fast.

"About 100 feet to go," Zim said over the radio that was being monitored by the crane operator.

"I'll take it slow," the man replied.

"Negative," Cobb said. Zim looked at him. "We need to get on the deck ASAP."

"Roger that," Zim said and clicked the radio. "No, keep the descent steady."

"Gonna be a good jolt when you hit," the operator replied.

"Acknowledged," Zim told him.

"Everyone brace," Cobb said. The ground came up pretty quickly, then the platform slammed onto the concrete road deck with a *Bang!* Metal on concrete resounded like the tone on a cello. A couple of the men hunched even lower. Nobody was hurt, though. He made a mental note to see if they could add rubber bumpers or something to the bottom. Immediately, they all vaulted the platform's metallic shield and jogged to the road's railing.

"Down and clear," Zim transmitted, and the platform instantly lifted off and headed back up, much quicker than it had descended. Above them, Master Sergeant Schardt had two more squads geared up and ready. They were the backup. The only problem was Shangri-

La only had two platforms for lowering men. They were using one, the recovery team was using the other.

Cobb took in the scene. They'd been set down on Interstate 40, maybe 200 yards from where Interstate 27 passed underneath. The section of interstate they stood on was 50 or so feet above the rail yard below them. He brought up his carbine and looked through the Acog sight. The three bright yellow Caterpillar generator sets were clearly within view, as he'd planned. The scope rated the closest at 210 yards. Moving his view up, he saw the dangling recovery crew, weaving back and forth in the light breeze.

He was about to transmit over his radio handset when he looked up. He swallowed at the sight. How many thousands of tons of steel were just…hovering…up there? It was astounding. He didn't appreciate the locals popping off rounds at them, however, standing under the massive structure which was hovering in the gloom of near nighttime, he understood a little more of their mentality. The vista was otherworldly. The gondola was also clearly visible, the armored glass catching the setting sun. Yeah, it was a visible target.

"Relief team, on the ground," he transmitted. "Recovery team ready?"

"Yeah," someone from the dangling crew responded. "Hope you got an idea; we're starting to feel like a worm on the hook with the world's biggest catfish below us."

Cobb chuckled and keyed the mic again. "No worries. Wait one." He clipped the mic to his tactical harness and addressed the men. "Marines, up."

"Oorah," the nine men barked and flicked off their safeties.

"Let 'em fly!"

All nine Marines fired their M203 grenade launchers at the same time. They'd been part of a unit which still used the older launchers. They'd been a favorite back in the day, but the military, in its infinite wisdom, was taking them out of service in favor of the M320 and the MK19. He would have loved to have a Mk19, which was basically a grenade machinegun, even considering how difficult it would have been to bring it down and deploy it. Its sustained rate of ass kicking was spectacular to behold. The M320 would have been nice too, because unlike the M203, you could dismount an M320 and shoulder fire it, just like the old, Vietnam era bloop-tube.

They didn't have a shit ton of grenades. Each Marine carried 10, which was just under half of their total supply. Cobb watched the dim flashes of the grenades arcing out and striking the mass of infected.

"Looks like a fucking pyramid covered in ants," an army private said.

The first nine grenades detonated in a staccato series of explosions. Cobb watched through his scope as dozens of former human beings were blown to bloody chunks. The insane, upward clawing to reach the dangling humans paused as the blasts echoed in the dead city.

"Give them another salvo," Cobb ordered, and nine more grenades popped out. This time, the explosion seemed to knock the base out of the infected pyramid, which collapsed toward the soldiers. "That's got their attention. They just need a target. Zim?"

"On it, Colonel." Zim and an army corporal took metallic cylinders out of their packs, pulled off the end covers, and struck them, igniting the phosphorous flares. As each flare was lit, they dropped it over the side. In seconds, hundreds of infected were running toward them.

"Why do they respond so fast?" a Marine asked.

"They're like a flock of birds," another Marine responded.

"Yeah," Corporal Tango said. "Only birds don't try to eat you alive."

"Let's thin them out," Cobb said. "Semi-auto, men." He raised his rifle, and a second later, all 20 men began firing quick, well-placed rounds. The infected fell, and in seconds, the pyramid had completely collapsed. A wave of infected rushed toward the bridge.

"Maybe we should have kept the platform down here." Zim thought.

"They can lower it faster than before," Cobb said, then paused. "Right?"

The wave of infected turned into a tsunami. "Switch to burst," Cobb yelled over the screeches of the infected. The soldiers blazed at the leading edge, dropping dozens who then tripped up others. The wave faltered under a growing wall of their own dead. Some slowed to tear at the injured, feeding on them. Cobb's stomach turned. But it was working.

"Generators are clear!" the recovery team yelled. "We're starting."

"Okay men, lets hold the line!" Below them, the infected roared with rage and advanced.

***

**The Flotilla**

**50 Nautical Miles West of San Diego, CA**

PO1 Anna Niles steered her bird toward the south and adjusted one of the three flat screen monitors which was showing her a 360-degree view of her flight path. She'd been excited when she trained in the operation of the new MQ-8B UAV, also known as the Fire Scout. How often did a 29-year-old woman get to operate a $14 million piece of hardware, especially when they weren't an academy graduate?

One of the strange things about the way the navy operated UAVs, or drones, was how they divided piloting responsibilities. One pilot handled takeoff and landing, the other operated the drone away from the ship. However, like the service loved to do, when the Fire Scout came online, they invented new specialties. She was an NEC8368, a Fire Scout UAV pilot. She got to take off, land, and fly. Sweet!

She'd started her career as an RQ-2 UAV pilot. She'd wanted to fly fighters. What kid didn't? Only, she didn't have the scores. She was a product of the video game generation. Operating a drone was second nature in many ways. When they started retiring the RQ-2s, she got promoted and moved to the Fire Scout project.

The team at Northrop Grumman who developed the Fire Scout had started with a traditional helicopter, the Schweizer 330SP. If you squinted, the Fire Scout still looked a little like one. It was the largest VTOL UAV, or Vertical Takeoff and Landing Unmanned Aerial Vehicle, in US Naval inventory—at least until the MQ-9 came out—and she got to play with one of the 30 in service. Anna was thrilled.

Then her team of three was assigned to the MQ-8B, tail number N22, and they found out they were taking their bird to the USS *Freedom*. She'd known the Fire Scouts were primarily deployed to littoral combat ships, but she'd hoped for the *Zumwalt* or something new and cool. The *Freedom* was neither new nor cool. Still, she got to be stationed in beautiful San Diego! And then Strain Delta hit.

The *Freedom,* along with her sister ship, the *Jackson* (a tri-hull *Independence*-class, unlike *Freedom's* single hull), happened to be out on exercises, having left a month earlier. They'd been just a day's sail away when everything fell apart. Admiral Hoskins had swept them into the task force, and they'd been doing what they could ever since.

The problem was, the LCS—the littoral combat ships—were small. Many in the US blue-water Navy snickered and called them little crappy ships. They *were* little, and as the *Freedom* was the first of her class, she was as problem riddled as you could imagine. Even seven years after her launch, things kept going wrong. A few of the older crew who'd been on board when Anna came over said they wouldn't have been surprised if the plague was just another malfunction on their ship.

Still, the ship's food lockers were nearly full of food that predated the warnings. Unlike those on many navy vessels, they weren't going hungry. However, three crewmembers had committed suicide since landside comms had gone down or upon hearing the areas their families were from had gone dark. It appeared to be the end of the world.

"What do you have, Niles?"

"Not much, Chief," Anna responded to the chief petty officer in charge of her division. They were near the hangar in the rear of the *Freedom*. Bigger ships had drone flight ops in the CIC. The *Freedom* didn't have room there, so she got to hang out aft, away from the officers. Suited her fine. "Looks like a zombie rave to me."

The monitor showed the darkening landing fields of NAS Coronado. Some fires still burned in places. Despite the rogue fighter blowing up the bridge, it looked like a million zombies were still roaming around. At least a thousand encircled the remains of the president's jet which continued to burn brightly. *Reminds me of Burning Man.*

"No signs of life?"

"Lots of signs of life, just none of it thinking," she said and banked the Fire Scout north to go along the eastern edge of the island. She'd located two small groups of Marines in the six hours since the drone had launched. Both times, they'd been rescued by a helicopter. She guessed 20 men rescued, tops. The casualties were over a thousand. All for a president. Sure, she'd voted for her, but was she worth a thousand lives when they seemed to be teetering on the brink of extinction?

"Marines got their asses handed to them," the CPO said.

Anna merely nodded, then thought of something. "What happens to us when we have to go ashore?"

"What do you mean?"

"Our food won't last forever."

The CPO stared at the monitors for a long time before responding. "Just keep your eyes open for survivors," he said and left.

"He didn't want to hear the truth."

Anna glanced at the voice. It was one of the Seahawk helicopter mechanics walking by the UAV bay with an armload of parts.

"Nobody does," Anna replied.

They'd been lucky to have only one instance of a man turning to a zombie, even if it was never figured out why he'd turned. The man was a young seaman on his first patrol. Most figured he'd gotten the infection from some snack from home he'd gotten a short time ago. Nothing else made sense.

Anna checked the endurance on her bird. Down to under two hours. Time to head for base. The Fire Scout responded smoothly to instructions and picked up altitude as it turned west. She could operate the UAV out to its operational range, or about 100 nautical miles. Further through satellites, though those were down. The captain had taken them closer to shore to facilitate the search sweeps. Once she landed her bird, another from the *Jackson* would take over. The other UAV would use thermal imaging since it would be dark by the time it was on station.

Once the UAV was on course, she keyed the mic on her headset. "Prager, the bird's on the way back."

"Roger that, Niles. How's she flying?"

"No problems. The actuator isn't sticking anymore." Prager was the mechanic on their team, and he'd replaced an actuator on the forward, high-resolution camera after the last flight. The bird needed maintenance and would have gotten it if they'd made port. Strain Delta had had other plans.

"When I fix something, it stays fixed," he said, and she smiled. PO3 Dan Prager was a competent flight mechanic. Along with PO2 Eva Perone and herself, they were a good team. She sighed as the UAV flew. She had no sense of future anymore. She'd been dating a man in San Diego. Alan was a nice boy. Was he running around Coronado looking for human flesh now? She started to think about her family in Omaha, but quickly squashed the thought. *I'm not going there again.*

At 10 miles out, she slowly descended. Fuel 10%, all systems normal. Well within the safety margin. The *Freedom's* beacon appeared on the radar, and she nodded. In another couple minutes, she'd initiate the automatic landing protocol. Of course, she could have landed it manually, but it was better to let the robots do their job. She yawned and checked the clock, which was why she missed the first flash.

"What was that?" she asked the empty room. A flash had caught her eye on the lower facing camera. She stared at it for long seconds, but nothing recurred. She grabbed the recording controls and rewound the footage. It took another minute to find it. A boat and brilliant flashes of light. Other things in the water. *What the hell?*

She looked at the UAV's fuel reserves and did a mental calculation. "There's enough," she decided. She took control back from the autopilot and executed a quick turn only a helicopter could accomplish. Staying under 1,000 feet, the Fire Scout swept back along its course. Eventually, she could see an RHIB of the type the Marines used. It was floating, alone and unmanned.

"What caused the flashes?" She descended another 500 feet, the hard deck for a patrol such as the one she was executing. The fuel light came on. She gritted her teeth and went into a hover. It was definitely an RHIB, but without the big gun often mounted on a Marine version. She focused as best she could. It was almost dark, and the Fire Scout didn't have a spotlight.

The gunnels of the boat were discolored. She flicked to infrared. The motor glowed, so it had been running recently. There were spots on the metal decking, and a wash of heat on one side. What could the heat be from? She went back to visual and recorded another minute of video as she rotated around the boat. The fuel alarm blazed again. Under 5% fuel. With a curse, she spun and raced for the ship.

She turned the UAV over to the computer which set it down with the display reading 'zero fuel.' She grimaced and sighed. The captain would have thrown her overboard if she had lost the UAV. Doing it in normal time would have been bad, but now? She got up and headed out to the flight deck.

Prager was attaching the little dolly which allowed a single person to maneuver the Fire Scout. The sea was calm and dark. A thin red line on the western horizon was all the light Anna could see. There were no stars yet, and the moon wouldn't rise until close to dawn.

Perone looked up from her work station when Niles came out and shook her head. "Crazy pilot," she said. "There's not enough gas in the tanks to make a martini."

"I hate martinis," Anna said. "I saw something weird. An abandoned boat."

"There must be a thousand abandoned boats in the area. One of the chiefs said there are hundreds of PLBs all around us." A personal location beacon was cheap and common, even on small craft. Nobody had time to check them. Bigger ships were equipped with EPIRBs, emergency position indicating radio beacons. The navy and a few other ships were checking those out, when they could. Not a lot was getting done; damn zombies!

"Yeah, I know," Anna said. "This is a Marine RHIB."

"From the assault?" Perone wondered.

"Don't know," Anna admitted.

"Help me get this bird indoors and tied down, and we'll look at the footage."

"Sure," she said and helped her move it inside. Their other hand, Prager, showed up just in time to help, and Anna told him about what she'd seen. In a short time, they were back in the operating cubicle, and she was pulling up the footage. Prager spotted something Anna missed.

"There," Prager said and pointed. Anna froze the frame. "Look in the water." A dark shape was visible.

"Too big for a body," Perone said.

"Shark?" Anna wondered. "If the Marines went zombie…"

"No," Prager said. Shape's wrong. Looks like a sea lion, maybe?"

"Sea lions don't attack people, do they?" Anna asked. The other two shrugged in unison. She ran the footage forward and stopped on the strange heat signature all over the side of the boat. "What's that?"

"I know," Prager said. "Saw it in weapons training. What you're seeing is warm blood splashed all over the side of the RHIB."

They stared at the screen for a very long time before Anna spoke. "I better call the chief and report this." She reached for the phone just as a series of gunshots rang out.

* * *

**Nightfall, Friday, May 3**

**Burlington Northern and Santa Fe Rail Transfer Yard**

**Amarillo, TX**

"Watch the right!"

Cobb shifted his weapon to the right, lowering it just enough to get a wider view, and saw at least a hundred infected sweeping up the overpass several hundred yards to the east. *Goddamn it!* This was the second time the infected appeared to be trying a flanking maneuver. He'd first seen this evolution in Texas, and he really didn't like seeing the mindless cannibals working together.

Their firing position was high enough that there was no way the infected could climb up. Not even a mindless cannibal could climb a massive, round, concrete pylon. From what Cobb had seen, it would be an unsurmountable obstacle. The mob rushing far to one side and up the overpass embankment argued to the contrary.

"Running low on grenades," Zim yelled over the roar of gunfire. They all wore modern hearing protection. It was one of the few useful things Sergeant Groves had provided. Her people had a whole case of the so-called 'smart earbuds' which were high tech, noise-cancelling earbuds that reduced the roar and din of gunfire to popping sounds, thereby allowing soldiers to hear and talk. Yay technology. Just in case, though, they all carried plastic plugs as backup.

"I know," Cobb confirmed. "Tango! Targets of opportunity, three o'clock!"

"On it," Corporal Tango said, and the Marines pivoted to fire as a unit. Nine M4s, wielded by well-trained marksmen, chewed up the infected before more than a couple could reach the top. It cost the Marines two magazines each, over 500 rounds to drop 200 or so infected.

Confident the problem was dealt with, Cobb went back to his weapons scope. He dropped several more infected before his magazine ran dry. "Reloading!" he called out as he did a quick swap. Like the rest, he stashed the empty magazine. You didn't survive what they'd survived without learning to save empty mags and everything else.

"Leakers on the left!"

Yet another group, smaller than the last but moving fast, had apparently gone all the way around the buildings at the base of the overpass to the interchange. They were now advancing quickly, and to his astonishment, quietly! Gods he missed CAS, close air support. A couple of fighters with precision, laser-guided bombs or an A-10 Warthog would have been nice. A little Brrrrrt! would have made the night better. Everyone loved the sound of the A-10's 30mm gun.

"Are they using tactics?" Zim asked, his voice full of astonishment.

"I hate to admit it, but they might be," Cobb said. "I started seeing signs that they were just before I was rescued." He didn't mention the mutations. He'd save that for later.

The army soldiers dropped the new group with considerably less ammo. However, their success came at a cost. The main force was now underneath them and below their angle of fire. "Switch to defend the sides," Cobb ordered. "Marines to the east, army to the west."

He did a quick tactical evaluation. They had a few seconds. "Ammo check!" While the men counted their mags, he called on the radio. "Recovery team, update?"

"First generator airborne," was the immediate reply.

Cobb looked through his Acog, which was set to light-intensifying now that the sun was gone. One of the massive, yellow, Caterpillar generators was ascending into the night sky.

"How long for the other two?"

"Number two is about half rigged. Say five minutes for them to get number one unhooked up top and lower the rig frame back down." The man was quiet for a moment. "At least another 15 for the last one."

His men finished counting their remaining magazines. They had an average of six each. They'd started with 15. "Noted. Keep me updated," he told the recovery team, then addressed his NCOs. "Have the men level out while we have a breather." He wanted everyone with roughly the same number of mags, levelling would do it.

"Roger that," Zim said.

"Got it," Tango agreed.

"They're coming from the south now," Tango said.

Cobb spun and observed the railway to the south. A leading edge of hundreds, if not thousands, of infected were coming. He cursed under his breath. "I was afraid we'd draw attention to ourselves," he said. "Check further out east and west, along the freeway."

"Too much smoke," was the report. The shooting had caused a few fires in the surrounding, abandoned businesses, and the resulting smoke was enough to obscure distant observations.

Cobb switched channels. "Cobb to Schardt."

"Go, sir," the master sergeant replied.

"You have eyes along the freeway east and west of us?"

"Let me check with the gondola." Long seconds passed during which Cobb went through another magazine, as did most of the men. "Oh, shit," Schardt replied.

"Yeah. How many?"

"A thousand plus to the west, more to the east. We're coming down."

"Negative, I don't want all of us down here if things start to go sideways." Cobb knew from talking with his sergeants that the platform was strong enough to hold a hundred men, but there wasn't the square footage. "Send the platform down with magazines, grenades, and two of the M-240s."

"Gonna have to get Groves to bring them."

Cobb suppressed a snarl. He'd sent someone to tell her to get the squad support weapons ready. She hadn't replied before they needed to push off or risk losing the light. "Tell her to move her fucking ass," Cobb snapped. "Master Sergeant, our situation is extremely kinetic. I want the platform on the way down in less than 5 minutes. We're going to be black on ammo not long after."

"Roger that, Colonel."

"Glad they found you, Colonel," the nearest Marine said between volleys of fire.

"Damned straight," an army private concurred. As he glanced at the private, he saw the Arkansas guardsmen glaring at him. When Cobb looked straight at him, the man's eyes returned to the battle.

"You men ever deploy like this before?" Cobb asked.

"Negative," Tango said. "We only went down in small fireteams with minimal firepower. The master sergeant wanted to send large groups, but the sergeants stood on a unanimous agreement to commit in force."

"Let me guess," Cobb said. "Groves never agreed."

"It's not for me to speak ill of a fellow sergeant," Zim said.

*Well, that makes it worse.* Cobb didn't say anything more out loud. Groves wasn't playing by the same book. He decided he would need to address the situation later, when thousands of former citizens of Amarillo weren't trying to eat him.

"Down to four mags," a Marine called out.

"Three," an army guy yelled.

"Grenades," Cobb ordered. "Buy us a little breathing space!"

The staccato *Pwunk!* of the M203s lobbing 40mm grenades sounded a second later. The men's aim was accurate, and most of their grenades impacted the end of the bridge embankments in both directions. The blasts were brilliant in the soldiers' night vision, each explosion sending brightly colored bodies cartwheeling through the dark sky.

Minutes ticked by and the soldiers went from burst fire to more selective semi-automatic. There were piles of bodies on both ends of the bridge. They'd been low on night vision, so Cobb elected for a starlight scope on his rifle. Most of the rest had PVS-7/14 helmet mounts. They had the binocular-style optics lowered over their eyes, making them glow like beady-eyed, green aliens.

Cobb checked his watch. "Five minutes, Master Sergeant!"

"M-240s on board. They only brought eight cans of ammo. I sent some grenades set too."

"Just lower it, now!"

"Big wave to the east!" Tango barked.

"Mother of God!" a Marine intoned.

Cobb raised his rifle and gasped. It looked like the tide rolling through the scope's night vision. Thousands, maybe ten thousand, infected rushed toward them. The satanic, growling screams of the enraged zombies turned his bowels to water. Their firefight had rung the proverbial dinner bell, and the diners had arrived.

"Send the platform down as fast as you can. Marines, grenades east," he ordered. "Fire at will!" The first volley of nine high-explosive grenades didn't seem to touch the zombies. The infected ran into the slaughter, then through it. Less than a football field length away, grisly death sprinted toward them.

"Little help?" he called to Schardt.

"Incoming," the master sergeant replied. Bodies exploded. A split second later the telltale chugging of a .50 caliber M-2 Browning machinegun reached them from above.

"Get some!" a Marine cheered.

The gunner worked his weapon back and forth slowly. The ball ammo had tracers mixed in every five rounds which caused brilliant streaks in their night vision. Even rounds that missed their targets, which were few since there were so fucking many, sent up shrapnel from the concrete roadbed which injured the nearby infected.

Based on the rate of fire, two of the big, beautiful Ma-Deuces had to be chugging away above. They and the constant grenade barrage staggered, then slowed the advance. Cobb glanced toward the salvage operation. The second generator was climbing slowly into the sky.

"Second generator airborne," the recovery team confirmed.

"Any zombies?" Cobb asked.

"No, you seem to have their full attention."

"Well, that's a load off my mind," Zim said.

Cobb chuckled. The men were professional, no doubt about it. He'd been in a convoy which came under fire in Afghanistan. The ambushers were hiding in a couple of houses, which were subsequently lit up by an A-10 Warthog. As the building came apart and burst into flames, a burning camel came running out. The men were laughing about it hours later back at base. "I said I wanted a Marlboro, not a Camel." Soldiers' humor, they called it. As black as the depths of space.

"They're coming from the west side too," Zim warned.

"Platform coming down," a Marine also warned.

"Heads up," Cobb said, moving clear of the rapidly descending, metal platform. "Army, grenades west." The platform hit the overpass with a resounding *Bang!* He instantly vaulted over the side to see what was inside. "Schardt, you're awesome," he said when he saw the two M240s that were set up and loaded, one to each side. "Tango, Zimm, get those 240s going! One on each side." He had to yell to be heard over the roar of gunfire. "Clear the danger zone!" he barked to the Marines. "Everyone on the platform. Detail to pass out magazines."

Zim tripped as he came over to man a machine gun, sprawling on the floor where two soldiers fell on him. Cobb didn't hesitate, he dropped to his knees behind the other machinegun and quickly checked its status. He gave the charging handle a jerk to verify that it was loaded and flicked the safety. Minus the night vision scope on his rifle, he only had the flashes of gunfire and the .50 caliber tracers coming from above to see by. The picture was no better than it was with night vision, though slightly more terrifying. The infected were less than 50 yards away.

Cobb's lips pulled back from his teeth in a rictus of barely suppressed terror as time slowed. The Marines took forever to clear the danger zone. The infected seemed to close in relentlessly as the Marines moved slowly aside. As the last Marine cleared the arc in front of Cobb's gun, the leading infected were so close, he could see the whites of their eyes.

Cobb squeezed the trigger. Machinegun training always stressed one thing above all else—trigger control. "Slow, controlled bursts" was the line you heard over, and over, and over again. Bursts kept the barrel from overheating and prematurely wearing out. They also allowed the gunner to pick off targets effectively. With only 200 rounds in a can, continuous fire would burn quickly through the ammo. The 7.62x51 rounds the M240 fired were considerably more powerful than the M4's 5.56x45 rounds. However, they were of little use if they penetrated soft body tissues without taking down the target. The training didn't cover a zombie charge.

Cobb held the trigger back and worked the gun barrel from side to side like a windshield wiper. The part of his mind not scared absolutely shitless tried to measure the movements, keeping in mind the M240's rate of fire which was around 700 rounds a minute. *You've got about 16 seconds.* Eleven rounds per second was deceptively fast when all of Amarillo had been transformed into flesh-eating monsters eager to snack on your face.

The rounds didn't tear people apart, unlike the .50 caliber rounds still raining down from above. In the near darkness, he could see bullets punching bloody holes through chests, stomachs, necks, and faces. The lower half of the face of a man who could have been a TV anchor exploded in blood and bone. The abdomen of a teenage girl who might have grown up to be a mother, an actress, or a scientist was torn open, and her intestines spilled out in pale rolls and tangled around her feet. An elderly infected was hit in the shoulder, the bullet dislocating his arm and leaving it dangling by shreds of flesh and tendon. Arterial blood sprayed like a fan in the strobe light of gunfire.

Cobb laughed. He didn't know why or where it came from. He felt tears running down his cheeks. It was pure butchery. He was distantly aware of the belt running out, the heat of the barrel singeing his fingers as he ripped up the feed cover. A Marine appeared, slammed another ammo can in place, and slipped the beginning of the belt onto the feed tray.

The smells—blood, cordite, sweat, fear, shit—combined to burn the images into his mind like a plasma torch. He'd remember the tableau for the rest of his days.

The feed cover slammed closed. "Go!" the Marine barked, slapping Cobb's helmet.

Cobb yanked the charging handle and pulled the trigger again. The infected were trying to climb over the dead and were being ripped apart by machinegun and small arms fire in their desperately insane desire to reach the 20 besieged soldiers.

A hand reached out and grabbed the M240's barrel just behind the flash suppressor. He clearly heard the sizzle of skin over the din of battle. He fired the gun, and the hand fell away. But then an infected used the newly dead one as a launching platform to hurtle over Cobb. He heard the grunt and yell as the infected hit the Marine who'd reloaded his weapon. In an instant, the infected were pouring over the side.

An infected man hit Cobb in the chest like a football lineman tackling a running back, bowling him backward and knocking the M240 over on its side. Teeth snapped at his face. Cobb couldn't reach his pistol. He grabbed one of his two knives and plunged it into the infected's chest over and over. The body jerked, falling away and taking the knife with it.

He rolled to his knees and clawed his M9 from his chest rig. He knew instantly he would miss his own Sig. He'd gone with the M9 so he'd have the same ammo and magazines as the rest of his command. He released the safety as he drew the weapon, rammed it into the face of another infected, and double-actioned it. Teeth and blood flew. He followed with a single-action shot. The infected jerked and fell. Another snapped at the gun like it was Cobb's hand. He killed it and two more replaced it.

For a time outside time, the men fought. The battle was hand-to-hand, gun-to-chest, knife-to-throat. The sound of gunfire became intermittent, replaced by the grunts of soldiers punching and stabbing and the ever-present screaming howls of the insane infected.

The soldiers roared and pushed the infected back. The Marines had attached bayonets to their M4s and were using them like pikes. It felt somehow medieval. Cobb took a shuddering breath and keyed his mic. "Recovery team, how long?"

"Finishing attachment of last generator. Five more minutes?'

"We're overrun," he said, extending his right arm and shooting an infected woman in the face. "Repeat, we're overrun. Have to withdraw."

"I think we've got this. Go!"

"Roger that. Schardt, you copy our last?"

"Affirmative. Lifting!" the master sergeant said. The platform lurched and began to ascend.

It groaned under the weight of 20 soldiers, extra ammo, grenades, and at least 200 infected. The steel cables linking them to Shangri-La, 500 feet above, sang and quivered under the unexpected strain. Hundreds more infected tried to climb up and over those already hanging on. The cable attachment nearest Cobb made an ominous pinging sound.

"Clear some of them off, or they could break the cables!" Cobb ordered.

All around the edges, the soldiers drew handguns or used their bayonets to shoot and hack at the hangers on. Dozens were killed and fell away, taking more with them. He was beginning to think they'd make a clean getaway when things went south.

A large group of infected had pushed back the Marines on their side. Tango barked for them to give him some space, and he brought the M-240 to bear. It wasn't something Cobb would have done in the most insane of situations. However, Marines lived for those moments. They started at crazy and moved on from there.

The big 7.62mm rounds tore through the infected like a scythe. He was so intent on doing his job, Tango didn't see the leaker who got past one of the Marines and bowled into him from the side. He let go of the trigger *almost* immediately, but not soon enough to avoid hitting one of the four heavy, steel cables supporting their platform.

The steel began to part. Cobb started to yell a completely ineffectual warning. But the damage was done. The rest of the cable parted with a *Pwing!*

The entire platform shifted crazily toward the missing cable, and for a terrible second, Cobb was sure it would flip completely over, spilling his entire command into the laps of the zombies. Men cried out in alarm, and everyone grabbed whatever they could to remain stable. The platform only shifted three feet lower on the broken cable's side, and everyone hung on except one man.

"Shit!" One of the army soldiers flailed as he was catapulted from the opposite side. Dozens of hands grabbed at him, but none got a good enough grip to hang on. He rolled over the crowd like someone being passed over a mosh pit. He landed in the hands of the ravenous infected.

"No!" Tango yelled and grabbed the man's outstretched hand. He caught it, barely. "Grab him, pull him in!"

The Marines grabbed at him, his face a mixture of hope and terror. A dozen infected's arms wrapped around him, pulling, dragging, and clawing. The platform continued ascending, and in mere seconds, the man had a thousand pounds dragging him back. The platform teetered on the edge.

"Anyone who can't reach him, move to the other corner!" Cobb ordered. Many of the men hesitated, but the platform tipped a little more toward the man hanging on, which was enough to make the rest go in the opposite direction. The platform began to level.

"Help me!" Tango ordered, and every soldier who could grabbed at the fallen man, creating a tug-of-war.

"Relief team," the recovery team called. "Relief team, we're in trouble here!"

"Goddamn it," Cobb said. He holstered his Beretta, and after a couple of tense seconds, located his carbine. Using the night vision scope, he found the distant recovery team. The last generator had just lifted off, with hundreds of infected clinging to and climbing on the framework. "Never a fucking break," he said and took aim. Using single shots, he picked off the infected one at a time.

"We're losing him!" someone yelled.

Cobb looked. The Marines were using knives, rifle butts, fists, and whatever they could to try and get the infected to let go. A couple snarled and fell off. Another's throat was cut, bathing the struggling man's face in blood. Several Marines recoiled from the spray, and with a scream, the soldier fell away into the dark.

Cobb closed his eyes for a second, taking a calming breath and wishing the man a quick death. "Help me with the recovery team," he said through clenched teeth. Some of the men raised their weapons to help Cobb, while the rest removed the last of the infected clinging to their platform or pitched bodies over the side.

"You got them, we're clear," the recovery team leader said.

"I hope it was worth the price," Cobb replied. The men stood, put their weapons on safe, and holstered their knives and pistols. The 19 men road the rest of the way up in silence. Halfway up, Cobb realized he didn't know the dead man's name.

* * *

**The Flotilla**

**150 Nautical Miles West of San Diego, CA**

Jeremiah Osborne climbed down the too-steep, metallic stairway to the technology deck. He'd grabbed a power nap, a beer, and some food, then returned to where the magic was happening. He expected to find his engineers working on their various projects—dissecting alien technology and trying to understand the best way to put it to work. What he found was a dozen overpaid scientists crowding around his new lost boy, Wade Watts. *What the heck?*

"...wasn't too difficult. I just adapted a flight combat simulator's interface."

"What's going on?" Jeremiah asked. Everyone looked up, some in surprise, some in annoyance.

"Mr. Watts just rewrote the operating system for an alien drive-controlled ship," Patty Mize said.

"What about the interface Alison wrote?" he asked.

Alison looked up from the computer and shrugged. "The geek's got game," she said. "Besides, programming is his thing; mine is electronics."

"Where are my programmers?"

"They all left when the navy evacuated people, along with half my staff," said Jack Coldwell, the only physicist still on board. He had a few assistants left, mostly grad students.

"Traitors," Jeremiah mumbled.

"You know," Wade said, "this alien stuff is really weird."

"No shit?" Maria Merino said from across the room and laughed. She was eating a SPAM sandwich, the only meat-like material still in plentiful supply.

"No, I mean the way it takes inputs. Earth technology is pretty standard—a lot of stuff uses 60 hertz because it's convenient. Not this stuff."

"Yeah, I noticed that when I wired the first controller," Alison said. "I ended up using 30 hertz because 60 kept glitching. Even 30 didn't work all the time, but I set up a continual input instead of a single pulse."

"It makes sense that 30 and 60 didn't work," Wade said. He picked up the multimeter he was using, which included an oscilloscope. "The wave form is 2.46 hertz, but in multiple forms. So, 2.46, 7.38, 29.52. You were off by just enough, even at 30, to make your pulses miss intermittently."

"Weird," Alison agreed. "Haven't seen many harmonics used in electronics."

"I wouldn't expect so," Wade said. "Once I figured out how it accepted signals, I started looking for some."

"And?" Jeremiah asked.

"I found them." He spun around a screen displaying a series of squiggly lines.

"I'm an aerospace engineer," Jeremiah said, "not an electronics or programming expert."

"They're discreet control feedback signals from the drive, power, and communications modules talking to each other." Watts pointed to a couple of the traces. They were all colored differently. "These are feedbacks from the drive."

"Just guessing," Alex spoke up for the first time, "but I think those are speed and positional data."

"Would have been handy to know in the middle of the solar system," Alison mumbled. Alex nodded solemnly. If they'd been able to return quickly, Lloyd Behm, one of the pilots on the *Azanti's* first flight, might have made it back alive.

"Some of these signals are *very* delicate," Jack Coldwell said. "This one on the power system may be the level of energy available. We compared it to the two power modules we have—the one you took to orbit to rescue the carrier and the one that has been sitting here, on the shelf."

"Does it give an indication of how much power the flight took?" Jeremiah asked.

"Yes," Jack said. "However, it took an hour of examining the waveform for us to figure it out. It adds up to about a hundred millionth of a percent."

"More or less," one of his assistants said. "It was almost too small to measure."

Jack shrugged, then nodded. "More or less."

"Of a percent?" Jeremiah asked. The physicist and his assistants beamed. "You're telling me the power module could make 100 *billion* trips to orbit and back?"

"Well, 50 billion," Alex corrected. "Estimated, because we had a 90,000-ton aircraft carrier hooked to the field on the return flight."

"Fuck a duck," Jeremiah said.

"Not by policy," Alex said. "We'll have to do tests, but it looks like mass may not affect power usage."

Someone was yelling up above, so Alex went to see what was going on.

"We need to run some tests," Jack agreed. "Bench tests with large weights. Maybe we can use one of the derelict container ships. They weigh about as much as an aircraft carrier. Float it for a day and see how much power it uses."

"Two tests would be better," an assistant suggested. "You know, one with the shield on, and one without?"

"You have control of the shield function?"

"Sure," Wade said. "I've isolated several of the signals and inputs. Some are switches, others are more like sliders."

"Potentiometers," Alison offered.

"Right, whatever," Wade said, waving a dismissive hand at Alison.

"You didn't date much, did you?" Alison asked.

"None of your…" He turned toward her and noticed she was leaning over the work bench. An impressive amount of cleavage was on display. Wade lost his train of thought mid-stream.

"Don't give the young man a heart attack," Alex said. Alison giggled, and Wade swallowed. The young programmer/hacker opened his mouth to retort but was cut short when a gunshot rang out on deck.

Several people jumped. Jeremiah looked at the ladder his chief test pilot had ascended a minute earlier. *God, not more damned zombies?*

A second later, Alex slid down the ladder with his hands, hitting the deck with bent knees to absorb the impact. "Lock the hatch!" he barked. He had an automatic pistol in one hand.

*Where did he get the gun?* "What's going on?" Jeremiah demanded.

"We're under attack."

"By whom?" he demanded.

"Seals."

* * *

Anna Niles jerked slightly at the first gunshot. After all, it wasn't the first time someone on the *Freedom* had shot a gun. She'd trained on all three required weapons—the M-16, the M9 pistol, and the M500—when she was promoted to petty officer. Sure, only a few rounds in each, but how many would a UAV pilot need to fire in the execution of her duties?

So, when the shotgun blast echoed, she stopped dialing the phone to tell the officer of the watch what they'd seen. Then, three more shots boomed out, two shotgun and one pistol.

"Must be zombies," Eva said.

"Maybe," Anna replied and got up. "Or maybe not."

She walked out of the UAV control bay and over to the hangar. Prager was standing next to the Fire Scout, a greasy rag in one hand and a water bottle in the other. He was staring out the open hangar door toward the extra-large landing pad where the Fire Scout had set down earlier.

"Is the well deck open?" she asked him.

"Huh?" Prager replied.

"I said, is the damned well deck open?"

"Uh, yeah," he said after a second. "They've been launching RHIBs all day." Yet another shot sounded. This time, it was clear that the shots came from below the landing deck or on the well deck under them.

Someone below yelled, fired three rapid pistol shots, then screamed. A long, ragged burst of automatic weapons fire sounded. One of their ship's four M-16s. *Oh shit.*

"Someone went zombie?" Prager wondered.

Anna didn't wait to find out; she turned and ran back into the bay. She yanked the desk drawer open, revealing the safe inside. It had a three-number punch combination on it. A sound somewhere between a bark and a roar sounded, making the hair on the back of her neck stand up.

"Get the gun!" Eva said. "Get the damned gun!"

"What the fuck do you think I'm doing?!" Anna screamed back and punched in the code. She twisted the lock, but it didn't move. "Shit, shit, shit," she said and tried to clear her mind. The CPO had changed the code the day he issued the gun. It was right after their sole zombie incident. The gun was locked in the safe where they kept the keys that allowed the Fire Scout to fire live munitions. The CPO had followed protocol and changed the code. *What's the fucking code?* she berated herself.

"Come on, damn it!" Eva said, shaking Anna's shoulder.

She shook off the other woman and screamed at her, "Knock it off, I'm trying to concentrate!"

Out on the flight deck, Dan Prager yelled in alarm. The barking roar came twice in close succession, each one sounding slightly different. The cognitive part of Anna's brain heard a brief, heavy, tempered metal scraping sound and knew her mechanic had just grabbed a big wrench or a crowbar from an equipment bench. A split second later, he gave a hideous scream which ended in a gurgle, then nothing. She heard more gunfire, this time from somewhere else on the ship. After what seemed like an eternity, the general quarters alarm blared.

"All hands, general quarters!" the captain said, his voice shaky. "Boarders. I mean, prepare to repel boarders." Someone near the captain yelled something. "Seals? What?" Glass shattered, and the captain cried out, then dropped the mic. The alarm continued to blare.

"I remember!" she said and punched 9-9-1 into the lock. She'd thought it was 9-1-1, but the CPO had told her that was too obvious. She turned the lock, and the box popped open. Inside were two red keys, a sealed envelope, an M-9 Beretta semi-automatic pistol, and two magazines. She grabbed the gun and spun before she realized it was too light. Turning it over, she saw that it was missing a magazine. There was a deep repeating reverberation through the deck plates, as if something heavy was being drug and dropped once per second.

Anna turned back and grabbed a magazine. The reverberations were closer. Her hands were slick with sweat, and the magazine went flying. She watched it hit the floor, dislodging a bullet, then bounce and slide under an equipment rack. "Fuck!" She grabbed the other magazine and turned back just as a monstrous shape blocked the light from outside.

The beast was so big, it barely fit down the hall. Eva was between her and it, frozen in shock. You didn't work at Navy Base San Diego without knowing about the seal population. The common harbor seals averaged 300 pounds. They'd sunbathe on buoys, boats, or anything else they could get on. They were tolerant of humans, to a point. The monster in the door was an elephant seal. Elephant seals could be as big as 16 feet long and weigh in at two tons. A score of bullet holes marked the seal's upraised chest and neck, several of which were bleeding profusely. It took no notice of the wounds as it turned its head and examined the compartment in a most un-seal-like manner.

Anna gasped. The seal was cunningly evaluating what it had found.

"What the hell?" Eva asked and took a step back. The elephant seal's protuberant nose, a characteristic of their species, wobbled as its strange barking roar sounded. It lurched its head forward, snatched PO2 Eva Perone in its blood-dripping mouth, and shook her like a ragdoll.

Eva screamed piteously, her voice shifting like a passing train, as the seal swung her body back and forth. The animal was so massive, its actions seemed to require little effort. On the third swing, Eva's head hit the bulkhead with so much force, her skull split. Brains and blood flew. The seal stopped shaking her, its eyes regarding the slightly twitching body for an instant before dropping it on the deck.

Anna screamed and slid the magazine into the gun. She remembered to release the safety before she pulled the trigger.

"The first trigger pull will be difficult," the firearms instructor had warned her. "It's called double-action. It cocks the trigger and fires in the same pull. After the first shot, firing the gun will re-cock it, and subsequent shots will only require a light pull."

The hammer went back and dropped with a loud click. The elephant seal's head cocked slightly as its black-on-black eyes regarded her. Anna pulled the trigger twice more. *Click, click.* Her hands shaking, she looked at the seal who looked at her. The doorway into the bay was extra-large to allow the fuselage of the Fire Scout to pass inside for maintenance. The seal fit through with surprising ease. Its huge mouth opened, and it reached for her.

"Don't forget to pull the slide back and load the chamber," her instructor had advised.

"Oh," she said as the seal struck.

* * *

"Goddamned harbor seals," Alex West said.

"They're cute," one of Jack Coldwell's young, female assistants said.

"Oh? Go pet one. There are about a dozen up on the deck, eating a crewman, right now!" The young girl looked agog.

"Strain Delta," Patty Mize said, her eyes narrowed in concentration.

"Yeah," Alex said. "You still armed?"

"You bet your ass," Patty said and produced her semi-auto handgun. "I've only got two magazines left."

"One extra," Alex said and brandished his much larger Glock. "Anyone else?" The room full of engineers, scientists, executives, and gamer geeks looked at him in fear and anticipation. "Swell." Something big thumped against the door he'd just closed and locked. He examined it. "Not watertight. Perfect."

"No harbor seal is getting through," Jeremiah observed.

"There are elephant seals with them," he said. "They're working together."

"What?" Jeremiah demanded. "As a team?" Above them, on the deck, they heard screaming and the sounds of something heavy being dragged, then banging on metal.

"Yeah," Alex said, "like a fucking team. I can see gunfire on every nearby ship as well. It's an attack across the entire Flotilla." A massive weight hit the floor just outside the door.

"What should we do?" an assistant asked.

The door behind Alex thrummed from a massive blow, bowing inward slightly. Alex looked around for options. There didn't seem to be any. The door was hit again, and the latch groaned. He and Patty squared off toward the door. Everyone else moved to the back of the work area, as far from the door as they could. The door was hit again and again. It seemed to have temporarily wedged closed.

Jeremiah searched for a way out. There was a service exit on one side of the room, only the doorway was bolted closed. It would take several men a half hour to get it open. Wade Watts was freaking out. He'd been rummaging around on the parts shelves, no doubt looking for a weapon. He wouldn't find anything useful on a rack of high-power capacitors, relays, and couplings. He was about to ask the programmer what he was doing with one of the alien power modules when the door screeched.

Jeremiah spun around in terror, his breath coming in gasps. Fight or flight, only neither seemed possible. A massive, black shape was dimly visible on the other side of the gap that had opened between the horribly disfigured doorway and the untouched, metal frame. Alex took a step sideways, aimed, and a fired a single round. In the metal compartment, it sounded like an artillery shell, making several people cry out and put their hands over their ears.

On the other side, there was a meaty *Smack!* as the bullet hit thick hide and flesh. The only response was a chuffing grunt, followed by a nasal roar. *Oh fuck.* Alex fired again, with even less results. There wasn't even a roar.

"I think you're just pissing it off!" Alison said.

Desperation got the better of him. Jeremiah ran over and grabbed a big crescent wrench off a table and pointed it at the maintenance hatch. "Someone give me some help!" A second later, the door exploded inward.

* * *

General Rose was staring at the big map attached to his office wall with magnets. A distinctive and familiar noise made him frown. *Distant gunshots?* "Mays?"

"General?" his aide called from the adjacent cabin.

"Did you hear shots?"

"Yes, General, but there usually are."

Captain Mays had a good point, though it didn't change the fact that they sounded different. Someone was always shooting a zombie or two. Or a dozen. Since he'd arrived with the remains of his command, there'd been constant fighting against the infected on many of the ships. Some was intense enough to cause the loss of an entire ship. Most of the fights hadn't been heavy on guns. A lot were hand-to-hand.

"Not like this," he said and walked out of his cabin to the bridge. Captain Sampson and his crew were around the radio listening to someone who sounded extremely excited. Or scared. "What's going on?" he asked.

Sampson spun, surprised by Rose's sudden appearance. "Something's happening all over the Flotilla."

"What?"

"Attacks," Sampson said.

"What kind of attacks?" Mays asked, coming in behind the general.

"We can't find out. The transmissions are walking all over each other. However, one navy ship, the *Freedom*, got through for a second."

"The guy was nuts," another crewman said. "He was screaming about seals."

"Navy SEALs?" Rose asked. Sampson shrugged. The wing doors of the bridge were open to the cool evening, and the sounds of gunfire were increasing steadily. Something was definitely wrong.

Rose walked back to his cabin and picked up his radio. "Rose to *Ocean Vista*, over." *Gotta change that name.*

"*Ocean Vista.* Go ahead, General."

"Tell security to secure all water-level entrances to the boat. There are incursions underway on other ships in the Flotilla."

"Only one entrance doorway is open," the man replied. "We have two people guarding it."

"Get an entire squad down there. Immediately."

"Yes, sir."

Rose nodded and put the radio down. Mays was standing by the cabin door, watching him, with a curious look on his face. "I know," Rose said, "but I'm not being paranoid."

"As you wish, sir."

"Whatever. Put First Platoon on alert. Get them geared up and ready. Something is seriously wrong."

Despite his doubts, Mays was a good aide and immediately did what he was told. Less than a minute later, the radio beeped for attention.

"That was fast," Mays said and answered. "Go ahead."

"Incursion on the port door," the voice said, the sentence punctuated by a series of shots. "A goddamned, big, fucking *seal!*"

"Navy SEAL?"

"No, one with flippers. It's as big as a man. Tried to bite Smith, so we shot it."

"Oh, shit," Rose said. "Close all doors." He ran back to the bridge. "Sampson?" The man turned. "Strain Delta affects all life. Dr. Breda said advanced mammals have bigger brains, and they can act intelligently." Sampson's brows knitted. "The damn marine mammals, Lieutenant. They're attacking to spread the virus."

"How…"

Shots rang out, clearly audible through the open doors. Rose looked at Mays who was already on the radio. "Does it matter how?"

"Two men wounded," Mays reported.

"What the fuck, Captain?"

Mays looked pained. "Dolphins jumped right through the open hatch."

"Were the men bit?"

"No, but they both have cracked ribs. Shot the fish and rolled them overboard."

"Tell them to shoot *any* animals they see," Rose said and stabbed a finger at him. "*Any*. You got me?"

"Yes, sir."

Rose turned back to Sampson. "Lock the damn ship down and try to spread word to the rest of the Flotilla."

Rose strode back into his cabin and opened his dresser. Inside were his battle rattle and weapons. "Better gear up," he said to Mays. More gunshots echoed. The porthole showed only darkness as he took off his uniform jacket and reached for his well-worn BDUs. His rifle and pistol were both loaded. He had a feeling he'd need both soon.

* * *

Jeremiah was considering using the engineering compartment's phone when the door burst open. He didn't know who he was going to call. It wasn't like OOE had an armed security contingent aboard. He'd been in such dire straights just before the plague, he'd cut his staff down to the bare bones.

The metallic door exploded inward, colliding with a table covered in tools, sending them flying like missiles. The table was crushed as though it were made of twigs. The elephant seal didn't act like a rampaging monster. If they had been in a movie of science gone amok, the seal would have been a mutant bent on killing everything, especially humans. Infected men and women seemed to exist only to murder and feed on uninfected humans.

The seal stood on its front flippers, framed in the doorway, little black eyes moving from side to side as it deliberately examined the room. Jeremiah felt a cold shiver run up his spine. "Oh, my God," he said. The seal instantly locked its eyes on him. Cold, deadly intent was evident in the seal's demeanor as it moved toward him.

"Now," Alex said. He and Patty fired simultaneously. Bullets smacked into the thick neck of the seal with little red splashes of blood. They continued to fire steadily with no evident effect.

Jeremiah noticed that the seal's neck and side were covered in massive scar tissue. He remembered seeing videos of male elephant seals battling each other for sexual dominance. Those battles basically consisted of them violently biting each other's necks until one decided it had had enough. The bullets must have seemed no more annoying than a particularly small challenger's nibble. The seal advanced toward Jeremiah, its forward gait reminding him of an overweight person trying to belly flop in the surf over and over.

"The face!" he yelled. "The neck is too tough!"

Both shooters instantly shifted their aim. Just as her gun ran empty, and the slide locked back, Patty's final bullets tore a chunk out of the elephant seal's 'trunk.' It reeled backward, mouth open and roaring. Alex switched to a two-handed stance and aimed carefully. He fired a single round which entered the seal's mouth and exited the top of its head.

The huge animal jerked, and all two tons of it crashed to the deck with enough force to knock over several benches and tables. Two of the benches landed on Wade Watts who had been screwing around with some parts. He let out a surprised cry but didn't try to free himself.

As often happens in the aftermath of a traumatic situation, several people stepped forward for a better look. This phenomenon could be observed after chain reaction traffic accidents, natural disasters, even war. In the aftermath of a briefly violent event, people just had to get a closer look. Sociologists believe it was the remnants of a simian reaction which benefitted our ancient ancestors in some way.

"Stay back," Alex warned.

Jeremiah jumped, realizing he was one of the ones moving forward. The elephant seal was twitching and pumping out a truly astounding amount of blood in bright red, rhythmic spurts. He reversed and backed away, looking over his shoulder at the access hatch. *This isn't over; I need to get out of here!*

"It's not dead!"

Jeremiah's head came back around. It was the same assistant who'd said seals were cute.

"You bastard—"

Alex yelled again, probably for the crazy woman to get back, when another, much smaller, seal flew in through the door and hit her square in the chest. Jeremiah had no idea how the damned seal had managed to launch itself the way it did. They appeared clumsy on land. It bit into her face as soon as they landed. Then, more seals poured through the shattered hatch like a jackpot on a deranged slot machine.

Alex started shooting as the young, seal-loving woman started screaming. Patty tried to shoot another seal, then realized her gun was empty. A big, fat, harbor seal rolled to a stop at her feet and snapped at her legs. Patty squeaked and backpedaled, clawing a magazine from her belt and desperately trying to fit it in place.

The seal caught hold of Patty's pant leg and shook her, hard. She flew sideways and hit the wall with a *clang*. She fell in a heap and didn't move. Alex continued to fire at the seals as they poured in. Jeremiah saw a couple of smaller seals take hits and go down before he turned back to the maintenance hatch. Without considering, he went to it and started turning nuts.

"Would you help me?"

Over the sound of gunfire, Jeremiah finally heard the voice. He searched for the source and realized it was Wade Watts who was trapped under the shelving. It looked like two had fallen creating an open area underneath, so he wasn't pinned. "I'm trying to get us out of here."

"Don't we have to live long enough to get out?" Wade demanded.

"How's helping you going to stop those crazy, fucking seals?" Jeremiah yelled.

"Like this!"

Jeremiah continued to strain against the wrench. The first bolt had yet to move. He glanced at the shelves and could see Wade underneath, holding up a device he'd built. Jeremiah's eyes narrowed. "Is that a…"

"Yes," Wade said. "Yes, it is. Get this damned shelf off me!"

* * *

The *Pacific Adventurer* was lit up like Christmas Eve. Lights all along the deck's edges illuminated the water. The men from Rose's platoon were spread out along the railings. The ship was 330 feet long, so the 44 soldiers were spaced 15 feet apart.

"Spread really fucking thin," Mays pointed out, which was why he and Rose were armed and, along with the navy pukes, helping guard the sections near the bridge. "We've closed the water-level doors. What can they do?"

A minute later, a dolphin rocketed out of the water and landed on the deck at his feet. Rose put a burst of 5.56mm from his M4 carbine through the dolphin. "Make sense now, Captain?"

There'd only been two other attempts by the dolphins. Rose was sure he'd seen one watching from the water as the others tried. But after the first try, his soldiers were ready. Shooting a human-sized target at 200 meters was what they were trained to do. Hitting something as big as a dolphin from only a few meters away was simple.

Other ships weren't as lucky. Through the crazy radio traffic, Rose heard intermittent calls about bitten people, attacking seals, biting dolphins, and people succumbing to the virus. *It's all turning to shit.* The attack was well planned. They'd waited for evening. It had probably taken days to get all the marine mammals in position. *How can humans fight this?* He remembered Dr. Breda saying days ago, "The planet is lost."

It had been an hour since the last attack. It sounded like they were largely played out around the Flotilla as well. He wondered how many had died or become zombies and how many more military ships had been lost.

"Hey, General," Mays called.

"What do you have, Tom?"

"Come look at this fish."

Mays was kneeling next to the carcass of the first dolphin that had landed on the deck. He'd shot it himself. Rose was reluctant to get up close and personal with the creature that had tried to kill him. Mays was using his Ka-Bar knife to hold the animal's mouth open.

"Those are some impressive teeth," Rose said.

"That's the point. Dolphins don't have teeth like this."

Despite his earlier concern, Rose leaned in closer. The teeth were about an inch long and pointy, with serrated edges. "Aren't those more like shark teeth?"

"Yes, they are." One of the navy men had come over. He looked uncomfortable in web gear, and even more so carrying a rifle. "I was a marine biology major before joining the navy. Dolphin teeth are tiny and rounded, not pointy. Those are definitely shark teeth."

"Then why are they in a dolphin?" Rose asked. The man shrugged. *Could it be the virus?* Dr. Breda insisted Strain Delta wasn't from Earth. Could the fucking thing mutate creatures? How long had the dolphin been afflicted? A week? Two? He stared at the teeth and wondered how long it took to grow them. *Years.*

The sound of outboard motors made him look out to sea. A RHIB was approaching his ship. He thought the crew must be overly brave. As it got closer, Rose could see it wasn't one of the smaller ones like he'd used. This one was longer and had an enclosed cockpit. There were gunners with .50 calibers on the front, along with six Marines in full battle rattle behind the cockpit. It looked like the USMC was still in the game.

"Ahoy on ship!" a loudspeaker blared as the engines slowed, and the boat came to a stop a hundred yards away. "Is this the boat with General Rose aboard?"

Rose moved back to the bridge wing where Captain Sampson was looking on. A young ensign reached into a cubby and handed Rose a bullhorn. "This is General Rose."

"General, this is Lieutenant Kennedy. Good to see you're okay. My commander sent me over to check on you. It's been mayhem everywhere. We had to shoot a dozen seals that were trying to get aboard my boat."

"We're good, Lieutenant. I put my people on alert as soon as the shit hit the fan."

"Glad to hear. We're going to check others. You sure you're okay?"

"We have a platoon, Marine. I think we can handle some wild fish." The lieutenant threw a salute at him.

Rose shook his head and returned the salute. "Crazy goddamned leather necks."

"Gung-ho bastards," Mays agreed.

They had just turned the boat, and the twin outboard motors were beginning to rev up, when it was slammed from below. The collision was titanic, cracking the boat's keel and shoving the center five feet above the waterline. The six Marines standing behind the cockpit were catapulted up and out, yelling as they splashed into the dark waters. The pilot slammed forward into the transom before falling limply as the boat dropped back into the water.

The forward and aft gunners had been buckled into their stations, so they weren't injured. Both yelled and sprayed .50 caliber bullets in wide arcs. Rose was too surprised to duck as bullets smacked into the water in a line just below him. All he'd seen were a dark shape lifting the boat out of the water and a flash of white in the *Pacific Adventurer's* powerful lights.

"Throw a rope to them!" he yelled at the equally stunned captain of his ship. He turned back just in time to see the massive, blunt head of a killer whale rise out of the ocean and rip the bow gunner from his position, gun and all. The same thing happened to the stern gunner a second later.

Mays got off a couple of shots during the second attack, though Rose couldn't be sure if any of the rifle shots had hit their mark. The small boat was attacked from below and torn apart, right before their eyes. Dark shapes were just visible below the water's surface. None of the ejected soldiers surfaced, and the killer whales swam off to find more prey.

"Sea monsters," Mays said.

"What?" Rose asked, surprised to see he was still holding his rifle and hadn't fired a shot.

"The missing navy RHIB? They said it could have been sea monsters."

"Sea monsters," Rose said and carefully searched the water. "Yeah." In the near distance, they could see the dim outline of a distinctive ship, its aft low in the water and a launch tower amidships. "Captain, do we have power? Can we move?"

"Certainly."

"Then let's go. We need to help out, and I'm sure as hell not getting in a small boat right now."

* * *

Alex aimed and fired as quickly as he could. All pretense of monitoring ammo use was out the window. He'd swapped to his last mag an undetermined eternity ago, leaving him with 13 rounds of .40 caliber. He felt like he'd fired at least 100 shots since then.

An avalanche of harbor seals had flooded in through the hatch after he'd dropped the elephant seal. He'd wondered where they were all coming from until he remembered the back of the OOE's ship was a low fantail that descended almost to water level. The idea was that it would be easier to load and unload spaceships. Turned out it was easier to load zombie seals too.

A seal stopped to maul the very dead research assistant. Another tried to climb over, and Alex took the two-fer. He fired, his bullet punching through the first seal's head and continuing into the torso of the second. They flopped around, biting each other and bleeding. A flood of sea animal and human blood flowed across the floor.

Everyone who was still alive and conscious was in the back of the room hiding. He cast a quick glance toward them. Alison was cowering with Coldwell and his assistants, their eyes wide in panic. They either couldn't move or knew there was nowhere to go. Jeremiah was trying to move a fallen equipment rack. Alex had no idea why. When Alex turned back, there was a crash and another elephant seal bulled through the corpses he had piled up.

"Oh, for fuck's sake, how many of you are there?"

It looked at him calmly, cocking its head. Alex responded by shooting it right between the eyes. The .40 caliber round dug a furrow in the animal's cranium, temporarily revealing gleaming, white bone before the channel filled with blood. However, the bullet didn't penetrate. The animal gave a honking roar and shuffled its huge, fat body toward him. Alex shot again, and the round punched into the beast's neck just below its head. Other than a stream of blood, there was no effect. The pistol's slide locked back, empty.

"Well, shit," Alex said and dodged sideways as the seal came at him. The damned thing was the size of a small car, though not as fast, or he'd have bought it right then and there. Despite the behemoth's lack of acceleration, it had quick reflexes. As Alex dove aside, it swung its massive head and clipped him, sending the surprised pilot flying.

He bounced off a still-quivering pile of not-quite-dead harbor seal and landed next to the ruined door. Fetching up against the wall, he saw stars and shook his head to try and clear it. He immediately noticed that he was lying on something hard. Reaching under him, he found a pistol. *Patty's gun!*

He rolled to a seated position and scooped up the gun. It was small. Way too small. *Jesus Christ, Patty, get a real gun!* However, any gun was better than none, even against a marine mammal the size of a Subaru. Since Patty had just reloaded it prior to her stint as an elephant seal chew toy, he raised the weapon and fired. He'd shot target pistols with more recoil.

The elephant seal turned and looked at him. It seemed offended. Alex emptied the magazine into the elephant seal which sat there and absorbed every bullet with no more effect than it would have if Alex had been insulting his parentage. The little pimp-gun locked open. He didn't know where Patty was. Even though she had another magazine, he wouldn't have time to reach it. *Well, this is it.*

The elephant seal reared up and moved toward him. He glanced around, looking for anything to fight with. Rocket launcher? Whale harpoon? Maybe a .50 caliber rifle? Nope. He sighed and waited for the hit.

*Craaaack!* A bolt of lightning as bright as the sun lanced across the room. It shot behind the seal, illuminating it like a photo strobe. The instantaneous boom which followed the flash made him think it *was* a lightning bolt. If the seal's bulk hadn't been between him and the event, he would have been blinded.

"You missed!" he heard Jeremiah yell. He looked behind him and saw Wade Watts with Jeremiah standing next to him. The chunky computer programmer and gamer looked like he was holding a damned satellite dish. The seal advanced on the pair. Alex tried to find another magazine for the gun, without success. Just as the seal attacked Jeremiah and Wade, the 'gun' fired again.

* * *

"Help me lift this thing," Wade said.

Jeremiah stared at the contraption. Wade Watts had used just about every piece of high-power conductor he could find, including a taser, which Jeremiah didn't think was in the shop. For that matter, most of the stuff in Wade's creation was a surprise to him. Now, he understood why the tech department went through so much money. Regardless, the contraption was huge. "Could you have made it a little bigger?"

"Just help me?"

Alex was shooting like crazy, dropping the small army of harbor seals. He obviously hadn't seen the elephant seal sliding down the stairs like it was at a water park. Blood and dead seals were everywhere, and while Jeremiah was no expert on guns, he knew Alex must be about out of ammo.

Jeremiah looked at the Frankenstein monster Wade had created, trying to find a place to grab. As an aerospace engineer, he knew better than to grab something with obviously high voltage. Wade held it by a rear section, which had started life as a ceramic insulator, and the taser. But there seemed nowhere particularly safe to grab it.

Then he spotted a pair of electrical gloves. After he pulled them on, he took another hard look at the contraption and made a face. The gloves probably wouldn't be enough. Then he spotted the rubber mat.

"Is it energized yet?"

"No, why?"

Jeremiah grabbed the rubber mat and tossed it over one of the shelves Wade had been under. He took hold of the strongest piece of the contraption and lifted. *Shit, it's heavy!* When he set it on the mat, the shelf underneath partially collapsed. "Well?" he asked.

"Good enough," Wade said and knelt behind the thing.

Across the room, Alex rolled over and pointed a tiny gun. Jeremiah didn't know much about guns, but he knew the little gun wouldn't do a damned thing against a couple tons of elephant seal. *Bang, bang, bang.* Yup, nothing. The seal reared up.

"Clear!" Wade yelled, and there was a *pop!*

"That's it—" Jeremiah started to ask. Then he realized all Wade had done was fire the taser. The overweight programmer shifted his grip to the back of the cobbled-together device, and he depressed a high-voltage relay. The sound was akin to that of the million-volt breaker Jeremiah had heard explode in a lab back in college. A bolt of lightning as thick as his forearm lit up the room as brightly as the surface of the sun. The explosion which followed knocked him backward off his feet.

The elephant seal froze, its attack interrupted. It turned to look behind it. Part of the thick hide on its back was blackened and smoking. Jeremiah hadn't been looking at the front of the gun, or he would have been flash blinded. He'd been looking at Wade's hands. He turned to track the shot and saw a hole in the bulkhead. Rather, several holes leading out to the ocean, all of them rimmed with red-hot, melted steel. *Mother of God!*

"I can't see!" Wade cried, rubbing his eyes.

"You missed," Jeremiah said.

"Reload the taser," Wade instructed and held out a black, plastic pistol—another taser.

"How?"

"Jesus Christ, you're a rocket scientist, aren't you?!"

Jeremiah cursed and looked at the gun's business end. The taser that was still attached was basically molten plastic. However, a high voltage connector, also partly melted, was attached to the taser's battery pack. The seal was looking at him. *Oh, fuck.* Jeremiah considered. Based on the attacking animal's behavior, he maybe had a couple seconds. It would take a lot more than a couple seconds to re-MacGyver another taser into place. The rest of the gun looked more or less intact. The seal turned toward him and Wade, obviously making the correct assumption that they were the source of the attack. Time was up.

The seal flopped forward twice and reared up. Jeremiah angled the gun upward as the seal struck. "Fire!" he screamed as the monster's mouth rammed down on the burned end of the weapon. He prayed there was enough metal left to conduct. God reached out and slapped him into oblivion.

* * *

Alex watched the elephant seal rear back to strike, knowing he was about to be unemployed. There was nothing he could do. The beast struck downward. Then there was a dazzling explosion of light and sound, and the top of the seal's head exploded.

Cooked chunks of seal meat and bone flew in all directions. A big chunk bounced off the wall behind Alex and landed in his lap. He stared at it, dumbfounded. It was charred through and through, with a curl of smoke rising from it. He shoved it off quickly, and it singed his fingers. *What the hell did they do?* The remainder of the elephant seal lay burning in the middle of the bay.

Wade got up on unsteady legs and swayed, pointing. "Jeremiah!" he yelled.

"What about him?" Alex asked. Anyone who was still alive was extracting themself from the burnt seal meat.

"He got hit by the Tesla gun."

*Is that what that was?* Alex made his way through the minefield of seal chunks to where Jeremiah lay in a heap against a bin of parts.

"Let me," Alison said. "I've had basic EMT training."

"I learn something new about you every day," he said.

She knelt next to their boss and evaluated his vitals. Her head came up in a second. "He's not breathing."

"I'm not surprised," Wade said. He was blinking quickly and squinting at everyone. "All I can see is outlines. I didn't know how much power it could throw."

Alison began CPR as Alex spoke. "What did you use to power it?"

"The alien power module. I didn't have time do to more than wire it to the Tesla coil. It was pure luck that it worked at all. I read Dr. Coldwell's files, and he said he didn't think it used electrical energy."

"I think we can confirm it does," Coldwell said, surveying the cooked seal carcass. "Great work improvising the weapon. I kept the Tesla coil around for fun. Never thought it would be useful."

"It probably won't be anymore," Wade said, squinting at the half-melted remains of the gun he'd slapped together. "I can see a little better now." He bent and retrieved the alien power module, brushing seal ash from it. "Doesn't seem damaged."

"We'll have to do some tests," Coldwell said. "I'll have Cynthia find the meters in this mess."

"The seal ate Cynthia," another associate said.

"Oh," Coldwell said. "Pity."

"Any luck?" Alex asked Alison when she stopped to check her patient's pulse.

"Yeah, he's breathing." She looked Jeremiah over. When she got to his hands, she hissed. "Oh, God, look at his hands." The heavy, rubber, insulating gloves had melted into his skin. "We need to get him to the infirmary."

"Unless the seals have eaten the medics," Alex said. "First, we need to see if anyone else can be saved and find some more weapons." A sound from the ruined hatch made him search the floor for a weapon. He found Jeremiah's discarded wrench and scooped it up. *And to think I used to like the circus!*

A pair of soldiers in full combat gear slowly peered through the entrance and took in the scene of marine mammal-induced carnage. "Hello? Anyone alive in there?"

"More or less," Alex replied. "Who are you guys?"

"Captain Mays, US Army," the older of the pair said. "You need help?" Mays was examining the still hot burn in the hull.

"Does it look like we need help?" Coldwell asked.

"We've got Jeremiah Osborne over here," Alison said. "He's badly injured. Can you help us get him to the infirmary?"

Mays yelled up to the deck and, in moments, the room filled with soldiers. Alex acquired a spare handgun and ammunition from Mays and felt much better for it. Two of the men were medics who evaluated Jeremiah and the others who were hurt. They found Patty Mize who had a fractured skull. Her prognosis was no better than Jeremiah's.

"The medics said we need to evacuate both of them," Mays told Alex. "Best we bring everyone over to the *Pacific Adventurer.*"

"Unique name for a military ship," Alex said.

"You can say that again," Mays mumbled.

"We can't just leave all this," Coldwell said.

"Why not? It's just junk," Mays said.

"This junk made an aircraft carrier fly."

Mays shook his head. "No shit? I bet the General would like to hear about this."

*****

# Chapter Six

**Midnight, Friday, May 3**
**Shangri-La**
**Amarillo, TX**

"It's a miracle we only lost one man," Cobb said as Governor Taylor and Clark listened. Others in the gondola were intent on the discussion despite having other duties. "I hope the generators were worth it."

"The report says the third one got a little shot up, but we can use it for parts," Clark said. He glanced at the governor, then quickly away. "The power was essential, though. We've got a lot of pre-plague meat and other food, but without the ability to keep it frozen, it would all be lost. We've been trying to find generators for days, but we didn't have the troops."

"You have our thanks," Taylor said with her signature smile. Cobb nodded.

Below them, salvage crews were still picking up the containers identified by Courtney Raines and her invaluable data. Cobb knew the data included information on refrigerated railcars containing food and the dates it was produced. Those cars were running out of the fuel that kept their refrigerators operating and, thus, were prime targets.

The cranes worked ceaselessly, each one lowering a pair of men with a framework to attach to the railcars. The infected still swarmed, but without any coordination. Lacking a single effort on the ground, they seemed confused and were easily distracted by spotlights or occasional flash-bang grenades. He could see a huge rail tanker, labeled diesel on the side, being lifted. It appeared Clark was correct; fuel wasn't the problem.

"If everything is okay," Cobb said, "I need to talk to Master Sergeant Schardt."

"Of course," Taylor replied. "Get some sleep too. We are looking at another trip to Houston. We know where a group of survivors have been hiding out."

Cobb rounded on her. "Then why aren't they up here?" She ground her teeth together. "Oh, right." He left without another word. There was something about the relationship between Taylor and the other 'leaders' of Shangri-La which didn't sit well with him.

He was already learning his way around Shangri-La. The military 'barracks' were only a few hundred feet from the entrance to the gondola. It was faster to cut through a couple of workshops and the infirmary than to take the roadways. Sure, the roads helped provide a feeling of comfort, but they were a waste of effort in his opinion. He hadn't been aboard a day and already knew their biggest problem; they were simply existing and had no vision for the future.

He reached the trailers that belonged to the military. The soldiers weren't lounging around like the last time. By now, they all knew about the loss of one of their own, and Cobb suspected the news hadn't been well received. He needed to get ahead of the situation. The problem was multifaceted. He had a severe shortage of NCOs and a complete lack of junior officers. The bird General Rose put on his shoulder didn't help. The rank and file felt a full-bird colonel was no longer a field officer. He was seen as a POG, a person other than a grunt. At least, until he proved otherwise.

He entered the unit where he'd first met the sergeants, but only Zim and Schardt were there. Both stood when he entered. Cobb waved them down with a grunt. "None of that shit," he said. Both men looked somber and uncomfortable. "We obviously need to talk."

"Of course, sir," Zim said.

"Colonel," Schardt said.

"I know nobody is happy, and I'm sure they're blaming me."

"Not as much as you'd think," Schardt said, making Cobb stop in surprise.

"The problem is that Private Davis was one of Groves' men," Zim explained.

"Ah," Cobb said. "Now I see." He'd only learned the dead soldier's name after they'd gotten back to Shangri-La. He wasn't used to fighting with men whose names he didn't know. He had pulled the men from a list assembled by Zim on a spreadsheet named 'Ready Teams.' They'd been rotating people to keep everyone from being on alert more than 12 hours a day. It was still tough duty, and part of what concerned him about the near future. "And where is Staff Sergeant Groves?"

"Staff Sergeant Groves is in her team's trailer," Schardt said.

"They have their own trailer? It was my understanding that the men were billeted together in one trailer and the women in another." The two sergeants didn't respond. They knew Cobb wasn't happy. "How long has this situation existed?"

"Since the staff sergeant came aboard, Colonel," Zim said.

"Right." He sighed and pinched the bridge of his nose with his thumb and index finger. It had been at least 36 hours since he'd gotten any meaningful rack time. However, this couldn't wait. He got up and removed his web gear. There was a rifle rack in the sergeants' office trailer, so after checking that his carbine was cleared and locked, he stowed it there and hung his web gear from a hook.

"Can the master sergeant ask the colonel what he intends?"

"I'm going to have a chat with Staff Sergeant Groves."

"Would you care to hear the master sergeant's advice, Colonel?"

"I'm always interested in a senior NCO's advice."

"I'd hold off on this one. Groves is too much of an unknown factor. Take some time to figure out her angle, maybe see if her situation settles itself."

"I respect that, Schardt, but the situation is too fluid right now. I need to let the staff sergeant know exactly how things stand."

"Understood, sir." Schardt looked nervous. "I would still suggest you don't do this."

"Duly noted. I'll be back in a few minutes, and we can discuss some new procedures for recovery operations, then I need some sack time."

"Roger that," Schardt said.

"Will do," Zim agreed.

Cobb nodded his thanks and turned to leave. He didn't notice the pair of sergeants exchange a look, wait a half minute, then head back into the trailer's back offices.

Outside, he looked at the line of trailers. Soldiers stood on the steps outside of two of them, smoking. Even in an apocalypse, they were following procedures. Each time they saw him, they saluted the way they would in the field, casually yet respectfully. Schardt appeared correct, they weren't holding him responsible for the loss of Private Davis.

He didn't know which trailer held the staff sergeant and her team, so he stopped and asked a couple of the soldiers who were smoking.

"Them?" a private asked. "Trailer on the end, near the edge." The other private nodded, his mouth a thin line.

No love for the staff sergeant there. He thanked the men and headed for the staff sergeant's trailer. "Colonel?" one of the men called.

"Yes, son?"

"Are we going to finally start looking for more of our people?"

Cobb walked back to them, climbing the stairs to get closer. Both looked apprehensive at his approach, perhaps fearful they'd said something they shouldn't have. "Where are you men from?"

"We're both 101st," the one who'd spoken said, and they both turned slightly so he could see the distinctive shield patch with "Airborne" across the top and a stylized eagle in the center.

"Fort Campbell." They nodded. "You guys were mobilized when the SHTF?"

"Yes, Colonel," the other one said. "We were trying to link up with III Corps in Texas."

"My unit," Cobb said. "Everything went to hell, fast."

"Yes sir, it did. We were in a flight of Blackhawks. Someone went zombie on all of them, except two. We set down near Texarkana and hid out. Kept trying to reach anyone by radio or GCCS, but MILSATCOM went down just before we crashed."

"Someone messed up GCCS," Cobb agreed. "Have you asked why we haven't started looking for more units?"

The first soldier who'd spoken looked toward the staff sergeant's trailer. "Sir, I'd rather not say."

"You've said everything you need to, Private," Cobb said, his jaw set. *That talk is* really *going to happen now.* "Things are about to change around here. What was left of III Corps went west, I believe, and they linked up with navy and Marine elements there." Both men perked up and looked less hangdog at the news. "I need to get a few things straight, and then we'll have a meeting."

"Looking forward to it, Colonel," the soldier said.

Both wore jump patches on their BDUs. How could they not be using these men for recovery operations? Jesus Christ, they were paratroopers! "We'll talk soon. I promise."

Both men came to attention and saluted.

"At ease, boys. We're in the field." Both smiled. These were good boys, and they were in a less-than-optimal situation.

Cobb strode toward the trailer at the end with meaning. As he passed the last row and turned toward the end, he caught sight of his destination. The words "Arkansas National Guard Territory' were painted on the side. He hadn't caught Groves' accent. It was possible her parents were from outside Arkansas or she'd been educated elsewhere. Either way, she was apparently seriously proud of her state.

On the metal steps, two men were using knives to scratch at the trailer paint. A second later, one of them noticed him and elbowed the other in the ribs. They both watched him for a bit until they recognized him, at least by reputation, and they immediately retreated into the trailer.

He would rather have showed up unannounced. However, things would go the way they would go. He wished he had his old command sergeant major from his lieutenant colonel days with him. He felt like he was flying without running lights. But he was committed.

He reached the stairs and climbed up. As he did, he could see that all the wall within reach of the stairs was covered in graffiti. Some was written in marker, but a lot was scratched on with knives. A fair amount was vulgar, and he stopped when he saw the common theme. Anti-minority. Actually, openly racist would have been a better description. One of the two soldiers he'd just spoken to was black. It was all coming together now.

Cobb entered without knocking. Inside the common area adjacent to the door was Staff Sergeant Groves, sitting behind a desk she'd obviously obtained from non-military sources. A corporal was lounging in a camp chair next to her, and the two soldiers who'd been vandalizing the barracks trailer were standing next to the staff sergeant. He closed the door behind him. None of them acknowledged his arrival or rose to their feet. Groves was messing with a laptop, and the corporal was staring at the same screen. The two privates pretended he wasn't there.

"Staff Sergeant," Cobb said.

"Yeah?" she replied without looking up from her computer.

"We need a word."

"So, go ahead."

"*Alone.*" His words were pointed and commanding.

She looked up for the first time, and he saw a hint of surprise, or maybe it was confusion, on her face. The corporal looked alarmed and leaned sideways to glance around Cobb. The two privates headed for the rear of the trailer where the bunk room was without being told. The corporal looked at Groves. She nodded, and he got up to leave.

Cobb stood for a second to see how Groves would react. Once they were alone, she closed her computer and looked up at him, the first time she'd made intentional eye contact. He searched for any sign of contrition or guilt. All he saw was, what, annoyance? Suddenly, he felt like he was in enemy territory, and he didn't know why.

"I want to talk about the op," he started.

"You come to explain why my man didn't make it back?" she demanded.

"Maybe if you hadn't taken your time bringing the M240s, he'd be alive."

"How dare you?" she snarled. "I brought them as fast as I could."

"Really? You weren't at the pre-op briefing, so how could you have known what might be needed?"

"I had other duties."

"Staff Sergeant, we have a problem."

"You've got the problem."

He continued as if she hadn't spoken. "Besides being insubordinate, you're terrible at your job."

She bristled as if he'd called her a nasty name. Then she visibly calmed herself, which somewhat impressed him. "I don't care what you think."

"Oh? Well, you should."

"What are you going to do, *Colonel*?" She spat the word 'colonel' at him. "You going to write me a poor fitness report? Hook me up with an article 15?"

"No, I'm relieving you of duty."

"You can't do that."

"Bet me? You are relieved, pending a review. I'll be evaluating the existing NCOs for potential promotion. I'm also having Master Sergeant Schardt evaluate the men you came in with. They are just as disobedient as you are. We're going to start actively looking for surviving military personnel so we can start assembling a proper force. There's been some radio traffic from out west. General Rose, my commander, went west. With any luck, we can link up with him. With any luck, we'll find him, and I won't have to run this shitshow anymore."

He looked at her and shook his head. "I don't know what happened to you, but you don't stop being an NCO just because the world came to an end. I didn't want this job, but it looks like I came along just in time."

"And you're leaving just in time."

Cobb turned his head at the unmistakable sound of a rifle bolt closing. All seven of Groves' men were filing in from the bunk area, and they were all armed. Her corporal was pointing his gun at Cobb.

"What the fuck do you think you're doing?" Cobb asked, looking from the corporal to Groves.

"Reestablishing the status quo," she said.

"You honestly think nobody will have a problem with you shooting a colonel?"

"Only if they find the body," she said, her smile savage. "It's a long way to Amarillo, and there are a lot of hungry zombies waiting for you. Come on, *Colonel,* time for a reckoning."

* * *

W*ell, this was stupid.* Cobb was fighting incredulity and a strong sense of failure. In more than 20 years of being an officer in the US Army, he'd never had someone take a swing at him, and now he was a prisoner of the people he was supposedly in command of. Worse, he was at gunpoint and completely at their mercy. His sidearm and rifle were back in the sergeants' trailer. He did have a knife in his pocket, but against eight armed soldiers, it was rather inadequate.

He needed time. "You really want to play this game?"

One of the men pushed him in the back none-too-gently with a rifle butt.

"What game is that?" Groves asked.

"Mutiny? Murder?"

"You looked around, Mr. Officer?" one of her men asked. "End of the fuckin' world, sir…"

"Stupid officer," another said, and they all chuckled.

"It doesn't have to go this way," he said, his mind racing. They only laughed more. He had decided to call for help from the soldiers outside, when he realized they weren't taking him out the front. They were moving down the center of the trailer to the back exit.

A narrow corridor ran down a length of tiny bunkrooms. Cobb had seen dozens of variants of the trailer. This one provided more, smaller sleeping areas, an equipment room at the back, and a rear entrance. When they reached the back of the trailer, he found it stuffed full. Not full of weapons, ammo, and such, but full of valuables.

The eight-by-five foot room was lined with stuffed shelves. He saw plastic bins full of gold and silver watches, plastic Ziplock bags full to bursting with gold rings and necklaces, stacks of gold bars, piles of gold and silver coins, even a massive bundle of $100 bills in one corner.

"Are you fucking insane?" he asked, unable to control himself. "This idiot behind me just said it's the end of the world." He gestured futilely at the piles of wealth. "What are you planning to do with this?"

The procession stopped as the soldiers digested this conundrum. Cobb took a chance and looked over his shoulder. He saw several of the men staring inquiringly at Groves. "Oh," he said, "what have you been telling this motley crew? You telling them this shit is somehow still valuable and more than pretty to look at?"

"Yeah, what's up with that?" one of the soldiers asked.

"Shut the fuck up, Dexter," the corporal snarled. "You were on welfare before the plague. You wouldn't know economics if it sat on your face."

The other men laughed, but Cobb could see them exchanging nervous looks, and he knew he'd hit a key point. "So, what's up with this plan?"

"Quiet," she ordered him.

"Or what, you're going to shoot me?"

She pulled a pistol out of her pocket and pointed it at him.

"Go ahead, pull the trigger so everyone comes running." She frowned a little. "Thinking stuff through isn't your strong point, is it?"

"This is bullshit," the corporal said and shoved something into Cobb's back. He heard a buzzing sound, and suddenly, the floor hit him in the face.

"God the fucker is heavy."

Cobb blinked and tried to clear his mind. The taser in the small of his back had packed a punch. He hadn't expected an intelligent move. Someone grabbed him under his arms and dragged him along the tops of the containers serving as the floor of Shangri-La. He lifted his head and saw that the edge was only a short distance away. A series of LED floodlights lit the perimeter of the floating city, possibly as a security measure so nobody walked off in the night. He knew people generally stayed away from the edge so they weren't the target of a random gunshot from the scared people below.

"I can walk, assholes," he spat. The men almost dropped him in surprise.

"Want I should taze him again?"

"Don't bother; I'll walk," Cobb said.

"Is the big colonel giving up?" The corporal laughed. "And here I figured you were some kind of wasteland badass or something."

Cobb ignored the mutinous prick. He'd taken advantage of being dragged and was ready for the endgame of their gambit. They reached the edge of Shangri-La in a few seconds. The rest of Shangri-La was relatively quiet. It was late, and most of the operations to salvage what they could from Amarillo had wrapped up. Nobody would see his body fall and probably be eaten by the ravenous infected.

"Any last-minute, pithy statements?" Groves asked as the two who held him turned him around, back toward the edge.

"Yeah," he said. "What happened to you?"

"To me?" she asked. He nodded. "Someone like you happened to me. I worked at the ANG USPFO in Littlerock. It was a sweet job, and I was good at it. I had a good crew too." She looked around at her men who nodded and looked satisfied with themselves.

USPFO was the postal and fiscal office, in charge of assets and paying bills. The stash made sense now. "How much did you steal?" Cobb asked.

Groves snorted. "Government wastes more than we stole."

"Did the officer in charge get wise?"

"The old major who was the USPFO office commander retired. The new one was a real smartass."

"Nosy bastard," the corporal agreed.

"He started getting too curious," Groves said.

"Meaning he did his job?" Cobb asked.

Groves ignored his question. "I figured he wasn't smart enough to figure things out, which was a mistake. When I realized he had found out what was happening, we pulled the plug and played it cool. He didn't have any evidence. Fucker was outta luck. He *knew* it was me, *had* to be me. But what could he do about it?

"So, he started making my life miserable. Wasn't enough that he stopped our side business, he started riding my ass. I showed up five minutes late, he wrote me up. Uniform not perfect? Same. Called in sick because I was sick of his shit? More of the same fucking attitude."

Cobb began to smile. Of course, the new major had changed his tactic. He couldn't get her for what she'd been doing, which could have gotten her arrested, but he needed her gone. So, he pushed her in every way he could.

"The day after I called in sick, the bitch major demanded a medical report. I didn't have one and told him to stuff it. The next day he filed an Article 15 on me."

"Let me guess," Cobb said, "malingering, insubordination, disrespect?"

"You fucking officers are all the same," she said and spit on the metal floor. "He wanted me out. But I had a friend, an old acquaintance in higher command. She'd gotten her star the year before, and she kept them from throwing me out. But I lost my stripes." Her face held nothing but rage, even though she'd been entirely responsible for what happened to her. "I was an E-4 with only two years to go, and the son of a bitch busted me down to buck private."

One of the men behind her smirked. Some of the others found it amusing as well. Cobb doubted any of them would ever let her see their amusement, though. "You weren't even a staff sergeant?"

"No," she admitted, then shrugged. "When the shit hit the fan, they mobilized all of us. Some dumb fucker put us in trucks and sent us to depots and armories. We were heading for the armory in Mena when a bunch of idiots went zombie. They'd brought food from home. Sucked to be them. During the craziness, the lieutenant in charge of our convoy had a little accident."

"ADed himself in the back of the head," a private said. Several others laughed, apparently enjoying the memory. Kind of hard to accidentally discharge your weapon into the back of your own head.

"Here, only my crew knows me. A staff sergeant from another unit had his face eaten off. So, I took his stripes." She shrugged again. "I knew the walk and could talk the talk. It was easy. The only officer left was a butter bar, gung-ho fucker. He didn't make it to the next day. I slipped some fresh chicken in his MRE."

"The rest was survival. We split off from the ones who wanted to go to the armory and get eaten. We moved around, grabbing up shit when we found it. Lots of good stuff.

"How much belonged to people?" Cobb asked.

"The dead and infected didn't care. The others? The strong survive. Anyway, we made a mistake. Broke into a big bank building. It was full of infected. Had to run for it. Ended up on the roof. We were running out of food when this fucking city floated over. We decided to move up."

"You know Schardt is on to you, right?" he asked.

"The old fart doesn't know shit. But you might be right. He's next. We'll give it a few days, and he'll have himself an accident. *Whoops!* Down he goes." Laughter all around. "Then, Zim. I'll be in charge. Maybe I'll put a bar on, make it all legitimate."

"You'll never be an officer," Cobb said.

She came back out of her reverie and stared at him. Cobb was standing up straight, chest out. Her face shifted into a look of loathing. "Boy scout, huh? Well, about time to fly, Boy Scout."

"Not so fast, Private."

Groves spun around. Master Sergeant Schardt was standing by the corner of the nearest trailer, 20 feet away, where he'd obviously been watching and listening. He stood casually, both hands behind his back, as if he were at parade rest.

Three of Groves' crew were still pointing their weapons at Cobb. None of them moved to aim them at the new arrival. Maybe they thought it was too much to hold a gun on a master sergeant while it wasn't too much to hold a gun on a colonel. Cobb would have laughed out loud if the situation hadn't been life and death.

"Why don't you take a walk?" Groves suggested.

"Why don't you stand down, while you still can?" Schardt replied. "I figured you might do something really stupid, so after Colonel Pendleton left to visit you, we followed him. Oh, and if you're wondering, I heard it all, especially how you're only a private."

Groves' face turned hard, and red crept up her neck. Cobb weighed the odds of an outcome that wasn't bad, and they didn't look good.

"The rank I was before doesn't mean shit," she said. Some of her followers nodded. The situation was fluid. "This motherfucker is not going to get anymore of my people killed."

"Your people?" Schardt demanded. "You mean the soldiers of the Arkansas National Guard who were ordered into active service in the United States Army by the US President a week ago? As the senior officer, Colonel Pendleton is in charge. These are *his* men, you idiot." Schardt cast his eyes around, making brief contact with each of the men who would meet his gaze. "You are contriving to commit treason with these men."

Several of the men shuffled their feet, and one lowered his weapon. Groves must have felt she was losing control because she aimed her pistol at Master Sergeant Schardt. His expression went from serious to dead calm. Instantly, Corporal Tango and Sergeant Zim rotated around from two of the trailers next to the one Schardt had been standing behind. They both held M4 carbines to their shoulders, were in a slight crouch, and had their cheeks welded to the butt stocks of their guns.

Schardt slowly moved his hands from behind his back. He held an M4 in his right hand, barrel down. His grip, like him, was calm and practiced. "You thought I missed the part where you said I'd have an *accident*? Whoops, there I go?" He cocked his head slightly, and a small smile played across his lips.

"Groves," Cobb said, but all her followers were raising weapons. They were trying to cover all three men at the same time. The two men with Schardt showed none of the same signs of indecision. If anything, they looked as calm as if they'd just picked up pizza for the kids on Friday night. "Groves!" Cobb said, louder.

She looked at him, her gun unconsciously drifting away from Master Sergeant Schardt. The look of confident arrogance was gone. Now, she looked worried and uncertain. Cobb thought it was his chance. "Put it down, Groves. Walk away. I'll move you in with the civilians. You can even keep all the shit you stole. Nobody cares."

"There's eight of us," she said, her voice almost a whisper. She looked back and forth, licking her lips. "We're not going anywhere. We didn't do anything wrong."

"I also didn't miss the part where you said you shot your officer," Schardt said loudly, his voice ringing out in the night. Groves saw he'd raised his rifle a little bit. Enough to gain a half second, maybe. "Make your decision, Private."

Cobb stayed perfectly still. He had a good view of Groves' face and half her crew from where he stood. For a couple seconds, he thought the situation would deescalate. He didn't think Groves had the guts or stupidity to make a bad situation worse. He had thought she wouldn't turn traitor and try to throw him off the side of Shangri-La. He was wrong about the standoff too.

Something in her eyes changed. Then the set of her shoulders and her overall body posture changed too. She'd made her decision. "Oh, shit," Cobb said just as she corrected her aim and shot Master Sergeant Schardt.

Everything exploded at once. A pair of Groves' more alert cohorts blazed away without bothering to raise their rifles, firing from the hip. Cobb had a perfect view of Tango and Zim. Both men responded coolly and quickly, sliding sideways and dropping to one knee. The result was that they were immediately behind the cover provided by the massive, metal, shipping containers they'd come out from behind.

The sound of the rifles wielded by Groves' people tore at Cobb's ears like icepicks. He'd removed his next generation hearing protection with the rest of his gear. He could see bullets from the two mutineers who'd opened fire immediately after Groves stitch up the side of the containers, trying to track Tango and Zim. They clearly had the older issue M-16s from the national guard, because the guns were on full automatic. The recoil of their guns on auto drove them up as they tracked sideways, missing the dodging men by a large margin.

Zim and Tango weren't guardsman. They were experienced operators, knew their weapons, and weren't afraid of being shot at. Both had their newer M-4 carbines on selective fire. They released 3-round bursts at their targets. Two of the mutineers were hit by the controlled bursts. They were close enough to Cobb for him to see and feel the bullets tear through the men's torsos.

One of the men screamed and dropped his weapon, clutching at the fountain of blood pouring from his neck. The other dropped like a sack of wet cement. A bullet had bisected his heart, killing him instantly. The reactions of the remaining six men were surprisingly varied and reflected the feelings of a group who'd chosen Groves because she could provide things to steal.

One dropped his gun and ran. Two ignored the weapons over their shoulders and put their hands to their ears against the fierce assault on their hearing. The remaining three raised their weapons and unleashed undisciplined fire toward Zim and Tango. They weren't firing crazily on full auto, they were jerking the trigger on semi-auto. At least, two of them were. The third jerked the trigger on his weapon while it was still on safe, with predictable results.

Cobb took a knee. He hoped the move would remove him as a valid target, and he was correct. They were much more interested in the far more deadly armed soldiers doing their level best to kill them. Zim and Tango were completely behind cover, confident the 5.56mm rounds couldn't penetrate the relatively heavy steel containers.

The bullets punched into the steel, and some even penetrated the facing wall, but because Zim and Tango were around a corner, the bullets had to punch through yet another piece of thick steel to get to them. Cobb could hear the rounds bouncing around inside. *Hope there's nothing explosive in there!*

The cause of the entire situation had spent the first few seconds screaming ineffectually at her men. Zim and Tango were timing their attacks, waiting for the remaining attackers to go bingo on ammo, at which point they became easy targets. Once they ran out, Zim and Tango both leaned out. Sadly, it was just as the dufus who'd been pulling the trigger on a safed gun finally figured out his dilemma, released the safety, and opened fire.

Zim, being older and more cautious, reversed immediately and retreated behind cover. Tango, being younger and a Marine, didn't seek cover. Instead, he placed three perfect shots in one of the two men who were reloading. Two bullets hit the man in the chest and one in the head, dropping him immediately. Only then did Tango return to cover, but not before a round from the dufus caught him in the chest.

"Oof," Cobb heard him utter as he fell back.

"Tango!"

Schardt was down, but not out. He raised himself up on an elbow and propped his M-4 on one leg. Cobb could see his lower extremities covered in bright blood as he sighted with a one-handed grip and put a three-round burst into the dufus. The survivors had completely forgotten Cobb, who waited for an opening, then kicked the right knee of the dufus who, despite being shot three times, was still up. The knee gave a satisfying crunch, and the dufus folded like a bad hand of Texas Hold 'em. He hit the ground and gagged on his own blood.

Something hit Cobb in the side of the head, and his vision exploded into stars. The impact knocked him over, and when his vision cleared, he saw Groves standing over him, her pistol pointed at his face. There was blood on her hand and the magazine well of the gun, answering the question of what had hit him on the head; she'd pistol whipped him. Rude.

"Enough!" she yelled. "One more shot, and your precious *colonel* dies." She continued to say his rank with as much contempt as she could manage.

Cobb took advantage of the pause in hostilities to take account of the situation. His head was bleeding, but not badly. It didn't feel like she'd fractured his skull, though a mild concussion did seem possible. He was having a little trouble focusing, and his senses were blurry. He'd been on the business end of an IED once, which had helped him decide to retire later. He was far luckier than the three men in the lead Humvee, all of which hadn't survived.

Master Sergeant Schardt was sitting in the same place. Cobb could see that he'd been hit in the left shoulder and abdomen. Both bullets had missed his armor. He didn't look good. Regardless, he continued to hold his rifle and look pissed. All Cobb could see of Tango was a foot sticking out from behind the wall. It was moving slightly, giving him hope the young Marine corporal was still alive.

There was no sign of Zim. Cobb suspected he was just out of view, waiting for his chance.

Of Groves' original allies, only one remained standing. He'd finished reloading his weapon and was looking from his leader to the bodies of his former friends. The dufus was still alive, but he was gurgling and spitting blood. Cobb was no longer concerned about him.

"We're getting out of here, and I'm taking this asshole with me," she said. "Zim, I know you're out there!" she yelled to be heard. "Wake up a chopper pilot. I want as much food and ammo as I can haul on board."

"You're not going anywhere," Schardt said. The effort made him grimace slightly. "You don't think the rest of the men heard this? They'll be here any second."

Her face darkened as the gears in her mind turned. A well-timed, distant yell came from the direction of the barracks trailers. "See?" Schardt said.

"You're right. Change of plans." She looked at her last man. "Kill him," she said. The mutineer's rifle moved, and Cobb knew he was out of options.

When Groves clubbed him, he'd fallen on his hidden knife. While the standoff proceeded, he'd slowly slid a hand under himself and gotten a grip on it. When she ordered her man to kill Schardt, he pulled it out and attacked.

Manufactured by Ka-Bar, it was made from high-quality stainless steel. The Ek Commando presentation knife had been a present from his men upon his retirement. He hadn't been able to leave it behind when he'd left his house to search for Kathy Clifford. Its handle was polished walnut, and it wasn't practical for field work.

He'd wrapped the handle with paracord during his exodus across Texas. He rammed the double edged, slightly diamond-patterned, razor-sharp, 6 ½ inch blade into her calf.

Groves let out a blood curdling scream and tried to jump away. Cobb held the knife in the wound, which tore her leg open halfway to her ankle. Her scream became shrill and inhuman.

Her last man hadn't fired. He was distracted by his leader's scream, and he turned to see Cobb holding the blade as blood poured out of the wound and over his hand. The man turned his rifle toward Cobb, at which point Schardt put three rounds into his center of mass.

As Groves' gun came down the barrel loomed like a tunnel, and Cobb saw oblivion as he looked down it. His eyes moved up to her face, which was frozen in a rictus of pain and fury. The corner of her mouth twitched into a smile. At least she was going to get to kill an officer before she died. Then her face disintegrated in an explosion of blood, bone, and brains. Her dead body fell across him with a thud.

Cobb breathed again. A second later, Zim appeared and rolled the dead mutineer off him. "Sorry I took so long, sir," he said. "Had to find another firing point, and it took a second."

The scene of betrayal flooded with soldiers. Many had small arms, and others were nearly naked, but all were confused and ready to fight. Cobb saw a pair of men dragging the man who'd run when the fighting started. It was done, then.

"Get a medic for Master Sergeant Schardt," he ordered as Zim offered him a hand up, which he took. "What about Tango?"

"I'm okay," the Marine corporal said. He was leaning against the corner he'd fallen behind. He tapped his armor, and Cobb could see a tear. "Round clipped the trauma plate, and the plate slowed it enough for the Kevlar to stop it. Knocked the wind out of me. Sorry to take myself out of the fight."

"No apologies needed, you three saved my bacon," Cobb said. Schardt looked like a mess, but he was still alert as a man in navcam with a medical bag kneeled down and worked on him. It was over, and despite his mistake in confronting the murderous traitor, he'd survived.

*****

# Chapter Seven

**Morning, Saturday, May 4**
**Classified Task Force**
**100 Miles West of Eureka, California**

A storm had blown in overnight and slowed the task force's progress to the south. Chamuel could have told Michael about it, had she desired to. Frankly, he was an asshole. He was the only one in the heptagon who was from a military background, and it showed. The bastard seemed to think he was a new Caesar or something.

She snorted as she sat in her mobility chair and let her eyes scan the monitors. Her working space was nearly covered in them. She missed their land-side installation in Portland where she'd had 20 monitors of various sizes and a pair of simply gorgeous 75" curved displays for live video feeds.

With the collapse of society and mass media, the need for the big displays was gone. So, when they'd abandoned the base and moved onto ships, she'd left them behind with a certain amount of sadness. She rode in their main ship. It had started life as a NOAA research vessel. The global weather monitoring room served her purposes quite well, and she'd asked Michael to have it modified for her use. He'd done it, if only to get her to shut up.

On the stern of the ship were three, large satellite uplink dishes. Chamuel had appropriated two of them. Despite Gabriel's releasing her virus to shut down the world's comms, Chamuel still had considerable assets for gathering intel. Dozens of military intelligence satellites, weather satellites, even commercial imaging satellites were accessible to her, thanks to the old legacy gateway via WWMCCS. Chamuel had to hand it to her, Gabriel had game.

As the sun was lighting the eastern horizon, Chamuel sipped her beloved Darjeeling tea and let her sharp eyes run over the hundreds of data screens set in her monitor wall. The door opened, and she glanced over to see who was coming, hoping it wasn't Michael. It was Azrael, their archeologist.

The tall, albino man had a steaming coffee mug in one hand and looked like, once again, he hadn't gotten much sleep. Chamuel went back to her studying, adding some new data from Europe to her notes. Eastern Europe had plenty of signs of life. Zombie life. The infected didn't seem overly bothered by radiation, which was good for them, since a good part of Eastern Europe would be radioactive for a millennium.

"Anything new?"

Chamuel was a little surprised her visitor had spoken. It wasn't uncommon for Azrael to come in, look at the screens while he drank his coffee, then return to his work without commenting.

"No," she said. "The fallout in Eastern Europe has followed Cold War era patterns. The windstorm, yesterday, over Turkmenistan carried the Mashhad fallout into Tajikistan. It's a shame; they were a pretty successful holdout to the virus until now." She brought up a satellite image on the largest of her monitors. The big city of Dushanbe in Tajikistan glowed in the evening light, its boundaries sharp. They'd built defenses and kept the infection from spreading. It was one of only 22 cities with any signs of power. Maybe 10 still seemed to be run by people, the others were probably lit due to automated power sources.

Chamuel put up another image next to it with a timestamp that was 48 hours later. Only a few lights showed now. They were dim and in isolated parts of the city.

"The fallout was intense?" Azrael asked.

"It shouldn't have been," Chamuel replied. "I think the radiation precipitated some other event. I'll keep watching to find out."

"The statue of Tajik, set under a golden arch in the center of Dushanbe, was beautiful," Azrael said. He shook his head. "So much lost."

"It's probably still there," Chamuel said.

"It's not the same."

Chamuel turned and looked at the archeologist. He looked thoughtful and a little sad. She wouldn't have guessed the man had emotions before now. How many billions were dead? How few who still thought for themselves had survived? And this man was moved by the loss of a statue? "Your priorities are fucked up," she said.

"Tell me something I don't know," Azrael replied. "I found the notes of the linguists from the 1950s. I gave them to Jophiel."

"Good news. Maybe we can get some answers out of the alien."

"Michael won't like it," he replied.

Chamuel had just turned to her monitors, but Azrael's comment caused her to turn back. "What do you mean?"

"There are pages and pages of conversations that were recorded once they could understand the Vulpes. Three of them landed. The government talked to them, and they eventually convinced the Vulpes we were open to discussion. The translations weren't perfect; those linguists were still guessing at some stuff. It was a context issue, I think. The government representatives probably made some offers they shouldn't have."

"What do you mean?"

"Well, the linguists thought the Vulpes were offering aid. They only realized, after the Vulpes left in their ship, that they weren't offering aid, they were *asking* for it."

"Holy shit," Chamuel said, "classic misunderstanding."

"Right," Azrael agreed. "Hundreds of wars throughout history started because of misunderstandings. Anyway, the linguists figured out more of it after the Vulpes returned to space, but they couldn't talk anymore. The last part is the one which will really piss Michael off."

Chamuel looked at him, waiting. Azrael finished his coffee and shook his head. "They said it would take about 50 years for them to come back because they were fighting a war. They looked forward to our help and would be coming with refugees. The biological specimens they left behind are from their foods and tissues. They left them so we could adapt the biology to match their different amino acid chains. We translated the requests, but never worked on the food problem."

"We invited them here, and when they showed up, we captured them," Chamuel said and shook her head. "Shooting down the ship was all on Russia, though. Our intel didn't think they had a directed energy weapon."

"So, what about Strain Delta?" Azrael asked, continuing his string of uncharacteristic loquaciousness. "You think it was a response to the Russian attack?"

"I don't know," Chamuel admitted. "I originally thought it could have been, but I really don't know. We understand so little about the Vulpes, I can't make predictions. All I've been doing is guessing how things proceeded afterward." She'd predicted the collapse of global society not long after the first CDC data came in and Project Genesis was activated. The fallback to save humanity. Some fallback. Only weeks into the catastrophe, and they were down to their last resources and final contingency base.

Azrael turned to leave.

"You're almost done?" she asked him.

"Just about," he replied. "There's a few interesting artifacts I haven't gone through yet. They're all of alien origin, so until Jophiel gives me a translation matrix, I can't tell what they're for. Nobody could figure them out in the 1950s, which is why they were all sealed away." He left without saying goodbye, which was his way.

Chamuel returned her attention to the screens. How would things have turned out if their government hadn't been so effective at keeping secrets? All the information, knowledge of the Vulpes, the alien technology, unknown secrets, all filed away and forgotten. Until it was too late to be of any advantage.

"If people knew how much of our tech is based on the few goodies the Vulpes gave us..." she said and sipped her Darjeeling tea.

During her time working for the NSA, where she'd been recruited as a member of the Heptagon inside Genesis, she found out just how much their government watched itself. Each agency spied on the others and their supposedly elected leaders. Nobody directed their resources inward to figure out what sort of old secrets were outside their own views.

Before she became Chamuel, as a younger woman, she'd seen *Raiders of the Lost Ark*. The story took place before WWII, during the tension of a building conflict. At the end, the ark is boxed up and put in a vast warehouse full of other unknown, world-shattering mysteries. Then she joined project Genesis as an associate researcher. She hadn't known 1/100$^{th}$ of what she knew now as a member of the Heptagon. But even then, she knew the warehouse existed, though it wasn't quite as simple as the one shown in the movie.

Over her time with Project Genesis she'd been to three warehouses in the United States. After joining the Heptagon as Chamuel, she'd learned there were 13 of them. She also knew other governments, big and small, had dozens more. The lifeblood of a nation was secrets, and the United States had gotten very good at keeping them. They were so good, they'd probably forgotten more than they remembered. *Apparently, they weren't as good as the Soviet Union, though.*

The directed energy weapon had been an unfortunate surprise. When the Vulples' ship came around the moon and tried to communicate, it had taken long days for anyone to realize what was happening, and more for the US's glacially moving intelligence agencies to understand. Eventually, they activated Project Genesis and initiated contact.

After seeing someone on an east coast weather satellite, Chamuel called up some data from the NRO, the National Reconnaissance Office. The delay in response was appreciable, making her narrow her eyes in consternation. Ever since Gabriel had killed the civilian internet and military MILSATCOMs, her connectivity had slowed. She'd estimated a 29% decrease in throughput, and it had ended up being 22%. Lately, it was down to a 33% loss. She pulled up one of her files on expected orbital asset degradation to correlate the decrease.

A few minutes later, she was still investigating the anomalous amount of throughput degradation. When Michael had her look into something, her habit of chasing squirrels (as she called it) drove him mad. It was one of the ways she found things other analysts didn't. She let her mind take her wherever it wished. Those squirrels led her to conclusions others would never find. It was a trait of her particular flavor of Asperger's, and it suited her line of work.

The answer appeared to be a missing telecom satellite which had been carrying some of her data. Only a single channel remained after the computer virus shut down the satellites, so she'd shared her data over dozens of different satellites. A monitor showed the typical mission control display with the missing satellite's orbit. A flashing, miniature explosion showed where it was when it experienced LOS, or loss of signal.

Chamuel stared at the location for a long time. In the dark recesses of her mind, connections came together. She pulled the satellite data log to verify when it went offline. It hadn't faded, it just stopped. The satellite was a relatively low altitude one, part of a special series of telecoms with limited use. It rode in a 655 km sun-synchronous orbit. Or at least it had, until it appeared to *hit* something. Something in orbit a few hundred miles west of the southern California coast.

She ran back the video of the last satellite passes over the Pacific coast. There were no NRO birds due for hours. The best weather satellites didn't have the resolution. However, a civilian imaging satellite used by a map company had done a California pass minutes earlier. It was supposed to stop recording shortly after passing over the ocean, but it was worth a look. Like everything else, it took longer than she would have liked for the imagery to come up.

The picture dominated one of her monitors when it arrived, so Chamuel could enhance and review it. She'd been imaging the so called "Flotilla" since it was first identified as a group of survivors. When the military arrived, she'd flagged it for Michael as a development to be observed. Because of the shortage of orbital assets, the pictures were from different angles, altitudes, and resolutions. But she had programs that would compensate for incomplete or badly angled data. The far west extreme of the new image was the target area.

Chamuel turned the newest image over to the processing software and went back to the data slowdown. Before long, another frame was added to the time lapse view of the Flotilla. Flipping between views revealed exactly what she was afraid of. The distinctive form of a supercarrier had first appeared a day ago, then it had disappeared, and now it was back. It simply was not possible. A 100,000-ton ship couldn't move far enough on her view to disappear and reappear in just a few hours.

She did something she rarely did; she gave the image gallery her full attention. Her screens were dominated by pictures from all over the planet. In minutes, she'd filtered the images to North America. Again, she lamented the lack of domestic surveillance capabilities. Maybe she'd ask Gabriel about 'borrowing' Russian assets? A half hour passed, and she had dozens of suspicious images, and a single damning one. She touched the intercom control on her mobility chair.

"Michael, Chamuel."

"Go ahead."

"We need a meeting."

"I'm talking with the facility manager at San Nicolas about our arrival. Can't it wait?"

"No," she said.

There was a slight pause before Michael replied. "Okay, give me five minutes."

As usual, Chamuel didn't travel to the conference room. The former NOAA ship didn't have any ramps for her chair, so she attended virtually and listened while Michael explained that Chamuel had called the impromptu meeting. "I assume this is important?" he asked as he finished and looked at her monitor/camera.

"Yes," she said. "The last 24 hours have seen a number of developments." She remotely accessed the conference room screen and began her slide show. *Even at the end of the world, Powerpoint dominates.* "As you know, our parent organization used the alien technology gifted to us by the Vulpes on their first visit to facilitate a considerable technological advancement period leading to our space program, the information age, and medical innovations, some of which were never released to the public.

"We've carefully monitored how the technological 'gifts' from out of town affected planetary technological development." She could hear several of her fellow Heptagon members chuckle. "Possible spin offs and unexpected side effects are the prime reasons the high-end medical treatments were not released. I consider this a mistake."

"Your position on this is well known and debated," Michael interjected.

Before she'd been made part of the Heptagon, Chamuel had been confined to a full mobility chair and could only control it with puffs of air. She had been born with part of her spine outside her body, and the medical treatments she was talking about had given her the use of both arms, improved vocal capabilities, and even movement in her legs. The miracles she'd experienced were something she'd lobbied to make available to others a hundred times.

She made a face but continued, "As I was saying, we've always monitored for signs of unexplained technological jumps. On the screen, you see a United States supercarrier, the USS *Gerald R. Ford.* This carrier is part of a group labeled the 'Flotilla' and is where the prisoner Lieutenant JG Grange came from. We know this grouping wasn't planned but resulted from the ships' proximity to San Diego. It, in and of itself, was not a concern of ours until the president came on site."

"I still think we should have shot her plane down," Michael said.

"I advised against it, and as you see, the situation resolved itself. I never ascertained if the collision was an accident or not. Either way, the president and her surviving cabinet members were all killed. With

NASA and CDC personnel being the only serious concerns, I reduced surveillance on the Flotilla. This proved to be a mistake."

"Chamuel made a mistake?" Jophiel scoffed. "I need to make a note of this on my calendar." Of the Heptagon, Jophiel liked Chamuel the least.

*You'd think with only three women, I'd get a little comradery from her.* "As I was saying, this was a mistake. You'll observe, on this frame, the *Gerald R. Ford* is more or less in the center of the Flotilla. In the next frame, the carrier is gone, and two small ships are sinking. We'll finish with the final frame in which the carrier is back. However, as you can see, the C-17 on the deck is gone."

"I fail to see why a ship sailing around matters to us," Raphael snapped. "I was in the middle of a cellular analysis run on the Vulpes' immune system."

"Why don't you all shut the fuck up and let her explain?"

They all looked at Azrael in surprise, even Michael. You usually needed to ask Azrael a pointed question to get any kind of a response. Between his earlier conversation with her and this outburst, Chamuel was at a loss to explain the change in the normally quiet man's behavior. Michael chuckled and gestured for her to continue.

"As Raphael said, this, by itself, doesn't mean much. However, a satellite also went missing last night—directly above San Diego. While I have no visual evidence, I'm forced to conclude someone in the Flotilla has salvaged one or more alien escape pods, and to make matters worse, figured out how to use the drives."

"How could they manage that?" Gabriel asked. "There might be some tech-oriented people there, but the majority of those people come from various freighters, pleasure craft, and military ships. Certainly no scientists."

"All except this ship," Chamuel said and called up a more detailed orbital picture of the OOE mobile launch ship. "This is the mobile launch ship that was customized by Jeremiah Osborne for his Oceanic Orbital Enterprises."

"A goddamned rocket scientist," Michael spat. "Great. Are you sure they figured it out?"

"I dug into recorded intel while I waited for this meeting," Chamuel said. "A couple weeks before Strain Delta went global, there was an emailed offer from Theodore Alphonse Bennitti III, a director at NASA, to Jeremiah Osborne. We knew NASA had noticed the escape pods entering the atmosphere despite our covering up the Russian shootdown of the ship we later captured. However, the unusual reentry paths made it unlikely they'd find any of them before the plague made the issue moot.

"After going over email communications from Mr. Osborne, I found this." She changed the display to a slideshow of an excavation revealing one of the alien escape pods, as well as a dead Vulpes. "He took the escape pod back to his facilities in San Diego. He sent several more requests to Director Bennitti for guidance, which were never answered, because everything was falling apart by then.

"In the end, the conclusion is pretty obvious. Jeremiah Osborne, with a well-skilled team of aerospace engineers and scientists, figured out how to open the pod and remove its redundant drives. He appears to have shared the information with the military and might well have constructed more than one working drive adaptation."

"Son of a bitch," Michael snarled. "Why didn't you see this?"

"Do you remember my initial report after the Russians started this dance?" she asked. "I said there was a 10-12% chance someone on the planet would figure out the alien drives." She shrugged. "You roll the dice enough times, you lose."

"Just down the road from our fallback base?" Michael asked. "That's bad luck."

"Pretty bad," Chamuel agreed.

"What's the chance they've figured out the escape pod's communications?" Gabriel asked, her eyes sharp and inquisitive.

She might be the only one in the group Chamuel considered a friend, though she was now reconsidering her position with Azrael. "We know there are six pods less than 500 miles from the Flotilla. If you recall, I considered the possibility that this was the reason the coast guard ship was in the Columbia River."

"We'd already recovered the local pod," Michael reminded her.

"I am aware; however, the ship was already heading north before we recovered it. In answer to your question, I'd say the odds are even, or maybe a bit in their favor."

Everyone was silent for a moment as they let Michael think. Chamuel was the Heptagon's tactical genius. She analyzed everything she saw and provided it to the team. It had been Michael's decision to let Gabriel unleash her virus on the world's data networks. Since the Strain Delta plague was already wreaking havoc, shutting down the data networks merely decreased the chances of anyone getting ahold of the alien tech, which Chamuel calculated would have made matters worse. Sure, it was a cold-blooded decision which ultimately cost more lives. However, it increased the species' chances of survival by allowing Project Genesis and the Heptagon time to work on the problem. She wondered if Michael was working on the problem or the situation.

*Oh, what a tangled web we weave,* Chamuel thought. Ultimately, who was worse? Chamuel for saying more people needed to die for the human race to survive, or Michael for actually pulling the trigger. *Whatever helps you sleep at night, I guess.*

"Okay," Michael said eventually, "I've made up my mind about this Flotilla. I'm contacting San Nicolas and telling them to neutralize it."

"All of it?" Chamuel asked. "Or a surgical strike on OOE?"

"What are the odds on each?"

Chamuel closed her eyes and let the factors roll through her mind. "Looks like a 40% chance of getting all the alien tech and those who understand if we target just the OOE ship. There's a 77% chance if we target OOE and the military, and an 82% chance if we target them all."

"All it is, then," Michael said. "Are we done?"

"What about Grange?" Jophiel asked. The elderly linguist had been unhappy about being asked to interrogate their prisoner, and she was obviously hoping this would get her out of the job.

"Run at least one more session," Michael said. Jophiel frowned. "Gear the inquiry toward seeing if our guest knew about their discovery of the alien tech. If she doesn't know anything, euthanize her."

"Very well," Jophiel said.

In Michael's standard, no-pleasantries fashion, the meeting was over. Chamuel looked away from the blank conference screen and back at her satellite image collection. She'd renewed her interest in the NASA fleet, which was still in the Gulf of Nicoya near Costa Rica. It was just sitting there, and she couldn't get any good views. *What is happening there?* Her complex mind estimated a 14% chance the military, with their NASA cargo, had surrendered control to the Russians and a 23% chance it was the other way around. However, she also calculated a 5% chance some sort of agreement had been reached. The probability grew every hour, so she kept a careful watch. An old US spy satellite would pass over later in the afternoon, then she'd know more.

A picture drew her attention. It was an image she hadn't shared because it had her mystified. Chamuel didn't like being mystified. A roughly round shadow obscured part of Amarillo, Texas, like a massive translucent cloud. It just hung there and hadn't moved for hours. As she did with Costa Rica, she only had weather satellite images, and nothing would be in view for more than a day.

She leaned closer to examine it. The best image processing software only managed to reveal a weird series of geometric lines, somehow reminding her of an integrated circuit. She chewed her lower lip and stared. *What the hell is that thing?* The computer had no answer.

* * *

**Shangri-La**
**Amarillo, TX**

"You definitely have a concussion," Dr. Clay said as she examined the x-ray on the back-lit box. Modern X-rays were computer images. Shangri-La's salvage team had found a FEMA lot shortly after getting the beast into the air. Among the dozens of residential trailers and truckloads of MREs, they found the old medical trailer, complete with a film X-ray machine and a stash of film. "I never thought I'd use an old model like this again," the doctor said, shaking her head.

"I've had worse injuries," Cobb replied. The doctor looked at him skeptically. "IEDs in the Stan. You'd be supri—OUCH!"

"Sorry," the teenager said. He was stitching the three-inch-long gouge on Cobb's head, put there by former Private Groves' pistol. He was the doctor's son, or at least Cobb thought he was.

"You got some painkillers?" Cobb asked. He looked at his *really* worn camo fatigues. He could add a nice splash of blood down one collar to the list of various stains.

"You should lie down for a day."

"Not right now," he said. She gave him the same skeptical look.

The door opened, and a Marine stuck his head in. "You okay, sir?"

"Fine, son," Cobb assured him. The young Marine nodded and disappeared. In the hours since the attempted coup, Cobb hadn't been more than a dozen feet from at least two soldiers. The Marines and army seemed to have taken Groves' attempt personally.

Inside the rear of the medical trailer were a dozen beds, each with a screen which could be pulled closed for privacy. Master Sergeant Schardt was behind one of the screens, sedated, hooked up to a life-sign monitor that was beeping away. Cobb had waited in the exam area for three hours while the doctor operated on Schardt. He'd been shot three times and was one tough son of a bitch. He complained the whole time he was carried to the medical trailer and didn't stop until she put him under.

"Anything new on the master sergeant?" he asked.

She didn't look away from the x-ray. "He's fine," she said. "I already told you, the bullet missed his bowel. There's no risk of septic shock." She walked over to a big, stainless-steel, floor-to-ceiling cabinet. It had been secured by several big locks which had all been drilled out. From the cabinet, she took out a handful of paper, single-use pill pouches. When she brought them to him, she leaned in and looked at the stitches with a critical eye. "Good job," she told the boy who was trimming the extra line. He grinned. "Only one package of two pills every four hours."

"Sure thing, Doc," he said, ripping open a package and dry swallowing the two pills inside. The paper was embossed with the FEMA logo and said Oxycodone—50 mg. *Yeah, the good stuff!* "I'll take it easy."

"No, you won't," she said and left. There were at least four people waiting on flimsy folding chairs in the waiting area. One middle aged woman was staring at the bloody smears on the floor with some alarm. No one had had the time to clean them up after Schardt was brought in. There were also six bodies covered with tarps behind the trailer.

The young assistant quickly wrapped a bandage around his head. Cobb tested it, then smiled at the kid who popped off a salute. Cobb smiled and saluted the kid back, then headed to the door. Outside, he found most of the surviving soldiers waiting for him.

Sergeant Zim stood at the front of the group. "Sorry, Colonel, I should have stopped you."

"There was no way you could have known the lengths Groves would go to," Cobb said. Zim had sat with him while Schardt was in surgery, the two going over what had happened. They'd grabbed guns and gear to hurry after him, only collecting Tango because the young Marine was coming to talk to them anyway.

"If we had, we'd have shot the psycho bitch days ago."

Cobb looked across the assembled soldiers and saw anger, regret, and grim determination. He knew they needed to hear something. "What's happened is over with," he said. "God knows, if the chain of command still existed, there'd be months of inquiries, court cases, you name it. As it is, we're through."

"What about Private Miller?" asked Corporal Tango who wasn't out of his gear and hadn't been seen by the doc yet. He was bare chested, a huge blue-black bruise growing on his abdomen.

They'd locked Miller in an equipment trailer while Schardt was tended to. Cobb had had to send them back to make sure it wasn't an airtight trailer. They'd all wanted to throw him overboard and feed him to the zombies. Cobb had had to remind them that doing so was no better than what Groves had planned for him.

"For now, he stays in custody. Zim, detail a squad to establish a detention area for the long term."

Zim nodded. Cobb could tell he was on the side of those who wanted to feed Miller to the infected. He hoped his feelings didn't become a problem.

"Changes," Cobb said. "From now on, all soldiers are to be armed at all times. No questions asked. Sidearm minimum, with four extra magazines each. I also want everyone to have a go-bag next to their bunk. Body armor, if you have it, and a radio. Zim will work with our supply people to make this happen. Those of you who have not qualified with a pistol recently will need to do so.

"Make no mistake, we're all sworn members of the United States Armed Forces. I don't care if you signed up a week before the plague or 20 years before. I left after my 20, more than a few years ago, but here I stand. We're in it for the duration. Look around you when you leave this meeting; these people need us. We're going to help. It's what we do."

They all looked at him for a second, then came to attention. Every man and woman saluted him and held it. He gladly returned the respect.

"Oorah!" the Marines barked.

"Hooah!" the army replied.

"Hooyah!" called the navy. The air force just stood respectfully. Cobb saw the army and Marines exchange grins, and he was glad they didn't take the interservice rivalry too far. Applause followed.

Cobb took Zim aside. "We need to talk to Governor Taylor."

"I guessed you'd be wanting to do that," Zim said.

Tango walked over, pulling a T-shirt over his still growing bruise. "You grunts aren't going anywhere without me."

"Corporal, you need to report to the doctor," Cobb said.

"She's busy, Colonel." Cobb narrowed his eyes. "I'll see her today, I promise, sir."

Cobb didn't believe him in the least. Of course, after his own insurrection against the good doctor, he was on shaky ground. If he ordered the corporal to see the doctor, she'd likely rat him out. He frowned, and in the long tradition of a soldier getting their way against the better judgement of their superior officer, Tango knew right away he'd won.

A huge grin crossed his face, and he walked over to the other Marines, talked to them for a second, then came back with a carbine and some fresh magazines that he stuffed into his freshly donned webgear.

"We're not going to fight," Cobb said.

"Just like we didn't with Private Groves?" the Marine asked.

Cobb snorted, then nodded. Zim handed Cobb his rifle and more mags. Okay, he saw how it worked. He'd also noticed everyone now referred to Groves as a private. Word had gotten around quickly. Once he'd checked his gear, he nodded. "Okay, let's go."

Shangri-La's headquarters was another trailer. This one, though, was a fancy, modern fifth wheel. The brand was "Mobil Suites", and it was painted gold and white. What's more, it had multiple slide out rooms and even a small 2nd floor which was raised up to give a view!

A trailer adjacent to it was immediately recognizable as a mobile army comms shack. Modular and portable, you could load it onto a truck or even a Humvee. He suspected he'd found Bisdorf's home while he was in Shangri-La. The profusion of antennas was enough to give it away. As they walked, he saw the heavyset man on the roof adjusting one of the antennas. Bisdorf spotted Cobb and started to wave, then he saw Zim and Tango marching alongside and froze.

He scrambled toward the ladder leaning against his trailer, and Cobb wondered if they were about to get into another firefight. They stopped and waited for the older man to carefully make his way to the ground. As Bisdorf hustled toward them, he looked nervously over his shoulder toward the command trailer.

"I can't believe you're alive," he said.

"Paul," Cobb said, holding up a hand to stop him. "What the fuck is going on?"

"I didn't have anything to do with it."

"With what, Paul?" Cobb demanded. The other man looked down, and suddenly the pieces clicked into place. "Oh, fuck me. She did it all, didn't she?"

"What?" Zim asked. "Who did what?"

"The governor sent us down there to die." Bisdorf was shaking his head, tears coursing down his cheeks. "She planned on our not making it back. Probably hoped the master sergeant would go all John Wayne when we got in the shit and come down to help, then she'd make it a clean sweep."

"Now?" Tango asked, knife-handing at Bisdorf. "With this fucker?"

"No, he wasn't even there." Cobb looked at the man. "What's she got on you, your wife?"

"My daughter," Bisdorf sobbed.

"Quickly tell me what happened." Cobb didn't notice Tango talking into a mic.

"When we found her, she had a dozen state police with her. She kind of insinuated her way into control. Nobody wanted it, but she had the air of authority. She hadn't been here a day before she had her cop buddies scoping out the place. A few days ago, they moved. They kidnapped our family members—my daughter, Clark's husband, and Hans Daimler's grandchildren. Staff Sergeant Groves fell in with her right away."

"The man from her group who went down with us wasn't accidental, was it?"

"No," Bisdorf said. "He was going to make sure you, Tango, and Zim got infected. He had syringes with infected blood."

"Mutherfucker," Tango hissed.

"You were the fly in the ointment. She needed time to get the military on her side."

"Paul," Cobb said. "You do know, if she'd succeeded, you guys would probably have been next?"

"It's my daughter," he sobbed.

"I get it. I don't suppose the people I came in with were actually in quarantine?"

"No," Bisdorf confirmed. "They're hostages with the rest. Amelia and her Angels are charged with caring for the hostages."

"She's in on it too?" Tango asked, shaking his head.

"Yes, she was with FEMA. She helped us originally, but when the governor came it all changed. They knew each other from before."

"I'm sorry; we never realized," Zim said.

Cobb patted the sergeant on the shoulder. "You had more than enough to do without watching them." He looked back at Bisdorf. "What were you doing with the antenna?"

"After you mentioned your people went west, I started looking for any signs of them. Taylor told me not to, but I didn't care."

"Did you find them?" he asked, feeling a thrill of excitement.

"I think so."

*Later*, he told himself. *First things first.* "What do you want us to do?"

"Can you help?" he asked. "*Will* you help?"

"Of course, we'll help," Zim said. "Damnit, why didn't you say something?"

"Would you if it was your family?" Cobb asked.

"Yeah, of course!" Bisdorf gave the sergeant a baleful stare. "Maybe. Fuck, I don't know."

Cobb backed a few feet away from the man, and his NCOs followed. He looked at the two and spoke. "What do you men think?" The looks on their combat weary faces said it all. He faced Tango. "Okay, get Privates Port and Betts up and have them bring their toys. I have a job for them. You too." Tango's tired grin became feral.

***

Lieutenant Governor Taylor looked up as the door opened. She didn't seem at all surprised to see Cobb come in. The two police officers who always seemed to be near her immediately came to full alert as he entered. The governor was sitting in a big, plush office chair behind a desk which would have been more at home in her old office than in a fifth wheel trailer. They were floating hundreds of feet above Amarillo, so it was a strange tableau indeed.

Taylor blinked twice as she looked him over—his disheveled appearance, his M-4 hanging on a 1-point harness from his web gear, his side arm and magazines. She paused when she noticed the blood-stained garments and the bandage around his head. "Ah wasn't expecting you, Colonel Pendleton."

"No, I expect you weren't." The view from the elevated level of the fifth wheel was impressive. The edge of Shangri-La was quite close, and the window was higher than the nearest trailer.

"What was all the shooting about?" Taylor asked.

"You politicians," Cobb said and laughed. He shook his head and sighed.

"Ahm afraid I don't know what y'all are talking about."

Cobb finished giving the room a once over, then moved to the side where a plush, leather chair rested and plopped down in it. Taylor's eyes narrowed, no doubt because it was real leather and his uniform was covered in real blood. The two officers looked from him to Taylor for guidance. She shook her head, and they relaxed slightly.

"You've got yourself quite a setup here," Cobb said. He removed a stick of chewing gum from his pocket, popped it in his mouth, and dropped the wrapper on the floor. This time, Taylor visibly scowled. "I mean, from Lieutenant Governor, an arguably less than useless job in Texas, to emperor. You've got the elevated house; all you need is to put on a chainmail dress and change Amarillo's name to Barter Town."

"Ah don't think that's necessary."

"Bless your heart," Cobb said. Taylor did a doubletake, and he smiled hugely. "You know, I was willing to ignore everything, until you decided I was an obstacle to your dictatorial plans."

"Maybe y'all forget you work for me, Colonel. You swore to do what elected leaders say."

"No, I work for the US Government. My oath of office is very specific, Governor. I do solemnly swear that I will support and defend the Constitution of the United States against all enemies, foreign and domestic; that I will bear true faith and allegiance to the same; that I take this obligation freely, without any mental reservation or purpose of evasion; and that I will well and faithfully discharge the duties of the office on which I am about to enter. So help me God. Nothing in there talks about working for you. You see, you think I took the same oath as the former Private Groves, which included obeying the governor of her state."

"Former? What did ya do, demote her?"

"You could say that," Cobb said. "If you consider being shot between the eyes demoted."

"What?" Taylor blurted, the bullshit, smiling façade finally failing.

"Yeah, you see, that is the cost of treason." As he said the last, he leaned forward and stared the governor right in the eye. He put on his best poker face and chewed his gum. Juicy Fruit wasn't his favorite, but it was all Tango had. From Cobb's experience, Tango was a typical Marine—tough as nails, gung-ho as fuck, and nutty as squirrel shit. "Especially ones who try to kill officers on the orders of wannabe tyrants."

"I was gonna try and talk sense with y'all," Taylor said, visibly getting herself under control. "But I can see y'all are just a fuckin' boy scout. Right, Colonel, a boy scout?" Cobb chewed and watched her. "Since y'all are a boy scout, I'll have to use it to ma' advantage."

Cobb leaned back in the chair and glanced at his watch as casually as he could. Unfortunately, Taylor noticed. However, she jumped to the wrong conclusion.

"You a little worried about comin' here and startin' shit?"

"Huh?" Cobb looked toward the door. The two state troopers were looking even more surly. In fact, he thought they looked positively murderous. Good. "You mean your two gorillas? It would take more than a couple pigs like them to make me nervous."

"Mutherfucker," the bigger of the two troopers snarled and took a step forward.

"Easy, Franks," Taylor said.

"Yeah, easy Franks, don't want to strain your brain by thinking." Cobb looked again and saw the veins standing out on the man's neck. *He is a big fucker.* "You were saying, Taylor?"

"Governor Taylor," she reminded him. Cobb kept up the deadpan and didn't respond. "I was sayin', since y'all are a boy scout, if ya' don't calm down, it might not be you who suffers."

He looked at his watch again and nodded.

"Y'all got a date?"

"No, I've been delaying," he said. She started to say something but stopped, her mouth hanging comically open. "You say being a boy scout is predictable? You're right. I wanted to make sure the innocents you were holding hostage were safe." The sounds of gunfire echoed across Shangri-La, and Cobb grinned widely.

Tango and Zim hadn't liked the idea of letting Cobb go into the lion's den by himself. However, he hadn't known for sure whether Taylor's toadies had seen them talking to Bisdorf. Once they learned about the hostages, they hadn't had time to recon or hope for a more favorable scenario. Decisive action was required. Decisive action which wouldn't initiate a firefight. There were more than a few Marines and soldiers who'd been to Afghanistan. Dynamic entry was a technique they'd trained for and done.

The shooting only lasted a few seconds. By the time Taylor thought to grab her radio and start yelling at her men, it was over. She began calling people by name, without response. After the fourth try, she looked at Cobb, her eyes wide in shock.

The sound of a mic clicking three times came from the radio hidden in his breast pocket. The all clear call. Mission accomplished. No complications. He smiled and nodded, letting his breath out slowly.

"You son of a bitch," Taylor said. "This ain't over!"

"We got Amelia and her Angels too. Cleaned them all up."

"What do we do, Boss?" Franks asked. Taylor started laughing. Her whole body shook, and tears rolled down her cheeks.

Cobb turned the chair to get a better view of the two troopers. They were looking from their boss, who was laughing hysterically, to Cobb, then at each other. Clearly, they were confused about what to do. He began to wonder if they were really cops at all.

"Boss?" Franks asked again.

She shook her head and wiped her eyes as she mostly stopped laughing. "What are you two waiting for? Kill him."

Franks and his partner unholstered their sidearms.

"Not here, you idiots. You think I want blood on my carpets?"

Still confused, they hesitated a moment before re-holstering their weapons. "Get up," Franks ordered him.

"Fuck off," Cobb replied, staring the man down. They hesitated. "Make me."

"Just get him out of here," Taylor snarled.

Franks nodded, and the two cops moved over, one on either side of Cobb.

"This is your last chance," he said to them.

"Or what, big army man?" Franks asked.

"Grab me and find out."

The other cop finally spoke. "To hell with this," he said and grabbed Cobb by one arm. Franks grabbed the other. Cobb raised his arms, almost as if he were going to help them get a better grip, then he covered his face with his hands.

"He's gonna cry," Franks said. They both started to laugh. Their mirth was suddenly cut short as two 7.62mm bullets passed through the big picture window, then through their heads. They fell limply to the floor where they proceeded to ruin Governor Taylor's nice carpets.

Taylor screamed, dove out of her chair, and hid behind her desk. She peeked around the corner and gawked at the two former state patrol officers. Franks' foot spasmed, beating a staccato rhythm on the floor for a few seconds as the rest of his body caught up with the news he was dead.

Cobb stood and waved. The two Marine snipers were about 250 yards away on one of Shangri-La's cranes. He could just make out Port's and Betts' M40A3 bolt action sniper rifles, their scopes catching the morning sunlight. Both men waved in reply, but stayed in position, ready to fire again. One shot, one kill. Marine snipers were among the best in the world, and using them was about the only reason Tango had let Cobb go through with his crazy plan.

"Oh God, oh God, oh God!"

*Right, one more loose end to tie up.* "Governor Taylor, you want to come out, please?"

"Y'all just killed two police officers!" she screamed. "A'll have you hanged, boy!"

It sounded like she was messing with the drawers to her desk. He suspected he knew what she was doing. "I didn't kill anyone. US Marines fired the shots. They were under specific orders to only fire if someone acted violently against me or tried to remove me from this office." Cobb kicked Franks' boot. The former cop didn't respond. "In a way, you killed them."

"You son of a bitch!"

"Oh, no doubt about it. My mom would have slapped the blonde off a woman like you." He moved sideways, closer to her desk, but kept it between him and the window. "I'm going to make you the same offer I made them. This is your last chance."

She stood up, a small pistol in her hand. He guessed it was either a .32 ACP or a .380 auto. Nickel finish—no surprise there. "No, this is y'all's last chance," she said. "You don't run for office in Texas and not know how'ta shoot, boy! Now you turn around, and I'm gonna hold this here pistol to your head while we get to one'a them sky-barges."

"Who's going to fly it?" he asked, not moving.

"Easy, Daimler will meet us there."

"Daimler? Really?"

"Bet yo' ass! He's been real helpful, giving me inside scoops on who's who since I got here. All he wanted was a piece o' da' pie. I plan ahead. We'll get on the barge, scoot on outta here. Winner, winner, chicken dinner. I knew these were a buncha' morons when I arrived. Computer geeks, CB talkers, rough necks. It was easy manipulating the bunch."

"We've freed his granddaughter," Cobb said.

"Dumb fucka, he ain't got no granbaby. He's worked with me all along."

"Really?" He spoke to his breast pocket. "You get that, Zim?"

"Yes sir, Colonel. I have a squad scooping him up right now." Taylor looked horrified. "Thank the governor for the tip."

"We've recorded everything you said, just in case we have to explain to someone later. Now, you want to give me the gun?"

She was looking around, only half paying attention to him. She looked like a cornered deer. Taylor looked at the dead cops and the window, working the angle. After a second, she smiled. "You shoulda' brought your own gun, Colonel. Your snipers can't hit me here."

"Just give me the gun, Governor," he implored her. "It's not too late."

"Oh, I'm afraid it is. I ain't going to no trial." She raised the gun to eye level and sighted. "Bah-bah, boy scout."

The window being punched by another round was accentuated by the front part of her face exploding outward. It wasn't the same clean kill as her two cops. Tango had placed himself perpendicular to Ports and Betts. The angle he had on Taylor wasn't perfect; he could only see the front half of her body. In typical Marine sniper fashion, he'd gone for the head shot.

Taylor made a gurgling sound followed by a scream. The gun hit the carpeted floor and bounced. She put her hands to what remained of her face. Blood pumped over her hands and down her shirt. Neither eye remained in place, so Cobb didn't know if she could see him. He shook his head at the waste.

Taylor staggered forward, and another bullet took the top of her head off, ending her suffering and her life. The body fell over the ornate desk and slowly slid to the floor, leaving behind it a thick smear of bright red blood and brains.

"Clean kill on the second shot," he told Tango through the radio.

"Sorry for the sloppy first round," the corporal replied, "sir."

"You earned your marksmanship badge, Corporal." Cobb walked over and picked up the gun. It was a .25ACP. Odds were, if she'd shot him with it, the bullet wouldn't have penetrated his Kevlar. "I'm promoting you to sergeant, by the way."

"Not sure if you can do that, Colonel."

"Who's going to complain?"

"You have a point, sir."

"Zim, do they have a meeting place?"

"Yes, Colonel. It's at the landing area for the barges."

"Pass the word. I want to see everyone there in four hours. Have whoever's flying this thing increase the altitude to a mile or so and get them to attend too. It's time we have a talk. First, I want a shower and a nap." *I've had a hell of a day.*

* * *

**Classified Task Force**
**Gulf of Farallones, California**

Jophiel took the headset off and dropped it on a cradle in disgust. One of the technicians yelped in alarm, and she stared daggers at the man, who looked away. "What the hell is wrong with this?" she demanded.

Behind the tech, a dozen more were using state-of-the-art laptops to analyze the CVR. A supercomputer was needed to turn neuro-stimulus into data which could be interpreted by another human. CVR—cognitive VR—was first tested two years ago, at which point the design was acquired by Project Genesis and remade into the device they now used. Not only could a user see what another was dreaming, they could enter those dreams and even manipulate the environment.

They'd hoped to use it with the first visitors last year, only it hadn't worked. "Brains are too alien," the Genesis scientists said, and they abandoned the attempt. However, their base ship, the *Ark*, still had the equipment. It proved to be a useful interrogation tool. Even if it didn't function on the aliens, it did on their fellow humans. This was the first time it had failed to work.

"We don't know, Ms. Jophiel," the head scientist said, looking confused and alarmed. Ever since Strain Delta had gotten free and caused the collapse of society, the seven members of the Heptagon, who only went by code names, had gained enormous power. There was no more oversight. There were no more senators or presidents to say what they could or couldn't do. Genesis military assets answered only to them. Michael ruled the group with an iron hand. Crossing him could result in expulsion into a zombie-plagued hellscape.

"Your answer isn't acceptable," Jophiel said in a cool voice. "Michael wants the last session completed so this patient can be disposed of. You are keeping me from completing it."

"We aren't keeping you," the scientist complained.

Jophiel gestured at the useless headset. "I don't concur." She glanced at her watch, a century old heirloom which had belonged to her mother. "I have a language compilation to run and will be back in 90 minutes. If you don't have this infernal machine working by then, *you* can explain it to Michael."

The scientist sputtered and coughed, barely managing to stammer a promise that it would be working before Jophiel hobbled out of the room.

***

Grange opened her eyes. She was again in the crisp hospital bed in the pure white, luxurious hospital room. Only this time there were mirrors on the walls, the furniture was trimmed in gold, and there was an ornate chandelier in the middle of the room. It had reminded her of *2001: A Space Odyssey* before, but now the room was a dead ringer. It was disconcerting being inside a memory.

"Hello, Pearl."

She turned her head and saw Bowman from the movie standing there. He was even wearing the orange space suit costume. "What the hell?" she blurted. She knew he wasn't real, but seriously?

"Do I surprise you?" Bowman asked and changed into the old man, also from the movie. "How about this form?" the ancient man asked, his hands shaking.

"Fine," she said, "just don't turn into the big fetus."

The old man smiled thinly. "You can understand me?'

"Perfectly," she said. "What's going on?"

"We have a few minutes to talk, and I need your help."

"I'm in no position to help anyone," she said. "I'm in some kind of mind-fuck prison. This isn't real. It's like a dream I can't wake up from. I've been here before, but I can't remember how or when."

"This is a simulation, created by our captors to facilitate interrogation."

"How do you know?"

"Because they tried to use it on me."

"You said 'our captors.' Are you a prisoner too?"

"Yes."

"Who are you?" she asked.

"My name would be too difficult for you to say or think about. My title was First Scout."

"I don't understand what is going on," she said.

"They do not want you to understand," First Scout replied. "I am sad to say you are an unfortunate victim. An analogy in your language would be a pawn."

"That suggests I'm nothing in the grand scheme," she said.

The old man smiled sadly. "Even a pawn can win the game, but I can make you much more." The room seemed to shimmer like she was looking through a window that was being flexed by an invisible force. "We do not have much time."

"I don't understand why I'm here or what is happening."

The ancient head lowered slightly, and the man sighed. "I do not have time to explain. I can only say that I need your help. If you do help me, you will go from being a pawn to a knight."

"Knights are the most strategic piece in a game of chess," Grange said. Her father had taught her to play when he was home on leave from the Coast Guard. The game was horribly complicated for a six-year-old girl, yet she'd managed to become a fair player. As the years passed, she'd largely given it up. The memories and complexities remained. "What do you want me to do?"

"The organization that holds you is known as Project Genesis. To make a long story short, they invited me here. We needed help; help we believed your people could provide. We were met with hostility instead of friendship. Our ship was shot down. The result of those actions was the devastation wrought on your people.

"It is within my power to give you specific abilities with which you can undo some of the damage. Those abilities will, however, come at great cost."

"How great?" she asked.

He smiled sadly.

"I see. She looked down at her body and sighed. "I'm not healed, am I?"

He shook his head.

"What will happen if I agree?"

"Something wonderful," the giant, floating fetus said.

"God," Grange cringed, "I asked you not to do that."

The baby shrugged.

"Tell me what I have to do."

* * *

"What do you have?" the lead scientist asked.

"Something…" the tech said, then shook his head. "It's gone now."

"All systems are nominal," another tech said. "It's as if nothing was ever wrong."

The scientist shook his head and stared at the various computer readouts. Indeed, everything was in the green. "Ghost in the machine?" he wondered. Some computer artifact of the billion lines of code. A digital hiccup. Whatever it was, it was gone. Jophiel was due back in 30 minutes, which gave him just enough time to grab a sandwich. "We've got 20 minutes to get a bite and hit the bathroom," he said.

His staff smiled and nodded gratefully. In seconds, they were gone. The computers hummed and whirred in their absence. Then the computers flashed, code rewrote itself, alarms sounded and were quickly silenced. Less than 10 seconds later, all appeared normal.

Inside the hospital room, on the other side of the one-way glass, Lieutenant J.G. Grange's horribly burned face smiled slightly before returning to its formerly blank expression.

* * *

Michael walked along the bottom of the massive silver ship. He reached up, his fingers just touching the surface. It felt more like glass than metal. *Such amazing engineering.* It vaguely reminded him of the silvery ship from one of the *Star Wars* movies he'd seen in his previous life, back before he'd dedicated it to the Heptagon. Only this one was a long, flattened triangle, somewhat like an old Indian arrowhead.

The ship rested on a barge, one of the huge oceangoing ones they'd appropriated when evacuation of the Oregon compound became necessary. The sun glinted off its surface like a mirror. Tests showed it was more reflective than any mirror humanity could produce. Too bad the fucking Russians hadn't tried to shoot it down with a laser.

Michael reached the aft section and looked at the hole. The metallic surface was burned and melted in a circle that was roughly five meters across. At the edges, the metal was merely distorted, but it became more burned and rougher closer to the center. In the middle was a hole, and components were visible inside. Such a small damage point, if you considered that the ship was over 100 meters long and 30 meters wide. Physical penetration into the interior was not even a meter across.

"Piss poor ship," he said as he examined it.

"Can I help you, sir?"

Michael glanced at the soldier and shook his head. The man wore the black camo of Project Genesis' combat personnel. He was one of the men assigned to guard the alien ship. "It's all good. We'll be at San Nicolas in just a few hours."

"Excellent. It'll be good to get off the water."

Michael grunted and continued his wanderings. He was tired of micromanaging the other members of the Heptagon. But, if he didn't, they'd wander off and do whatever they wanted to. He should have only been concerned with defensive matters—protecting the United States from alien invasions and all the red, white, and blue shit. The Russians kinda fucked up his main goals. So he'd run the Heptagon and Project Genesis.

"Colonel Baker to Michael."

Michael touched his radio's ear bud. "Go ahead, Colonel."

"Both Hunters are up and running. We're going to need a couple hours to get the Wasps airborne."

"What's the issue?" Michael asked. He'd given the orders two hours ago; the attack should already be underway.

"We were attacked by infected animals. Seals of several types. We lost a tech who was working on the Hunter subs to a damned whale."

"No shit," Michael said. "Losses?"

"Three guards and the tech."

Michael scowled. They had plenty of guards, but the tech was a definite loss. He briefly considered taking the Flotilla. If they had people smart enough to figure out the alien drive technology, they could be an asset. He'd read up a bit on their mirrored internet records. Jeremiah Osborne was a brilliant, if flaky, aerospace engineer, and his company profile listed dozens of scientists and hundreds of technicians. It was likely that more than a few had survived Strain Delta.

He shook his head. No, that's a bad idea. Too much risk of the military intervening.

"Standing by, sir."

"Colonel, send the Hunters out. ETA to the target zone?"

"About an hour, sir."

"Very good. Have them do recon and verify there are no subs. Chamuel is certain there aren't, but she's not infallible."

"ROE, sir?"

"Rules of engagement are, at this point, fire if fired upon. If detected, avoid contact."

"Understood," Colonel Baker said and cut the connection.

Michael wanted things to move along. He didn't like incomplete tasks. At least Jophiel would soon be done with the troublesome Coastie. Considering how little useful intel he'd gotten out of her, he wished she hadn't been blown clear of her ship's explosion. Damn, she'd cost him a lot of assets too. He was beginning to look forward to seeing her tossed to the fish.

Thinking about fish reminded him of Colonel Baker's reports. He went back to the soldier guarding the alien ship. "Corporal?"

"Sir?"

"We've gotten reports of infected animal attacks at base." The man's eyes got wider. "Seals and whales. Get an additional detail up on deck. Orders are to fire on any approaching animals." He looked around the barge and frowned. It was low to the water. "You know what, make it two squads. Also, pass the word to the other ships."

"Sir!" the corporal replied and immediately turned to his radio.

*Delegate*, he reminded himself. Everything was well in hand. They'd be at the base by afternoon, then they could get the alien unloaded and begin interrogation. *Need to remember to praise Gabriel for getting the language licked and Azrael for finding the language records from the 1950s.* He was looking forward to a direct interrogation of the Vulpes once they got set up in San Nicolas.

As Michael watched, soldiers begin to show up on deck and set up defensive positions. He nodded and smiled. So far, so good. Now, if they could just deal with this Flotilla, it would be one less thing he had to worry about. Gunfire and the roar of a wounded seal from the other side of the ship confirmed his successful planning. What would Genesis do if he wasn't there?

* * *

**The Flotilla**
**150 Nautical Miles West of San Diego, CA**

Jeremiah was at the ASCE, American Society of Civil Engineers, awards ceremony. OOE was receiving the Columbia Medal for creating the *Azanti*, the first viable SSTO—a Single Stage to Orbit rocket plane. The audience was on its feet, clapping and whistling as Jeremiah took the stage. The society president was holding out the medal; it was only the second time it had ever been awarded.

He reached the president and shook his hand. "You deserve this," the man said, putting the medal in Jeremiah's hands and closing them around it.

"Thanks," Jeremiah said and turned to face the crowd. The medal clasped between his hands started to get hot. "Thank you everyone..." He paused. The medal was getting hotter still. "Ouch," he said and tried to drop it. He couldn't let go. "Hey, someone help!" The crowd got to their feet, applauding even louder. "This hurts!"

His hands were smoking. Jeremiah turned to the president. "Help!"

"You deserve this," the man said and laughed as Jeremiah's hands burst into agonizing flames. He screamed.

* * *

"Easy, Boss. Hold him while they give him some more morphine."

Jeremiah opened his eyes and tried to breathe through the agonizing, mind-shattering pain. Alex West was lying across him, which, for a second, made him think the pilot had succumbed to the plague and was eating him. But after a few more seconds of agony, he realized that, just like in his dream, all the pain was in his hands.

In the corner of his vision he saw a man in camo lean over and look at him. "Jesus, let me get an IV in."

"Just jab him," Alex said.

Jab me, what?!

The soldier looked pained but left for a second and returned. Jeremiah felt another pain in his arm. Relief flowed from the injection point outward. The pain didn't disappear, but he didn't care about it anymore. As the pain ceased its onslaught, he felt like he'd been submerged in the warm embrace of a goddess.

Slowly, over what felt like ages, the fog cleared from his mind. He was in the small infirmary on his ship. Alex West and Alison McDill looked like they'd been through the ringer. He could hear the soldier who'd given him the delicious drugs nearby, no doubt helping somebody else. *Why are we all in the infirmary?* he wondered. *Oh, the seals.*

"Is everyone okay?" he asked or, rather, croaked. His throat was dry. There was a water bottle on the table next to his bed. He reached for it with his right hand but found his arm wrapped with bandages to his elbow. "What the fuck happened to me?"

"You don't remember?" Alex asked.

"I remember the seals, and you fighting them." His brow furrowed as he tried to think. "But nothing after the elephant seal busted in." He held up his left hand. It was bandaged too, but only past the wrist.

Alex looked at Alison who looked back at him. They looked upset and uncertain. The situation wasn't helped by the drugs flowing through Jeremiah's body. He was forced to try and focus as a new fog grew, this one from the drugs. *Maybe a little less of the good stuff next time?* It reminded him of college and all the better parties.

"How is he?" Wade Watts had walked over, a pair of oversized sunglasses covering his eyes. The overweight computer geek looked at Alex and Alison who didn't reply. "You didn't tell him?"

"Not yet," Alex said.

"What happened to your eyes?" Jeremiah asked Wade.

"You gotta tell him," Wade insisted.

"Is it related to my hands?"

Neither of the other two said anything, so Wade did. "I found some high-voltage generators among the parts on the shelf. I won a science fair in high school by making a tesla coil. Accidentally set the gymnasium on fire, too. Anyway, the notes the military stole explained that you'd discovered the alien powerplant could channel energy, though your physicist didn't know what kind of power or how to control it." Wade laughed and shrugged. "The seal was kicking people's asses."

"Patty Mize is dead," Alison said. "Got knocked against a wall, broke her neck."

"Maria Merino also," Alex added. "She got cornered up on deck along with three ship's crew."

"Jesus," Jeremiah said.

"They were really hard to kill," Alex said. He sported a few bandages as well.

"So I slapped a sort of lightning gun together. It was all I could think of."

"Did it work?"

"Yeah!" Wade exclaimed with a huge smile.

"How did you direct it?"

"I used a taser, if you can believe it."

"Brilliant!"

"Yeah, except I missed. The seal came at me, and you helped me hold the gun. It was fucking huge. There wasn't time to reload the taser, but I think it was fragged anyway. So, when the elephant seal attacked, you grabbed the gun and rammed it in the seal's mouth."

Jeremiah looked at his hands. "Oh. How bad?"

"We only have a navy corpsman," Alex explained. "He restarted your heart."

"I was *dead*?"

Alex nodded. "For about five minutes. The aftermath of the fight was kind of crazy. He doesn't think you have any neurological damage, but your hands were…"

Alison touched his shoulder, and he looked at her. "There isn't much left of your hands. They're trying to get a surgeon."

"Can they repair them?"

"Jeremiah," Alex said, "there isn't enough left to fix."

Jeremiah stared at the bandages for a bit. The level of pain made more sense. They hadn't said it, but the surgeon was probably coming to amputate. *Well, I'm alive!* Considering several people were dead, he was lucky. His father had always taught him to find something to hold onto when things seemed the worst. "Hey," he said. They looked concerned. "Who's going to wipe my ass for me?"

The three stared at him, dumbfounded. Then Jeremiah chuckled, and they relaxed. "I'm the one with barbecued fingers," he said. "Don't be so damned morbid."

"I'm sorry, Boss," Alex said.

Jeremiah started to hold up a finger, then remembered he didn't have any, so he just waved his bandaged hand. "First off, there's nothing to be sorry about. We got attacked by an act from fucking Sea World." The pilot looked down. "I'm alive. I got rich using my brain, not my hands. We'll figure something out. We have alien technology, maybe we can make some cool *Terminator* arms or something."

"You're taking this really well," Alison noted.

"How else can I take it?" he asked. "Besides, the corpsman gave me some really good shit." They all chuckled. "How about bringing me up to date?"

"You sure you want to do that with that much morphine in you?" Alex asked.

"You went to college, didn't you?"

Alex smiled and nodded. "I was at West Point, so the drugs were less of a thing." Jeremiah shrugged. "Marine animals attacked the entire Flotilla. The attacks seemed coordinated and timed. There were hundreds of seals of all types, some not commonly found in this area, and dolphins and killer whales. The killers sank dozens of smaller boats." He thought for a second. "Almost all of them. The seals got onto a lot of the small navy ships too. It was bad. Real bad."

"Coordinated?" Jeremiah asked, blinking. "My God, how is that possible?"

"Nobody knows how any of this is possible. There are nine navy ships still responding and around thirty private ships. I think the captain said 30, anyway. We've come together in a tighter group.

Since the weather is good, we're close right now. We don't know how long we can keep it up. There's a low-pressure front due in 36 hours."

"What good does getting close do?"

"Overlapping defenses," Alex explained. "The navy ships can detect the larger whales. Most of the surviving ships have armed crew as well."

"We didn't," Jeremiah said. "How come we're even alive?"

"General Rose, the army guy who came in on those big transports? He'd taken over a couple ships and saw we were in deep shit. They came alongside and put a platoon on our deck. Just in time too."

"I'd shake his hand, if I could." Jeremiah offered some more dark humor.

"He's got his hands full. His troops are distributed across all the civilian ships. The attacks have largely ceased, but they're still probing defenses."

"This is like a bad 90's monster movie," Wade said. "There has to be an evil mastermind controlling them."

"Maybe aliens," Alison said.

"You might not be far from the truth," Jeremiah said.

Alex started to laugh, then stopped when he saw the expression on his boss's face. "Wait, you're serious?"

"Did we or did we not find a dead alien fox on a spaceship?"

Wade was staring off into space, his mouth hanging open. "Oh, shit."

"What?" Jeremiah asked.

"I came on board the *Ford* with some others who'd evacuated with the general who rescued us. One of the survivors was a reporter, Kathy Clifford."

"I know her," Alex said. "Hot."

"Right, her. Anyway, she's still playing reporter. She's got all kinds of recordings. Captain Gilchrist gave her access to the *Ford's* media room for the Flotilla news thing she was doing."

"Is that who was sending those stories?" Jeremiah asked. "I thought they looked professionally done."

"Right," Wade agreed. "But she was also spying on everyone and everything. Says it's what a reporter does. A real reporter anyway. She's got gigabytes of images, conversations, even recorded radio traffic. She just kinda blends into the background."

The others nodded. It was an interesting story.

"Anything else I should know while my brain is still working?" Jeremiah asked.

"Just that there's another military fleet. It came from the east coast. Started in Norfolk, went to Cape Canaveral, then through the Panama Canal. They picked up a bunch of scientists, including some from the CDC, and a NASA guy named…" he made a face as he tried to remember. "Beretta, Benini?"

"Bennitti?" Jeremiah barked.

"Yeah, him!"

"Holy shit, Theodore made it!"

"Is that the guy who hired you to investigate the asteroids that turned out to be alien ships?"

"Bingo," Jeremiah said. "I should have known, if anyone could figure out how to survive, it would be Theodore. He could fall into a truckload of manure and find a gold ring."

"Well, I was there when one of the people who'd come with us from Fort Hood, Chris Brown, arrived with news. He'd overheard that the fleet has an alien and its ship."

"A live alien?" Jeremiah asked. Wade nodded. Jeremiah blinked, his drug fogged mind working. *Was it an invasion then?* "Amazing." Everyone nodded in agreement. "What's the plan?"

"Unknown," Alex admitted. "The surviving military is talking about it. I suspect the whole Flotilla will get underway, maybe move everyone onto a few of the biggest ships for safety."

*Fewer and fewer of us,* Jeremiah thought. He drifted a bit, and when he could concentrate again, the pain had started to return. The only one in the infirmary he recognized was his surviving physicist, Jack Coldwell, and the corpsman. It looked like Jack hadn't come out of it untouched either. He was getting some stitches in his head.

"You okay, Jack?"

The much older scientist only moved his eyes as the needle was in a very precarious location. "Hey, Jeremiah. Yeah, I'll be okay. When they were shooting the seals, a ricochet bounced off a tool bench. This is from a piece of shrapnel. Looks worse than it is. I waited until the important cases, like you, were dealt with."

"Real shit show, right, old friend?"

"Without a doubt."

"Hold still please," the corpsman said. He appeared to be in his early thirties and was extremely businesslike in his bedside manner.

Jeremiah watched the stitches go in, waiting until the corpsman was done before he inquired about more drugs. However, before the man was finished, a pair of navy people came in. One was a woman in her forties, the other a man in his fifties. The man had a caduceus logo sewn onto the epaulettes of his blue camo light jacket. The woman rolled in a big cart similar to the ones mechanics took on jobs. It had all manner of military jargon stenciled on it, along with another caduceus logo.

"Is Jeremiah Osborne here?" the doctor asked. Jeremiah raised his mostly bandaged, right arm. "Sir, I'm Lieutenant Commander Peterson. I'm the surgeon off the *Reagan.*"

"I thought the *Reagan* sank."

"It did, sir. I happened to be taking out an appendix on the *Ford* when my ship went down." He didn't look happy. Jeremiah wondered if doctors went down with their ships, like captains did. "I am here to see about your injuries."

"Help yourself," Jeremiah said, waving his hands. "I'd like a side order of drugs to go with the exam, please."

"Corpsman, can I see his chart?"

"Of course, sir." The man left Jack's head half stitched and quickly retrieved a clipboard and handed it to the doctor. "Permission to continue with my other patient?" Dr. Peterson nodded, and the corpsman returned to the abused looking physicist.

The doctor examined the chart for a minute while the woman, obviously a nurse or similar, parked the two big roller bags. Dr. Peterson clucked a couple times as he flipped pages, then addressed the corpsman again. "No issues with the Demerol?"

"No, sir."

"Good. Well, Mr. Osborne. I'm going to give you a little more painkiller, but not much. I need to unwrap your hands to get a better look, and you need to be conscious for the exam." Jeremiah saw the nurse unfolding the portable cases to reveal some impressive machines.

"Is that an x-ray?" he wondered.

"Yes. I had it and my PA, my physician's assistant, with me on the *Ford*. Some of their permanent gear wasn't installed yet." He gestured at the bandages. "Do I have your permission to proceed?"

"Oh, sure." Jeremiah looked at the bandages. "This is going to hurt, isn't it?"

"If the corpsman's report is competent, yes."

Jeremiah glanced at the young man. He was tying the last of Jack's stitches and expertly cutting the excess with a pair of scissors. If he was aggrieved at having his competence questioned, he showed no signs of it. Jeremiah sighed and made himself more comfortable. "Okay, let's get this over with."

"Do you want a screen?" the PA asked.

"A what?"

She rolled her eyes. "A screen to block your view of the injuries."

Jeremiah shrugged. "Doesn't do me much good to deny what happened."

"Very well," she said and prepared a syringe.

The doctor had been correct. It hurt. A lot. Jeremiah concentrated on breathing. That was about all he could do. The PA glanced up at him a couple of times while she unwrapped the bandages, but only slowed when she noticed he was sweating and breathing fast. "Doctor?"

"I noticed. Mr. Osborne, please breath slower. You're hyperventilating."

"No shit," Jeremiah hissed as a piece of gauze came away with a flap of skin. "Fuck, fuck, fuck."

"Almost done," she said.

Despite his words, he looked away. The ceiling was constructed of acoustic tile. Let's see, five tiles from back to front. Ah, God! One, two, three...eight side to side...Fuck! Oh, God.

"I understand you were hurt saving some people's lives."

"W-what?" Jeremiah asked, the words barely penetrating the agony.

"How were you hurt?" the PA repeated.

"I don't precisely remember," he said.

"He shoved a bloody lightning gun into an elephant seal's mouth and pulled the trigger," Jack explained.

"That'll do it, I suppose," Dr. Peterson said.

"All done, Doctor," the PA said.

"I need a drink," Jeremiah gasped.

"Not with Demerol in you," the doctor said, coming closer.

The PA had put a sanitary board across Jeremiah's chest and covered it with a drape and tools. The bloody bandages were in a bucket on the floor. Dr. Peterson put on sterile gloves and gently took Jeremiah's right arm just below the elbow and lifted it. Jeremiah looked for the first time, then wished he hadn't.

When he was a child, a neighbor's tool shed had burned to the ground. He had gone over to help them clean up the mess. Inside, they found the reason. A raccoon had chewed through a power cord and started the fire. Half the animal's body was outside the burned structure. Jeremiah's hand looked like the part that hadn't gotten out.

His left hand looked slightly better. The flesh was broken in places, and some bloody red muscle and white bone were visible. A tear rolled down his cheek.

"I'm sorry, Mr. Osborne. There's no way we can save either hand."

"I know," he replied.

"Both elbows look good, and I'm reasonably confident we can keep enough musculature on your lower right arm for a prosthetic attachment." He went on to describe what they could do with the facilities they had. "While more advanced facilities might be available somewhere, time is of the essence. Damage of this degree has to be mitigated. Infection will be almost impossible to avoid."

"What do we do?"

"I want to take you over to the *Ford,* immediately, so we can amputate and save what we can."

"A-amputate," he said with a catch in his voice. "I see. Very well."

"I'll let the helicopter pilot know. Captain Gilchrist has okayed the procedure, given the important role you played in the Flotilla's long-term survival."

"Do you have to put the bandages on again?"

The PA moved over. "We have a special burn covering for cases like this. It's a wet bandage with topical pain killer. They won't feel great, but they'll be easier to remove than the others were. The corpsman did a good job with what he had available." The corpsman was standing by the door with his medical bag over his shoulder, waiting.

"Okay," Jeremiah said. "Let's go then. Jack, please let my people know?"

"Of course, Jeremiah," he answered.

Rewrapping his hands wasn't as bad as unwrapping them had been. It was easier, too, because he was still trying to come to grips with the fact that he was soon going to be handless. *Why both of them?* he asked himself over and over.

When they finished, they crossed his wounded limbs over his chest and secured them with more bandages. A pair of his own men came in and locked their arms together to make a sort of chair for him to sit in, so they could carry him to the flight deck. He would have complained he could walk, but he knew otherwise. His whole body wasn't responding correctly. He didn't know if it was the drugs, the wounds, or the shock of what was about to happen.

Up on deck, one of the navy versions of the Blackhawk, a Seahawk, waited, its rotor idling. Most of his surviving staff were there as well. As he came into view, applause broke out. He couldn't help himself; he started to cry. It didn't help that Alex West came to attention and saluted him.

"Well done," Alex yelled over the increasing sound of the helicopter.

"Don't let anyone drink my scotch!" he yelled back to the pilot, who laughed and nodded. Wade Watts also tossed Jeremiah a half-assed salute before he was loaded into the chopper.

He was in good enough shape to be strapped into a seat, so he was spared the indignity of a gurney. Dr. Peterson and his assistant were helped aboard by the helicopter's copilot, and they strapped in as well. The copilot even showed Jeremiah some pity and put a headset on him, setting the mic to vox.

"Thanks," he said.

"No problem, sir. We'll have you on the *Ford* in just a couple of minutes." The helicopter took off a short time later.

Jeremiah watched as they lifted off the deck of his ship. The *Azanti* still rested where they'd landed her. A slight smile crossed his face. Regardless of how things worked out, she'd flown in space. She'd really flown. Faster than light. Something no other human ship had ever done. He had wanted to go into space himself. But now, that dream was over.

The helicopter tilted forward and away from the ship that had been his home since the plague destroyed the world. He had a good view of the Flotilla from above as the helicopter continued to climb and angled away. When they'd flown back from the *Ford* a few hours ago, the ships had been scattered and far more numerous. As he'd heard, the few that were left were clustered around the sole remaining functional carrier, the USS *Gerald R. Ford.* There appeared to be more helicopters in the air than ships in the water. Aircraft circled around the outside as they approached their destinations, careful to avoid clustering in the middle.

"Is this all that's left?" he asked over the microphone.

"A few ships lit out a short time ago," Dr. Peterson explained. "You can still see some over there."

Jeremiah followed the doctor's gesture to the west and could see a ship steaming away. It was maybe a mile distant. It looked a lot like his ship. Perhaps it had also been an oil platform service ship? There was a flash, and the ship seemed to lift out of the water and split in two in the middle. Fire, smoke, and water exploded into the sky as the two parts fell back down.

"That was a goddamn torpedo!" the pilot yelled, and he banked hard toward the carrier just as another explosion flashed.

* * *

**USS *Gerald R. Ford***
**Combat Information Center**

"Sonar contact!"

Captain Gilchrist slid out of his chair in the *Ford's* CIC and moved through the maze of workstations and screens. Normally, a good part of it would be used for launching and recovering fixed wing aircraft, like fighters or E-2 Hawkeye early warning craft. He had exactly three flight-worthy, combat aircraft left after the fiasco at Coronado so most flight ops were rotary wing.

When the damned seals and whales attacked, everything went insane. Who would have thought so many ships would be vulnerable to seals? Navy SEALs, sure, but the marine mammal variety? The animals had flopped onto fantails and slinked up walkways, and dolphins had jumped 12 feet out of the water to land on decks and bite people. Reports included mutated creatures too. *Mutated?!* Carrier captains had to be good at dealing with adversity, or they'd never get the job. But this was insane!

Only five combat ships remained after the attack. A day ago, there'd been nine. The Marine amphibious assault carriers had proven particularly vulnerable with their open well decks. The only one still reporting in was the *Essex*, and they were preparing to abandon ship. An outbreak of infected had caused a fire in the hangar deck.

Twice, Gilchrist had tried to send a damage control team to help, but both times he'd been diverted.

He wanted to know how so many ships without low-to-the-water access had also had sudden outbreaks of infected. They'd lost the *John Paul Jones*, and nobody knew why. A lookout had seen gunfire on the bridge, then all comms were lost. The *Carl Vinson* had seemed fine, then was quiet. She was drifting a mile to the north. He didn't have the time or personnel to check on her. Both of the littoral class ships were gone as well.

All he had left were the *Ford*, the *Russell*, an *Arleigh Burke*-class destroyer, the *Ingraham,* the *Rodney M. Davis,* and the *Vandegrift* which were all *Oliver Hazard Perry*-class frigates. He also had the *Arctic,* a *Supply*-class, fast combat support ship. He was most worried about the *Arctic.* Without her, they would quickly run out of food and fuel.

The surviving ships pulled in around the *Ford* and the *Russell* for whatever safety they could provide. General Rose, on his bloody cruise ship, had distributed his sparse number of soldiers between the civilian ships to shoot seals and whales. The Marines were largely scattered as well. They'd taken the worst of the losses in Coronado, and many more during the attack. Dozens of RHIBs had sunk, lost to the seals and whales. They were down to using helicopters to move people around. All told, as the Brits would say, it was a right proper cockup.

"What do you have, son?" he asked the sonar tech.

"I've been getting weird transients since 09:44, sir," the tech said and pointed to the screen. The colored plot showed the various things surrounding them. The techs had been trying to track the damned killer whales, without much success. The infected whales were quiet compared to normal whales. There wasn't much conversation between zombies, apparently. "There's been so much garbage from fights on ships and that yacht full of ammo exploding…"

"I understand, Seaman. Get to it," Gilchrist prompted.

"Yes, sir. I've been spending all morning isolating the garbage. I was tired of trying to do it on a spot-by-spot basis. I finally got it all sorted out a few minutes ago, then I picked up a new set of screws approaching. These are definitely underwater. I'd swear it's a sub, sir."

Gilchrist narrowed his eyes as he examined the computer representation of the signal. The data didn't match any known submarine. Any American sub would approach on the surface, especially in such a chaotic situation. He was about to call for his XO to contact the *Russell* when the sonarman sat bolt upright, a hand over his ear that wasn't covered by an earphone.

"Torpedo in the water!"

"Commander Tobias, battle stations!" Gilchrist barked.

His XO called out orders, and the CIC lighting took on a reddish hue. Several crewmen who'd been off duty came rushing in over the next several minutes.

"Report on sonar contact," Tobias said as a crewman used a grease pen to mark the aggressor on a plotting board.

"Contact is changing aspect," the young seaman said, his face contorted in concentration. "It's *really* weird, sir. The main contact sounds more like a torpedo than a subma…it's gone!"

"They go silent?" Tobias asked.

"No, it just faded out, like it accelerated out of range." The seaman looked up at Gilchrist. "Computer estimated the speed at over 350 knots."

"Impossible," Tobias said.

"What about those Russian VA-111s?" Gilchrist asked. His XO looked concerned. The Russians had developed a supercavitating torpedo capable of over 200 knots.

"Weren't they supposed to be powered by rocket engines?" the sonarman asked, still listening. "The torpedo in the water sounded conventional, but also fast. Maybe 150 knots."

"Who makes a sub faster than a torpedo?" Tobias asked his captain, sotto voce.

"Nobody," Gilchrist answered. "Do we have a plot on the torpedo?"

"Affirmative," someone said. "Torpedo is true and active, bearing 295 degrees, course 99.5 degrees, range 2,900 yards. Speed 152 knots."

A list of ships was written on the board in blue grease pencil. A sailor had already marked the firing location of the submarine, with its escape direction. A squiggle indicated it was no longer being tracked. A red dotted line marked the torpedo's course, and a red circle indicated the probable target. "Target is the *Propseridad.*"

Gilchrist looked at one of the seamen tasked with monitoring the ships in the Flotilla. Unfortunately, her job had gotten steadily easier over the last day and a half. She was reading from a laptop.

"Sir, the *Prosperidad* is a Venezuelan-flagged oil rig resupply ship that was in San Diego, taking on materials, when the plague hit."

Gilchrist was decidedly not happy. As if zombies weren't bad enough, he was bobbing in the middle of a tight knot of ships with zero screen. It wasn't where a carrier boss wanted to find himself when a skunk suddenly appeared in their midst. He would normally have had his own nuclear attack subs to screen at a distance, not to mention a trio of destroyers keeping an eye out 12 to 25 miles away. The board indicated the attacker had been less than 10 miles out when he'd fired.

He turned to Tobias. "Get some ASW assets in the air, now."

Tobias was scanning the board that listed their aircraft, where they were, their status, and their availability. "We can launch that

Viking in 5 minutes," he said and grabbed a phone, "but we don't have any ordnance to mount on it!"

Gilchrist nodded. "Shoot it." S-3 Vikings were fine ASW planes. They were equipped with MAD, or Magnetic Anomaly Detection, and they flew low over the ocean, looking for telltale signs of big hunks of submerged iron and/or nuclear reactors. They were effective, and naturally, they'd been taken out of service. The *Ford* only had one aboard. The S-3 Viking and the now lost F-35 Lightning had been on the ship for ACT, or Aircraft Compatibility Testing, which was part of the *Ford's* evaluation as the first in her class. *Now last in her class.* Having a few of the older planes on board also helped them test the new EMALS, Electromagnetic Aircraft Launch System. The Viking was no longer in direct service. Instead, carriers relied on screening vessels and submarines now.

"They're fueling and moving it onto the elevator now," Tobias said. "A couple of electronics repair techs are filling in for the MAD operators."

"This should be interesting," Gilchrist said. "See how long before any surviving destroyers or frigates can equip an ASW helicopter."

"Torpedo time on target, 10 seconds," the sonarman announced.

"I've got a visual from one of our Seahawks," a technician said. One of the flatscreens showed a jiggly picture of a ship sailing away from the camera. It was a wide, fat ship with a big, open rear deck and two folded cranes. It reminded him of Jeremiah Osborne's ship. If they were under attack, having the injured CEO coming aboard for treatment would complicate things. Gilchrist didn't know the nature of his injuries, only their severity. He was concerned how having him aboard would impact their plans to exploit the alien technology.

"Impact!" the sonarman called out.

On the screen, the *Posperidad* lifted and split in half, a textbook torpedo attack amidships. The explosion was a big one, too.

"Holy shit," someone said. Others exclaimed as well.

"Quiet," Tobias snapped, and the chatter fell off.

Gilchrist didn't blame them too much. Few, if any, of them had ever seen a live fire exercise. In this case, a lot of people had just died. The stricken ship was sinking, *fast.* "See about getting an SAR bird airborne." Tobias nodded; he hadn't hung up the phone yet.

Minutes ticked by as the off-duty sonar techs came rushing in, and the other combat stations arrived. Tobias announced that an E-2 was being moved onto an elevator. Seconds later, the hull vibrated, and they could see the S-3 Viking shoot off the end of a waist catapult on one of the deck monitors. He silently hoped they didn't rip the nose off the old airframe. In the books, the EMALS was easier to finetune than the old steam catapults. But the reason they'd been on test runs and not on a shakedown cruise was because the damned thing was proving harder to dial in than the contractor had said it would be.

The Viking clawed its way into the sky, only dropping a meter below the deck before beginning its ascent. A huge cruise ship was only a quarter mile away, and Gilchrist ground his teeth together as the Viking barely cleared the pleasure craft. It was like running flight ops in a fucking bathtub. As soon as it's gear retracted, the Viking banked westward, toward the attack.

"When is a helicopter coming in that can be equipped for ASW?"

"Beeker said the bird with Osborne is landing now," Tobias said.

"Tell the airboss to rearm that damned helicopter in record time."

"Torpedo in the water!"

"We need to maneuver," Tobias snarled.

Gilchrist wondered if there was something worse than a cockup.

* * *

**USS *Vandegrift***
**Bridge**

Commander Jeremy Richards, Captain of the USS *Vandergrift* was proud of his ship. The *Oliver Hazard Perry*-class guided missile frigates were quietly referred to as the ghetto navy by the admiralty, and they were being phased out faster than the much more prestigious and heavily armed *Arleigh Burke*-class destroyers were coming online. Regardless of what the brass thought, the *Vandegrift* had enjoyed a distinguished service since her commissioning in 1984. Well, except for the drunken orgy by her CO in 2012.

Richards had known the commander. He also knew the former CO of the *Vandegrift* hadn't done anything a hundred navy commanders hadn't done before him, except he had broken the first rule—don't get caught. Especially if you were in a foreign military port. So, Richards had gotten the command. It would have been the last for the *Vandegrift*, which had been scheduled to be decommissioned later that year, and the ship would have likely become a target for weapons testing. Only now, things had changed. A damned virus was turning people into flesh eating zombies.

He glanced behind his command chair on the wide-windowed bridge. The ship's plaque read Exercitatus, Conservatus, Paratus. Skilled, maintained, prepared. *Who can prepare for a zombie apocalypse?*

"Captain," the radio operator called. "The *Ford* reports a torpedo attack on a civilian ship, bearings follow."

"Torpedo attack?" Richards demanded. "Who fired a torpedo?"

"Unknown. We're the only unobstructed warship; they want us to move out and screen ASAP. They've launched something called a Viking."

The XO looked at Richards and laughed. "I thought they retired those."

"They did," Richards said, "couple years ago." He shrugged. Who knew? Looking around the bridge he shook his head. Half the crew was down or missing. They'd had a small outbreak of the infection shortly after arriving with the *Ford.* Some sections were severely shorthanded. He picked up the phone and punched in engineering. "Engineering, bridge. Report power status."

"Bridge, engineering," the reply came immediately. "Turbine one is at 10%, providing power and station keeping. Turbine two is down. I was going to pull a fuel booster pump for maintenance, it's been acting up."

"Belay that. Bring number two online, we're moving."

"What's up, Captain?"

"Looks like someone's shooting bloody torpedoes."

"What? As if flesh eating infected aren't bad enough?"

"I know, right? Give me as much as possible on number one and spin up number two as fast as you can." He hung up the phone and turned to his XO. "Cast off from the *Arctic* immediately." They'd been alongside since taking on fuel, providing security against seals, of all things. "Signal our people on the supply ship to stay aboard; we don't have time to get them off."

He watched as his crew went to work. The helmsman was a new seaman recruit. He had come aboard when they left San Diego last month to rendezvous with the *Ford* on her sea trials. His XO would have normally called the senior helmsman, but she was in sickbay after being bitten by a rat. Six others were with her. The corpsman in charge said she had a staph infection. He'd have to transfer them to the *Ford* for treatment once this torpedo stuff was dealt with.

"We're clear and ready to maneuver," the XO informed.

"Port rudder, all ahead, one-quarter."

"Port rudder, all ahead, one-quarter, aye-aye," the helmsman said.

"Take us to battle stations," Richards ordered. "Sonar, coordinate with the Viking. Find the damned sub."

* * *

**USS *Gerald R. Ford***
**Media Center**

"Was that a catapult launch?" Kathy Clifford asked.

The young navy media specialist looked up from her sudoku puzzle and blinked. "Yeah, it sounded like the EMALS." The alarm had sounded a few minutes ago, but it had sounded several times since the marine animal attack.

"I thought there weren't any more fighters."

The woman shrugged and went back to her puzzle.

Kathy scowled and opened her laptop. In a second, she found the deck camera, but there wasn't anything to see. The men were moving some stuff around, but she didn't see any planes. Like the last time she'd checked, a cruise ship was visible ahead of them. None of the ships were moving since they'd come closer together.

The marine mammal attack caused her the most frustration since they'd been in space. Nobody would give her any details, and she had the misfortune of being on the only navy ship that had been untouched by the crazy attack. She'd gotten some secondhand stuff. A sailor knew another sailor who'd heard from a guy on another ship that sharks had been leaping up and biting people. Another had said seagulls were divebombing civilian ships. A cook had said sea lions had swum in through the well deck on the *Essex* and attacked the Marines.

*What a crock of shit*, she mused and flipped around the camera views. Suddenly, she saw an elevator bringing up one of the AWACs planes. "What's that called?" she asked the woman.

"An E-2 Hawkeye," the woman said. There were a dozen civilians in the media center. None of them took any notice. The space had been designated as a gathering spot when on alert. She'd protested, but the deck officer was unimpressed. The ship's media library was up and running, so the civilians were streaming movies. She had her sights set on something higher than watching Shrek for the fifth time.

The Hawkeye was pulled off the elevator, its wings folding down and locking in place. In just a few seconds, it was being maneuvered into location behind one of the catapults. Its engines spun up, it was hooked to the catapult, and it fired off into the air. It all happened so damned fast! She had to remind herself the *Ford* was a new carrier and had never been deployed.

"I bet they know more in the radio room," she said. Nobody even looked at her this time. Kathy scanned the monitors one more time. When she didn't see anything interesting, she took her laptop and left.

Her roaming of the interior spaces on the *Ford* had quickly taught her where the various departments and compartments were located. The fatigues they'd given her were devoid of patches or insignia, so she wouldn't pass scrutiny. However, they were enough to get her into most areas without an extra look. The communications section, which she thought of as the radio room, was two decks up and forward. It only took her a minute to get there.

The room was twice the size of her media room, and the wall was lined with workstations and instruments. Nobody took note of her arrival, so she walked along the length of the compartment and got a feel for it. She wasn't up on military jargon and listening to it brought back painful memories of Cobb. Not a day had gone by since they'd left him at Fort Hood that she didn't think of him.

Much of the radio operation looked like it was ship-to-ship or ship-to-air. The carrier didn't have a ton of airplanes up, but there were a lot of helicopters to keep the operators busy. The problem was, of course, all the operators were wearing headsets. Techs were moving around directing traffic or acting as assistants. She relied on her reporter skills and listened to every word she could hear.

It was a skill she'd cultivated over her entire career. The best reporters weren't the ones who talked or wrote the most. Rather, they were the ones who listened the best. She'd learned the art of questioning a prospect in school, then, as an intern for a network, she'd lucked into an experienced mentor who explained that the schools had it backward. The best reporters knew when to shut up and listen and when not to ask penetrating questions.

Listening proved to be the ideal tactic. As she was casually watching a radio tech key data, she heard someone say, "Mr. Jeremiah Osborne." She did her best to mosey over for a better listen. The speaker was a woman working helicopter traffic on the flight deck. The helicopter was designated a medical evac, special code SAR, or search and rescue.

"Can I help you, Ms. Clifford?"

"Morning, Chief Kuntzleman. Why is Jeremiah Osborne arriving via medivac?"

The older chief looked around and shook his head, a small smile crossing his face. "You're amazing, you know?"

"So I've been told." She lifted an inquisitive eyebrow, and he shook his head again.

"Mr. Osborne was critically injured in a zombie incident on his ship."

"Human or seals?"

"You don't miss much, do you?"

"I try not to."

"Seals, like most of the attacks on the Flotilla." He glanced around and leaned closer. "Fifteen minutes ago, a private ship that was leaving the vicinity was torpedoed. No, we don't know who did it. The ship was identical in design to Osborne's ship."

"Oh," was all she could say for a long time. Kuntzleman was about to leave when she finally spoke. "Is Wade Watts with Osborne?"

"I doubt the captain would let him set foot on the *Ford* if this were the last ship afloat and there was no land left anywhere on the planet."

It was Kathy's turn to snort. Captain Gilchrist did seem pretty good at holding a grudge. She made a note to see if it was a common trait among ship captains. Or were they more eccentric, each with different traits? They seemed more like old feudal lords, each ruling their own little part of the world.

She moved around a bit more, noticing that Chief Kuntzleman kept an eye on her. He seemed willing to tolerate her presence and was simply making sure she stayed out of trouble.

In her wandering, she passed the satellite communications system. Kathy recognized a lot of the equipment from remote broadcasting jobs early in her career. She was a little surprised at the age of the equipment, despite its being installed on a brand-new carrier. It wasn't used or worn out, just old enough that she'd worked with it 20 years ago.

She caught the chief's eye. "Is this the system Wade got going?"

"Yes, ma'am," he replied. "Did a top-notch job of it, too. Then he went rogue."

She didn't argue with him. Wade obviously thought he was helping, they obviously thought he wasn't. Wasn't worth arguing with them. She did her best to appear interested in everything else while actually studying the satellite system as intensely as she could. It took five tense minutes to find what she wanted. An ear-to-ear grin spread across her face. Kathy turned and left so quickly, Chief Kuntzleman didn't notice until she was long gone.

Back in the media center, she logged back into the ship's network and entered the common access code she'd noted while in the radio room. Instantly, she had full access to the satellite feed Wade Watts had restored. After looking at the interface for a moment, she saw a log of military assets connected to the *Gerald R. Ford.* Among them were the ships immediately adjacent to them, all of which she recognized by name. However, there were a bunch of others as well.

KRSOC, GCC, Dagger, TCC, ADF-C, USARJ, AMSSPS-NSF, and others. The only one she recognized was KRSOC, which was the military intelligence facility on Kunai, Hawaii. She had no clue about the others. *What the hell was Dagger? Some kind of weapons program?* The list suggested locations they had contact with. She clicked on ADF-C, and it brought up an interface that allowed her to plug in headphones and talk.

"Oh, wow, it's a satellite two-way radio interface." She quickly disconnected. Using this she could broadcast to anyone who was linked with the military satellite communication system, MILSATCOM. Kathy backed out to the main menu and started to close the program. She thought it would be better to mess with it later when there was less chance Kuntzleman might be watching. Then a subsystem off the main menu caught her eye.

The entry read, "VHF radio connection." She had direct access to the ship's radios. The same grin she'd had on her face in the radio room cut across her features again. Grinning from ear-to-ear, Kathy grabbed a pair of headphones and plugged them into the jack on her laptop. She logged onto the VHF radio, hit mute, found the frequency presets, and started moving around, listening. When she heard the call for help from a large fishing boat, she opened a recorder app and linked it. This was going to be some good stuff.

* * *

**Classified Task Force**
**Gulf of Farallones, California**

"What the fuck happened to recon?" Michael snarled over the secure comms. It took a couple seconds to get the reply. The other end was only a few hundred miles away, but a version of VLF, very low frequency, communications was being used. It took the computer time to send the signal and more time to get the reply.

"Sir, I'm sorry. We spotted a high value target, identified by the computer as the Oceanic Orbital Enterprises launch ship. I took the shot."

Michael's eyes narrowed as he calmed himself a little. The Hunter sub commanders were chosen based on their skill as submariners and their independent initiative. In simulations, Chamuel had warned him they were likely to go their own way in pursuit of part of an objective. As was often the case, the damned savant had been correct.

"Very well," he said at last. "Upload your reconnaissance data."

"Uploading, sir."

Michael watched the report build a virtual battlefield and fill it with data on the big laptop screen. They were still a couple hours out of San Nicolas, forcing him to run operations remotely. But it was better than when they were in the northwest. At least they had direct communications now, instead of the slow satellite relay.

He was encouraged by the status of the so-called Flotilla. Less than 30 ships total, only nine military ships. Because the report was assembled from sonar data, the number of non-military ships wasn't 100% accurate. There was an old oil platform to one side of the Flotilla, and the ships were in a circular formation around the carrier. *Curious.*

"Chamuel, this is Michael."

"Go ahead."

"The Hunters are at the Flotilla. There's an old oil platform that looks like it has been modified. I need to know what it's for. Oh, and the ships created a defensive cordon around the surviving supercarrier, apparently prior to one of the Hunters sinking a ship without direct authorization."

"I thought you issued hold and recon orders?" Chamuel asked.

"I did."

"So, they went ahead on their own initiative?"

Michael ground his teeth together as he answered. "Yes, as you predicted."

"Interesting. Very well, stand by. I have a satellite passing over now."

Michael grunted in acknowledgment of the delay and used the time to examine the remaining military ships. When the Flotilla was called to his attention, he'd been concerned. It had contained 29 military ships, including a pair of Marine amphibious assault carriers, three supercarriers, and a considerable number of escorts. It was a formidable force, a far larger force than Chamuel had considered probable. Then the savant spotted the second fleet coming through the Panama Canal.

It was immediately obvious the fleet coming through the canal meant to link up with the other one, and he couldn't allow it. Strangely, Chamuel had predicted that wouldn't be a problem. She told him the Russians would take care of the second fleet. Michael knew the Russian government was toast, so how were they going to deal with the second fleet?

The answer came in the form of a squadron of Russian submarines on the western side of the Panama Canal. Chamuel had fed the Russians intel suggesting the American government had caused Strain Delta, just as the Russian state was collapsing. The Russians were almost certain to lose their ships, but they would take out the remaining American ships first. The savant had said, worst case, the Russians would nuke a couple US cities. Since the cities were not vital to the survival of the species, they were no major loss.

"I have your information," Chamuel said two minutes later.

"Go ahead."

"The oil platform belonged to an organization known as HAARP, the Human Advancement and Adaptive Research Project. They were outlawed from the United States three years ago."

"I remember them," Michael said. "Eugenicists or something?"

"It's more complicated than that. HAARP was not trying to improve the human genome; they were trying to find ways to remove vulnerabilities. Fun fact—Project Genesis was at least partly responsible for their creation."

"Really?"

"Oh, this gets better and better. There is a 50% probability they've either found a cure for Strain Delta, or at least, a way to treat infected material."

Michael considered. *Was it possible to take out the Flotilla while capturing elements of this HAARP?* His memory of the HAARP thing was less than perfect. Such details weren't in his wheelhouse. "Who's the main person on this project?"

"Dr. Lisha Breda. She's a biologist with some physics and computer training. Their board of directors were largely biologists in practice, though I show a 99% probability none of them were on location and are all dead. The rest were simply shadow figures used by Genesis to gain a say in HAARP's development. Wait one."

Michael took the time to continue evaluating the military ships for risk as well as to review the Hunters' assessment of manpower remaining. *Wow, the Marines took it in the ass during their assault on Coronado.* He had to hand it to Chamuel, feeding the president the location of the Flotilla had been a master stroke. It took her out of the equation and nearly decimated the Flotilla's combat forces.

"Okay, additional information," Chamuel said. "The platform has been abandoned by HAARP. They are now aboard the ship I'm indicating on the images you received from the Hunters."

Michael examined the image. The indicated ship was a supply or support ship of one kind or another. Chamuel also indicated another ship with it, a tug. The only issue was that she thought an adjacent ship had soldiers billeted on it. Since there was an Osprey and attack choppers on it, he considered it a possibility.

"What are the odds we'll be able to cure the alien bug?"

"Not good in the short term," she explained. "However, since the language barrier with the Vulpes has been breached, the odds are steadily increasing. Within five years they pass 50%, and they gradually climb to 99% inside 25 years. However, the addition of Dr. Breda significantly increases those odds in the short term."

"Got it, thanks." He cut the connection and looked at the imagery. The carrier had one of the old guided missile frigates deploying ASW assets, looking for the sub. That might work in his favor. The other Hunter was in the middle of the Flotilla, quietly relaying live views to Michael. Slowly, his normally non-emotional face broke into a grin.

Michael used his comms to contact Colonel Baker. "Colonel, change of plans."

*****

# Chapter Eight

**Late Morning, Saturday, May 4th**
**Shangri-La**
**Amarillo, TX**

Cobb felt partly human for the first time in days. He'd gotten three hours of sleep, a shower, a shave, and even some chow. He wasn't sure which he liked more. If forced to choose, he'd probably pick the hot shower. Immediately after getting cleaned up and donning a clean uniform, he looked in on Master Sergeant Schardt. He was recovering from his surgery. Dr. Clay insisted the master sergeant would be fine. She noted Schardt had apparently been shot at least twice before.

Newly promoted Sergeant Tango and Sergeant Zim accompanied him to the landing field. Cobb had wondered how many people would show up. Neither man had given him any idea. However, Cobb found out for himself as soon as he turned the corner and saw the open landing area crowded with thousands of men, women, and children. The sound of their combined voices immediately reminded him of the last time he'd gone to a sporting event.

The nearest people noticed him, and news of his arrival traveled through the crowd in a wave. It was disconcerting to hear the conversation quickly slow and die out. He wondered if the meeting was a big mistake, especially without more security. Then he saw, once again, that his people had been thinking ahead. It looked like every soldier on Shangri-La was already there, divided into two groups, up by the elevated docking area where Bisdorf's barge sat. The modified houseboat was serving as an improvised stage.

"We got this," Tango said quietly.

Cobb nodded and strode forward. Because they came in from the side opposite the houseboat, they had to move through the middle of the crowd which parted for him respectfully. The looks he saw could mostly be described as curious, though more than a few seemed upbeat or, possibly, happy.

He reached the ladder and climbed up into the back of Bisdorf's sky-barge. The man was sitting on a stool behind the controls, basically in the same place Cobb had first seen him. Now, however, there was a woman in her twenties sitting with him, holding the older man's hand. Bisdorf was smiling so hard his face was almost split in two. The woman appeared tired and malnourished; however, she was no worse for wear.

On the far side of the boat was Daimler. The man's hands were behind his back, tied with stripper cuffs. He'd apparently tried to fight when a squad of soldiers came for him. Luckily for him, he fought badly. None of the men were injured, so he only got roughed up for bad behavior. If the German had wounded any of the men, Cobb knew he would have found himself flying down to Earth. He had a swollen eye and a split lip. Considering how pissed the soldiers were about the whole hostage thing, he was lucky to be alive.

Cobb turned and cast his eyes over the crowd. Several thousand people watched expectantly. Clark climbed into the boat, and a much thinner, light-skinned, black man followed close behind. Clark immediately came over to Cobb and held out a big, beefy hand.

"I can't thank you enough," he said, "and I can't apologize enough."

Cobb glanced at Clark's partner who looked like he'd been crying. He nodded. "I understand, I just wish you'd said something. Anything. But I understand that you were afraid."

"Perry is all I have," Clark said, and took the other man's hand. "We survived Houston falling, and with Daimler and a few others, we got this place going. When that German SOB turned on us and helped Taylor take over, it all happened so fast. She promised to let the hostages go, eventually. We were beginning to realize she was lying when you came along. It was hard to trust you when Sergeant Groves fell into line so quickly after getting here."

"What's done is done," Cobb said. "Will you help us?"

"Of course, this is our home. Help is all we ever wanted to do."

"Thank you," Perry said. His voice had a strong Cajun accent. "For everything."

"It's probably not over," Cobb said.

Clark produced a small, battery-powered bullhorn and handed it to Cobb. "We found a 20-foot container full of these. We dumped most of them over the side, but Perry is a bit of a hoarder."

"I just like stuff," the other man said with a guilty grin.

The bullhorn looked like one of those you'd buy at a sporting goods store, made for a coach to yell at his team. It wasn't exactly mil-spec, which meant it was probably better. It would do. He checked the controls, turned it on, and looked at the crowd once more.

"Shangri-La," he said and adjusted the volume down a notch. The little bullhorn was more powerful than he'd expected. "I am

Colonel Cobb Pendleton, United States Army. I've only been here part of a day, but by now, you've all heard at least a little about me."

"Paul Bisdorf found me and a group of survivalists in Junction, Texas. We were trapped. As we were being rescued, we lost a good man. Without that lost man, we would have all died. The man who saved us took a real risk, and I'm grateful." To the side Bisdorf nodded his thanks. "When I got here, I found out how many soldiers had also been picked up. I didn't come planning to take over and be their commander, but fate had other plans.

"I was duty-bound to assume command. When you are a soldier, you do what the job requires, not what you want to do." He looked to both sides and saw dozens of soldiers, his soldiers, nodding in agreement. "I found out what had been happening here as events unfolded."

He took a minute to lay it all out, knowing many of those listening were hearing it for the first time. He told how Clark, Bisdorf, and others had figured out the alien drive and used it to get Shangri-La off the ground, only to have Shangri-La coopted by Governor Taylor with the help of Groves. He told how Taylor saw Cobb's arrival as a threat to her power, and through Groves, tried to kill him. He told how she was going to have her state troopers outright assassinate him when the subtle attempt didn't work. He heard audible gasps and cursing from the crowd.

"We turned the tables on her after Paul admitted what was going on." He explained that Taylor was holding many hostages to ensure their loyalty. "I tried to get her to surrender and see the reality of the situation. She decided to fight, and she paid with her life and her men's lives."

Cobb paused and let that sink in before continuing. "More than a few helped former governor Taylor. Among them was Hans Daimler." He glanced back at the German who looked indifferent. "He is the man who figured out the very technology that made this place possible. There was also Amelia, who used her so-called Angels to help Taylor perpetrate her hostage scheme, all in the name of helping ensure no infected came aboard.

"We tried to catch her, however she must have been tipped off, because she and a dozen of her helpers managed to escape in one of the sky-barges." Cobb had been disappointed to hear about her escape. At the same time, he thought it was okay. More than enough had already died for Taylor's ambitions. "This means there are still people here who are against me. That's fine. I'm not in charge of Shangri-La."

"Who is?" someone yelled.

"I'm turning it back over to those who started it." Cobb turned. "At least to some of them." He glanced at Daimler and shook his head. "Clark and Bisdorf will be in charge, until there is an election. We're the military. We follow the orders of a civilian leader. For now, it'll be whoever you choose. At least until someone in the order of succession or in the general chain of command is found.

"So, for now, we move onward. We'll continue to find people, rescue those we can, salvage where we must. Mr. Daimler has agreed to continue working in exchange for some limited freedom. Haven't you, Mr. Daimler?"

"Ya, I see little choice," the man said.

"He'll be closely supervised, of course."

"Bet your ass, he will," Clark growled, though the megaphone didn't pick it up.

"We have a second chance. I find it ironic that the name, Shangri-La, was picked by Paul and the others. Shangri-La was a mythical town, hidden in the clouds. A safe place of wonder. Well, that's what we have here. I hope we can put this behind us. I'll do what I can, and I will lead our small band of soldiers to keep us safe. That's our job. It's what we do."

He put the megaphone down and sighed. A second later, someone started clapping. Then someone else. In seconds, thousands were applauding. The ovation went on for almost a minute before tapering off. *Now what?* he wondered. Behind him, the pure and beautiful voice of Paul Bisdorf's daughter rang out.

"O beautiful for spacious skies, for amber waves of grain,"

"For purple mountain majesties," the crowd quickly picked up. "Above the fruited plain!

"*America! America!*" It became a roar. "God shed His grace on thee."

"And crown thy good with brotherhood from sea to shining sea!"

A pair of navy sailors leaped onto the back of the boat and produced an American flag. It wasn't big, and it looked a little tattered. They spread it wide between them and held it high. Cobb turned and came to attention, saluting the flag. All his men did likewise. He didn't know when he'd begun to cry, but tears rolled down his face. Where there was Old Glory, there was still hope.

* * *

**USS *Pacific Adventurer***

**150 Nautical Miles West of San Diego, CA**

General Rose covered his eyes with a hand as another navy helo screamed overhead. Like the last two, this one wasn't ferrying people between ships. The torpedoes slung under the stubby winglets left little doubt what it was doing.

"They haven't found the sub yet," Captain Mays said. It wasn't a question.

"Not with this level of activity," Rose agreed. Of course, he knew about the torpedoing. Everyone in the Flotilla knew by now. All the civilian ships would have lit out for parts unknown if they hadn't been scared shitless. He had to admit, he was. An army general had no business being on a fucking cruise ship while torpedoes zipped around and blew shit up.

He'd briefly considered calling Gilchrist on the *Ford* to find out what the fuck was going on. The Captain would have to take his call. After all, Rose *was* a damned O-9, and the captain was only an O-6. At least, Rose was pretty sure he had the navy rank correct.

Mays listened to his radio for a moment then turned to Rose. "Sergeant Grady on the *Looper* reports they've contained the outbreak. He wants to know if he should hop a ride back."

"Tell him to detach a squad for security. Call WO3 Peppers and have him get over there to bring the rest of the platoon back."

"Right away, sir."

Rose nodded. Sergeant Grady was in temporary command of a platoon due to a distinct lack of officers under his command. He figured he should pin a bar on the man's shoulder when there was time. Most of his men had been dispersed to help the surviving Marines deal with the crazy damned seals and shit, not to mention the weird virus outbreaks on ships where none had occurred for days. His platoon was the last to accomplish its mission, and according to Mays, they hadn't lost a single man in the operation. In the distance, he saw one of his V-22 Ospreys banking toward the *Looper*, a huge tanker a half mile away and closer to the carrier than his *Pacific Adventurer.*

The Ospreys had proved invaluable in the operation. He cursed the idiots in the Pentagon who'd kept the army from getting them, while simultaneously thanking the fates who had six of them sitting at Fort Hood when the plague hit. They'd been there for a Marine joint-forces operation which had never happened. When he'd arrived at the Flotilla, the onsite Marine commander had wanted them back. Rose had told the man to kiss his stars, so they had stayed.

He wanted a cigarette and regretted smoking a couple during the evac from Hood. He sighed. There were a lot of regrets to go around. Rose turned and looked to the east. Just 150 miles over the horizon was California. Probably 349 million zombies too. At least the zombies didn't have torpedoes. He wished Grange had checked in, and he knew he had to consider her lost. Maybe a strange virus outbreak on her ship had taken her out as well. Who knew?

A shadow passed under the ship. *Fucking whale again.* He leaned out a little, gun at the ready. It was even bigger than the killer whale he'd seen an hour ago. Moving quicker too. "What other kinds of whales are around here?" he asked Mays.

"I have no clue, sir. One of the navy kids running around the boat said killer whales shouldn't be here, so it could be anything."

"Great," Rose said and searched the dark blue waters. Nothing moved. The whale hadn't looked quite right. At least, his mind couldn't reconcile it with the way a whale should look. He recalled the dead dolphin's changed teeth and shuddered. Mutant whales; that was all he needed. His mind conjured up an image of a whale big enough to chomp his former cruise ship. *I gotta get some rack time, soon.*

He moved to the bridge wing and watched as a group of seals tried to get aboard a mega yacht a short distance away. Unlike a lot of the private ships, this one had little difficulty defending itself. A dozen men in store-bought camo lined the side of the ship, pumping shotgun and AR-15 rounds into the seals. Though muted by the echoing cracks of their weapons, Rose was pretty sure he could hear them whooping in excitement.

"Ah, America." He laughed and shook his head. They used to joke that the hardest part of a zombie apocalypse would be pretending you weren't having fun. Well, at least a few people seemed to be having fun. He was just glad it was one boat he didn't have to rescue. Marines had had to save an even bigger mega yacht earlier. It was full of some social media mogul's executives, friends, and family. They'd had at least 20 men for security, all armed with tasers and batons. The mogul was solidly anti-gun. Funny, he didn't seem overly disturbed when a squad of US Marines rappelled down from a Super Stallion.

"Warrant Officer Peppers reports he has Sergeant Grady and 24 of his men aboard, and one squad staying behind."

"Understood. Things seem to be winding down. Vector them to the *Vista* to offload, rearm, and get some grub and a couple hours of sack time."

"Roger that, sir."

Rose knew that if he was tired, his men were probably on their last legs. They were all good men and women. You didn't push good soldiers past their breaking points. Unless you had no choice.

A distant gunshot made him turn his head. There were no distant ships in that direction, only the unusually shaped *Helix* which now belonged to Dr. Lisha Breda. Curious, he raised his borrowed pair of binoculars to his eyes. A dark shape rising a short distance out of the water was against the rear of the ship, and tiny black figures were swarming over the side. *What the fuck?*

He spun the distance control on the binoculars and squinted. The tiny figures resolved into humans with compact machineguns moving in tight groups.

"Mays!" Rose yelled. "Get Peppers to hightail it to the *Helix*."

"Right away. What's going on?"

"They're under attack. Not by animals, by humans. Fuck, tell him to hurry!"

* * *

Dr. Lisha Breda yawned and watched as Weasel presented his latest results. The man was both crazy and unrelenting. As they'd transferred her belongings from her former home to the ship, he'd hardly stopped working. Even when most of the gear was crated and being moved, the man had spent time scribbling in a paper notebook and mumbling to himself.

"Is that normal?" Lisha had asked Oz.

"It is for Weasel," Oz said, a twinkle in his eyes.

*How did so many crazy people end up working for me?* As soon as the equipment was settled into a workshop on the former supply ship,

Weasel went back to work. She guessed you'd call it rapid prototyping. He wasn't satisfied with the equipment he'd brought with him, so he was stealing stuff from wherever he could find it. A couple of coffee machines, some high-voltage power supplies, and the only functioning microwave from the galley all fell victim to his single-minded determination.

"How am I supposed to make lunch?" the cook demanded.

"Hand out MREs," she said. They'd found at least a thousand in the ship's hold. There were also cases of potted meat, which she already knew were safe, regardless of their production date. Same as SPAM. It was likely because of the manufacturing process. She hated both but disliked the idea of joining Grant Porter in the Pacific Ocean even more.

"Done," Weasel announced.

Lisha moved over to the workbench expecting…what? The machine they used to resurrect Frankenstein? She blinked in surprise. The device looked even more like an industrial microwave oven than the previous version, albeit with a main case and door that made it look like a Hollywood prop. It appeared more finished and less like something a kid would build. Though only slightly. "This works?"

"It should," Weasel said, moving around and checking the different electrical connections and electronics. Several of the controls were made from breadboards, a tool used by engineers to test electronic assemblies. "Yeah, we're good."

"How do we test it?" Oz asked.

Lisha went down to her new lab, under the substantial crew quarters, and returned with a large handled case. She found an empty spot on the floor and opened it to reveal an array of petri dishes and sample vials. She handed a trio of vials to Weasel. "Give these a shot."

He examined the vials. One was marked "Grant Porter—Cerebellum Sample" along with a date and sample code which was meaningless to him. The second was labeled with the name of a deceased lab tech who'd been infected in the initial wave and contained a sample from his femur. The third said "Commercial Beef, >INFECTED<" along with the date and another code.

"I figured you'd want to clean a bunch of food or something," Weasel said. He looked disappointed.

"Are you going to eat it afterward?" she asked.

"Uhm…" He looked quite uncomfortable.

"Maybe we should take baby steps before we jump in with both feet?" she suggested.

"Okay," he said and turned to his machine.

As he set about adjusting the controls, she removed her portable, high-power microscope and moved a few tools on a bench to make room. When she turned back, he was closing the door on the machine. "Ready?" she asked.

"Yup," he said. "Want to do the honors?"

Lisha examined the power connections, the profusion of electrical tape, and the butt connectors. "You know what? It's your invention. Have at it."

"Sure," he said, earlier transgressions already forgotten.

*He's more like a cat than a human.*

He touched a control. An LED bar lit up red, then the bar began to shrink. As it shrank it changed to yellow, and when it was almost to the end, it turned green. The machine beeped as though Weasel had been microwaving a Hot Pocket. "Done!"

Lisha had been expecting to see the lights dim or to hear the snap and crackle of discharging high voltage. It hadn't made any noise except the beep at the end. He opened it and took out the samples with his bare hands. She cringed and opened her mouth to yell. Weasel turned and held them out. They showed no signs of being hot. She flinched a little.

"They're fine," he said. "Not hot at all."

Her eyes narrowed slightly. She knew the process he'd developed with radar frequencies was low power, yet radar could still produce heat. Plus, in order to make food safe they had to cook it to 400 degrees. This seemed contra-intuitive. She reached out and took the glass vials. As he'd said, they were cool—exactly the same temperature they'd been when she'd handed them to him.

Lisha took them to her microscope where more samples waited. The waiting samples were animal brain matter kept in nutrient fluid. Part of the problem with Strain Delta was that it wasn't an actual virus. She couldn't make a reagent test, so she was forced to check via microscope. You couldn't see detail on the thing, but you could see clumps of it move in brain matter. Mammal brain matter was the best. She had a few hundred samples from her meager supply of primates which had all been harvested to make test vials.

Lisha took the meat sample first. It was from a batch of steaks that had once been in the base cooler. They'd been brought on board just before Strain Delta exploded, and they had tested positive. She carefully took the sample Weasel had treated, put it in the first primate brain test medium, and gave it a shake. She did the same with the other two samples, then put them in a rack.

"I use five minutes," she explained to them. "I tend to notice changes in only a minute, two at the most. So, I established five minutes as the baseline."

"Sensible," Weasel said. Oz nodded.

While she was waiting, Lisha got up and examined the machine Weasel had made. As she examined it, she realized the chamber that held the sample had no back. "Is this supposed to be open?" she asked incredulously.

"Well, yeah," Weasel said.

"But…" she gestured at it. "What about radiation?"

"There's very little of it," Weasel said.

"Oh, I feel a lot better!"

"It's not energetic. The radar frequency I used doesn't rebound well. The only time it was ever used was by the British in World War II."

"Okay. If this works, can you put a back on it anyway?"

"Yeah, sure. No problem."

The timer chirped, and Lisha returned to the microscope. She slid the sample with the added meat under the lens. After several minutes of looking, she could find no signs of the telltale alien virus clumping and trying to rebuild the brain. She used a green sharpie to mark it good, then tested the bone sample. Same result, it was clear. She picked up the last vial, the one with the sample of Grant Porter's brain.

Lisha felt a sort of connection with this sample. Grant had been her researcher, her friend, and for quite some time her living Strain Delta test subject. She'd removed half his brain, only to have him get up and walk around, and eventually enable her to identify the alien bugs' strange operating frequency of 2.46 Hz.

"You okay, Doctor?" Oz asked.

"Yeah," she said and put the sample under the microscope. There were no signs of active Strain Delta. "Weasel?"

"Yes?"

"You are a genius."

The man beamed at Oz who clapped him on the shoulder. Lisha looked at the machine again, considering the mechanics involved in its function. "I want you to get with the mechanical engineers and see about making portable versions of this," she said. "You know, you've probably saved the human race."

"Really?" Weasel asked.

"Yeah. We can't cure people; their brains have been reformed. I want to see how your treatment affects their behavior though." She thought for a second, then remembered what she'd been about to say. "We can purify food and water and maybe scrub early forms from people." She took a second to explain how the types combined to create the dangerous versions.

After a minute, Lisha stopped, realizing she'd gone off on a tangent. "Sorry," she said.

"No, don't be," Weasel said. "Nobody ever explained to me how the virus works." He gestured at the machine. "Since you say it's mechanical, the treatment makes sense."

"How so?"

"It's all energy." Lisha shook her head; she didn't understand. "You figured out high temps kill it. But it can't be killed if it's a machine. Heating is just a higher energy state which deactivates the virus or machines. Radar imparts energy. Microwave ovens heat denser matter more effectively. It's why water boils quickly, meat cooks well, but light stuff doesn't.

"My machine uses a specific frequency based on a harmonic of the 2.46 Hz you told me about. It's directly affecting the machines."

Oz snapped his fingers. "A reset code?"

"Yeah," Weasel said, "maybe. Or the little machines are very vulnerable to that frequency of radar." He rubbed his chin and looked at the machine. "We'll have to mess around with it."

"Once we get some field versions going, sure. Using it as a food and water treatment machine is a priority. You invented it; what are you calling it?"

Weasel looked at his machine for a second, frowning. Then the frown became a grin. "Call it a Februus."

"Sounds Latin," Oz said.

"It is. Februus was the Roman god of purification. February was his holy month, and it was named for the Februla which was a spring purification festival that occurred during that month. There's a lot more mixed up in there."

"Sounds good to me," Lisha said.

A banging sound somewhere on deck made them turn in that direction. There'd been plenty of maintenance and construction on the *Helix,* but Lisha thought the sound was…strange. Oz cocked his head and moved toward the door leading out of the old storage room that was now Weasel's Workshop.

"What is it?" Lisha asked.

"I'm not sure," he said. Then a long rattle of gunfire sounded. Oz instantly drew the gun he always wore.

"Doctor, get down over there."

"That's the soldiers shooting at seals again," Lisha said, though Oz's nervousness made her less certain.

"That sounded like an MP5," Weasel said and produced his own pistol.

Where did he have that hidden? Lisha wondered. Am I the only one on my crew not armed?

"A small caliber machine pistol of some kind," Oz agreed, then turned his head toward Lisha. "None of the Zombie Squad or the army soldiers General Rose sent carry a weapon like that. We've been boarded."

"Boarded?" she asked. "What, like pirates?"

"I have no idea—" Oz didn't finish the sentence. An explosion blew the door off its hinges, sending him flying backward. The door rebounded off the floor, expending most of its energy. However, it was still a big steel sheet, and it landed on Weasel, pinning him to the floor.

Lisha cringed behind the workbench, holding her microscope and many of Weasel's tools. She peeked around the corner. Oz was up on one knee. In the flickering fluorescent light, she could see him run a forearm across his forehead, wiping away bright red blood. He grasped his pistol in both hands just as a trio of figures rushed through the door.

They crouched down as they moved, squat, short-barreled guns tucked against their shoulders. They were dressed entirely in black. Armor covered their bodies, blending in with their black uniforms. Helmets covered their heads and ears, and slightly reflective face shields obscured their features. They moved as one, spreading out and sweeping the entire room.

Oz fired three quick shots at the one closest to him. Two shots hit the black clad figure's chest, and the last ricocheted off his helmet with a bright spark. The shots to the chest staggered the man who unleashed a burst from his gun. Bullets ricocheted off the walls, and one narrowly missed Lisha's head. She heard the bullet pass by her ear. It was a sound she'd never forget.

She pulled back with a little yelp. There was another burst of machinegun fire. Oz responded. *Bang, bang, bang.* Another burst, and the shooting stopped. Lisha crawled around the table to the other side, toward Oz. When she looked, he was lying on his face, blood pooling around him. She thought he was breathing, but she wasn't sure. She heard a click and looked up; one of the black-clad men was pointing his deadly gun at her head.

She closed her eyes and waited for death. Nothing happened. She felt a pair of hands drag her roughly to her feet. The man raised her chin. She opened her eyes and saw that he had a miniature screen built into the armor on his forearm. On it was a picture of her. She instantly recognized the less-than-flattering picture from her Wikipedia page.

"We have her," she heard one of them say, the voice muffled by the full-face shield. If there was a reply, she didn't hear it. The man nodded. "Take her. Let's evac."

"I'm not going with you," she said and tried to pull away. Another one produced a little vial and squirted her in the face. She gasped and shook her head. She tasted something sweet, and her vision swam. "You son of…a…bi…" She fell down a long, dark tunnel into perpetual night.

* * *

"Osprey inbound!" Mays said.

"They're coming back out," Rose said. The black clad soldiers were fast and well trained. Even from more than 200 meters, he could see the way they moved. "Goddamn it, they have a hostage." *Fuck, it's Dr. Breda.* It had to be. She was on the chunky side and black. How many overweight, black women were on the ship?

"It won't arrive in time," he realized. Rose dropped to one knee and flipped open the cover on his rifle's scope. Mays followed suit. It had been a lot of years since he'd been on the qualification range. Some skills you never forgot, but they did get rusty. He spun the wheel on the advanced sight, and the ship came into focus. A soldier, one of his, leaned over a railing and fired at close range. One of the attackers went down.

"They got one," Mays said. Instantly, three of the attackers fired short bursts, and the soldier fell.

"Damn it," Rose cursed. "Try to slow them down." He spun the magnification on his weapon and settled the crosshairs on the chest of the man closest to the aft of the ship. He read the distance on the scope—*220 meters*—did the mental calculation and raised his point of aim five inches. He flipped off the safety with his thumb and squeezed the trigger. The rifle bucked, and he rode the natural recoil back to the target.

His shot was high and struck the metal superstructure behind the target. The man spun and kneeled, searching for the shooter. "Perfect," Rose growled. He settled again with less drop and squeezed off another round. The sea was almost dead calm, with very little roll. The bullet crossed the 220 yards and hit the man square in the chest.

"Nice shot, sir," Mays said and fired his own weapon.

Rose grunted and evaluated the results. His target had been knocked back on his haunches. However, he was back up in a second with no apparent injury. "Fuck," Rose snarled. As he looked, he noticed the attacker who'd been shot at almost point-blank range appeared to be up and moving, though less steadily. He'd been hit. "They've got some really good armor," he said to Mays.

"I noticed." Mays and Rose both fired again, though neither hit. Unfortunately, the bad guys had figured out where the attack was coming from. "They can't do much at this range with those poodle-shooters."

Heavy slugs tore into the superstructure over their heads. Paint and metal shrapnel spalled in every direction. Rose yelled a curse and rolled sideways into his ship's bridge. A heavy machinegun on the enemy's submarine had opened fire.

"Mays, can you get a sight on that gun? Mays?" Rose looked back and saw Mays lying on his back, eyes staring blankly up at the sky. Half his chest was a bloody mass of shredded meat. "Fuck!"

Machinegun fire raked the *Pacific Adventurer* around the area he and Mays had been shooting from for several seconds, then it stopped. Guessing they were reloading, Rose propped his rifle back on the railing and looked for targets. There were none. The sub and the mysterious enemy combatants were gone.

* * *

**Classified Task Force**
**Gulf of Farallones, California**

"You again?" Grange asked as the old woman entered the room. "I've told you everything I know."

Jophiel stopped and looked at the patient. Was something different about the young Coast Guard officer?

"I just have a couple more questions."

Grange reclined and put her hands behind her head. "Ask."

"Do you remember seeing anything strange at the Flotilla?"

"You mean, besides a zombie apocalypse?"

"Of course. Maybe flying boats or things like that?"

Grange laughed and shook her head. "No, nothing."

Jophiel questioned her just long enough to be sure she wasn't hiding anything, then left without another word. There was no need for any more pleasantries. She'd finally completed the task Michael had put before her, which meant the annoying Coast Guard officer was of no more use.

She removed the CVR helmet and put it on the holder. The techs looked anxiously at her. "Whatever you did fixed it." They seemed to sag in relief. "You can begin shutting down the system for transport to San Nicolas."

"Thank you, Jophiel," the team leader said. She left without further comment. She needed to get back to her office. The translation matrix was nearly complete. It would have been finished if Michael hadn't wasted her valuable time making her act as an interrogator instead of a linguist.

After the door closed, the techs waited until they were sure she was gone, then cheered and high fived each other. None of them noticed that one of the many computers running the Cognitive VR system had changed screens for a moment, then returned to the original. The team leader addressed his staff.

"Well done. Let's go down to stores and get the crates. The Heptagon will want us to unload quickly. Rumor has it someone else is being brought in, some doctor who might have a cure, and Michael wants her questioned using CVR."

None of them looked forward to more interactions with the Heptagon, however they'd at least be on a base where extensive facilities existed. The ships were nothing more than improvised environments. Many of their families and friends had been evacuated to San Nicolas shortly after the plague went global. It was an extra insurance policy to keep them loyal and hardworking.

Less than a minute after they were gone, the door opened, and a pair of women came in. "Hello?" one called.

"Where the hell is everyone?" the other one wondered.

"No clue." The leader was a specially trained physician, and she carried a small, steel case. "This is that Coast Guard officer, right?"

"Yeah," the assistant said. She held up a tablet and read the instructions again. "I don't understand why we're doing this. Didn't someone say she was going to be disposed of?"

"Maybe the scuttlebutt was wrong," the leader said. "God, look at her. It's a waste of time, really."

"The orders are signed by Michael," the assistant said. They opened the adjoining room and went inside. The smells of burned flesh, anesthetic, and bleach were almost overpowering. Both women quickly put on sterile masks. They didn't completely block the stench, though they did help. "Goddamn. Hard to believe she's still alive."

"Just open the kit, so we can get out of here."

The assistant administered the first drug, while the team leader prepared the special hypodermic. "Ready?" she asked. Her assistant tapped her watch.

"One minute."

"Oh, right." They waited, trying to ignore the smell. The watch beeped. "Here we go," she said and stuck the needle into Grange's thigh, then depressed the plunger. She immediately moved back as Grange screamed through the breather and arched her back up off the stained sheets.

"Gah, I never get used to that," the assistant said.

A second later, Grange fell back on the bed and lay still.

"Okay, we're done," the supervisor said. They packed up their gear and left without a backward glance.

A minute passed, then two. Suddenly, Grange's chest began to rise and fall quickly, as if she had just run a marathon. Her eyes snapped open, and she looked around wildly, gasping. "What? What?" It took long minutes for her breathing to slow and her mind to clear.

"It worked," she croaked once she could speak. "Okay. Next."

She heard a click as her restraints released. She sat up, her putrid bandages fell away, and blood dripped onto the bed. She showed no indications of pain, and she didn't acknowledge the horrible burns. Instead, she spun sideways and put her feet on the cold, metal floor. She grabbed the monitor leads and pulled them from her chest, and she roughly yanked the IVs out of her arms, paying no heed to the sprays of blood which stopped in an instant.

Grange had great difficulty walking. She staggered toward her destination, the medical room's door. It beeped and slid open as she approached. With each step, she left a bloody smear behind. Her balance became increasingly better. There were three lockers in the attendants' area. She pulled one open and took out the contents. With each passing moment, she moved with less difficulty.

Ten minutes after the injection, she opened the outside door and walked into the hallway. A passing technician glanced at her curiously, wondering why she was wearing a tinted face shield. However, it wasn't the strangest thing he'd seen since joining Project Genesis, so he just shook his head and continued on.

The mysterious medical tech, wearing surgical gloves and a face-mask, stopped at an access hatch. The door beeped and opened as she reached it. It swung open and she stepped through, closing it behind her just as the CVR crew came into view carrying big crates and drinking sodas.

The team leader opened the medical bay's door and put down his crate. He was reaching for a clipboard to begin inventory when he noticed the bloody footsteps. "What the fuck?" he asked. The steps were clearly leading out of the still open isolation room to the clothes locker. There were bloody smears on the locker's handle, and a towel lay on the floor looking as though it had been used in surgery.

"She's gone!" a tech cried out.

The supervisor ran over to the window and looked inside. There were more bloody footprints, and pieces of charred skin lay on the floor along the path. A tech ran out into the hallway and returned a second later.

"Nothing!" he said. "No signs at all."

The supervisor's eyes darted all over the room, searching for answers where there were none to be had. The intercom buzzed, and they all stared at it. The supervisor nodded toward it, and one of the assistants picked up the handset. "Just a second," he said and held it out. "It's Michael. He wants the patient terminated. What should I say?"

"We're dead meat," another tech said. The supervisor could only nod.

* * *

**HAARP Ship *Helix***

**The Flotilla**

**150 Nautical Miles West of San Diego, CA**

The V-22 Osprey took up the entire helicopter landing pad and then some. Luckily, the *Helix* had a completely open aft deck, since the Osprey's twin rotors cut a massive swath as it sat idling. General Rose and a squad of his best men came down the rear ramp and onto the ship. A group of navy corpsmen who had arrived earlier were busy tending to casualties.

Rose already knew he'd lost five of the seven man squad assigned to protect the *Helix*. The ship had also had a small group of defenders, referred to as the Zombie Squad, of all things. Bunch of crazy rednecks with guns. Still, they'd gotten the only kill on the attackers, but it had cost them their lives. Five bodies lay under sheets. A man named Jon Osborne was being carried out on a stretcher by a pair of corpsmen. He was in a bad way, but he was alive.

"You men know if he's any relation to Jeremiah Osborne?" Rose asked.

"No sir, sorry," the first corpsman replied. "He's unconscious."

"Understood. Take him to the carrier with the other wounded."

"Roger that, sir."

Sergeant Grady came out of the ship, carrying his M-4 in both arms. He had a look of tired determination on his face. "Sorry we were late, General," he said.

"Not your fault, Sergeant. Any leakers left on the ship?"

"Negative, it's clear."

"Casualty count?"

"Five of our men KIA, two injured. Five crew also KIA, including all their shooters. The attackers largely ignored anyone who didn't resist. They were clearly after Dr. Breda."

"Any clue why?"

"No, General, sorry. They took a case full of samples."

"And they left my Februus Device behind."

A somewhat overweight guy walked out of the main hatch. He held a bloody rag to his balding head and looked a little like a crazy, homeless man.

"Who are you, and what's a Femur Device?"

"Paul McDaniels. They call me Weasel. *Februus* Device," he said, carefully pronouncing the first word as if Rose were a child. The general's eyes narrowed dangerously. "It's a radar powered, sterilization machine."

"Weasel, I'm lost. What the fuck are you talking about?"

"Can I get a Band-aid or something?" he asked. When he took the rag away from his head, blood flowed freely, and Rose was pretty sure he could see pale, white bone.

"Jesus, man, you've got a good gouge on your head. Corpsman, get this man prepped for evac."

"No," Weasel said. "I need to stay and work on the Februus."

"I need to know what this thing you're talking about is. Corpsman, can you stop this guy from leaking all over the deck?"

"Yes, General." The medic examined Weasel's injury, while he described the invention he'd created to the General.

"Are you saying you invented a cure for Strain Delta?" Rose asked.

"No, its just a way of deactivating the nano machines."

"The what?"

"Strain Delta isn't a virus, it's a machine. The Februus Device deactivates it."

Rose rubbed the bridge of his nose and watched the corpsman work. A big flap of Weasel's scalp was ripped. It was a bloody wound, but not a dangerous one, as long as it was dealt with. The corpsman, who was closing the wound with staples, was doing a top-notch job of taking care of it. Weasel was a pretty tough character, only flinching as the staples were clicked into his flesh. Behind them, the injured had been loaded into the Osprey. The engines revved up, and the big VTOL craft rose off the deck, angled over the side, then turned toward the carrier.

"Weasel, pretend I'm not a scientist, or an engineer, or whatever you are, and explain this device to me."

"In simple terms, we can use it to purify anything that will fit inside."

"Anything?"

"Yes. Food, water, animals, whatever. But Dr. Breda said it wouldn't *un-zombie* anything, because Strain Delta modifies the brain to this weird 2.46 hertz frequency, almost like a computer. Oz said it might be possible to read the programming and change it, or something."

*For fuck's sake.* "Okay, sorry I asked. So, it can make clean food? Even from the infected stuff?"

"That's the whole point," Weasel said, frustrated.

"Is the machine hard to make?"

Weasel got a vacant look, and his lips moved. Rose wondered if he'd just lost his last marble. "No, not really. You have to sacrifice a microwave for the magnetron, and you have to collect a few other parts that shouldn't be hard to find. Probably have to manually control the cycle because I built mine with a breadboard."

"So, yes?"

"Yeah, isn't that what I said?"

Rose's radio buzzed for attention. "Weasel, when your head is fixed, get some rest."

"I'm not tired."

"Okay. Can you make some more of your…"

"Februus Devices?" Rose nodded. "Sure. I'll need some parts."

"Tell Sergeant Grady what you need. Give him a list." The sergeant was off to one side, standing by the ship's railing. He gave Rose a 'thanks a lot' look. "I have a call I need to take."

"Sure, sure," Weasel mumbled as the corpsman finished treating his wound. Rose sighed and clicked the radio. "General Rose."

"General, this is Captain Gilchrist on the *Ford*."

"Captain, you calling to say you found the sub?"

"We're hunting what appears to be two subs, General."

"I need you to avoid sinking them."

"Sir, you cannot be serious. They've sunk one ship already."

"Yes, and they sent commandoes aboard this ship to kidnap Dr. Lisha Breda."

"The woman from that genetics project?" Gilchrist asked. "That's unfortunate, but is she worth risking more sunken ships, especially one of our few remaining military craft?"

Rose considered the question. If they had the treatment device that she'd helped develop, and she was one of the only people still alive who understood Strain Delta, was she worth the risk? She was one of the only people he liked, and he realized he wasn't willing to let her go. But he needed to make a logical decision, not an emotional one.

Suddenly, something came to mind. He remembered the flight from Hood to the west coast. Part way there, one of his transports had been attacked in an airport outside Truth or Consequences, New Mexico. Could these seemingly random events be linked? It seemed unlikely, but it was what he had to work with. He explained the attack to Gilchrist and how he believed the two were linked. "I also believe Dr. Breda is of crucial importance to our survival."

"General, risking assets right now goes against my better judgement for the sake of those in harm's way."

"I understand. Will you do it anyway?"

"I will. I have an old Viking ASW plane following a sub heading north. The damned thing is fast, goes almost 300 kph. Luckily, the Viking is faster. I can't risk losing the Viking, though. If there's any sign of a counterattack, I'm calling it off."

"Understood. The sub must have a base. If you can find it, I'll do the rest."

"Shouldn't we leave it to the Marines? We don't have a bunch, but this is what they're trained to do."

"They're providing security for the Flotilla. I'm betting this sub is heading for an island. If it is, the fuckers are in *my* territory. Keep me up to date, Captain. And thanks."

***

**Joint Combined Evacuation Fleet**
**150 miles West of Puerto Escondido, Mexico**

Theodore Bennitti wandered the deck of the USS *Bataan.* A nearby crewman, tending to a recently returned Osprey, glanced his way, making sure he didn't stray too close to the still spinning VTOL aircraft's blades. Theodore was too busy to notice; he needed fresh air and open spaces to think.

Back at the Cape, his office had been located in The Plaza, Kennedy Space Center's HQ Building on Merritt Island. It had been five kilometers from the launch complex's northern end. As a director, he'd had an easterly view from the 3rd floor. It had been a decent vantage point from which to watch launches, and he'd seen many in his time at NASA. The new building being built a block away was seven stories tall and would have had even better views, but now it would never be completed.

On nice days, he would walk out to the extensive grass lawns around the Plaza to think. At night, the sky was beautiful. In the 70s, before the population explosion in Florida, you could often see the Milky Way. With society's collapse, all light pollution was gone. He guessed the spectacular views were back.

He had a lot to think about, and the flight deck was a near-perfect place to think. They were sailing through calm seas as midday approached. Since the Russians were no longer hunting them, the environment was much calmer—you could feel it in how much calmer the crews were.

Theodore had gambled the Star Fox would be enough evidence to convince Captain Chugunkin the plague wasn't an American construct. It was a gamble because they couldn't let the captain physically touch the alien. For safety, they kept her away from all human contact. He and Dr. Gnox were concerned the Russians would believe the alien was nothing more than a fancy, animatronic creation or CGI.

He'd found out from Gnox only minutes before the meeting that Nikki, the alien they'd called Star Fox before, had made major strides in learning English. What neither had known was the extent of those strides. By the time Captain Chugunkin met the alien face-to-face, Nikki was not only conversant in English, but Russian as well.

How was that possible, he wondered?

* * *

The purpose of the conversation between Nikki, Captain Chugunkin, and Theodore's group of scientists was to convince the Russian guests not to start a war. However, Nikki had other plans. She started by revealing how the Russians shot down their starship in orbit. Captain Chugunkin was confused and offended by the suggestion.

"How could my government have shot your starship down?" he demanded. "You can fly between the stars, but we shoot you down with a missile?"

"It wasn't a missile," Nikki replied, speaking first in Russian, then in English, thereby announcing she'd learned Russian. "It was a directed energy weapon, a particle beam with more than a gigawatt of power."

Captain Chugunkin's mouth turned into a thin line, and Theodore knew a truth had been told. A truth the captain hadn't been expecting.

"The weapon was fired from the following coordinates." Nikki rattled off some numbers, and Captain Chugunkin's face paled. "In addition," the alien said, looking at Theodore and his team, "this happened after you invited us to return."

"What?" Theodore gasped.

* * *

He shook his head as he walked, mumbling to himself. His government, always good at keeping secrets, had kept a doozy. Who would have thought the much-hyped Roswell incident had really happened? Or at least, the popular version had happened to cover up Star Fox's species making first contact with humanity.

* * *

Admiral Kent hadn't been quick to buy into this new revelation, even after Nikki provided a litany of names from the 1950's US military and government. Theodore and the other scientists had less trouble accepting the new paradigm. Certain technological innovations beginning in the post WWII era were far too convenient.

So, the US had invited the aliens back, but they hadn't bothered to prepare for their return. They'd been too busy covering up the initial contact and profiting from the technology gifted to them. Then the Russians, in a typical overreaction, shot the aliens' ship out of the sky.

Chugunkin wasn't happy with the situation, especially when he realized the aliens had shared tech with America, but not with them.

That was one of the things Theodore wondered about. The Russians had kept pace with the US technologically in many areas, even exceeded them in some. A common school of thought suggested the Russians would have exceeded the West had they possessed a better form of government. The particle beam was a huge mystery. Where exactly had they developed this technology? Had they developed it at all, or was its origin extraterrestrial as well?

In the name of mending bridges, Kent agreed to share the details for making the salvaged alien drives work. Nikki hinted that she could do something about the nanovirus. However, she told them their ship was the problem. The mothership, which was shot down, crashed somewhere in the western United States. That was news to Theodore. Nikki's ship, which was in the Bataan's hangar, was more of a ship's boat, maybe a captain's yacht; it wasn't intended for long flights.

"When the mothership was critically damaged, and we were forced to enter Earth's atmosphere, our ship's computer issued an order to abandon ship. Escape pods were scattered all over the northern hemisphere."

"What about the virus?" Dr. Gallatin asked.

"It was an accident," Nikki replied. "A result of the attack."

"Accident?" Kent demanded. "Our planet is dead!"

"I am not an expert," Nikki said. "You must understand that what you are calling a virus is really a machine."

"We understand it is a machine," Gallatin replied angrily.

"Do you?" Nikki's whiskers twitched, and her ears vibrated. The Vulpes weren't exactly the same as foxes, just similar. They appeared less mobile than the terrestrial species. "Then you understand such machines are useful for much more than causing diseases?"

Gallatin opened his mouth, then closed it with an audible pop. He shook his head. Dr. Curie spoke in the silence.

"You mean they're, what, tools to you?"

"Tools with a great many uses." Nikki leaned closer to the window separating her from them. "Any tool can be dangerous, if proper care isn't taken. Its name is not pronounceable to you."

"We call it Strain Delta."

"I know," Nikki said. "The tool your Strain Delta came from, I will call it Pandora, was a dire accident. We did not expect to be attacked. I am not a member of the crew. My job was to negotiate with your race. I must assume the damage to our ship was in the engineering section, which is where Pandora was stored."

"We did this to ourselves?" Gallatin asked, still shaking his head.

"The Russians did this," Kent snarled, glaring at Chugunkin.

"If we had known there was an alien starship coming, maybe we wouldn't have shot it down." Chugunkin said.

"Knowing your government, I doubt it would have mattered," Kent replied.

"This is not productive," Theodore intervened. "At this stage, we need to work together to fix this, or at least salvage something from it."

"We need to find my ship," Nikki said. "Without more of my people and my ship's resources, there is nothing else I can do. If what you say is true, Pandora will continue to wreak havoc until your race is lost. Or worse."

"Worse?" Kent gasped. "In the name of God, what could be worse?"

"You don't want to know."

After the meeting, Chugunkin agreed to assist them in any way possible. Theodore spent a few minutes talking with his fellow scientists.

"What could Nikki have meant by worse?" Gallatin asked almost immediately.

"A worse plague? What can be worse?" Curie asked. "Jesus, Theodore, the damned thing is reprogramming humans into cannibals!"

"Grey goo," Theodore said.

"Pardon me?" Gallatin asked. Curie looked confused too.

"A theory of nanites. Many speculate about a special kind of self-replicating nanite, like these. Only, instead of doing simple jobs, or even reprogramming people, these are dissasemblers. They only exist to replicate and take things apart. They replicate and disassemble until there's nothing left except primordial elements. Grey goo. A whole planet of grey goo. Theoretically, a galaxy of it."

"That's fucking worse," Gallatin agreed.

* * *

"Grey goo," Theodore mumbled, shaking his head.

"You okay, sir?"

He glanced at the deck crewman, confused. "Oh, sure," he said, realizing he'd probably been talking out loud. The man nodded and went back to his duties. Theodore was once again alone on the aircraft carrier. Water stretched away as far as he could see. Other ships were within sight, but as far as he knew, they were alone on an endless sea of water going on forever. Just like the universe.

He turned to go inside; he needed to make some notes. The walk had cleared his mind, just as he'd hoped. A thousand things still rolled around inside his head, but there was some coherence to his thoughts now. Just as he reached the hatch going down, a thought came to him.

How had the alien suddenly become so good at not one, but two, languages? He'd spoken to Wilma Gnox right after the big meeting, and she'd confirmed she'd kept her language interactions to mundane subjects and terms. There had been no discussion about the plague. So, exactly how had Nikki known they called the plague Strain Delta?

* * *

***Ocean Vista***

**The Flotilla**

**150 Nautical Miles West of San Diego, CA**

Rose grabbed his radio the instant it beeped. "General Rose."

"It's Captain Gilchrist. The Viking shadowed our bogey to San Nicolas Island."

"San Nicolas?" Rose asked, wracking his sleep deprived mind. "Northwest of San Clemente?"

"Yes," Gilchrist replied. "It was a navy weapons testing facility. About 20 years ago it was deemed largely off limits. Classified research."

"Like stealth subs that can go faster than a jet?"

"Not faster than a jet, but fast, yeah," Gilchrist replied. "Thanks to that bastard Watts, we have some space assets back. One is a National Reconnaissance Office bird with a recent view of San Nicolas. It's interesting, because I shouldn't have access to data on a classified installation. A small squadron of ships just docked there, including one with a big, shiny something aboard."

"Something?"

Gilchrist hesitated. "If I had to guess, I'd say it's related to the alien escape pod thing Osborne brought aboard."

"No shit," Rose said.

"No shit."

"Are there any defenses you can see?"

"As a matter of fact, yes. My analysts have identified two SAM sites, a radar installation, a big aircraft hangar, and some of the weirdest looking helicopters I've ever seen at the airstrip."

This is some skunk works shit, Rose thought. These fuckers must be the ones who took out my aircrew in Truth or Consequences. But why did they take Lisha? "Captain, have you spotted the submarine?"

"There's a shadow that I think is the sub."

"Captain, it is my intention to attack the island and retrieve our kidnapped doctor."

"General, that's a US installation."

"Which is harboring unknown people who attacked my forces, sank a private vessel, and kidnapped a scientist."

"You have a point. However, I can't risk running surface assets out that way. There's still a sub out there, and I have a feeling it is going to be trouble soon. The Viking is coming back now."

"What can you do then? You don't have any bombers left, do you?"

"No, and I don't have any helicopters to spare either, not with those SAM batteries."

Rose cursed.

"However, I do have cruise missiles."

"Well, that sounds lovely!"

"They likely have the ability to down them, so I'll have to overwhelm them. The *Russell* has 12. We used a lot during the Coronado fiasco. It might be enough to do the job."

"I'll take what I can get. Hold one." He looked up. "Lieutenant Drake?" Drake was his newly assigned aide. Rose had grabbed the man from his extremely limited supply of officers. He had been in logistics at Fort Hood, but he had served in a combat brigade when he'd been a 2nd lieutenant.

"General?"

"I want all four Osprey's spun up and ready to go. Find Master Sergeant Ayres and tell him I need the two best, most rested platoons ready to mount up. Full assault ruck." He looked at his watch. "We dust off in 15 minutes. Time to get some payback."

*****

# Chapter Nine

**Afternoon, Saturday, May 4th**
**Classified Genesis Facility**
**San Nicolas Island**

Pearl Grange sat quietly in the storage locker and waited. The voice whispering in the back of her mind had slowly become more understandable. After she'd woken up, all she could understand were the most basic ideas. Go straight ahead. Open the door. Wipe the blood away. Put on clothes.

Now that she'd sat in total darkness for several hours, the voice was becoming clearer and clearer. A constant flow of information and ideas. Where things were located on the ship, crewmember schedules, what areas to avoid.

*How am I hearing all of this?*

*From me.*

*Who are you?*

*First Scout.*

*I'm going insane.*

*No, you are not. The Pandora injection they gave you is attuned to psy-lock.*

*The what injection is attuned to what?*

There was silence for the first time, and she silently congratulated herself on achieving a moment of sanity.

*They have given you an injection which enables me to talk to you.*

*I don't understand how you can speak in my brain.*

*It is not important for you to understand. You said you would help me.*

*I didn't think it was more than a dream.*

*It wasn't, but I still need you.*

*I hurt.*

*The medication used to dull your nerves before the Pandora injection is wearing off. Before long, you will feel everything.*

She could feel her cracked and burned skin inside the gloves she wore and shuddered. Burns were among the most horrific injuries. She'd been in a burn ward during her time in Afghanistan. A young Marine was brought in with badly burned legs from an IED. He kept screaming that he wanted to die. She started to shake in fear.

*We will hurry.*

She wasn't encouraged. *I need to keep my mind off this. Tell me how you know about this ship.*

*My psy-lock allows me to interface with any computer. The room they have me in is ingenious, no doubt built with knowledge we gave your race the last time we were here.*

*You've been to Earth before?*

The kinds of things it said and the way it talked led her sci-fi loving brain to a conclusion—aliens. It made sense. She even saw the crazy haired guy from TV saying, "Aliens".

*Yes, years ago. We wanted to come to your planet. Humans we talked with offered us a safe haven. We gave them technological gifts to aid you toward the goal, help raise your technological level. When we returned, we were attacked.*

*Who attacked you?*

*We do not know. My ship was damaged, and we crashed. The psy-lock allows me to talk with computers through my mind. The injection you got gives you a similar ability.*

*I have computer telepathy?*

*Yes. I am trapped in this isolation cage. I cannot contact my ship. I need to. If you can get on the ship, we can make this happen.*

*What will happen if you contact your ship?*

*Something wonderful.*

*Yeah, you already said that.*

*It's time.*

"Right," she whispered out loud and got to her feet. Tortured nerves and muscles screamed, and unfortunately, she felt some of it. She dearly missed the yummy drugs.

*I don't know if I can do this.*

*Think of your dead shipmates.*

Her jaw muscles bunched, which hurt. In her mind's eye, she saw the faces of her crew, all dead because of the bastards who were all around her. Maybe she could get some payback. Was that worth some pain? Was it worth a lot of pain? She pushed through the agony and got to her feet. The pain faded, a little.

*Okay, where to?*

* * *

***Ocean Vista***

**The Flotilla**

**150 Nautical Miles West of San Diego, CA**

All four of the Ospreys' huge blades spun at idle as the ground crews finished pumping fuel into the VTOL craft. Rose stepped out of the barge's built-up structure, doing his best to ignore the pain in his knees caused by his ruck. He hadn't carried anything close to a combat load since the 2nd Gulf

War, and then it was just to load aboard an APC while his firebase was moved.

Master Sergeant Ayres was helping a private secure a difficult piece of equipment when he saw Rose. The senior NCO's face darkened, and he left the private to puzzle out the problem by himself and walked over to his commander. "General, what do you think you're doing?"

"Getting ready for this mission."

Ayres made a face and looked over Rose's gear, taking in his harness, extra ammo, weapons, and camelback. "Sir, when's the last time you went out on an op?"

"Been a few years," Rose admitted.

"Been a few years since prohibition ended too."

"Master Sergeant, I'm going. It isn't up for discussion." He walked forward and looked at the men arrayed on the deck in rough formation. There were 92, which was nearly half of his combat ready forces. They all looked tired. He understood. He felt pretty ragged himself.

"You ordered a lot of machineguns, General."

"Yes. The enemy we're facing has improved body armor. We'll brief the men en route."

Rose heard a striking sound and turned to see Ayres lighting a cigar. "Master Sergeant, you do know it's against regulations to smoke on duty?"

Ayres puffed the cigar to a cherry red and shook out the match before answering. "If a three-star general can waddle onto a Marine Osprey near the end of the world to attack some secret base to rescue a biologist being held hostage..." He took a big drag on the cigar, "...I can smoke a damn cigar on the transport."

"Fair enough," Rose said and raised his voice. "We were attacked a couple of hours ago. An unknown organization sank a civilian ship, then kidnapped a scientist who's working on a cure for Strain Delta." He didn't bother explaining it wasn't really a cure. "These same sons of bitches were the ones who took out our scouts in Truth or Consequences on the way here. They killed four of us then and six more now, not counting civilians. I'm not inclined to let this stand. Who wants some payback?"

"*Hooah!*" the men roared.

"Master Sergeant, load them up!"

All four Osprey had M-240s mounted on their rear doors for close air support. Rose fully expected the landing to be opposed. They were going to come in low and fast, but the adversary had already demonstrated technological prowess beyond what they'd normally encounter. So, he was going for a multi-pronged attack.

"All men aboard," Ayres yelled over the roar of the twin Rolls Royce engines. Even at idle, the turboprops were loud.

Rose raised a hand over his head and made a swirling motion with his finger. The master sergeant spoke into his headset, and the roar of the engines rose to a crescendo. A second later, the V-22 Osprey climbed into the air. He could see out the rear door which was locked half-open to allow the machinegun to work. The other three Osprey took off after and followed.

He linked through the aircraft radio and called the carrier.

"David actual to Passkey."

"Passkey actual, go ahead David."

In the time between his decision to commit and the beginning of the operation, Rose had ferried notes over to the *Ford* with his order of battle and some code names he'd created.

"Operation Roundhouse has lifted off."

"Roger that. Will initiate Counterstrike at the agreed upon waypoint. Good luck, and God speed."

Rose nodded and left the radio on the tactical channel, just in case.

***

**Classified Genesis Facility**

**San Nicolas Island**

Lisha Breda gasped and opened her eyes. Her heart was racing, and she couldn't catch her breath. She was in a drab room that looked like it was made of metal, sitting on a hard, uncomfortable chair before a similarly manufactured table. She tried to move her hands and found they were tied behind her back.

"What's going on?" she demanded, her breathing beginning to slow. "Why am I tied up?" There was nobody in the room to answer. She looked around and tried to figure out where she was and how she'd gotten there. "Hey!" she screamed at the top of her lungs and immediately regretted it. Her head throbbed as though she'd been at a heavy metal concert.

The door opened, and a tall man in blue coveralls walked in. He had short blonde hair and wore sunglasses despite being indoors. "Ah, Dr. Breda, you're awake."

His walk and tone of voice suggested he was military. "Why am I here?" she demanded. Slowly her memory was returning. There had been an attack; her people had been killed. "What did you do?!" she yelled, straining painfully against her restraints.

"Doctor, my name is Michael. I'm the leader of an organization that was established to protect the United States from alien invasions."

"Oh? Looks like you fucked that up pretty thoroughly."

Michael smiled, but his tone was without humor. "Accidents happen. However, I can assure you, things would be much worse if we had not been here to manage the situation."

"Manage? Like kidnapping me?"

"Doctor, please." He seemed to take no real notice of her insults. "We need to know if you found a cure for Strain Delta."

"You couldn't have called? Maybe sent an email?"

"We don't have the luxury of common courtesies," he said as if he were explaining things to a child. "We've seen evidence someone in your Flotilla has learned to use alien technology. Care to fill me in?"

"I don't see how what we've learned matters. And no, I don't care to fill you in on shit."

"The knowledge is essential to saving the United States, and by default, the planet."

Lisha glared daggers at him. "I don't feel like being cooperative when I'm tied to a chair, Michael or whatever your name is."

The door opened again, and a pair of black clad soldiers came in. Her memory had returned sufficiently for her to realize they were dressed and equipped like the ones who'd attacked and taken her hostage. She tensed. They had her sample case.

"Does this contain the cure?" he asked.

"Fuck you."

"If I cut you free, will you cooperate?" She nodded, and he gestured one of the men toward her.

The soldier moved behind Lisha, and she heard the *schnict* of a knife locking open. A second later, her bindings were cut. She pulled her hands around and massaged her wrists. Both had angry red welts from the bindings, which were likely stripper cuffs. She looked at the sample case and shook her head.

"Did you just steal the first thing that looked useful?"

Michael glanced at the soldier who'd cut her free. The soldier shrugged. "Are you saying this isn't the cure?"

"I'm saying this is a sample case. It holds deactivated Strain Delta as well as samples of human brain matter that I use for testing."

"Deactivated? So, you did cure it."

She didn't reply.

"Fine, I have what I need. You'll brief our people on the cure, and I'll get rid of the Flotilla."

"What?"

He removed a radio from his pocket and spoke. "Colonel Baker, you have a go to attack. Make it quick. No surviving ships."

"You son of a bitch," Lisha snarled and leaped, hands outstretched for his face. Michael intercepted her jump with a backhanded blow, spinning her to the floor. She hit and saw stars, spitting blood from a split lip. "Take her to a long-term cell. Inform the team to prep her for CVR."

She tried getting to her feet. She needed to get her hands on him, scratch his eyes out, and throttle the life out of the bastard. Strong hands grabbed her and pinned her arms behind her back. The soldier applied so much force, she was afraid her joints would dislocate. She cried out as she was cuffed again. When she tried to kick one of the men in the groin, leg restraints were added. She screamed as they carried her out like luggage.

* * *

"Enjoy your stay," Michael sneered as the screaming scientist was hauled out. He switched channels on his radio. "Security. Any sign of Grange?"

"No sir, not yet."

Michael spat a curse before replying. "Now that we're docked, I want two full platoons searching the ship. She probably crawled off somewhere to die, but I detest loose ends."

"Yes, sir."

Michael cut the connection and stared at the empty chair and sample case. It wouldn't be hard to get answers from the doctor with the CVR system. It always worked in the end. Still, the mystery of Grange's disappearance from the medical ward bothered him. *Could the medics be involved?* It was possible they'd gone soft. Those types didn't understand the necessity of breaking a few eggs to make omelets.

Like everyone assigned to Genesis, they'd all undergone psychological evaluations, and they'd proven they were loyal and had flexible morals. Of course, all good medical types had limits, or they didn't make very good healers. But how had she managed to get out of bed?

He picked up the radio again. "Michael to Dr. Meeker."

"Yes, sir," the doctor answered.

"You are aware of the missing prisoner?"

"I have heard."

"Is there anything unusual in her chart?"

"Hmm, just a second." Michael heard keys clicking. The doctor was already in the island's medical facilities, as were most of the staff from their ships. Migration onto the island had been planned out well in advance and had proceeded quickly once they'd finally docked. Hundreds of island-side staff were waiting and leaped into action as soon as the first ship tossed lines ashore.

"She was in pretty bad shape, obviously. We've been keeping her alive, as you requested. Low level injections of stabilizing nanovirus. The full healing package was administered just before we made shore."

"What?!" Michael roared. "What did you say?"

"I said we administered the full healing package."

"We were done with her, damnit. Why would you do that?"

"I have your orders here, in the file."

Michael cursed again, took out his handheld tablet, and accessed the files on Lieutenant JG Pearl Grange. He didn't understand much of the jargon or the details of her physical condition. But he didn't have to be fluent to know how bad her injuries were; he'd seen her scorched skin and the exposed muscle and bone. The fact that she'd come out of the water alive was amazing.

The nanovirus treatment to keep her alive was science many on Earth would have given untold fortunes to obtain. The treatment he'd apparently authorized was nothing short of the hand of God. It had only been used 11—now 12—times.

"Is there anything else?" Dr. Meeker asked.

Michael cut the connection and made another call. "Gabriel, it's Michael."

"Yes, Oh Beloved Leader?"

"Will you ever stop being a smartass?"

"Only when you stop being a power-hungry asshole."

Michael was careful to avoid letting any of his anger slip into his voice. "I need you to look at a medical order."

"Of course," she responded with far more civility than he expected. Michael sent her a virtual link to Grange's file. "Gimme a second."

Michael checked a status report on his tablet as he waited. He left the interrogation room and walked outside. He enjoyed the cool May weather on San Nicolas. The big, silver alien ship was suspended from numerous cables as some of the crew swung it off the barge toward a heavy hauler surrounded by a couple dozen project personnel. They were being very slow and very careful. Michael had made it quite clear what would happen to the crew if they dropped the ship.

"What's the problem?" Gabriel asked, bringing Michael back to the present.

"Can you confirm the digital signature on the order to administer the healing package?"

"I saw the order and was confused," Gabriel said. "Weren't you insistent on disposing of the woman?"

"I was and am. Just check."

"Okay." A few seconds went by. "Digital signature is a perfect match…"

"How's that possible?" Michael demanded.

"Let me finish. I was going to say it was a perfect match to the signature on an order you approved last week. This is a forgery, albeit a really good one."

"Who could do this?"

"I could, of course. Maybe Jophiel, though I doubt it. Chamuel could, if she had time. But none of us did."

"How do you know?"

"Every order has a tracking tag that looks like a simple data string, part of the information. It's a checksum I wrote into the process so you would know whose computer things were signed on. According to the checksum, you signed the order on your computer…a week ago. Whoever faked it didn't know about this copy."

"I still don't understand," Michael persisted.

"You cannot insert this order with an origin code. Even a fraudulently copied order would show what computer it was written on. What you have here is the same as a letter arriving in your mailbox, mailed from you, with the matching post office cancelation on the stamp."

"So, how is this possible?"

"It's not."

Michael wanted to argue with the woman, but her statement was so definite, it gave him pause. Gabriel was a lot of things, incorrectly confident was not one of them. "Noted," he said and cut the connection.

He walked into the main building, then down to the labs, and found the isolation wing. The Vulpes' module was already installed, having been lowered in the massive elevator designed for extremely heavy freight. He wasn't surprised to see Jophiel already there, facing the glass wall of the isolation module, a headset on and a large tablet held in both hands.

He walked closer and listened to her speaking in a strange, trilling voice, punctuated with a sharp click that was caused by her snapping her teeth together. After he had been watching for a minute, Jophiel shook her head and turned. She jumped a little, surprised to see Michael standing behind her.

"Scared the shit out of me," she said, using a hand to push some of her waist length, white hair out of her eyes. Her voice had an unusual slur to it.

"What were those sounds?" he asked. "The clicks?"

She grinned and took a plastic appliance from her mouth. It looked a little like a denture upper to him.

"This is to help with some of their vocalizations. Azrael noticed that the researchers back in the fifties were complaining about guttural stops and inflective accents. Those clicking snaps. Our mouths lack the parts." She held up the plastic piece and shrugged. "I had this fabricated."

"So you can talk to it now?"

"Yes, I'm 100% certain we've figured out the language." She looked back at the fox-like alien who sat on his pallet watching them. "He won't talk to me, though. I can tell I'm saying things he understands because of his reaction to the first thing I said."

"What was the first thing you said?"

"Hello, what's your name?"

"Makes sense," Michael replied and stared at the alien. "Can you translate for me?"

"Sure," she said and resettled the appliance in her mouth.

Michael stood within inches of the glass and tapped on it. The alien cocked his head. "I know you can hack our computers," he said. When Jophiel didn't speak, he looked at her. She had a shocked expression on her face. "Later," he said, then nodded toward the alien, and she started to click and trill in its language.

The alien turned his gaze from Michael to Jophiel, obviously intent on listening. Michael saw why she was certain he understood. When Jophiel got to the end of her translation, the alien's head snapped around, and he skewered Michael with his tiny, black eyes. *Bingo.*

"Ask him where Grange is hiding."

"I don't know how to say a person's name," Jophiel said.

"Just say the burned woman."

She spoke to the Vulpes who, this time, didn't take his eyes off Michael. When she finished, the alien showed his tiny, razor-sharp teeth. Michael was sure the alien wasn't smiling.

"Okay, fine," Michael said. He took out his tablet and typed, "Ariel, this is Michael."

"Go ahead," came the text reply.

Michael spoke aloud as he typed. "I know you're still working out all of our alien guest's biology, but have you learned enough to produce a sedative?"

The response took a little longer this time. "Yes, I believe so, but there is some risk."

"I understand. Prepare an anesthesia. I'm going to authorize you to do some exploratory surgery. It seems the Vulpes can communicate with computers."

"Is that so? That means I'll have to operate on his brain, the most likely source of such an ability."

"I would rather you didn't," said a new voice in English with a slightly nasal tone and high pitch.

Michael let the grin spread across his face as he looked up from his screen. The Vulpes had risen and walked over to the glass which was only inches away. Michael typed, "Make the drug; standby on the surgery."

"As you wish." Michael thought the simple, typed response managed to convey his disappointment. He'd wanted to operate on the living alien since he fell into their hands. He glanced at Jophiel who looked shocked and annoyed, no doubt miffed the alien had learned English before she learned Vulpes.

"I'll repeat my question," Michael said, now speaking into the microphone which would relay his voice into the isolation chamber. "Where is Grange?"

"You should release me," the Vulpes said.

"Why don't we start simply? I'm Michael, leader of the Heptagon. Do you have a name?"

"I know who you are. I am First Scout, leader of the mission to your solar system."

"You haven't been very cooperative."

"You shot down my ship and killed most of my crew."

"You brought a plague with you."

"I don't owe you an explanation, human."

"Is that how it's going to be?" Michael asked.

"I will say it one more time, let me go."

Michael tapped his tablet, sending another message to Ariel. "When you have the anesthetic ready, I want the Vulpes unconscious."

"There is some risk," the biologist replied.

"Noted." Michael looked back at the alien. Although he was only about half as tall as Michael, it felt like First Scout was staring at him eye-to-eye. It was a little disconcerting. The Vulpes didn't say anything more. Michael turned to leave.

"What should I do?" Jophiel asked.

"See if you can change First Scout's mind," he said and departed without waiting to hear what she said.

Once he was outside, Michael made another call.

"Go ahead," Gabriel said.

"Our alien guest can use his mind to talk with computers."

"Really? Is that how the medical records were altered?"

"Yes."

"Why only do that?" Gabriel asked. "Why didn't he try to, I don't know, get loose?"

"Where would he go? He arranged the nanovirus healing for the Coastie we had in custody."

"Strange. Can you ask the woman why?"

"She's missing."

"I thought she was a crispy critter. The nanovirus wouldn't have completely healed her, would it?"

"No, but it healed her enough that she was able to slip out. Since there's no indication of any broken locks, I think the Vulpes helped her gain access to secure areas too."

"I am really beginning to like the fox." She laughed.

"You would." *Fucking hackers, worse than graffiti artists.* "Don't get too attached, I might have to kill him."

"A suboptimal solution, I would say."

"I agree. However, I can't let him continue."

"The telepathy must have some limits, or he would do more. Why not jack up power on the isolation field?"

Michael stopped and nodded. She had a point. The isolation cell had a faraday cage which was part of the alien isolation protocol. However, going in and giving the alien his own survival rations might have created a weakness. "Can you enhance the isolation field to cut him off from our computers?"

"I can see if I can figure out how he performs his tricks, sure."

"Do it," Michael ordered. As he spoke, Michael wandered outside to the alien ship. It was on the hauler, and the handlers were prepared to move it. The specialists would begin taking it apart soon, and he hoped there would be a lot of useful technology inside. They were in the endgame of the fall. Once the last few vestiges of government were wiped away, the reconstruction could begin.

Michael was so pleased, he didn't see the figure dressed as a medical technician climb onto the heavy hauler, then into the alien ship.

* * *

**Operation Roundhouse**
**Approaching San Nicolas Island**

"On the deck, Pepper!" General Rose called over the Osprey's intercom.

"I'm not an expert on these fucked up birds," the pilot replied.

"They have SAMs, Warrant Officer. How are you at dodging missiles?"

"On the deck, you bet!" The Osprey angled down toward the waves.

Rose watched out the rear door as the water became precipitously close. Radar had a difficult time telling aircraft from waves below an altitude of 20 feet. Waves seemed to be skimming along below them close enough for him to reach out and grab a fish. He had a brief stab of fear; what if a killer whale jumped up and hit them? *Sea monsters.* The thought made him chuckle. *Here, there be monsters!*

"We've reached waypoint Alpha," Pepper said over the intercom.

"Roger that." Rose switched to the fleet channel. "David to Passkey."

"Passkey, go ahead."

"Waypoint Alpha, I repeat, we've reached Waypoint Alpha."

"Acknowledged. We're shipping your package."

"Roger." Rose grinned. Let's see what the fuckers think of this.

* * *

**USS *Russell***

**The Flotilla**

**150 Nautical Miles West of San Diego, CA**

The *Arleigh Burke*-class destroyer, the USS *Russell*, came about onto a north-westerly course and centered her wheel. "Authorization for fire mission," Captain Paine informed the weapons control officer in the CIC.

"Roger, I concur. Stand by to fire."

The missile technician fed the details into the computers which quickly assigned targets and transmitted the data to the missiles nestled in their cells. "We have a green board," the technician reported.

"Affirmative," Paine replied. "Fire."

On the *Russell's* deck, nine doors opened with mechanical precision. An instant later, plumes of fire erupted from the blast channels that carried the fire of the rocket engines away from the relatively delicate missiles. The light metal sheeting covering the cell exploded outward as the first Tomahawk cruise missile blasted skyward, angled slightly, and leveled off. Three seconds later, the second one followed, then the third. Eleven seconds after boosting out of their cells, the missiles' launch rockets burned out and fell away. The missiles extended their stubby wings, and their turbofan engines screamed to life. Twenty-four seconds after the first missile launched, the entire wave of missiles was airborne.

Thirty thousand feet above them, an E-2 Hawkeye from the *Gerald R. Ford* took command of the missiles. The weapons had already descended to 10 feet above the mean wave height and reached their cruising speed of 550 mph. At this speed and altitude, they would pass over a ship before most occupants heard them coming.

"Inform David their package is in the mail."

* * *

**Operation Roundhouse**
**Approaching San Nicolas Island**

"Here they come, General!" Pepper said over the intercom.

Rose moved closer to the back door and tried to find them. The sunlight made the sea look like a wrinkled mirror reflecting a million brilliant flashes of light. He squinted and saw a phalanx of tiny, moving darts just above the water. "Got'em," he said.

The cruise missiles caught up to them in a heartbeat, blasting past the four Ospreys so quickly, Rose couldn't make out more than their basic shape.

"Hooah!" the man manning the M240 yelled as the missiles flashed past.

Rose checked the gear on his battle harness and tried to forget that he hadn't done what he was about to do in thirty years.

* * *

The controllers on the Hawkeye watched the developing situation via their APS-145 radar. At the aircraft's current altitude, they could see more than 200 miles. Normally, in the current AO, the radar would be clogged with airborne targets, since both the Los Angeles and San Diego flight corridors were within range. Now, however, they only saw a couple dozen targets, including the cruise missiles, the Ospreys, and the various helicopters searching for the elusive submarine.

The cruise missiles passed the four Osprey, then split into two groups, one of four and one of five. They were staggered and locked on targets, designated to arrive every 10 seconds. In less than a minute, they would hit the unsuspecting island.

"We've got aircraft lifting off from the targeted island."

The skilled radar technicians analyzed the reading and concluded the targets were drones. They reported the new development and continued orbiting the area.

***

**Classified Genesis Facility**

**San Nicolas Island**

Chamuel sipped some soup and dabbled with her screen's configuration. The food on the ship had been drab because of the limited stores available. The alien plague was inconvenient. Even so, she continued on as best she could. She reached over and touched the air conditioning controls, dropping the temp by two degrees.

She was quite happy now that she'd brought her workroom online. She had an entire wall of high-tech monitors giving her at least four times the viewable data, and she was glorifying in the sheer level of output. Plus, her preferred brand of Darjeeling tea was now available. All in all, it was a pretty darn good day.

She'd just finished her soup when a screen flashed. She had customized her rig so the entire screen instantly became dedicated to whatever data had triggered the alert. The island's defense alerts were routed through her data gathering programs as they were sent to Michael's soldiers. A series of radar cross sections were detected to the southeast. Strange.

Chamuel didn't immediately consider the alert of major importance. The sensors were extremely sensitive, and when she'd activated her base system, there'd been dozens of such alerts in the logs. She'd wasted an hour going over them, only to realize they were meaningless things like flocks of birds or waves. She'd turned down the sensitivity and reduced the range, but something had triggered them again.

She noted that Michael had ordered the Wasps into the air and the Hunter back from the Flotilla. This meant Michael had what he wanted and was about to finish off the Flotilla. That was fine with her. The sooner any organized opposition was cleared from the playing field, the sooner they could work on stabilizing the situation.

She'd already seen the recording of Michael getting the Vulpes to speak. First Scout was an interesting name. Chamuel plugged it into one of her tracking programs; it was one of a thousand things she was watching. She examined how the new name and the Vulpes' knowledge of English correlated with other facts, until the proximity alarm sounded again. Then again!

She pulled up the detail. Exactly nine radar returns, both times. *Oh, fuck.* She pulled the data and put it into a comparative file. Her eyes scanned the information as quickly as the computer. She extrapolated size, speed, and altitude. The conclusion was almost immediate. Cruise missiles.

"Michael!" she yelled into the island communications network.

"What now?"

"Inbound cruise missile attack. Nine of them. First strike ETA thirty seconds!"

* * *

Michael had been reading orders on his tablet while he walked from the dock to the main building when the first radar alarm went off. Before he could look, Chamuel overrode it. He trusted the tactician to know whether something was worth his time as the military leader of the Heptagon, so he continued on.

"Michael, sir."

"Go ahead, Colonel Baker."

"The Wasps are finally ready."

"Very good, launch them. Program them for assault on the only remaining *Arleigh Burke*-class first."

"Understood."

A moment later, the scream of jet turbines echoed over the island, and he caught sight of the drones rising from the runway. They took off in pairs until all six were airborne. The Wasps bore a distinct resemblance to the F-18 Hornet, which made sense since they were based on it. A lack of cockpit and the addition of more advanced engines gave the Wasps a vaguely insectile appearance. The name was fitting.

Besides being smaller and faster, the Wasps had gained considerable range and endurance. All six were heavily armed with air-to-surface missiles that were just as advanced as they were. The Flotilla had minutes to live.

Michael had just entered the main building when Chamuel yelled her warning over the radio.

"Cruise missiles?"

"Yes!" she insisted.

"Mother fucker," he snarled and ran, changing his radio's channel back to Baker's. "Inbound missile attack!"

"The radar warnings were overridden."

"Chamuel was *wrong*. Prepare for attack."

"Activating defenses."

Michael cursed as he climbed the two flights of stairs to the operations center where Baker worked. The room had armored windows and had served as a control tower in the days when San Nicolas was a navy airfield. Just before he punched his access code into the keypad by the armored door, he heard the *Brrrrrr!* of the close-in defense cannons firing.

***

**USS *Vandergrift***

**Conducting ASW Operations**

**175 miles Northwest of San Diego, California**

"Got it, Captain!"

Richards raced over to the sonar board with its lines of signal traces. A tight squiggle amid all the other noise showed the telltale sound of a supercavitating trace. It had to be one of the skunks they'd been trying to find.

"Where's the Viking?" he asked his XO.

"Seventy miles north, out of range."

"Two Seahawks are vectoring in; they'll be in position in five minutes."

"Not soon enough," Richards mumbled.

"That's gotta be it, sir!" the technician insisted.

"I think you're correct, son," the Captain replied. "Weapons, standby on starboard launcher. Program bracketed spread."

"Targeting solution is set," the weapons officer replied.

"Fire."

On the deck the triangular Mark 32 torpedo tube sounded an alarm as it came alive and rotated. High power motors whined as the tubes pressurized. Five seconds later, the first door opened, and a Mark 46 torpedo was ejected. By the time it hit the water, a second had joined it. Less than a minute later, the launcher rotated back to its centerline, having launched three torpedoes.

"Torpedoes away," the weapons officer announced. "All three running hot and true with linked guidance."

"The damned sub is five times faster than our torpedoes," the XO whispered.

"More like eight times," Richards replied. "But we have to get them on a defensive footing before—"

"Enemy torpedo in the water!" sonar called out.

"Flank speed!" Richards ordered. "Hard into the bearing. Prepare to launch remaining torpedoes."

"Time to impact…" the sonarman paused as he calculated. The *Vandergrift* leaned to port as her rudder came over hard, and she turned. "Time to impact, *ten seconds!*"

"Transmit the skunk's bearing and range to the *Russell*," Richards said. "Tell Captain Paine I said good hunting."

The radio man quickly relayed the information. Ten seconds later, the enemy torpedo exploded under the *Vandergrift*, tearing her in two. The ship's magazine exploded, killing Captain Richards and his bridge crew instantly.

* * *

**USS *Russell***

**The Flotilla**

**165 Nautical Miles West of San Diego, CA**

"Captain Paine, radio transmission from the *Vandergrift*. They're under fire, and they provided the latest coordinates for the enemy skunk."

Paine looked at the sheet, then up at a monitor. It showed a telescopic view of the *Oliver Hazard Perry*-class frigate steaming almost directly away from the *Russell*. She was leaning hard as she turned to port. There was a flash, then she was engulfed in a blast amidships. He knew from the way she lifted in two parts, she was dead. A secondary explosion blew the forward section apart. "Captain Richards offers us good hunting."

"Damnit," his XO snapped.

"Fire control, range to target?" Paine asked.

"Twelve miles, Captain."

"Fire mission. Give me a spread of four ASROCs on that bastard."

On the *Russell's* deck, five more cells opened, the anti-submarine rockets blazed into the sky.

* * *

Though she was dead, the *Vandergrift's* two Seahawk helicopters had survived. One was miles away, still ferrying crew between the Flotilla's ships. The second had AQS-13F sonar aboard. She was hovering just 20 feet above the water. A crewman was using a cable to lower a buoy into the dark waters where it could pull a continuous signal. They had a good return and were tracking the submarine when the operator suddenly pulled his headset away.

"They got the *Vandy*," he said. "Motherfuckers!"

"Stay on mission," the commander snapped. "You still got the bastard?"

The sonarman replaced his headset and checked his instruments. He smiled predatorily. "Yes, *sir,* I sure do."

"Continue to relay data." The pilot had a panoramic view of the area. He'd seen their ship die. His jaw hurt from clenching his teeth. Almost all their friends were dead or dying, and there was nothing he could do except hope for payback.

On the horizon opposite the *Vandy*'s burning hulk, a series of flashes and contrails announced the *Russell's* response.

"ASROCs!" his copilot crowed and pointed. "Four of them!"

"Yeah," the pilot agreed. "And Seahawks from the *Davis* and the *Ford* are about to drop two more fish." In addition to the three torpedoes the *Vandy* had launched before she died, there would be nine torpedoes in the water. *Dodge those, you fuck.*

"Enemy sub is accelerating to…*135 knots!*" the sonarman said in disbelief.

"It has supercavitating tech," the pilot said. He'd been briefed when they'd been reset for active ASW. He just wished they'd had time to give him some weapons. The enemy was so fast, they couldn't dip and fire, so they needed to maintain active lock.

"They've got it bracketed," the sonarman said, leaning closer to his screens. "It's running, but no way is it going to get away!"

"Good," the pilot said. He saw two of the ASROCs launched by the *Russell* burn out. The torpedoes parachuted into the water, adding to the drama. No sooner were they in the drink than the sonarman exclaimed. "What's wrong?"

"The sub turned, then it split into a dozen returns instead of one."

"How is that possible?"

"It isn't," the sonarman replied.

"Drones maybe?" the copilot suggested.

"They wouldn't sound *identical* to the original. I can't tell them apart!"

"Then neither can the torpedoes," the pilot said. The sea in the distance erupted in explosions. In less than a minute, all the torpedoes had detonated, sending white plumes into the air. "Any idea if they got the real submarine?"

"I still can't tell them apart," the sonarman said. He monitored the signals until the surviving decoys went dark. "Okay, I got him again. Shit, he's heading toward the Flotilla at 95 knots."

The pilot called the carrier and advised them of the development. He checked his helicopter's fuel level and was about to order a pursuit of the submarine when his sonarman called out.

"I have another sub. It just appeared, one mile northwest. It's going shallow."

The pilot unconsciously searched the horizon. If an enemy sub surfaced, one of the warships could take it out with an anti-ship missile. No matter what weird decoy drones they had, it was a hard to stop a Harpoon. Then he spotted it, a long dark spot breaking the surface. "Got it," he said and pointed.

"I see," the copilot said and raised his binoculars to his eyes. "It doesn't have much of a sail. I don't think it looks like any submarine I've ever…" He stopped and focused the glasses. "Something just came out of the hull."

"Are they evacuating?" the pilot asked. He set the helicopter for auto-hover and picked up his own pair of binoculars. The vessel was boxy and seemed familiar. It flashed, and a line of white smoke shot upward from it, angled, and came right at him. "It's a RAM launcher," he said. He grabbed the controls and added power, the autopilot instantly disengaging in response to the control input. As soon as the engine responded he turned away as quickly as his craft could. "*Russell*, be advised, another sub inbound!"

The RIM-116, rolling airframe missile, accelerated to Mach 2 in a second and crossed the distance between the sub and the hovering Seahawk in a flash. The pilot tried to bank away, but they were stationary and only feet above the water. The missile struck the helicopter square in the belly, turning it into a fireball.

* * *

**Classified Genesis Facility**
**San Nicolas Island**

"How many missiles?" Michael demanded. The six battle stations in the control room were each manned by a different person. To one side were six consoles in a row, the controls for the Wasp operators.

The defenses were largely automated—all they required was an operator to engage them and specify a priority. The cruise missiles, which were coming in a wave, had only been recognized as a threat when they were seconds out.

"Initially, six to ten," Colonel Baker said. A central monitor showed the airspace around San Nicolas. The missiles were in two groups. One was coming straight in off the sea and was targeted at the complex he was standing in. Radar showed three missiles total still in the air.

On an adjacent building, the roof-mounted Phalanx CIWS, or Sea-Wiz, came alive and spun around. *Brrrrrr!* The gun's six barrels fired seventy-five 20mm rounds per second. The system was designed to fire a maximum of 500 rounds per burst, with a cooldown period to keep the barrels from overheating. The magazine held 1,550 rounds, giving it a total firing time of about 21 seconds.

"Kill," an operator said.

Michael saw an almost comical burst of smoke over the water. The gun moved back and forth, as if it were shaking its head disapprovingly. Its tall, conical dome had earned the weapon system the nickname R2-D2. Inside the top of the dome was its radar, which was completely independent from the installation's. Each of San Nicolas's two Sea-Wiz had their own generators. Michael appreciated redundancy when his ass was on the line.

"Acquiring another."

Brrrrrr!

"Kill," the operator said again. He sounded businesslike and unstressed. Michael nodded. The team was well trained, as he'd come to expect from Colonel Baker. It was a good thing, or Michael would have had to take this oversight out on Chamuel's ass.

"West radar alarm."

"Far side of the island," Baker said.

Michael moved next to the radar operator and looked over his shoulder. A group of 10 signals flickered in and out. "Why can't it resolve them?" he asked.

"The system wasn't designed to shoot down US-made Tomahawks," Baker replied. "We have to let them get in closer."

"Sounds dangerous."

"Without a doubt."

"Engaging," the operator said.

The second Sea-Wiz was more than a mile away, on the other side of the island's low range of hills. A monitor showed the weapons system jerking and spinning, then spewing bullets. A few seconds later, the sound of its firing echoed over the base as a distant, but subdued, *Brrrrrrr.*

"They must have some intel on us," Baker said. "A live image or something."

"Gabriel is certain nobody has satellite recon," Michael assured him.

"Radar," Baker said, "report any high-flyers in range."

"I have a bird at Angels-30, just over the horizon."

"Emissions?"

"Stand by," the man said. A second later, he replied. "Confirmed. Looks like early warning radar."

"AWACs," Michael growled. "Damned E-2, probably from the *Ford.* How the fuck did they find us?"

Baker looked at the radar data. "He's well outside our RIM-162 missile range."

"Order the Wasps to take it out."

"Yes, sir," Baker said and nodded to the drone operators.

A few seconds later the Sea-Wiz tech yelped in surprise.

"What do you have?" Baker asked. The man didn't respond; he was too busy working his console. He'd gone from calm to concerned in seconds. Colonel Baker moved closer and cursed. "Damn it."

"What?" Michael demanded.

"They overwhelmed the far side defenses."

On the screen, the distant Sea-Wiz let off a burst, then turned and fired a much shorter burst before stopping. It jerked back and forth as if confused or distressed.

"Can't you reload it?"

"Takes an hour," Baker said. No sooner were the words out of his mouth than the screen flashed and dissolved into static.

"Far side Sea-Wiz and radar destroyed," the technician reported.

Outside, the nearby defensive gun let out another burst, and Michael glanced nervously from the weapon to Colonel Baker. In the back of his mind, he wondered if it was time to run for the bunker.

"We're not showing any more inbound," the radar technician reported.

Michael let his breath out slowly. The fucking Flotilla had just gone from a nuisance to a serious threat. He guessed having the sub commander sink a ship was a bigger mistake than he thought.

"Switch defenses to the RIMs," Baker ordered. "Get a team to reload the Sea-Wiz, *fast!* Also, dispatch a recon drone to the radar station and give me a report on possible salvage." He turned to Michael. "We have three more in storage, but they'd take a week to install. They were earmarked for future expansion."

"How long to intercept that Hawkeye?"

"Ten minutes." Michael made a face. "If we go supersonic, it'll significantly reduce their operational time. What do you want more, the Flotilla or the E-2?"

"Both," Michael said. Baker looked at him in exasperation. "Fine, detail one to take care of the Hawkeye and have the other five proceed to the Flotilla." Baker nodded and gave the orders to his drone pilots. Michael's jaw muscles bunched as he waited. *This needs to be done, damnit.*

* * *

Grange watched from her hiding place on the huge, heavy crawler as her tormentor, Michael, walked past, mumbling to himself. Her pain was temporarily forgotten in the terror of what he would do to her should she fall into his hands. Death was certain, though she now knew death could come in many ways and at many speeds. Michael probably wouldn't be merciful if he found her skulking around, especially if he figured out what she had done.

*I'm at the ship*, she thought and waited for First Scout to reply. Just then there was a loud *Brrrrr!* as a Phalanx Sea-Wiz came alive. She jerked and put her hands over her ears. The drugs they'd given her seemed to have heightened her senses, among other things. *Come on, all hell's breaking loose!*

*Under either side, just behind…and touch it.*

*I lost you for a second,* she thought. The Sea-Wiz fired again, a longer burst. Jesus Christ, it was a war zone. Men and women, some in black combat armor and others in blue coveralls, were running everywhere.

*You are at the edge of my psy-lock's reach…instructions.*

*Damn it, how am I supposed to do this without you?* Grange sat on her haunches and breathed. The pain was slowly, but steadily, getting worse. She knew it would eventually consume her.

*Wait where you are,* First Scout said.

*What are you going to do?* Suddenly she jerked as a jolt of thought entered her mind. In a second, he'd sent her the floorplan of his ship. It took a few seconds for the information to settle into her brain. It felt like Legos falling into place. The whole process was the most disconcerting thing she'd experienced in her already bizarre life.

When Grange could finally concentrate again, she thought about the ship and found it was as if she'd been aboard it a hundred times before. It wasn't an overly complicated ship, and it reminded her, superficially, of her own ship. Unfortunately, thinking about the *Boutwell* brought back painful memories.

*It is important not to dwell…you need to proceed before…*

*I know,* she thought back and returned to thinking about the plans. A room near the bridge was highlighted in her mind. She looked back from it to the exits. There were two. One under each of the forward flares of the stubby wings. *Got it.*

*Do well.*

*No shit,* she thought and forced her tortured body back into motion.

Unfortunately, the toolbox she'd been hiding behind hadn't provided much cover, so as soon as she got up and slouched toward the ship, she was spotted.

A black uniformed man who was running by came to a sudden stop. "What are you doing up there?"

She ignored the shouted question and forced herself to move faster. She didn't want to look back, afraid she was about to be jumped. But by the sound of the man's voice, he was more confused than upset. *Probably can't understand why someone dressed in medical isolation gear is up on a hauler.*

Grange reached her destination. The hull looked like stainless steel, polished to a mirror finish. There were no signs of seams or locking mechanisms. Reaching up without thinking, she touched first one spot, then another, then ran her hand between the two. Despite never having touched the spaceship before, the movements felt familiar, as if she'd done them every day of her life. A pinging sound echoed, and a hexagonal outline appeared. In quick, mechanical movements, the 'hatch' retracted an inch and quickly slid to the side and disappeared.

"Hey!" the person who'd questioned her yelled. "Supervisor!"

"Time to go," she croaked, dismayed at how horrid her voice was. She reached inside and found the handle she knew would be there and pulled herself up. Her arms screamed in protest, and she had to drag herself belly first over the lip of the hatchway. She felt her partly healed skin separate and warmth spread. *More blood*, she thought. A hand brushed her foot as she was pulling it in, and she squealed in alarm.

"What are you doing?" A head poked in after her. A man in his thirties, wearing a black uniform hat, looked pissed. Grange touched the side of the interior, next to the hatch, and it closed a lot faster than either she or the surprised man expected. "Hey sto—" The sounds of running and Sea-Wiz fire were cut off, along with the man's surprised exclamation and his head.

"Oh fuck!" Grange screamed and pushed herself away from the bloody, severed head. Interior lighting came on, and she was face-to-face with the dead man's wide, staring eyes. "Oh, oh God," she gasped and wretched. "I didn't mean to kill you," she said. The head had no reply.

*I can't do this,* she thought as tears rolled down her cheeks. The salty tears stung as they touched the burned flesh on her face. First Scout's thoughts didn't reach her anymore. Apparently, closing the ship's door had cut her off completely from the alien. *I'm on my own.*

She examined the interior. The hallways were round and about three feet tall. She was going to have to crawl. Her pain was getting worse, and she didn't want to look at the dead man's head anymore, so she set out toward her destination. The sooner she got there, the sooner it would all be over.

***

**USS *Gerald R. Ford***
**Medical Center**
**The Flotilla**
**165 Nautical Miles West of San Diego, CA**

"What's going on?" Jeremiah asked.

"There's an emergency, Mr. Osborne," Dr. Peterson replied. He was in scrubs and his hands were bare, but he held them up in front of him to avoid contamination. An assistant was removing his blood-stained smock and replacing it with a fresh one, careful to avoid his hands.

"What kind of emergency?" Jeremiah demanded. The drugs were wearing off, causing his pain to grow, along with his impatience. His forearms were covered with pen marks and painted red with betadine in preparation for the coming mutilation. The doctor ignored him, and his temper flared. "Goddamn it, I'm still alive and want to know what's happening!"

Peterson glared at him. Jeremiah refused to break eye contact. The doctor sighed. "As I understand it, some unknown faction has high-tech, miniature submarines. They've already sunk a private ship and a frigate and shot down a helicopter. Now, they're coming after the rest of the Flotilla. So, if you are lucky, you'll be under general anesthesia when we sink, and you'll be spared the "fun" part of drowning. Is that better?"

"Holy shit," Jeremiah said. Peterson grunted and called for an anesthesiologist.

Jeremiah lay on the gurney and thought. Who would want to attack the Flotilla? Aliens? Naw, they'd just blow us up with ray guns or drop rocks on us. Wasn't the virus bad enough? Alien tech would change the way war was fought. "What?!" he suddenly blurted.

A woman in medical scrubs was checking the IV he'd had in his arm since arriving. After checking it, she picked up his chart and asked him to verify his name and ID number.

"Is any of my staff here?"

"I'm sorry? Please pay attention."

"I said, is any of my staff here?!"

She looked at his chart. "Civilian, ah. Look, Mr. Osborne, you've been injured. We need to go over these details before your surgery."

"Screw that. I need to talk to someone from my staff."

"If you don't cooperate, this will complicate your treat—"

"Fuck my treatment. Do you want to survive?!"

The woman sighed and left, which was fine with him. "Is there anyone here with an IQ above room temperature?"

"Mr. Osborne?"

Jeremiah turned his head and saw a pretty, blonde woman looking down at him. Her face was instantly recognizable, and the CEO part of him switched into media-relations mode. "Kathy Clifford, good to see you."

"Jeremiah Osborne, isn't it? CEO of Oceanic Orbital Enterprises."

Jeremiah nodded. He noted the tiny recorder clipped to her borrowed camo shirt and wondered if anyone else realized she was recording everything she saw.

"One and only," Jeremiah confirmed.

She looked him over, stopping at the thick, blood-soaked bandages on his hands. Her professional smile turned to honest concern. "How were you injured?"

"Classified."

"Mr. Osborne, we're all one, big, happy family."

"Not for much longer," he mumbled, thinking about the killer subs.

"I'm sorry, what does that mean?"

*Good hearing too.* He considered. There might be a chance to leapfrog the military mentality. The nurse was back, and he knew he didn't have much time. "Ms. Clifford, I'd love to give you an exclusive."

"Great."

"However, I'm about to go into surgery. If you'll arrange to get a message to my associates, I will give you the interview afterward." She frowned.

"I'm not against carrying a message for you, but what makes you think I can?" Jeremiah stared at the camera. She looked back at him for a second, then quickly glanced down at the device and back up. A sly grin appeared on her face.

"Mr. Osborne, please?" the nurse asked.

"I need a couple minutes," he said.

She glanced at the clipboard she was carrying and frowned. "I suppose I can give you two minutes."

"Thank you." She moved off, and he gestured with a mangled hand for Kathy to come closer.

"Can you at least tell me how you were injured?"

"I was burned by a lightning gun while we were fighting infected elephant seals." Her eyes sparkled with intense interest, and he knew he had her hooked. "Okay, listen, I need to talk quickly."

After he'd given her the message, and she'd hurried off, he relaxed and tried to prepare himself for what was coming. He'd had a good life with his hands and was going to miss them. Still, he'd miss life more, so if he had to lose them to keep living, they would go. *I wonder how hard it will be to find a good counselor after the zombie apocalypse is over?*

Alone, without any distraction, he was again aware of the growing pain. He thought about getting someone's attention, then realized he would probably catch shit for delaying, then hurrying them.

"Mr. Osborne?"

He followed the voice and saw another medical tech, a man with an NCO rank insignia. "Yes?"

"I wasn't expecting you to be conscious." The man looked him over, a confused look growing on his face. "It says here you were shot four times."

"Shot? No, I was electrocuted."

The man leaned over him and looked at Jeremiah's hands in confusion. "Where's your ID bracelet?"

"The plastic one? They put it on my ankle since my hands are fucked up."

"Oh." The medic moved Jeremiah's blanket to examine the plastic bracelet. "*Jeremiah* Osborne?" Jeremiah nodded. "I didn't know there were two Osbornes here. Sorry."

"Who's the other one?" Jeremiah asked.

The man looked at his clipboard. "Uhm, Jon Osborne, from the *Helix*."

"Jon Osborne?" Jeremiah sat up and swung his legs over the side. "Show me?"

"Sir, should you be up?"

"Just show me." The medical tech shrugged and moved down the line of wounded waiting for treatment. Jeremiah had no idea there were so many. Most appeared to have been bitten, clawed, or burned. He felt guilty for being moved to the front of the line, ahead of some of the others.

"Here he is," the tech said. Jeremiah turned and gasped. "You know him?"

"I should; he's my cousin." It was definitely Oz, and he looked bad. Bloody trauma bandages covered his chest and abdomen. Not one, but two, IVs poured blood and fluids into his body. A compact life monitor beeped, and a mask fed him oxygen.

"I need to get him prepped for surgery, sir."

Jeremiah nodded and backed away. He hadn't seen Oz for years and had no idea he'd been in the Flotilla. *I hope he makes it.*

"Mr. Osborne!" an outraged nurse exclaimed. "What do you think you're doing?"

***

Kathy walked as quickly as she could, sliding down ladders the way she'd learned from the sailors, to her media center. A few of the people sharing her space looked up as she entered but didn't say anything. They'd ignored her all along anyway.

She'd been studying her newly acquired hack into radio traffic, until she'd heard about helicopters bringing in injured, then rushing to rearm and take off to fight the attack. She'd had some questions, and in just a few seconds, Jeremiah Osborne had answered several of her most urgent. She still didn't know *who* was attacking, though at the moment, it didn't matter.

She opened her laptop and logged in, quickly entering the ship's radio system. She put a headset on. It took her a minute to figure out how to use the interface to transmit. As she worked, she tried to control her breathing. *I need to exercise,* she chided herself. After surviving zombie-infested Mexico, exercise hadn't seemed like something she needed to do.

"There it is," she said. She examined the virtual control for a moment before entering the data. "Calling OOE ship *Azanti.* Come in?" She shook her head at the name, wondering what it meant. *Azanti? Sounds French.* She repeated the call twice.

"OOE, who's calling?"

"This is Kathy Clifford on the *Ford.* I have a message from Jeremiah Osborne. Please listen. Wade Watts is on your ship. He needs to know something."

"Go ahead, I'm recording."

Kathy relayed the message.

* * *

Captain Gilchrist watched the developing battle as the Tomahawks found their targets. The E-2 fed the carrier data as missile after missile was intercepted.

"Where the fuck did they get a Sea-Wiz?" Commander Tobias asked.

Gilchrist grunted in response to his XO's question. It was asked rhetorically, out of frustration. Their mysterious enemy had a lot of shit it had no right to own. It was possible to get ahold of a Sea-Wiz through some of their less scrupulous allies, but stealth submarines that could move at over 100 knots? Not so much.

"There's a hit!" Tobias yelled. The radar return from the Hawkeye showed debris flying into the air. One of the two radar installations on the island had been destroyed.

"General Rose reports he is beginning his landing," the radio operator said.

"God speed," Gilchrist said. Tobias nodded.

"E-2 reports they have inbound bandits."

"Damnit," Gilchrist said.

"Had to happen sooner or later," Tobias said.

Gilchrist sighed. The worst thing about the situation was being unable to protect his people. In normal operations, an F-18 would be hovering nearby, ready to intercept any threat to the *Ford's* extended eyes, the E-2 Hawkeye. He didn't have a single fighter left. There were some on the other carriers, however none of them responded, and they appeared overrun with infected. Or they were on fire. "Tell them to try and evade."

The orders were relayed, and hopes were passed along. The E-2 was powered by a turboprop, a jet engine pushing a propeller. Its top speed was 350 knots. Radar data showed the intercepting craft were the size of Hornets and flying just under Mach. He knew the pilot would do everything he could—fire chaff and flares and try to hide in clouds. But it was all in vain, and the radar blip for the valiant, little plane blinked out.

"E-2 is down," the formal report came back. Not only had Gilchrist lost his only E-2, but his visible range had been reduced by more than half. One of the last things the E-2 had shown was five more of the Hornet-like planes heading toward the Flotilla.

"Inform all ships to prepare for air assault."

* * *

**Shangri-La**
**Amarillo, TX**

"Hey Cobb."

"What's up, Paul?" Bisdorf's big frame dominated the doorway to Cobb's new office. They'd insisted he take the former governor's space. He'd promptly had temporary walls put in to add space for the senior NCOs and what would eventually be the civilian leadership. It was more comfortable than what he was used to. Even a Lieutenant Colonel didn't get a corner office with a view in the US military.

Bisdorf walked in and put a digital voice recorder on Cobb's desk. He didn't like the desk; it was too ornate. The only thing he wished he had back was the window. The three bullet holes were a constant reminder of what he'd been forced to do to rid himself of Governor Taylor.

"What's this?"

"Play it," Bisdorf said.

Cobb picked it up and pushed play. The first few seconds were static with an occasional crackly sound that reminded him of dogs howling. Then it cleared, and he heard a clear voice. "Roger your location, *Russell.* Confirmed ASW Seahawk down to missile fire. Recommend we prepare…<crackle>"

"That sounded like navy traffic," Cobb said, looking up at Paul.

The big man smiled and nodded. He'd been eager to help as much as possible after the truth came out.

"There's some kind of battle going on."

"I heard. Is there any more?"

"Just one bit." He took the player, set it to a different recording, then handed it back. "I thought this was a news report. A couple of stations are still on the air, though it's playing in a loop. Listen."

As soon as the voice came through, Cobb sat bolt upright.

"This is Kathy Clifford on the *Ford.* I have a message from Jeremiah Osborne. Please listen. Wade Watts is there. He needs to know something."

"Kathy!" he cried.

Bisdorf hit pause. "You've met her?"

"Yeah, she's my girlfriend."

Bisdorf nodded slowly. "Way to go, my friend."

Cobb felt his cheeks getting warm. "It just kinda happened."

"Doesn't it always?" Bisdorf laughed.

"I knew the guy Wade Watts too. Play some more?"

Bisdorf nodded and un-paused the recorder.

"Go ahead, I'm recording," another voice said.

"The sub that sank those ships is coming back. They won't be able to stop it, you need to…" the transmission dissolved into static.

"That's it?" Cobb asked.

"I'm afraid so. Atmospheric skip can work like that sometimes."

Cobb backed it up and played the clip again, listening carefully. "They're being attacked. Do you know where this is?"

"I heard San Diego in the background."

Cobb nodded. It matched what he knew about General Rose's destination. If Kathy and Wade had made it, it was all but certain the rest had as well. Who was attacking them? She'd also talked about sunken ships. My God, where they in danger? They had to be.

He jumped to his feet and headed for the door.

"Where are you going?" Bisdorf asked.

"I need to see Daimler, and you're coming with me."

* * *

**Operation Roundhouse**
**San Nicolas Island**

As the low, coastal island grew slowly closer, General Rose held his breath and prayed to whatever deity happened to be listening and gave two shits about grunts. *Please don't notice us.*

"Eagle to Roundhouse."

He perked up. Eagle was the callsign for the navy AWACS. "Roundhouse. Go ahead Eagle."

"Package delivered. One headlight is out. High beam only. I repeat, high beam only."

"Acknowledged. You get that, Pepper?"

"Yes, *sir*! Altering course for the ridge. Since we don't have clear radar, we'll be at high risk if we try to dust off. Once they spot you landing…"

"I got it, Warrant. Cancel the rappel. Wait one, and I'll advise on LZ." Rose secretly heaved a sigh. He wouldn't have put money on his ability to rappel down from a hovering Osprey. Frankly, it had the potential to be disastrously embarrassing. He switched channels. "Roundhouse to Passkey."

"Passkey actual, go."

"We're about to arrive at Grandma's House."

"Acknowledged, Roundhouse. We have unexpected guests, so I don't know if we'll be here much longer. Grandma's might be the safest place. Best of luck, Roundhouse."

Rose cut the channel and sighed. They were attacking the Flotilla again. *Can we take out the objective quickly enough?* It was worth considering. He still considered Lisha to be the #1 objective. Killing the fuck out of the bastards and finding out who they were was a bonus.

San Nicolas's beach passed below the Osprey as the pilots slowed and started climbing toward the low mountain opposite the objective. Rose glanced at his tablet, examining the map. Part of his mind wondered where they'd get new computers or have the ones they had repaired. He'd realized when they did the inventory aboard the *Pacific Adventurer,* he only had one. Six more were scattered among his command.

On the screen, he'd marked three potential landing zones. With one of the base's two radar installations taken out, his best choice was the LZ just behind the hill, almost in view of the main base. There was no way in hell anyone at the base would miss the sound of four fucking Osprey settling in. But, if he deployed closer to the far beach, they'd have more than a mile to cover, partly up hill, in unknown territory. If these bastards had stealth subs, who knew what other toys they might possess. Speed was the better option.

"Pepper!"

"General?"

"LZ #5, if you please."

"Roger that. ETA 30 seconds." Above the rear door, the jump light turned red, and everyone started final checks on their gear.

* * *

Chamuel's tea was cold, and her eyes were dancing back and forth across the massive monitors. She half expected Michael to come raging in at any minute, and he might have had a good reason. She moved her mobility chair slightly so she could concentrate on another screen. She stared at the big, weird shape over north Texas, wishing there was an NRO satellite she could re-task to get a better look. Sadly, the US government had been too short sighted to task more satellites with watching the mainland.

"Something is happening," she mumbled, flipping between screens faster than most people could follow. She was so tense, her distorted back muscles were spasming. She'd created a file of unexpected events:

- The sudden attack of the cruise missiles.
- The Flotilla understanding at least part of the alien tech.
- The *thing* floating over Texas.
- The cure apparently discovered by Dr. Lisha Breda.

There were hundreds of trembler alarms all over San Nicolas. They were there to detect people setting foot on the island. For years, they'd guarded against unwary boaters who'd decided the island was a good place for a picnic. Nine times out of ten they were set off by a sea turtle, a seal, or a group of birds feeding in the surf.

Usually one or two would go off near each other. This time, when the alarm sounded, dozens triggered at the same time.

Chamuel accessed the cameras near the sensors and saw four V-22 Osprey flash over at low altitude, heading almost directly for the destroyed radar position. A ground attack by a Marine unit. However, the Marines had been neutralized; the probability was 92%. But what about the east coast fleet?

She'd been ignoring them for quite a while, sure the Russians would attack them sooner or later. After all, she'd been sure the intel leaked to them blamed the US government for the virus. She reviewed the last NRO satellite pass over the Nicaraguan coast. Nothing! No signs of a battle, no signs of American surface ships, and no signs of Russian subs.

"No," she said and slammed her fist against the computer tray, nearly sending her keyboard flying. "What's happening?"

Chamuel spent minutes reevaluating the data while simultaneously evaluating the chances of the ground assault succeeding. She kept dozens of files with other odds. Chances of a world government surviving were less than 1%. Chances of a regional government surviving were 2%. Chances of a new government emerging in the aftermath, taking into account Strain Delta, were 3%. She tabulated new data, and the last datapoint changed. Changed alarmingly to 25%.

All thoughts of the attacking force were forgotten. *Michael can deal with it.* She searched for the east coast fleet. She found it at last, just west of Isla de Cedros, or less than 200 miles from San Diego. As she observed the fleet, she input data. All the previous US ships were there. Further, reconnaissance satellites showed six Russian submarines. They weren't hunting, they were ranging ahead in a clear vanguard formation.

She updated dozens of files with numbers representing the new developments. Something she'd considered effectively impossible. The key to her predictions was math. She'd learned the beauty of math at a young age, quickly proceeding from basics into algebra, geometry, trigonometry, plane geometry, and calculus. She'd mastered all of them before she graduated from high school. She would find out years later, Genesis had arranged her scholarship to MIT.

Once in the university environment, she had truly exploded, and she had been free to pursue topics her high school was completely unprepared to teach her. Combinatorics had briefly fascinated her, as well as computational equations and logic. She had moved into applied mathematics and found her first love—game theory.

Then, while finishing her first PhD, she had discovered quantum mechanics. When she started mixing this new area of interest with game theory, a whole new way of thinking was born. She might well have been known to the world as another Sagan or Hawking if Genesis hadn't harvested her. She had disappeared from the world, having only published a single paper on game theory.

At Genesis, she had developed her new mathematical system for predicting the actions of macro societal responses to events and situations. She had called it Game Mastering, for lack of a better term. The more she fine tuned it, the more accurate it became. By 2001, she knew the 9/11 attacks would happen, 21 days before the attacks. She had predicted a 99% probability of a space shuttle being destroyed during reentry before 2004. She had also predicted the Arab Spring as well as dozens of other major events. Genesis shared the details on some, but not on others. Her predictions were always based on her further estimates of secondary events.

To point, prior to the virus, the only major event she'd failed to have on her radar was the alien ship arriving and getting shot down by the Russians.

"It's the aliens," she realized. "How could I have been so blind?" The one factor that had been stymying her since her first failure was the aliens' involvement. She stared at the east coast fleet steaming north toward the Flotilla. "They've got a live Vulpes," she said.

She input a flurry of data that caused probabilities to spin across her worldwide model. There was no denying it, every plan Genesis and the Heptagon had made had less than a 15% probability of succeeding now. A number she kept out of sight was her own little piece of the puzzle. Her chance of surviving. Until minutes ago, it had been in the 90% range. She looked and saw that it was now in single digits. To be precise, 6.9%.

She did what she'd never done before, she factored her team into the equation, looking for individual actions that would alter the 6.9%, as well as the global survival probability, the biggest number she tracked. What was the chance humanity would survive? Since the disaster, the number had slowly been climbing. Only minutes ago, it was comfortably above 60%. After adding in the new information and factoring in alien interference, the prognosis reversed. It had been above 60% before they released the information about the global virus shutting down satellite comms. Now it was under 10%.

"A complete inversion of the curve," she said and laughed. She'd been so sure of herself, she'd missed how *well* it was going. An early teacher in high school once said; "If all your calculations are perfect, better go back and check again."

"There has to be a way to salvage this," she said to the empty room. She looked at the inputs from seven names, hers among them. One at a time she subtracted their inputs, then in pairs, then in every possible combination. Her headset buzzed at an incoming call. She glanced at the time; six minutes since the tremblers went off. She took her headset off and set it on her desk. Chamuel continued to run permutations until, suddenly, one small change caused global survivability to jump to over 80%. She stared at the results and dug into the math. It was not a solid number. She removed a few uncertainties, and it went down to 69%. Still, the results were undeniable.

She pulled up some cameras. The four Osprey sat on a stretch of roadway with their rotors idling. Troops had disembarked and broken up into squads to race up and around the hill. At the base, alarms were sounding. Black-clad Genesis security teams were emerging from the buildings.

Chamuel input some new numbers. The probabilities altered again. Her path was clear now. The number for her own survival hovered around 28%.

*****

# Chapter Ten

**OOE Ship**
**The Flotilla**
**165 Nautical Miles West of San Diego, CA**

Wade Watts stared at the recorder after listening for the second time. Stealth submarines? A desperate assault on an island to rescue a kidnapped scientist? Warships being sunk and unable to stop the attacks? "Holy fucking shit!" He looked at the radioman who'd brought him the message. "Is this true?"

"A ship was sunk. We saw it," the man said. "Another supposedly was too, but we didn't see it."

"Fucking hell, let's get out of here!"

"The boss hasn't ordered it." Wade looked at him horrified. "Look, dude, I'd turn and book if I could. Those seals and shit took out most of our remaining crew. The captain says we don't have enough people left to safely get underway. This ship looks high tech and shit, but it's really an old clunker. Even with a full crew, we're lucky to make 12 knots."

Wade sighed and flopped back in his chair, which moaned in protest. He was surrounded by electronic components in the space he shared with Alison McDill. Jack Coldwell was across the corridor. They were in new workspaces because the old ones were splattered with seal blood and gore. It had been easier to move.

The crewman looked at him for a minute, then set the recorder down and left. Wade didn't intervene. It was clear the man and his ship were of no use in preserving Wade's life. "Fuck my life," he said to the empty room.

Osborne's instructions were simple. The execution was less simple. There was no way in hell Gilchrist would take Wade's advice, even if it were covered in gold and dressed like a prostitute. "But," he said, tapping a finger on the desk, "there's always mob rule…"

He got to his feet and climbed the three ladders to the deck. *Why didn't they put elevators on these ships? They had elevators on cruise ships.* Walking out onto the deck, he examined the ships around them. They were a motley collection of commercial and private pleasure ships. A few hundred yards behind them was the hulking shape of the supercarrier, the *Ford.*

Wade went to the bridge and found the radioman who'd brought him the message and a balding, overweight, Asian man with decorations on his epaulets suggesting he was the captain. Wade cleared his throat and they both looked at him.

"You heard the message from Osborne?" he asked, looking at the captain.

"Of course," he said. "Do you want to use the radio?"

"You bet I do."

* * *

Everything came together incredibly quickly. By the time Wade reached the bridge, five ships were alarmingly close together. The captain was looking unhappy at the proximity of so much gross tonnage.

"Are you sure about this?" he asked Wade.

"Yup," Wade replied and helped Alison and Coldwell begin attaching gear to the bridge wall. The captain and the radioman, who might have been the only remaining crew on the ship, watched the work suspiciously. By the time the device was bolted in place, the nearest ship was calling them on a bullhorn.

"Ahoy, we're ready!"

"I'm on it," Alex said, trotting onto the bridge. He'd been resting in the ship's medical bay, and Wade had completely forgotten about him.

"You know what we're doing?" Alison asked.

Alex winked. "Soon as I listened to the recording Wade left in the shop and looked around, I figured it out. Gloves?" he asked the captain. The man took Alex out onto the walk along the bridge's superstructure. Wade went out on the bridge wing to watch. The nearest ship, a fishing boat about half their size, tossed over a line. Alex caught it, hooked it to a machine, and pulled the rope over until he reached a metal cable, which he attached to a metal cleat.

"Make sure it's metal on metal!" Wade yelled at him.

"No shit, kid. I've been doing this longer than you."

Wade frowned and returned to the bridge. The captain and the radioman were talking when a long, skinny military ship off their bow exploded. He gawked instead of ducking. The shockwave hit the boat, blew the windows out, and sent him sprawling.

* * *

**Operation Roundhouse**

**San Nicolas Island**

"Around to the other side!" General Rose yelled to the sergeant and gestured with his hand. A bullet came so close to taking his hand off, it nicked his glove. "Fuck!" He pulled back around the corner of the blockhouse which stood among the smoldering remains of the radar installation.

The bastards who ran the island didn't lack martial prowess. They'd responded to his landing in good order, deploying at least two squads to try and pin Rose's men down and stop them from advancing. Rose decided to take the two squads nearest to him and pretend to be pinned, while his fourth squad swung around the edge of the hill and approached the enemy's installation. If he was right, once his men attacked the base, at least part of the forces pinning him down would wheel about to avoid getting caught in a flanking maneuver, and Rose could then use his superior numbers to rush them.

"Get that M240 set up by that burning truck," he ordered a nearby corporal. The man nodded and went to set up the machinegun. They already had one 20 meters in the other direction. He'd suffered two wounded and would bet the enemy hadn't suffered any. That was fine, as long as they thought he was stuck.

He heard a double click on his radio. The flanking squad was in position. Rose got Master Sergeant Ayres' attention.

"Sir?" he called over the crackle of gunfire.

"Flankers in position. Have the two M240s provide covering fire. Heavy weapons team in the rear. We're going to advance."

"Roger that, sir."

Rose took a couple of breaths and clicked the radio twice in reply. Normally, he'd have used their secure squad comms. The problem was that his enemy had US equipment, so he couldn't count on any level of security. In seconds, gunfire echoed up from the flank. Instantly, fire faltered from the enemy pinning his men down. Rose smiled.

"Advance by squad!"

* * *

"We've lost all surveillance on the west side of the hill," Colonel Baker said.

Michael slammed his radio down on the counter. He'd been trying to reach Chamuel for 15 minutes, ever since the damned Ospreys appeared out of nowhere and dumped a shitload of fucking troops in his lap. At first, he just wanted answers, but now he needed some guidance.

"The savant bitch won't answer her radio," Michael snarled. Baker looked at him, waiting for orders.

"Subs have begun attacking the Flotilla," an operator said. "Captains report they are targeting screening vessels so the Wasps can get past the anti-air screen."

Michael nodded. They'd tried to get the Wasps in close enough to start sinking ships, only to lose one to a missile. The next generation drone they'd been working on was based on a stealth design and would have been a different story. The Wasp wasn't stealthy, but it was fast, highly maneuverable, and carried a ton of firepower.

"We have a highflyer over the Flotilla," one of the Wasp operators said.

"What is it?" Michael demanded.

The pilot checked his radar and scratched his chin. "It's not a fighter or an E-2. If I had to guess, I'd say it's either a Greyhound or some sort of civilian turboprop."

"Ignore it."

"Roger that, sir."

He could have ordered a wave of anti-ship missile fire, however, between the carrier, the destroyer, and the remaining frigate they still had six Sea-Wizes as well as other anti-missile defenses. Unlike a short time ago when a wave of Tomahawk cruise missiles arrived, they were expecting an attack. Their defensive fire would be much more accurate. It wouldn't do any good to force their hand; that damned *Arleigh Burke* could still have 50 or more missiles in her tubes.

"They have to be here for that damned scientist," Michael said. Yet another failure to predict a response. Chamuel was less than worthless now. Fine, he'd kill the bitch himself when this was all over. The thought of choking her brought a grin to his face. *I wonder if she'll predict her own death?*

"Subs got the last frigate."

"Excellent, finally some good news," Colonel Baker said.

Michael barely nodded. He picked up his radio and checked to be sure it was still working. Like most of their technology, it was nearly indestructible. He made a call. "Have Dr. Breda moved to the bunker."

"Yes, sir."

"Have you found Grange yet?"

"The personnel were pulled from the search when the attack began."

He suppressed the urge to yell, instead acknowledging it as the correct move. With both subs holding two squads of his elite soldiers, only two platoons remained on the island. A quarter of them were in stationary defensive positions to guard against the unexpected. "Very well," he said and cut the call.

"Dockside facilities under attack!"

Michael ran to the waterside window and looked. He could see figures clad in US Army camo moving and shooting. The few security stationed there were going down, *fast.* The goddamned soldiers had either landed more people or flanked his defenders on the hill. Son of a bitch, this General Rose was good. He wished he'd had a chance to serve with him.

"Pull back a squad from the hill to deal with these leakers," Michael ordered. "I'm going to get my battle rattle. You should do the same."

Baker opened a locker and revealed a battle harness, armor, a helmet, and a nice little combat MP5 submachinegun. Michael nodded, exited, and climbed down the stairs. He wasn't in a hurry, he was just being certain. Had he waited a few seconds, he might have noticed that one of the dockside soldiers wasn't fighting. The man had set up an observation scope and was observing the control tower.

***

**The Flotilla**

**165 Nautical Miles West of San Diego, CA**

"Wake up!"

Someone slapped his face. Wade spluttered and waved the hand away. "I'm here," he moaned. The back of his head felt like white hot fire. He opened his eyes and saw carnage. The big bridge windshields had been blown out, and the radioman he'd been talking to only moments earlier was lying a few feet away, his face turned into bloody hamburger. The man wasn't moving. A pair of hands grabbed Wade and hauled him to his feet.

"Wade, snap out of it."

"My head hurts." Wade focused on the person holding him. It was Alex West. He was bleeding from several cuts but looked a lot better than the radioman.

"Yeah, so does mine. The damned alien drive doesn't want to work. Alison is down. You know the most about this shit."

"I…can't," he said, slipping back toward the dark. Alex slapped him again. It wasn't a brutal slap, but it was a painful one, carefully calculated to focus his attention. "Ow, damn it!" The hand was coming again, but Wade blocked it with his own.

"There, that's better." Alex pointed out one of the shattered windows. Another ship, a tanker, was in flames and sinking. "We don't have much fucking time, Kid! If you sleep, you *die.*"

"Dead?"

"Very."

He turned and found the alien drive where he and Alison had installed it. The device was simple; so simple, he'd laughed when he saw it. Playstation comes alive, flies to space! He felt a little giddy through the pain. *Must have a concussion.*

Doing his best to concentrate, he examined the alien drive and control unit. It only took a second. "Got it," he said. "The connection to the power module was destroyed."

"So, it won't work?" Alex asked, agog.

"Not with the power module." Wade looked around, almost falling from a dizzy spell, then spotted what he was looking for. He *carefully* bent and took a radio from the dead radioman. "He won't be needing this." Flipping it over, he took the back off, removed the battery, and dropped the radio. He moved back to the alien drive and improvised the same power connection he'd seen in the initial diagrams on the key drive. "There," he said, "it'll work now."

Alex blinked, looking from Wade to the control.

Wade walked over to a chair and sat down. He went to hold his head with his hands and found it was soaked in blood. *What a fuckin' day.*

Alex turned the controller on. With reflexes developed through hard practice, he gently moved the X axis up. The OOE ship slowly rose out of the ocean.

Wade turned his head and stared out the window. The ship next to them was also rising out of the water, courtesy of the metal cable they'd sent over and Alex had locked down on a cleat. Despite his pain, he grinned. "This is cool."

"They've connected other ships," Alex said, pointing.

Wade could see that at least four other ships were connected. They were all rising as well, though they appeared to be lagging behind the OOE ship and the first one connected. "I wonder how far we can extend it?"

"I'm afraid we're going to find out." Alex found another radio and spun the frequency dial. "OOE to the *Gerald* R. *Ford.* I need to talk to Captain Gilchrist, immediately."

* * *

The submarines circled the remainder of the Flotilla. This time, Michael's orders were more specific. Target the warships in the fleet first. Unfortunately, it was difficult because of the repeated explosions of ultra-high frequency sound coming from one side of the Flotilla. The sound pulses didn't follow any pattern, and they were playing hell with the sonar gear. Without the sonar, they couldn't target.

The Hunter subs were marvels of technology, not the least of which was their supercavitating system which allowed amazing speeds. They were also coated in a material that made them all but invisible to active sonar, as long as they weren't using the supercavitating system. At just over 100 feet long, their crew was 11, and they could carry 20 additional passengers. In this case, they both carried Project Genesis commandoes.

Their biggest Achilles heel was weaponry. Each sub had two torpedo tubes, one forward and one aft. They only carried eight weapons each, loadable in either tube via a central magazine system. The torpedoes were supercavitating as well, though they only had a range of 10 nautical miles. The modified RAM missiles were useful, but not against warships. Plus, the subs had to surface to use them. They skulked together ten miles from the Flotilla, waiting for the strange bursts of sound to end.

After ten minutes, the senior captain finally got impatient enough to bend one of Michael's instructions. He slowed to a stop and rose to just below the surface. The sub's periscope broke through the water, and the commander examined his quarry from extreme range.

The commander stared at the screen for a long moment, shaking his head, then rubbing his eyes. It had been a long, few weeks since the plague arrived, but should he be seeing things?

"Tell me if I'm seeing flying ships," he told his XO.

"You're seeing flying ships," the woman replied.

The captain scanned the tableau and spotted what he was looking for. "The carrier isn't flying. Tell the other Hunter to fire on it with us. At least it will be gone." He continued to observe as the weapons officer programmed the supercavitating torpedo.

***

The port Sea-Wiz fired a medium length burst. *Brrrrrr!* Captain Gilchrist glanced at the air defense screen that showed the ammunition status for the *Ford's* remaining three Sea-Wizes. It was clear the skulking enemy drones were testing for a weakness. Damnit, this was not a winnable scenario. He never thought he'd die in such a way.

When one of the subs sank the last frigate, he knew the endgame was underway. He kept hoping Rose would succeed in his crazy assault. There was a chance, if the general succeeded, he could lift the siege on the Flotilla as well.

Tobias moved away at the summons of someone from communications, returning a moment later with a strange look on his face.

"What's wrong now, James?" he asked his XO.

"That crazy nerd, Watts, is on the radio from OOE. He says he wants to get us in the air again to avoid the sub."

"Oh, for the love of God," Gilchrist said. "Why is anyone listening to that miscreant?"

"He has a point," Tobias said. Gilchrist could see it pained the man to admit it. He was pointing to one of the many camera monitors around the carrier's CIC. This one showed the second most ludicrous scene Gilchrist had seen in his years as a naval officer, the first had been when he looked out from his carrier's bridge into space. At least six ships were floating off the water, like they were suspended from a child's mobile. The monitor wasn't high-resolution, but it appeared they were loosely connected with ropes or cables.

"Do it," he ordered.

"We have our own device here," Tobias whispered to him.

"After the last time, I'd rather not mess with it." He gestured to the screen. "Floating a little bit above the water is fine. I can live with that." He shook his head. In the long run, he didn't know if it would help. Between the sub and the drones, it only temporarily took care of one problem. He didn't think it altered the endgame.

"It's going to take some time to get us close enough to pull a cable," Tobias told Gilchrist after a minute.

The captain nodded. Supercarriers weren't designed to maneuver gently. You needed tugs and lots of patience to bump around a hundred-thousand tons of steel. The smaller ships in close proximity made it a disaster waiting for a wave. Luckily, the seas were nearly dead calm.

"Radar reports contact with the subs again," Tobias said.

"Relay the info to the *Russell*, but I fear he's wasting ASROCs." Earlier, they'd expended nine torpedoes in one attack and gotten squat. The *Russell* only had three left at last count.

"Captain!" the radioman called. "I have Admiral Kent on the *Bataan*!"

"Belay the order to the *Russell* and stand by." He pointed at the radio operator, then at the speaker above his chair. The radioman gave him a thumbs up. "Admiral Kent, good to hear from you!"

"You too, Captain Gilchrist. We've been trying to reach you through MILSATCOM, but it's still pretty FUBAR."

"We've managed to restore some functionality, though it isn't reliable. We're engaged with aggressors who may be responsible for that problem."

"I've been monitoring your comms. You've got aggressor aircraft and two subs of unknown capabilities? Can you give me the coordinates on those skunks?"

"They've submerged," Tobias whispered to him. "The Viking is bingo fuel, but the enemy craft have ignored him, so he's been circling the Flotilla at 25,000 feet. He says he has good positioning on the subs; they're sticking together for some reason."

"Excellent," Gilchrist said, then turned back to the radio. "Admiral, we have them positioned with an old Viking we had aboard, though it won't be able to hold the lock for much longer; it's bingo fuel. How far out are you?"

"We're 190 miles south of your location."

"Sir, with all due respect, unless you have some Hornets…"

"All we have are Harriers. None of the *Nimitz*-class were in port when the shit hit the fan."

"Then I don't know what I can do."

"If I told you, you would either think I'm nuts or a traitor."

Gilchrist blinked at the speaker. He'd known Kent, met him several times at the Puzzle Palace. He would have never accused the admiral of either. "Tobias, have the Viking relay to Admiral Kent moment-by-moment positioning on the enemy skunks."

He watched as his XO relayed the orders. He had no idea what the admiral had in mind. He was about to ask for an update on how long it would take to get the stupid flying ship thing moving when the torpedo hit.

* * *

**Classified Genesis Facility**

**San Nicolas Island**

The painkillers had worn off, and hell had returned in full force. Grange crawled for a time on her hands and knees, leaving bloody trails as she went. Then she moved through a tiny hatchway, which opened at her approach, to a higher level. Her hands and knees were in unspeakable agony, so she started crawling on her belly. It felt like a year or fifty had passed. Maybe it was a century.

"I'm done," she croaked. "I'm done." She lay her head on the cool, metallic floor and tried to keep breathing. "I'm sorry," she whispered, wondering if First Scout could still hear her with his psy-lock trick. She closed her eyes.

After some time, she opened her eyes. She saw a wall of the same light gray, semi-pliable, plastic material she'd seen when she entered the alien ship. The halls were more like tunnels, ovoid in shape, about 3 feet tall by 5 feet wide. There seemed to be no top or bottom in their design. Hatches like the one she'd entered through were spaced irregularly along the corridor. Every few feet, light sources were embedded in the widest points. The illumination was subtle—

enough for her to see most detail, yet somehow lacking the intensity she'd need to read. It just felt…wrong.

The air tasted rich, like a forest. Memories of trips to the woods bounced around her mind. There were unidentified smells of living things and water. The humidity seemed high, and the temperature was slightly below what she considered normal, at least from what she could tell from the small areas of her skin that still possessed nerve endings.

Grange lifted her head a little and looked down. She'd taken off the medical helmet, so her face had been resting on the 'floor'. Some of her burned skin, along with blood and mucus, were matted there. She was in one of those eddies of pain she'd been feeling. Short times when the pain overwhelmed her nervous system, and she wasn't conscious of it. She knew the agony would return, sooner or later. If she just lay there, it might not be sooner.

*I want to live,* she thought. Others want to live too, though. What had First Scout said when she had asked him what would happen? "Something wonderful." He hadn't said she'd be healed, or even survive. *I'd still like to live.* Somehow, she found the energy to move, despite the pain she knew would follow.

Yet another hatchway presented itself. This one didn't open automatically. She touched the center of the hatch in an intricate pattern, and it slid aside. With the last of her energy and resolve, she pulled herself inside. She *knew* she had to close the hatch behind her which she did with a simple touch.

She was in a room shaped like a flattened sphere. In the center was a cylinder running from the floor to the ceiling. The only light was coming from the cylinder which seemed to be full of swirling liquid. Grange sagged onto her side and stared at the strange display. "Reminds me of a lava lamp," she rattled.

"Touch this pattern on the *Pandora* control," echoed in her mind.

"Pandora?" she wheezed. Everything was beginning to look ethereal, and she didn't think it was due to the alien lava lamp. With a feeling like a dream, she reached out with her hand. The side of the *Pandora* chamber was icy cold, even through her burned fingers. She started pressing a pattern. Then she reached the end. Her hand moved downward, still vainly typing, but the patterns didn't translate through her fading consciousness. Her hand hit the floor. This time, she was done.

She lay on the floor, fingers just touching the cylinder. She blinked and tried to breathe, but she couldn't. She closed her eyes. Something fluid flowed across her hand, and a feeling like electricity shot up her arm. Grange opened her eyes and instinctively tried to pull away from the jolting sensation. A glowing, pulsating, fluid mass was affixed to her hand.

The pain of her failing body forgotten, she turned and tried to pull her hand away. She didn't know where the sudden energy had come from. *Was I just dead?* The wall of the *Pandora* chamber was gone, and the mass was floating in space, levitating, except for the pseudopod-like mass attached to her hand. It stretched thin and pulled back.

"No!" she croaked. It crawled up her arm as if it were eating her. It reached her elbow and a section of unburned skin, and her entire body arced as if she'd been hit by a live wire. "Aaaaah!" she screamed. Grange thought she'd plumbed the dark extremes of mortal pain. She'd been wrong. Horribly, dreadfully, hideously wrong.

The pain grew with every square inch of skin that was subsumed by the glowing matter.

The worst part was that the pain knew no limits. It ratcheted higher and higher. The part of her mind that was still able to form coherent thoughts begged for death, screamed to whatever god, goddess, demon, or devil was listening. She thrashed like a fish on a lure as the stuff reached her shoulder and moved onward. She screamed until her lunges ached, and blood sprayed from her lips. Then it moved up her neck to her face.

The stuff entered her mouth, and the pain ended. So did her consciousness.

Pearl Grange ceased to exist. Something else was born.

* * *

"Michael?"

"Go ahead, Colonel."

"Dr. Breda is gone."

Michael paused from loading gear. "What did you say?"

He heard a slight pause on the other end of the line. "The security team I sent down to get her found her cell empty. A top-level code was used to open the cell."

"Find Chamuel."

"She's not in her suite of offices."

Michael struggled with his rage for a long time, so long that Colonel Baker had to clear his throat to let Michael know he was still there. "There's more, or you wouldn't still be waiting."

"None of the Heptagon are in their quarters. The bunker entrance has been sealed from the inside."

"Traitors," he growled.

"What are your orders?"

"Order a combined attack of the Wasps and Hunters. All out. Destroy them at any cost."

"We'll lose assets, sir."

"They'll lose more."

"Understood."

* * *

**The Flotilla**

**165 Nautical Miles West of San Diego, CA**

"Damage control reports the flooding is under control," Tobias said.

"Very good," Gilchrist acknowledged. They'd been hit three times, but the *Ford* was still afloat and still under power. He smacked the arm of his chair. *Goddamn, what a ship!*

How a modern supercarrier could handle being torpedoed was somewhat of a mystery. Except for an exercise where the USS *America*, CVN-66, was sunk in a weeks-long exercise, no US supercarrier had ever been sunk in combat. They'd lost the *Reagan* the day before, but that appeared to have been from internal explosions related to infected, not enemy action. The fact was, Gilchrist's ship was built to be nearly unsinkable.

Of course, "unsinkable ship" was a term that hadn't been used in maritime architecture since a little incident with a ship named the *Titanic.* The *Ford* possessed redundant watertight zones and advanced damage control which made her extremely difficult to sink. The biggest risk was a magazine or fuel explosion. Luckily, she didn't have much of either. All they had to do was keep her from taking on too much water or losing both reactors.

"Viking is breaking off," Tobias announced.

"I guess Kent couldn't swing whatever he wanted to do," Gilchrist said. He looked at the various computer monitors. Every ship except the *Ford* was floating in the air like a strange puppet show. Even the *Russell*, yet it was still able to fire weapons. *Good show, Paine, good show.*

"*Ford,* this is Admiral Kent, be aware you have incoming ordnance. *Serious* incoming ordnance."

"I wonder what he means?" Tobias asked.

"Missile inbound from the south-east."

"Do not engage with the Sea-Wiz!" Gilchrist barked. He could see the direction of the new attack was from the heading of Kent's task force. "Inform the *Russell* to do the same."

"Weapon is hypersonic!"

The fire control officer was examining the radar data, and he suddenly looked up in shock. "Captain, weapon matches the profile of a Kalibr missile. Russian, sir!"

"Oh, shit," Tobias said.

Gilchrist nodded. It was too late to order anti-missile fire. The weapon reached them in seconds and passed over. He breathed a sigh of relief and watched the radar track.

"It's heading for our two skunks."

"What can a single, anti-submarine, cruise missile do against them?" Tobias wondered.

Gilchrist didn't comment; he thought he knew the answer.

When the missile reached its destination, the engine cut out, and it fell below mach. Shortly thereafter, it split and released a torpedo, which parachuted into the sea. On impact, a rocket engine ignited.

"It's supercavitating!" their sonarman said, pumping his fist in the air. "Let's see how you like it!" He jabbed a finger at the sonar track. "They're trying to run. Impact in five seconds."

"They'll only get one."

Gilchrist shook his head. "Sonar, safe your board." The man looked at him. "*Now*, son!"

The man removed his headset and pressed a safety button, protecting his gear. Four seconds later, the supercavitating VA-111 Shkval torpedo's radar showed it was within a kilometer of a submersed target and detonated its warhead.

On the monitor facing the engagement, there was a brilliant flash of light below the water. Immediately, the surface was turned into a titanic blast of water which spread, and climbed, and climbed, *and climbed*! Alarms went off on the bridge.

"Nuclear explosion!"

"That would be what Kent meant by treason," he said, laughing and shaking his head. "Mr. Tobias, it would appear that, for the first time since WWII, the Russians are fighting on our side." On the screen, a small mushroom cloud was forming. "How far away was the blast?"

"Twenty-three miles," a radarman reported, staring at the screen with huge eyes.

"We're fine. Helm, steer course 299 to minimize the swell effect. I don't believe the subs will be a factor anymore. However, be prepared for the fighters. Whoever sent this attack will not be happy."

* * *

**Classified Genesis Facility**
**San Nicolas Island**

"The subs are both off the scope," Colonel Baker told Michael. "The telemetry from the Wasps indicates it was a nuclear sub-surface explosion. One of the subs had just reported the Flotilla ships were using alien tech to hover out of the water, then that it was under attack by a single cruise missile-launched torpedo. The chatter scrambled, then they were gone."

Michael wasn't mad anymore. He was glad he'd settled on his current plan when he did. He'd salvage what he could and put the pieces back together later.

"Order the Wasps to destroy the rest of the ships, civilian ones first. Fire everything they've got. Get in close to reduce the chance of intercept. If they can overwhelm us with a dozen cruise missiles, we can do it with 20 Maverick missiles. And yes, I know, we'll probably lose the Wasps."

"Acknowledged, sir."

* * *

Baker shut off the radio and turned to the UAV pilots. "You heard Michael, clean them up. Reserve one weapon each, and we'll use them on the carrier after the civilians and the *Arleigh Burke* is gone."

The five remaining pilots nodded. The sixth, his UAV shot down, was assisting the others. Baker watched them coming around at high speed before coming in low and fast. They were using their afterburners for the first time. Michael was right, even if they survived the assault, one or more might not have enough fuel to make it back.

He glanced at the door and settled his pistol in its holster. It felt like everything was going sideways. He didn't know where Michael was. The military leader of Project Genesis had said he was getting his combat gear. It shouldn't have taken him half an hour.

Baker walked over to the armored glass which afforded the tower a 360-degree view of the airstrip and surrounding buildings. Their forces on the hill had given ground, but they were still pinning the men down. The fighting by the dockside buildings was less defined. As long as it wasn't organized, they weren't in any real danger.

Down on the airfield, a small Cessna Citation, in nondescript black paint, was parked. It was fueled and ready, and Baker had his multi-engine jet rating. Maybe it was time to consider a career change.

Movement in the corner of his eye made him turn. There'd been a small explosion down by the dock, probably a grenade. He was about to look away when he saw them; two men on the roof of a warehouse. One man was kneeling, balancing a big, blocky tube on his shoulder. There was a puff from it and a darting shape came flitting directly at him. He'd trained with the FGM-148 Javelin man-portable anti-tank missile system and knew it by sight.

"Well, fuck," he said, just before the missile slammed into the control tower and detonated, turning the structure into burning wreckage.

* * *

**The Flotilla**

**165 Nautical Miles West of San Diego, CA**

"They're coming in hot!" Tobias called out.

"All bearing Sea-Wiz on automatic," Gilchrist ordered. The computers could target and fire them far faster than humans could. *This is it.*

The radar showed five mysterious planes approaching at Mach 2. The enemy was using improved Maverick missiles which could do nearly Mach 3. They'd barely been able to shoot them down one at a time. Considering five planes were coming in at once, it wouldn't end well. At least they seemed to have a shorter range of 10 nautical miles.

When the fighters passed within 10 nm and didn't fire, he knew they were willing to spend themselves to get the kill. "It's much harder to defeat an enemy that doesn't care if he survives," was the teaching. It was why suicide bombers were such tricky adversaries. Well, maybe they could take a few of them with them. The Sea-Wizes came alive as the fighters came under seven miles. They could begin firing at five.

"Holy crap!" someone yelled. All five enemy fighters dropped off the radar.

"Stealth?" Gilchrist asked.

"No," Tobias said, listening to the chatter. "Spotters said all five went into the water."

"General Rose," Gilchrist said and laughed. "You magnificent bastard!" Tobias looked at him, uncertain. "They must have been drones. Our good General Rose took out their controllers."

"I take back almost everything I've ever said about the grunts," his XO said. Gilchrist smiled and nodded.

* * *

Kathy hung on and prayed during the fight. What else could she do? She'd done everything she could think of to help save the day. She'd hijacked the cameras with her laptop and seen the rest of the Flotilla take off in the almost magical way the alien tech worked. All of them except her ship.

She didn't know why the *Ford* hadn't gone airborne. When the first torpedo hit the ship with a sickening boom and everything shook, she stopped worrying and concentrated on prayers. She'd done it a few times in her life. She didn't know if they helped, but she did know they didn't hurt.

When the *really* big explosion happened, she'd stared in shock and horror. *Was that a fucking nuke?* She listened to the bridge chatter. Yeah, they were evacuating the flight deck. The *Russians* had fired a nuclear torpedo and destroyed the subs. Only the fighters remained.

Her laptop was recording everything. She'd set all the channels to record and had her 10tb external drive soaking up the feeds. It was an orgy of information that would take weeks to sort out. Maybe she'd even survive to tell someone about it or write the book she'd been thinking about.

Then she heard people yelling in the hallway, and she was afraid the carrier was sinking. She stuck her head out and looked. Two sailors were high-fiving each other.

"What happened?" she asked.

"The enemy are toast! The fighters crashed for some reason."

"That's awesome!"

Kathy went back to her space with a grin on her face. She was about to sit down at her desk when she saw the rat. She'd seen rats on the *Ford* before, just after coming aboard. The first person she'd complained to had laughed at her.

"Ships have rats," the sailor had said.

"It's a brand-new ship!" she had complained.

The sailor had laughed again. "Maybe it's a brand-new rat."

"Shoo!" she said and waved a hand at it. The rat turned and looked at her in a most un-rat-like manner. "Oh, oh no." At the sound of her voice, the rat cocked its head. It was a movement she'd seen more than once from an infected. It hunched and leaped at her.

A shotgun boomed, splattering the rat all over her desk and the wall behind it. The civilians and dependents in the room screamed, many diving under chairs or into corners.

Kathy shook her head, swaying on her feet from the deafening explosion that had been a foot from her head.

Chris Brown stepped up next to her, racking another shell into his shotgun. "Sorry," he said over the ringing in her ears. "I came to see how you were, and I saw the rat." He took a shell from his vest and fed it into the gun. "Didn't have time to warn you."

"I'm not complaining," she said. Then she examined the gore on her desk; it was a mess of blood and rat pieces. "Hey, this explains why random outbreaks have been happening. There are rats on all the ships, and they're infected."

"Makes sense," Chris said. "I'll inform Commander Tobias so we can do something about them." He headed for the door.

"Can you tell me about that nuke?" she called after him.

"What nuke?"

"Never mind." She went back to her desk and wondered where they kept the cleaning supplies.

* * *

**Classified Genesis Facility**
**San Nicolas Island**

The underground dock shook, and dust rained from the ceiling. His personal guards grabbed weapons and looked up, as if they could see through the rock. Michael picked up his radio.

"Brady, report. What was that?" Only static answered him. "Brady, damn it, answer!" Still nothing. He looked at the loading process and frowned. They needed another ten minutes. Grabbing his tablet, he called up the connection with the island's computer. None of the datalinks with the command tower were live. None of them. "What the hell?"

Michael flicked to the video surveillance system and found that the tower cameras were offline as well. Out of frustration, he moved to the dockside camera. Situated on a rooftop, the camera was facing the docked ships. He used a finger to turn the camera and watched as the burning remnants of the control building came into view. Something walked in front of the camera which immediately refocused to show a US infantry soldier in camo looking into the lens. The man cocked his head and said something.

The camera had no audio pickup, so Michael didn't know what he said. However, another man appeared a second later. The two looked over their shoulders at the burning building and back at the lens before they flipped the camera the bird. Michael turned it off. "Son of a bitch."

"Hurry up," he said to the men. He didn't bother trying to contact the troops that were still holding out. They couldn't get to the dock in time, and there wasn't room for more than a few anyway. There were seven more seats. A low growl escaped his throat. The Wasps were toast, the Hunters were gone. But the goddamn Flotilla was probably still there. *Okay, you want to play it that way? Sure, fine.*

He opened another program on the tablet. He entered a password, scanned his fingerprint, then entered another password. "Targeting Online." A map covering about ¾ of the planet came up. He used a finger to center it just to the west of San Diego. The map was one of Chamuel's and was about an hour old. As he zoomed in, the icon for the Flotilla appeared. He clicked on it. "Target Selected—Click and Hold to Confirm."

"You're goddamned right," he said and mashed the icon with his finger for the required five seconds.

"Target Confirmed—Launch in Progress."

"Okay, let's get the fuck out of here."

* * *

Rose crouched behind the ruined WWII era flower planter and tried to catch his breath. His shoulder throbbed where the body armor had stopped the bullet. Goddamn, it still hurt. It had knocked him down, and he was sure he'd been hit. He had caught a bouncer back in 1990. It had only been a big chunk of a Russian 7.62mm, but it had felt like a piece of sewer pipe in his thigh. After a few seconds, he was sure it hadn't gotten through his armor. This hit didn't have the deep down, messed up feeling the previous one did.

"You okay, General?"

"Fine," he lied. "How about you, Master Sergeant?"

"Just another day at work, General!" Ayres couldn't be more than 10 years his junior. The man had no fucking right to look so chipper.

"You find out what the explosion was?"

"Yes, sir. The squad you sent to flank the dock blew the shit out of the base control tower. All kinds of antenna and armored glass. Said some guy with bird colonel insignia was running things. Ain't runnin' shit no more."

"Good," Rose said. "Damned good. Now, if we can just convince these bastards to call it quits."

"Comms are back!" a corporal yelled. "I got the carrier."

"How's it going?" Rose asked.

"They said the fighters splashed about the time our boys blew the control tower."

"Musta been drones," Ayres said. Rose nodded.

"Said the subs sunk too. We got them on the ropes, General!"

"Maybe we should ask those guys if they want to call it quits." Ayres said.

Rose was chewing it over when a sound like an air raid siren echoed in the distance. A second later, a shape rose above the hill to the north. The ground vibrated, then the sound hit them. The roar of the rocket engine was horrendous.

"General, this is Pepper. You see that? It's a goddamned MX! They're supposed to have all been destroyed."

"ICBM," Rose said. The roar was decreasing as the missile accelerated into the sky, banking southward. He addressed the corporal with the radio, "Give me that radio, son, I think I know where the missile is heading."

* * *

**The Flotilla**

**165 Nautical Miles West of San Diego, CA**

"Persistent bastard, isn't he?" Gilchrist asked. "Radio, notify Admiral Kent. Advise him to stay clear of the blast range."

"Can we shoot it down?" Tobias asked. You didn't train to down ICBMs aimed at your ship.

"The Sea-Wiz can do it, in theory. San Nicolas is only 180 miles away, so this is a super short shot for a missile like that. It'll take about 9 minutes. Tell the operators to train their weapons for vertical attack."

"What about the alien drive?" Tobias asked.

"I had it taken apart," Gilchrist said and shook his head. "Between the crazy ride and how it affected the nuclear plant, it seemed too dangerous. No, the Sea-Wizes are our only hope."

As Tobias gave the orders, Gilchrist shook his head. He knew better. There was no reason to explain that the MX carried as many as 10 warheads. A MIRV missile, multiple independent reentry vehicle, it was designed to rain hell on Soviet cities and missile complexes. The cone-shaped weapons would come in at 10 times the speed of sound. The Sea-Wiz might get one, maybe two. Even if they missed, they wouldn't be the nuke the Russians had used on the enemy subs. These would be 500kt city killers. At least it would be quick.

*I wish I knew why. Why did all this happen the way it did?* Now he'd never know.

* * *

**Classified Genesis Facility**

**San Nicolas Island**

Rose didn't have to tell his men what was happening. You couldn't grow up without seeing videos of nuclear missiles launching and learning about the Cold War. They knew all their friends and family were dead, so they went crazy. The defenders weren't ready for the ferocity unleased by Rose's soldiers. He'd never been prouder.

In only a few minutes, they'd backed the black clad defenders into a bunker's opening from which it was proving impossible to dislodge them.

"Want me to have them use the last Javelin?" Ayres asked.

"If they've fallen back here, it means their leadership is inside," Rose said. "I want them alive to answer for this." *Plus, Lisha is probably in there.* He very much wanted to see her alive. "See if they want to give up."

A man used a bullhorn to relay the terms of surrender. Someone on the other side took a shot at him.

"Okay, answers that question," Rose said. He examined the tactical situation, trying to determine the best angle of attack without resorting to rockets or grenades. He wasn't having any luck. "Ayres, you think you can use an M240 over by that building and force them back inside with grazing fire?"

"Maybe," the master sergeant said, rubbing the stubble on his chin. "We're getting low on ammo, though. Hey, what's going on?"

Rose turned back to the bunker just in time to see one of the black clad figures come flying out as if he had been thrown by a giant. Rose's men were too surprised to do more than watch. All shooting came to an immediate halt as another man rolled out. This one's head was smashed flat. It was not a pretty picture.

"What the hell is going on?" Rose wondered. A trio of black clad soldiers came running out. Rose was about to raise his weapon when a flash of light came from inside the bunker. The beam bisected one of the men neatly in two. A gurgling scream was cut off as the body fell into two parts. "Oh, shit! Was that a laser beam?"

"Everyone down!" Master Sergeant Ayres yelled.

Rose couldn't see what followed. He heard two more screams, the last one going on and on. After a couple seconds, he stuck his head up so he could see, painfully aware of how far up his helmet rested above his eyes. All three enemy were down. The second man was still alive, amazingly. His left arm and a significant portion of his torso lay several feet away. The screaming was piteous.

"For the love of God, Ayres," he hissed and pointed.

The master sergeant nodded and raised his M4. A single shot ended the enemy soldier's agony.

"Advance to the bunker entrance," Rose ordered, and gestured with his hand. The troops were a little hesitant. He couldn't blame them; they'd just watched a fucking laser beam slice several people into chunks. He'd suffered only six casualties. Frankly, that was far less than he feared after seeing the raiders move and shoot aboard the *Helix*. He was hesitant to jump to conclusions, but it appeared these soldiers weren't as well trained or equipped as the ones who'd kidnapped Dr. Breda.

Four men reached the bunker doorway, two on either side. They took out mirrors on poles and used them to check inside. A second later, they signaled the all clear. Despite the pain in his knees and shoulder, Rose was among the first up and moving across the open space. He didn't look down as he passed the man Ayres had killed with a mercy round.

"What do you have?" he asked one of the privates who'd checked the bunker with a mirror.

"Bodies, sir. Someone or something cleaned house."

A corporal was already moving inside, playing the tactical light on his M4 around and whistling. Rose and Ayres followed him in. It was a slaughterhouse. There were at least another ten men, all dressed in the same black combat gear and all diced up in the same hideous manner.

"Anakin Skywalker, your table is ready," one of the soldiers said.

"What does that mean?" Rose asked.

The man looked at Rose with an embarrassed expression. "Sorry, General. You ever see *Star Wars*?" Rose nodded. "These guys look like they were sliced up with a light saber."

"Ah," Rose said. *Sure, like the fucked-up dude in the cantina.* He shook as he moved across the room. The area where the chopped-up dudes were appeared to be an equipment bay, a place where you could don equipment and armor. Two walls were lined with lockers and gun safes. Multiple charred lines were traced along the walls. One of the lockers was smoking, and the metal still glowed dimly. *How much power had it taken to do this?*

The men were examining the door on the far side. A half dozen soldiers had gathered, and they were muttering to each other. "Make a hole," Ayres ordered, and they moved aside. The door was designed to protect high-security facilities—two-foot thick, high-carbon steel, with massive reinforcing plates and locking bolts. They were cut roughly down the middle and then pealed back as if they were made of aluminum foil.

"Mother of God," one of the men hissed.

Rose shook his head. The edges of the cut still glowed softly and felt hot even from several feet away. *What could have done this?* The door had been torn away from the room, indicating that whatever had done it and killed the enemy, had come from deeper in the bunker. Had it come up, opened the door, killed everything, then gone back inside?

"Lieutenant Drake is coming up," Ayres let him know.

Drake had taken a squad to deal with the port distraction and had ultimately taken out the headquarters. He came in using a piece of pipe as a crutch and being supported by a private. Only two more men were with him. "Sorry we missed the party," Drake said, looking around. "Jesus, who gave you the chainsaw, General?"

"Long story, Lieutenant." Rose looked at the men with him. "This it?"

"Yes, sir. It was expensive. Worth it?"

"I think you saved the Flotilla." Drake nodded and leaned against the nearest wall which hadn't been cut up by…what, a light saber? Rose added the ten men Drake had lost to the six from his own group for a total of 16. They also had three men still ambulatory. He'd lost just about a third of those he'd brought to the island.

"The ones we fought had that fancy armor and could really fight. Good thing there were only six of them. What about this lot?"

"More like weekend warriors," Rose said. "Decent training, but average armor. Hit them, and they went down." He explained the light beams and how they'd found the slaughter. "No clue what did it."

"Darth Vader?" Drake suggested. Several of the men chuckled nervously.

Rose pointed at him and looked around at his men. "Now I understand that reference." They laughed more heartily. Good, it lightened up the scene a bit. "Who the hell is this Anakin guy?"

"Long story," Ayres said.

"Later then," Rose agreed. "Set point, and let's see where this leads. Lieutenant," he said and glanced at Drake, "stay here with the injured."

"Yes, sir," the lieutenant agreed. He didn't look thrilled. Rose nodded and moved in behind his men as they moved out.

* * *

Michael watched his personal detail load the last case into the sub. They were ready to go. Thanks to his traitorous, former allies, they'd had plenty of room for extra gear. Genesis had six more installations like San Nicolas. None had the level of staffing they did here, though. It was unfortunate, but you did what was necessary to survive.

He checked his tablet. Five minutes since he'd launched the missile. The Flotilla would be getting theirs soon. Time to go. He entered the shutdown command on this tablet. In ten minutes, the base would completely shut down. The various labs, warehouses, and facilities would lock their doors, and data would be erased. Nothing as cliché as a self-destruct. He kind of regretted that now. How nice it would have been to have a loud countdown ending in a huge explosion.

Michael looked at his tablet. He still had one more nuclear missile… "Maybe after I'm at the next base," he said.

The heavy, reinforced door to the bay rang like a bell. Michael spun and stared at it in surprise. He checked his tablet and confirmed the sea door was still closed. They were 50 feet below sea level, if the inside door suddenly opened while the sea door was also open, it would be bad. He accessed the cameras and searched for the ones outside the bay. "There they are," he mumbled and clicked on the sub bay cameras.

Everything from where he was to the tunnel leading to the ocean came up. He scrolled, looking for the one just outside the door. Had someone set off a breaching charge? He wanted to see topside, but he still hadn't found the correct camera. He finally found it and expanded the image to fit his tablet's screen.

The corridor was dark and lined with concrete. Its only purpose was to access the sub bay. No need for anything fancy. Standing outside was a single figure. Michael could see its head moving as it examined the door. He zoomed in to see who it was. One of the damned soldiers who'd landed on the Osprey?

The figure wore no clothes and appeared to be made of silver, like an unfinished sculpture. A radiation or bio suit? The figure stopped looking at the door. Its head turned and stared directly at the camera. That was no suit. He could see no signs of a face mask or joints. It was a silver figure of pure mercury.

"Oh, hell," he said. "What are you?"

The figure cocked its head as it seemed to observe the camera, then turned back to the door.

"Well, whatever you are, enjoy trying to get out of that corridor when all the doors lock."

It pointed a silvery hand at the door, and the camera image flashed white. The display read "Thermal Overload." Michael's head spun around to look at the door again, just as a spot on it started to glow. In an instant, the glow went from warm red to brilliant white. Without thinking, Michael dove to the floor.

A brilliant beam of light stabbed though the door and cut laterally across the sub bay. One of his men was caught in the beam and cut cleanly in two. He barely had time to scream before the two halves of his body fell bloodlessly to the floor.

"Take cover!" Michael yelled.

"What is it?" the leader of his security detail asked.

"No idea, just kill it."

The cutting beam turned off and something grabbed the glowing edges of the door and *ripped it outward.*

"Jesus Christ," Michael hissed.

As soon as the door was sufficiently open, the silvery figure stepped through. Michael and his men gawked in open mouthed amazement as the bay's lights reflected off its skin. Its movements were robotic. *God, it's some kind of alien robot!* It was the only conclusion that made any sense. He looked around at his surviving men crouched behind machinery and equipment.

"What are you crouching there for? Shoot it!" Five compact machine pistols came up and opened fire.

Bullets bounced off the metallic creature with bright flashes of light, almost like photo strobes. All five of his men dumped their magazines into the shiny figure. For several seconds, it looked like the red carpet at a Hollywood release. The bullets shattered and flew in every direction. Since the sub bay was a metallic structure, it was like being inside the barrel of a shotgun as pieces of bullets flew like hail.

Michael ducked behind a cart and felt several pieces hit his body armor. One found a soft spot on his neck and another in the small of his back. He cringed and jerked as the fragments penetrated his skin. They hurt, though neither felt bad enough to be dangerous.

The men's fire tapered off, and Michael heard a buzzing which quickly grew and became a roaring, snapping sound. Someone screamed. He heard magazines falling to the floor, and yelling. He found his position in relation to the sub and crawled toward it.

The battle continued out of his view. Bolts were closed, and there was more gunfire. He heard thumping footsteps and a yell, followed by a sound like wet cement hitting the floor. Something wet splashed across the floor just before him. It looked suspiciously like entrails. He was halfway to the ramp leading to his escape when the shooting and screaming stopped. A silver foot stepped directly in front of him, and his blood ran cold.

Not one to face his fate on hands and knees, Michael got to his feet. The silvery being was imperfectly human. Its shoulders were overly stooped, and its arms seemed too short. It was also short, not much over five feet. He towered above it. Death shouldn't be so physically insignificant. Michael thought he could pick it up and crush it like a toy. Yet his six men, the most highly trained of the Project Genesis soldiers, veterans of special forces and SEAL training, had been slaughtered, and there was not a mark on this being.

He squared his shoulders and stared down at the being only a few feet away. It mostly reminded him of an artist's mannequin he'd once used in school a lifetime ago, before Michael, when the world was a very different place. Its head moved slightly, and he knew it was examining him, trying to understand, trying to decide. Michael considered his MP5 hanging on its sling. The floor of the bay was littered with empty brass, testimony to the futility of reaching for his gun.

"Fuck you," he snarled. "Get it over with." The figure raised its right arm.

"Wait," someone yelled.

Michael turned toward the ruined door and saw a big, somewhat portly soldier stepping through, flanked by a squad of men, all in identical US Army camo. Michael's sharp eyes picked up three black stars velcroed to the front. "Lieutenant General Leon Rose?"

"Who the hell are you, and what the fuck is that?"

"My name is Michael. I *was* the best hope for mankind's survival until you came along. I suspect this thing is some alien creation. To tell the truth, I thought you'd created it with salvaged alien tech."

"Let's take a second," Rose said. "I'm arresting this man for treason."

Michael sighed and shook his head. "You don't know what the hell you're talking about or what you're dealing with."

The silver figure raised its arm and pointed a finger at Michael's chest. Michael looked at its face, smooth and featureless.

"What? You want to say some—" A brilliant beam of light lanced through Michael's chest, ending his life.

* * *

Rose jerked as the beam slashed through Michael's chest. Whatever the 'weapon' was, aiming and firing it was nearly instantaneous. Michael's body dropped like a marionette cut from its strings.

"Shit!" Master Sergeant Ayres yelped, and the men who'd come in with General Rose brought their weapons up. The silver figure's head came around with fantastic speed.

"Stop!" Rose barked, holding up his empty hand. "Easy men, we don't know what we're dealing with."

The figure lowered its arm and stepped forward to examine its handywork. Its head moved so little, it was difficult to tell exactly where it was looking. Rose was pretty sure it was watching him. It felt like bugs crawling up his back.

"Will you talk to us?" he asked. The figure moved around the room, checking the dead men, and stopped to look over the docked submarine, which was the first time Rose noticed it. *So, this Michael was running.* "We're looking for a hostage, Lisha Breda."

The silver figure stopped its examination and turned toward the door. The men tensed, their weapons shifting nervously.

"Don't initiate hostilities," he said. "That's an order."

The figure walked toward the door. Rose limped aside and gestured to his men to clear the way. Those past the ruined door did their best to flatten against the walls. The figure moved past them as if they didn't exist.

"Looks like Iron Man and the Silver Surfer had a lovechild," Rose heard a private say.

He had an idea of who the Silver Surfer was but did know Iron Man; that had been a good movie. Could the soldier be right that he was looking at a super-advanced suit of armor? If it was, whoever wore the armor was small. Damned small. As the thing passed by, he noticed it only had three fingers and a thumb and walked stiffly, as if it weren't used to its legs. There was no sign of instability, though. It didn't trip over the piles of spent brass or stumble as it stepped through the ravaged door.

"What do we do?" Ayres asked, watching the figure fade down the hallway.

Rose scanned the room again. He was *really* interested in the sub. It was pretty big, and he suspected it was one of the ones that had been attacking the Flotilla. The silvery figure was almost out of sight when he decided.

"Follow it," he said, gesturing with one arm. "Not too closely though."

"Yeah, I wouldn't want to piss it off," Ayres agreed.

Rose checked his watch; eight minutes since they'd seen the missile launch. The fate of the Flotilla would soon be known. They left the scene of death behind.

*****

# Chapter Eleven

**The Flotilla**
**165 Nautical Miles West of San Diego, CA**

Kathy Clifford finished feverishly packing the files she'd recorded over the last couple of weeks into a single archive file. Luckily, she'd been sorting as she'd recorded, so the data was saved by priority based on what she considered important. Using compression software she'd saved from her days as a reporter, she'd gotten the total down to ten 50-gigabyte files.

When she'd gained access to the ship's data systems and radio, she'd found the link Wade had established with MILSATCOM, which led to several off-site data archives. She didn't know what any of them were, and it didn't matter. The ship's communications specialists were using the restored connection sparingly, so she took advantage of the low outbound bandwidth. The collections of files were being uploaded to a dozen active storage locations.

"I don't see why you're bothering," Chris said. After he'd told one of the CPOs about the infected rats, he'd returned to help her clean up the mess he'd made. While he was there, they'd overheard the radio conversation between Captain Gilchrist and General Rose. They only had a few minutes to live.

"Because I want someone to know what happened," she said. He shrugged and sighed. *Besides, it's something to do,* she thought. *Better than spending my last minutes of life crying.*

"I wonder what happened to Cobb?" Chris asked suddenly.

Kathy looked up at him. "Why are you bringing him up all of a sudden?"

"Because I know you had a thing for him," he said. "I keep thinking he's out there, somewhere, doing a Mad Max thing across the wasteland."

Kathy snorted and laughed. He'd already done his Mad Max thing when he came after her in the Mexican desert. Then, they'd fought their way back north, rescuing dozens of Mexican civilians fleeing the infected in their own country. So many tangled fates, all coming to an end now. Of all the ways she'd thought she would die since the world fell apart, in a nuclear fireball was not one of them.

Suddenly, she didn't want to die without trying. She accessed the radio controls and selected a wideband frequency. A handy pop-up warned her that sending such a broadcast was against US Military regulations. She clicked her understanding and put the headset on.

"What are you doing?" Chris asked.

"Saying goodbye," she said. Kathy glanced at her watch. They had about five minutes. She cleared her throat and broadcast, "This is Kathy Clifford coming to you from the Flotilla. We're about 150 miles west of San Diego.

"For the last eight days, I've lived with thousands of others who were trying to stay alive. Strain Delta has killed most of society. Nobody knows how many people are still alive. Most of the living are no longer intelligent and only seek to kill and eat anyone that's not infected.

"I've seen much and recorded all I could. I documented that aliens were involved with Strain Delta, though not how or why, how their ships were found, and even some information about how they work. I've seen an aircraft carrier fly and have gone to space inside it. Maybe we could have used it to fight the plague? We'll never know."

"Some unknown force attacked the Flotilla hours ago. They kidnapped some scientists, then began sinking ships. A battle occurred. A force of US Army soldiers landed on the island where this mysterious enemy existed. I believe they won, but do not know. The only thing certain is that this enemy retaliated by launching a nuclear missile at us. It will be here in…" She glanced at her watch. "…Less than three minutes. There's just enough time for me to send this last broadcast.

"So, this is Kathy Clifford reporting from the USS *Gerald R. Ford* in the Flotilla. Good luck to those who survive. Good night and good luck."

"Edward R. Murrow?" Chris asked.

"Seemed apropos." She smiled sadly.

"Want to watch from the deck?"

"Won't matter more than a millisecond where we are," she said, then shrugged. "Sure, why not."

She glanced at the computer's progress first. Most of the files were uploaded to various sites. It looked like they'd all make it to one place or another in the next couple of minutes. She left the laptop open and followed Chris up the ladder to the flight deck.

She was surprised to see it crowded with hundreds of people. Many more than she'd expected. It looked like the news had spread. Some held hands. Others watched the sky. A few cried. Chris put an arm around her shoulders, and she leaned into him.

"Thanks for everything," she said. He nodded.

"There it is!" someone yelled.

Everyone looked around until they saw a sailor pointing east. Wasn't the missile supposed to come from straight overhead? But there was something to the east, a glowing point quickly approaching.

"No, it's up there somewhere," another person said. Heads turned to look for the missile.

"Two missiles?" Kathy wondered. Then everything happened at once.

* * *

"Du bist verdammt verrückt!" Daimler cried.

Cobb laughed. He'd served in Ansbach, Germany for a year. He knew a fair amount of German. Yeah, he was crazy alright!

"Halt die fresse und flieg!" he yelled back. Shut up and fly.

"Schiesse!" was Daimler's reply. Most people knew that word.

They'd been chugging along at a couple hundred miles per hour, which was standard cruising speed for Shangri-La. Cobb had Daimler flying the monstrosity, under the close supervision of Tango, who'd been more than willing to shoot the traitorous German when his duplicity was revealed. However, Paul Bisdorf said nobody was better at flying the beast than Daimler, so Cobb had made a deal.

"Behave yourself and do as you're told, and we'll discuss the terms of your imprisonment later."

At a cool 500 mph, they would make the Pacific coast in just under 4 hours, and thereby avoid having to stop to let the shield down for fresh air. They'd climbed to 25,000 feet to avoid any air traffic (as if there would be any) and hauled ass.

Navigation was via IFR, which Bisdorf jokingly referred to as I Follow Roads. They'd traced Interstate 10, passing just south of El Paso, and were approaching Tucson when Bisdorf picked up the radio call. "You better listen to this." He put the broadcast up on the speakers in the gondola.

"…attacked the Flotilla hours ago. They kidnapped some scientists, then began sinking ships. A battle occurred. A force of US Army soldiers landed on the island where this mysterious enemy existed. I believe they won, but do not know. The only thing certain is that this enemy retaliated by launching a nuclear missile at us. It will be here in…less than three minutes. There's just enough time for me to send this last broadcast.

"So, this is Kathy Clifford reporting from the USS *Gerald R. Ford* in the Flotilla. Good luck to those who survive. Good night and good luck."

"Edward R. Murrow," Bisdorf said, nodding. "Good choice."

"Okay, ve stop," Daimler said.

"Bullshit," Cobb said. "Punch it!"

"Dumpkopf, did you not her ze woman? Nuclear bomb!" Daimler pronounced the last words as clearly as he'd ever said anything.

"We have a shield," Cobb said.

"We don't know what it can do," Bisdorf pointed out. "Stopping a nuke seems bold."

Cobb looked at Daimler who was staring back at him. He reached down and unsnapped the retention clip on his sidearm. "Bullet or nuke, which do you think will hurt more?"

Daimler cursed in rapid fire German, manipulated the controls, and suddenly, the ground started going by faster. A *lot* faster.

"You should have been a Marine, Colonel." Tango laughed.

"Tucson to San Diego," Bisdorf was muttering, "call it 360 miles. Flotilla is 150 miles offshore, so 500 miles. Less than 3 minutes, better make it two." He closed his eyes for a second. "We need at least 4.2 miles per second, or…" He opened his eyes wide. "…about 15,000 miles per hour! Just under orbital speeds, in the fucking atmosphere."

"Do it," Cobb told Daimler.

The German continued cursing and looked down at the controls. Clearly, they weren't designed for anything like the speed they needed. Cobb could see the numbers on the knob ranged from 1 to 500. At one time, it had been 1 to 200, but it had been updated when he brought the former prisoner down to drive. Of the knob's 360 degrees, 1-500 took up about 90 degrees. The man removed a plastic tab, looked at the scale, and spun the speed control almost all the way up.

"Oh, hell," Bisdorf gasped.

Cobb looked in the direction of their travel. The leading edge of the forcefield had been visible before, like a contrail. Now, it was glowing like the sun, and streamers of plasma were flowing along the leading edge. Looking down, he could just see the ground passing at an alarming speed.

"We're high enough to clear the mountains, right?" he asked Bisdorf.

The big man was looking at the timer on his phone. "You are planning to stop a nuke with this thing, and you're worried about flying through a mountain?"

"Well, when you put it like that…"

"Wooohooo!" Tango cried as he looked out the front of the gondola. "Looks like *Star Wars*!"

"We probably look more like *Independence Day* from the ground," Bisdorf said. "Okay, 10, 9, 8…"

Cobb looked expectantly at Daimler who had been messing with the wiring on the controls. He had just enough time to wonder what the man had been doing when Bisdorf yelled, "Zero!"

Daimler touched a button, and they stopped. Shangri-La didn't slow down, it just *stopped.*

"Oh, that was cool," Bisdorf said.

"Quit sightseeing and find the Flotilla!" Cobb yelled. According to his watch, they had less than a minute, and that was if Kathy's estimate was correct. They were floating over the open ocean. *Have we overshot and ended up near Hawaii?*

"There," Tango said and pointed. "San Clemente Island."

There was a long, low island at about 2 o'clock.

"You sure?" Bisdorf asked.

"Marine, remember? We trained there."

"We're about 75 miles short," Bisdorf said and looked at Daimler. "If you did what I think you did, about 5 milliseconds." Daimler reached for the controls. "*Milliseconds.*"

"Ya, ya," Daimler said. He typed something on a simple keypad and touched the controls. The island disappeared and plasma flashed across the nose of the shield. Then there were ships in view.

"Over there!" Cobb said, pointing. The unmistakable shape of an aircraft carrier was clearly visible, surrounded by dozens of other ships.

Daimler was muttering again as he resumed manual control. Shangri-La turned and accelerated normally, in hundreds of miles per hour instead of thousands. He watched carefully and dialed back the speed. As if he were parking his Mercedes Benz, he settled Shangri-La over the flotilla as smooth as could be.

Cobb ran from side to side, looking at the edge of Shangri-La, then down at the ships. "I think we're bigger."

"Better hope so," Bisdorf said, and gestured for Daimler to go lower. They descended quickly. After a second, Daimler touched a button and the gondola was pummeled by airflow.

Cobb grabbed the mic for Shangri-La's PA system. "Nobody look up! Shield your eyes."

"Some idiots are going to look up," Bisdorf said. Cobb shrugged.

"Shield off," the German said. He slowed the descent, and they came to a stop only a hundred or so feet above the carrier. He touched a control again. "Shield on!"

"Any last words?" Cobb asked.

"Oohrah!" Tango said, and the world turned brilliant white.

* * *

**Classified Genesis Facility**
**San Nicolas Island**

Following the silver figure wasn't hard. Where it encountered doors, it simply cut them down or tore them open. It seemed to be heading somewhere specific. Rose wished it would get there, because his shoulder was killing him.

They encountered people on multiple occasions, and they always got out of the silver thing's way and put their hands in the air when they saw Rose and his men. Everyone was wearing khaki uniforms or blue coveralls. No insignia were visible. The one exception was a black clad soldier who drew down on their silver friend and was promptly cut into not-quite equal halves. Rose would have shot the man to put him out of his misery, but he was dead before they got to him. A few of the people they passed looked at him questioningly.

"Go topside and wait," he ordered them. They all complied, and a few ran. There were hundreds of personnel. He marveled at the size of the operation. It helped him understand how the government seemed to lose a few hundred billion dollars every year. There was simply no way this was anything other than a US Government black-ops. Maybe something to do with DARPA, the Defense Advanced Research Projects Agency. Whatever it was, the guy named Michael, who was roasted by the silver Iron Man, was obviously in charge of defenses, because there was no sign of continued opposition.

Finally, they reached another heavy door, like the one leading outside the bunker. Rose got to watch close up as the silver figure carved the door open and pulled it apart. The entity didn't use its hands to bend the metal. It gestured like it was using its hands, but never actually touched the metal.

"Freaking Magneto," the soldier who'd been using comic book analogies said.

The being stepped through, and Rose hurried to see where the door led. It was a room with a big glass cage. Inside the cage was a fox. *All of this for a zoo exhibit?* The fox was standing on its back legs and gesturing at something.

The silver entity turned, and a beam of light lanced from its hand. It was a much smaller beam than the one that killed Michael or was used to cut steel doors like they were butter. As soon as it fired, the glass cube threw off electric sparks, and the fox nodded. The silver thing went to the glass cube and pried one side open.

I can't keep calling it the silver thing, Rose thought. How about Mercury?

The fox stepped out and looked up at Mercury whose head was inclined down to look at it. Then the fox turned its head and examined the soldiers. It looked back at Mercury, eyes narrowing, and stared for a moment. After a time, it once again looked at the soldiers, picked out Rose, and walked closer. Rose realized he should have been prepared to defend himself, but the creature looked like it should be stealing chickens, instead of deep inside an unknown government base.

"You are General Leon Rose," it said in perfect English.

"Son of a bitch," he said in surprise.

"I am to be addressed as First Scout. I've been a prisoner of this installation. My defensive avatar," the creature gestured at Mercury, "believes you are not part of the people who held me here."

"No, we're not," Rose said. "Who, or what, are you?"

"You would call me an extraterrestrial. An alien."

"No shit!" the comic book private said.

Rose shot him a withering glare. Ayres grabbed the man's battle harness and jerked it. The private shut up.

"The organization that held me here is called Project Genesis. They were formed in 1956, following my race's first contact with your government. They were established to manage contact with my race when we returned. It didn't go well."

"What part of the US Government ran this place?" Rose asked.

"It was a…" First Scout's eyes glazed over for a second. "It was an off-the-books operation loosely under control of the NSA, though they never fully understood what Genesis was for. The leaders of Genesis are known as the Heptagon, six scientific specialists and one military leader to manage the operation."

"How do you know all of this? How can you speak English?"

"I have the ability to read computers from afar."

"Woah!" the private said. This time Ayres pulled him from the room. Rose smiled. The kid was enthusiastic, but he had poor impulse control.

"That cage was a faraday cage, and it severely limited my abilities. Once my defensive avatar freed me, my full abilities came into play. Where is the one known as Michael?"

"Mercury burned his heart out."

"Mercury?" First Scout asked.

"Oh, I've been thinking of your avatar thing by that name. It's skin kinda looks like mercury." First Scout stared at him. "Humans like to name stuff." He shrugged. Mercury was staring at Rose, at least he thought it was.

"Very well, I will call it Mercury too." First Scout looked at the machine, which nodded. First Scout did an unmistakable doubletake. "Anyway, I was able to make contact with another prisoner, a female of your race named Pearl Grange."

"She's here?" Rose asked excitedly. "We lost contact with her."

"Grange discovered Project Genesis when they were moving my ship here. They sank her ship for her transgressions. She was able to get free and activate my avatar," he gestured. "Mercury. I'm sorry, but she was badly injured and died in the effort."

Rose looked down and shook his head. "That's unfortunate. However, there's another prisoner we're looking for."

"And I am looking for the rest of the Heptagon," First Scout said. He gestured, and Mercury began moving again. Soldiers nearly fell over themselves getting out of its way.

"Follow them," Rose ordered.

First Scout wasn't fast, owing to his short stature. He was maybe three feet tall, yet Rose felt like he was in the presence of a much larger being. He was as self-assured as any command officer Rose had ever met. First Scout was used to giving orders and having them obeyed.

The procession continued until they came to a small elevator. Mercury used its patented door opening maneuver to reveal a stairwell adjacent to the elevator shaft. It was clear to Rose that the avatar was a defensive automaton.

First Scout and Mercury went down the stairs. Rose took point behind the descending pair, and Ayres insisted on being right by his General's side. The stairwell went around three times and exited through a Mercury-mangled door that revealed a small area with yet another heavy, blast door. First Scout gestured to Mercury who opened it.

On the other side of the door was a bunker holding seven people. Rose looked past First Scout and Mercury. There were three men and four women. One of the women was in a mobility chair and standing next to her was Lisha Breda. She spotted him, and her expression went from confused fear at the site of First Scout and Mercury to excitement.

"Can that woman come out?" Rose asked First Scout.

The alien turned its pointy head and looked at Rose. "She is not one of the Heptagon?"

"No, she was kidnapped."

"Then she may go."

Lisha looked down at the woman in the mobility chair and seemed unsure.

"Lisha," Rose said and gestured, "come on."

"What is that robot going to do with them?" Lisha asked.

"I suspect they're going to die, and I couldn't care less."

"Then I'm not leaving."

"What?" Rose asked. "Lisha, a lot of people died to rescue you."

"And these people risked their lives to let you win," Lisha said, her eyes flashing.

"Lisha, I cannot stop them from doing whatever they want."

"You can *try*."

He sighed and shook his head. Why do some people have to be so fucking compassionate?

"First Scout?"

"I have been listening," the alien said. "I have no intention of letting them go."

"Haven't enough people died?"

While Mercury stood next to the bunker door, waiting without moving, First Scout turned his head and regarded Rose. "Perhaps you are not aware of how I came to be in that cage? My ship was shot down from space. Most of my crew is dead. My ship is badly damaged. We were invited long ago, and this is the reception we got.

"After my ship crashed, they captured me," He gestured at the men and women. "They did experiments on me. They tried to manipulate my brain to get more answers. They tortured Grange, who you expressed some concern about. By any definition you believe, they are *evil.*" Mercury's head turned slightly toward First Scout as if it were listening.

"Not all of us," the woman in the mobility chair said. "I am a tactical expert; a mathematical analyst." She indicated a man who must have been an albino. "Azrael is an archeologist. Gabriel is a computer expert, a hacker. We didn't lay a hand on you."

"And the others?" First Scout asked.

"I cannot say what they may or may not have done."

"You will not say, you mean?"

Chamuel shrugged. "I joined Project Genesis for a lot of reasons. One was the medical treatment I got, which was derived from your technology. We're humans; we make mistakes. One was shooting your ship down. The next was allowing Michael to lead the Heptagon. We can't change the first, you dealt with the second. We're not perfect, but we'd like to help now."

"First Scout," Rose said. "Most of our planet is dead. The virus came from you, didn't it?"

"An accident," First Scout said. "You call it a virus; for my people, it is a machine. The best name would be *Pandora.*"

"Apt title," Chamuel said.

"It is a powerful machine," First Scout said. "Powerful and potentially deadly."

"Its purpose doesn't change what it did," Rose said, "and I'd like to learn more. But the point I am trying to make is that there has been enough dying. I'd like to help you, and I hope you can help us. I am a soldier, but I'm asking you to stop the fighting. Let's work together to sort this out, fairly, without indiscriminate killing. What do you say?"

First Scout stared at him for a long time with his beady little eyes. He looked back at the six members of the Heptagon and Lisha, then spoke. "Why do you defend them?" he asked Lisha. "Were you not their prisoner too?"

"Because Leon is right. There's been enough killing. These people didn't make the decisions, that was Michael."

"I brought us all down here," Chamuel said. "I stopped helping Michael and brought everyone down here, because I knew General Rose would prevail without our help."

"You let Michael die, then," Rose said. Chamuel nodded. "Hard call."

"Not really," Chamuel said. "Michael was an asshole who treated Genesis like his personal toy." The other five Heptagon members nodded in agreement.

Rose could see a variety of expressions among those who called themselves the Heptagon. From fear to resignation. He was sure there was guilt there, to varying degrees. But he didn't want to be the one to make a summary judgement. That's what courts were for.

"We'll have to hold a trial, review evidence, then decide." He looked at First Scout. "This is *our* way. Justice will be served."

"And if they are guilty?" First Scout asked.

"Then a punishment will be decided. One that fits the crime."

"Our futures are tied together now," First Scout said. "Very well. We will see what comes of your justice."

Rose nodded, then wondered what the alien meant by their futures being tied together. Mercury turned and walked out with First Scout right behind. There was much to do; he'd have to figure it out some other time.

* * *

**The Flotilla**

**165 Nautical Miles West of San Diego, CA**

Kathy stared in amazement as a roughly round…*thing* flashed across the sky and stopped a few miles away. It was many thousands of feet up, floating like a cloud. Then it zipped sideways and stopped directly above them.

"Are you seeing this?" she asked Chris.

"Uhm, a floating city or something flitting around?"

"Okay, I'm not hallucinating. Oh, shit!"

The object plummeted toward them. There was a shuddering *Boooom!* and a blast of air sent people flying all over the carrier deck. Chris had his arm around her, so the two were merely knocked on their butts. The strange construct stopped descending only a hundred or so yards above them. Kathy tried to take it all in, but it was *huge*—many times the size of the carrier, which she also thought was huge. Her mind tried to reset her sense of large to a whole new scale.

"It's made of containers!" Chris said, pointing.

Kathy's eyes ran over the regular shapes and realized he was right. Hundreds of steel containers, all welded together. In the middle was a glass structure, like a gondola, hanging underneath. It was obviously run with the alien technology, but by who? She thought she could see people in the gondola. In fact, one seemed familiar.

Then, sound suddenly changed, and a shimmer was visible in the distance. A second later, the world was consumed with light. She screamed and put her hands over her eyes. Everyone around was yelling as well. She thought she could see the bones in her hands through her closed eyes. It only lasted a second, then quickly faded.

Kathy took her hands away from her eyes and looked around. In the distance, fire seemed to swirl around. In fact, it was in all directions. The water flashed and roiled, but she couldn't feel any heat.

"The nuke hit," Chris said, then pointed up. "That thing shielded us."

"Wow," Kathy said. "It must be the same shield that was around the ship when we were in space."

"You know what?" Chris asked. "I think they came to your call."

"What?"

"Your Edward R. Murrow transmission?" He pointed up again. "They heard it and came to our rescue."

Her vision had almost returned to normal. The light had changed again, and when she gazed to the side, she saw that they were flying. The structure above them, the carrier, and all the ships of the Flotilla. To one side, fading into the distance, a mushroom cloud was still climbing into the sky.

She turned back to look at the gondola. Cobb stared down at her and waved. Tears of joy rolled down her cheeks.

*****

# Chapter Twelve

**Morning, Monday, May 6th**
**Formerly Classified Genesis Facility**
**San Nicolas Island**

Cobb stood to the side with Kathy, watching and listening. She hadn't let him out of her sight. Daimler flew the whole Flotilla and Shangri-La to the island of San Nicolas, figuring it was close and a good place to hover after they set the ships down. Turned out to be fortuitous, because it was where General Rose had gone to fight the unknown enemy force.

The Flotilla was set down a short distance from the island's docks, and Shangri-La took up a position over the island. Admiral Kent's fleet arrived later in the day, vastly increasing the number of ships and military personnel. A few other ships which had fled also returned. And there had apparently been a reunion between two surviving aliens, First Scout and Nikki.

Cobb was pretty much beyond being surprised. The sails of a pair of Russian nuclear attack subs at anchor just offshore might have come close, though. Frankly, he was glad to see General Rose and an admiral. He was thoroughly out ranked once again. When there was time, he planned to write a full report on what he was forced to do on Shangri-La, hand over command of the troops who'd found refuge there, and retire again. Nobody needed an old, former lieutenant colonel. Well, judging from the look on Kathy's face, maybe one person did.

He, along with Paul Bisdorf and Clark, were invited to a meeting as representatives of Shangri-La. All the players were assembled in a conference room inside the former Project Genesis facility. A lot of it was shot to shit, and a few buildings were wrecked. Others were in use as temporary detention facilities while the status of the former Genesis workers was sorted out. Still, it was the largest enclosed area they could find.

It needed to be enclosed so First Scout and Nikki wouldn't be exposed to direct sunlight; it was dangerous to them. Not only had the aliens evolved in less intense light, but their basic biology was different. They needed to avoid too much exposure to Earth's environment and its contaminants. They sat on specially modified chairs which lifted them to the level of the conference table. There was no sign of the frightening, metallic guardian named Mercury. Cobb had seen it once and didn't want to see it again, especially after he'd heard from Rose what it could do.

Other attendees were the Russian senior officer, Captain Chugunkin, and his XO, Captain Lieutenant Svetan, Dr. Lisha Breda and Wade Watts, who'd worked out a way to remove Strain Delta from things, Admiral Kent, and Captain Gilchrist. There were also a NASA scientist named Bennitti, a virologist named Gallatin, and another female scientist named Gnox. God help him, but Cobb felt like there should have been elves and dwarfs talking about a ring.

Dr. Breda was talking. "Our new process doesn't change the overall fact that even with the Februus device, we cannot stay on this planet."

"I'm not willing to give up the United States," Admiral Kent said.

"There's nothing left to give up," Bennitti said. "With the alien drives, we can do salvage operations, but we're just feeding off the corpse." Kent scowled.

"Also," Lisha continued, "tests I've done with the Februus show that it merely neutralizes the nanovirus, it doesn't destroy it. Introducing an active unit reboots everything."

"That is in line with how Pandora was designed," Nikki said. Cobb had heard that they'd decided they wanted their species to be known as Vulpes, which he thought meant "fox." Fitting. "Once we finish repairs on our ship, I can do more tests. However, Pandora is designed to be self-sustaining." The little alien shrugged, a gesture it seemed to have picked up from the humans around it. "There is no simple fix. Maybe none at all."

"Then what can we do?" Kent demanded. "Float around on that crazy city they're building?"

"Why not?" Bisdorf asked. "We built Shangri-La with a few dozen roughnecks. Given a better labor force and help from the Marines, we could build something 100 times bigger in weeks."

"Will the drives support it?" Kent asked.

"Easily," First Scout said. "They were not designed for the uses you have put them to, however we can provide you the field calculations. Considering the low density of your metals, I am confident a single unit will support a structure 10 kilometers long."

"Holy crap," Clark yelped. "What about power?"

Cobb already knew some of the answer. Based on some tests, the unit that powered Shangri-La had lost 5% of its total capacity from taking a direct nuke. The engineers were stunned, but he wasn't. After all, the aliens flew around the galaxy with the damned things.

"Your nuclear power plants are usable," Nikki said. "I reviewed the designs and—"

"How did you get those?" Admiral Kent demanded hotly.

"They are in the Project Genesis databank," the alien said, returning the admiral's glare. "We have full access. As I was saying, I've studied your primitive nuclear power system. The overload you experience inside a shield is the result of a feedback loop. It can be easily cured. The shield will enhance some radioactive processes. I believe you have a device called a radioisotope thermoelectric generator? Even a modest one will provide all the energy needed to operate a drive system for hundreds of years."

"It's still a temporary solution," Rose said, getting in between the admiral and the alien. "The animals are mutating under your Pandora. It's dangerous for us and will get more dangerous."

"With that sort of power source, there's no reason to keep the bases Earth-side," Bisdorf said. People around the table gawked at him.

Clark rubbed the stubble on his chin and nodded. "The device provides a forcefield for atmosphere, gravity, and everything you need. Why not put it in orbit?"

Cobb watched the discussion bounce around and shook his head, glad he wasn't in the middle of it. He looked at his girlfriend. She was looking at him. "What?" he asked.

"I was just thinking about what comes next."

"Lunatics are talking about fucking space colonies," Cobb said.

"No, I mean you and me."

"Well, I did cross the wastelands for you."

"You did," she cooed and snuggled against him. "But I mean…"

"What, should we get married?" he asked.

"Oh, I accept."

"Hey, I didn't really ask."

"Sounded like it to me."

Cobb felt his face getting hot, and she grinned. That was when he noticed the little lens clipped to her shirt pocket. "Is that what I think it is?"

"Yes, and I have evidence you asked me to marry you."

"Okay, I'll admit you're right. What I want to know is whether you were recording the whole meeting." She grinned sheepishly. "You're going to get me in trouble."

"Oh, you'll get used to it."

"Fine," Kent was saying. "We'll start with this Shangri-La and expand it. Rose, who do you want in charge of security?"

"I'm going to tap Brigadier General Pendleton over there, if he can stop smooching with that reporter long enough."

Cobb's head spun around when he heard his name. "General, what?"

"I said I want you in charge of Shangri-La's security while they expand. We'll put these Heptagon people on your place too. Less chance of losing track of them floating in space."

"Sir, I was thinking I'd retire."

"Denied," Admiral Kent said. "The general staff serves at the discretion of the president, and we don't currently have one to release you from active duty."

Cobb was about to complain that he wasn't general staff, when his mind finally processed how he was addressed. "Wait…did you say brigadier general?"

"I'm pretty sure that's what I said," Rose replied.

"Oh…I don't know if you can do that."

"Are you going to tell a general and an admiral what they can't do?"

"No sirs."

"Good. Then remember when a lieutenant general and a vice admiral tell you to shut up, you have to listen." Kent had a tiny grin on his face that Cobb didn't like at all.

"Yes, sir."

"Good."

"With time, other plans could be made. But we'll have to see." First Scout said.

"We'll see," Rose agreed.

*****

# Epilogue

**Shangri-La**
**Low Earth Orbit**

Kathy Pendleton watched the ship approach Shangri-La. Docking was still tricky. Even with the alien's help, balancing the force field as the two came together was tricky. She liked to come out and film ships returning from Earth, not because it made great footage, but because the people loved it. It was heartwarming to know people were still being rescued, supplies were still coming up, and plans were moving forward.

The sound of cheers echoed from East Side where a baseball game was underway. She'd wanted to watch, but this particular ship was important to her. It had once been a nuclear submarine. Now it was what they called a Phoenix. Not a class, but a type. They were airtight vessels that were designed to drop down to the surface to recover groups of survivors. This one's previous name had been the USS *Wyoming*, SSBN-742. It was now named the *Grange*, RS-01. Rescue Ship 01, named after Lieutenant JG Pearl Grange, who was lost on-mission after the collapse.

Six more ballistic missile submarines were in one stage or another of refit in berths at the shipyard. Kathy understood they'd proved ideal for the job. Because of the side effects from the alien force field, a nuclear power plant on a navy vessel could be set in permanent standby mode and still create enough power to run the craft for decades. Maybe centuries.

The next ship was to be the *Cartwright*, RS-02. She'd interviewed survivors and her husband about the name. She was doing a TV segment for each ship. They were all to be named after people who died trying to save others during the collapse.

The *Grange* completed her transition through the force field and began to settle into her berthing cradle. Kathy picked up her laptop and ever-present voice recorder and walked toward the yard. Not far away, a crew was using a gravity manipulator to move a tank the size of a 747 into position. It was part of the planned 100-unit expansion of their aquaculture farm. Population growth was straining the algae tanks. Having to maintain strict Strain Delta quarantine didn't help production. But nobody wanted to start from scratch with clean samples. Another full, atmospheric purge was something nobody wanted to do.

By the time she reached the gangway for the *Grange,* the sail hatch was already open, and crew were emerging. The contamination dome had been locked down on the aft deck, where nuclear missiles used to be housed, and people in biohazard suits were opening the hatch. She was distracted by the appearance of a handsome man in combat fatigues with a bag over his shoulder.

Cobb trotted down the ramp, stopping at the bottom to salute a flag which hung next to the ship, before stepping back onto Shangri-La. Kathy pranced over and leaped into his arms.

"Oof!" he said, dropping his bag and laughing. "Careful, I'm an old man."

"Phft," she snorted. "You look chipper to me, General."

A squad of Marines marched by and wolf-whistled. Cobb gave them his general's stare, and they stood ramrod straight as they marched on. Kathy wasn't fooled, she saw the glint in his eye and the smiles on the men's faces.

Kathy took his hand as he picked up the bag, and they walked down the pier. The berth next to the *Grange* wouldn't be empty for long. It already had a sign saying *Cartwright* by the gangway. She saw Cobb looking at the sign as they walked by.

"He was a good guy, huh?"

"Yeah," Cobb agreed. "One of many." They walked in silence for a while.

"How many this time?" she eventually asked.

"We have 29 on board. It was 30, but one had the bug. The test didn't pick it up until it was too late. If we'd known, we could have cut the cruise short and come back to hit him with Februus." He shrugged. It happened sometimes; the test wasn't perfect. The jury was still out on the treated ones too. The Februus Device was 100% effective for stopping the bug, if you got to it before the brain was messed up. The problem, as Dr. Breda explained, was that the bug wasn't destroyed. Its progress was frozen in time at the moment the victim was 'reset.' If they got even one live bug, it would pick up where it left off in a matter of seconds. It made those who had been infected potentially dangerous.

"We stopped by the seed bank, too, for another load."

She nodded. The Antarctic seed bank held some of the only pure seeds on the planet. They didn't show any sign of Strain Delta. Turned out, extreme cold helped slow the virus. On some of the first missions after the Battle of San Diego, people from the Amundson-Scott station at the South Pole were rescued and found to be bug free. They'd stayed on Earth and gone to manage retrieval of specimens from the seed bank. They were already used to extreme cold, so it was a natural fit.

"When's the next trading mission with Atlantis?" she asked.

"Next week. They want to take the *Cartwright* to show it off."

"Looks like the Europeans are moving along pretty quickly," Kathy said. She'd seen recordings from the first trip to the European version of Shangri-La. It was only 1,000 yards on each side and growing a bit slower. They didn't have aliens helping them.

One of President Paul Bisdorf's first acts was to establish formal relations between Shangri-La and Atlantis. They were still evaluating Atlantis's quarantine procedures, and on the second trip, they delivered a new Februus Device. Again, they couldn't be too careful.

"I'd like to go."

"I know," Cobb said. "Paul says another month of setting up their procedures and harmonizing them with ours, and it should be safe." Kathy frowned. "The refit of the *Pacific Adventurer* is almost finished. We're going to use it for shuttle service back and forth."

Kathy laughed and shook her head. "A cruise ship in space. Now I know I'm dreaming." She looked to the west and saw that the sun was about to drop behind Earth. Shangri-La was orbiting to the night side. In order to afford access to the planet, she did two orbits a day. At their altitude, that meant 16 hours of daylight and 8 hours of night, broken up into two cycles per day. Everyone had blackout curtains on their apartments.

"How about Kitezh?" The Russian orbital city was the third in the string. It was the closest in size to Shangri-La and would probably be bigger in another month. Despite a smaller population and some political strife between the various Russian and former Soviet people living there, they worked hard. The Vulpes had gifted them a good number of drive modules and the associated hardware, but they refused to assist the Russians. The Vulpes had a healthy suspicion of them and had only helped the Russians at the insistence of Admiral Kent as part of the overall bargain.

First Scout said he was willing to reconsider their relationship with the Russians after a time, if no more shooting took place.

"You really want to go there?"

"Of course," she said. "I hear the food is good."

"If you like beets and sour cream," he said, and they both laughed. Part of the mutual aid agreement had included instructions for manufacturing Februus Devices. She'd heard rumors that the Russians were trying to reclaim territory back on Earth. First Scout and Nikki had both said it was ill advised, then washed their tiny hands of the matter.

"And what about the *Mayflower?*" she asked.

"No decision on when to start yet," Cobb said. "Maybe not for a year or two. Still a lot of survivors down there."

"The longer we wait, the greater the chance of losing it all up here."

"Paul knows," he assured her. "Hey, is that a baseball game I hear?"

"Yeah, wanna go watch?"

"Sure," he said, and they changed course. "Oh, hey, did you hear Tango's girlfriend is pregnant?"

"Oh?"

"Yeah, seems everyone is getting knocked up. You'd think people would be a little more careful. We've brought up more than enough condoms, for crying out loud." He'd walked a few feet before he noticed she hadn't said anything. He stopped and looked at her. "What?"

"Well…" She felt her cheeks getting hot. Like most men in these kinds of situations, she could see the wheels slowly beginning to turn, like putting a manual transmission in gear with a bad clutch.

"Wait…you mean…you…and me…?" He trailed off.

"Yes, dear, you and me." She put a hand on her belly.

"But I thought you were on the pill?"

"I was," she said. "I went to the doc. He said a lot of people are in our situation. The pills are getting old." She shrugged. "They lose their effectiveness." He looked flustered. "We don't like condoms."

"I know. But damn, baby, I'm almost 50. It's a little late to start a family."

"It's never too late. Why do you think everyone's getting preggers?" She knew he'd been a bit conflicted when they'd gotten married four months ago. His wife had only been gone for two years. They'd never been able to have children, and he thought it was his issue. A lot of guys came back from the Gulf War sterile. Turned out he was wrong.

"The timing…" he said.

"The timing is what the timing is. Cobb Pendleton, you are going to be a daddy. So, are you going to whine about it or soldier up?" His eyes narrowed, and she winked at him.

"You got me, Boss," he said. They resumed walking. "Dad," he said, then nodded. She was smiling so hard her face hurt.

* * *

General Rose sat on the uncomfortable bench and watched the baseball game between the only two teams on Shangri-La, the La-Las, who were civilians, and the Leathernecks, who were Marines. Being an army general, he didn't have any skin in the game. His people weren't very interested in playing games yet. He needed to work on that.

One bench down, Admiral Kent sat with a teenage girl—his granddaughter. Against all odds, she'd been found alive in Miami Beach with a large group of 33 survivors. It was the second biggest find to date, and the numbers were beginning to go down. Shangri-La's official population was 13,559, not counting those in decontamination, quarantine, or newly arrived. Sure beat the hell out of a couple hundred living on boats off of San Diego.

The distinctive *Chink!* of an aluminum bat hitting a ball was followed by cheering, and a 20-something woman with flowing red hair ran like crazy. Rose smiled and applauded despite his somber mood. Six months and still no real progress.

The discussion months ago about long-term solutions had yet to yield results. It was a combination of President Bisdorf's unwillingness to take risks and the aliens' unwillingness to give more technology. He was just a general, so he did whatever the civilian leadership told him. Even if Shangri-La was a miniaturized version of the United States, it still resembled it.

As of last month, the courts were up and running. Just yesterday, he'd been walking along the east market and saw a no-shit lawyer's sign hanging on a building. There were a hell of a lot of libertarians on Shangri-La—the guy had better be careful. Rose smiled and shook his head.

Of the thirteen-thousand plus residents on Shangri-La, almost half were military, former military, or dependents. That was good and bad. Good in that there were a lot of people who weren't risk adverse and knew how to fight. Bad in that there was a pretty stark division between service and civilian. He knew they had to be careful it didn't balkanize their society. He and all the other officers had insisted the first president *not* be military for just that reason. He knew he'd annoyed more than a few who'd wanted to put up Pendleton as president. He smiled, thinking of Cobb in the hot seat. Might still happen, just not for a few years.

As if his thoughts had summoned him, Cobb came in with his wife on his arm. The two looked cozy together. Rose didn't fancy reporters much, but she was extremely popular on both sides. Well, with everyone except Gilchrist who wouldn't acknowledge she existed. He was still salty about her spending days recording everything on his boat, then hacking his comms. He wouldn't see reason, even when it was explained to him that her hack had saved their lives.

Gilchrist had yet to set foot on Shangri-La. He and the *Ford* were a planet-side base. He'd allowed his carrier to have a drive module installed. They floated near whatever area of operation needed assistance. Repairs had been done, aircraft and fuel provided, and the *Gerald* R. *Ford* was now the first (and probably only) fully functional, flying aircraft carrier.

He seemed satisfied. After what the man had done to keep people alive, neither Rose nor Kent had any problem letting him do his own thing. It was a necessary job, too. They'd proven invaluable during the operation in Washington, D.C. Rose shuddered just remembering it. Must have been a million zombies. A week of operations, and they hadn't gotten into the Smithsonian. They'd eventually decided to forgo further operations until the flesh-eating population had thinned out some.

Few people were found alive in any of the government bunkers. A few small groups of government employees were, but nobody in elected positions. It wasn't until after that fiasco that everyone agreed on the elections which made Bisdorf president.

Cobb saw him and waved. Rose waved back. He wondered if Kathy had told him she was pregnant yet. He'd found out from Lisha, who'd found out from the horse's mouth. Lisha thought Kathy was a friend. He needed to remind her that reporters didn't have friends.

They found a place to sit, and he glanced at his watch. The sun dropped below the horizon, and the baseball field's lights came on automatically. As usual, Lisha was late. They enjoyed their time together and were happy leaving it there. After two marriages, he was the first to admit he wasn't good at it. Lisha was a bit of a mystery, and he wondered how much was under her quiet demeanor that he hadn't figured out. *Chink!*

Some popcorn sounded good, so he walked behind the bleachers where they kept the popcorn. There was a small line which he didn't mind. Like the ballgame and the movie theater that was under construction, it meant people had some hope for the present and the future.

"Evening, General."

"Mr. Gregory," Rose said. "I saw your sign yesterday. How's business?"

"You don't appreciate the law, do you?" Gregory was a tall, gray-haired lawyer they'd rescued from Washington, D.C. One of several, he was the one who'd taken it upon himself to champion the cause of the Heptagon.

"Appreciate isn't a word I'd use in relation to leeches."

"Amusing," Gregory said with a chilly smile. "I was talking to President Bisdorf about the need to start the trial for those accused of being with the rumored Genesis conspiracy."

"Accused, rumored, right." His turn to get some popcorn came, and he got a small bag. When he turned around Gregory was still there. "What exactly do you want?"

"The President wants you to represent the accused."

Rose laughed so hard he almost dropped his popcorn. "Wait, you're serious?"

* * *

"I don't know if I'm ever going to get used to this," Alex said as the stars redshifted out the forward cockpit window of the *Azanti II*. A bluish light was steadily growing.

"It's pretty cool," Alison agreed. "Doesn't really look like *Star Trek*, though."

"Can't have everything," Wade agreed.

"What is *Star Trek*?" First Scout asked.

"A type of entertainment," Alex explained.

"I see. Please monitor the shield flow on the forward focus."

"It wasn't this complicated the first time we flew FTL," Alison said.

"From what you have said," First Scout replied, "it was a miracle you survived."

"Thanks?" Alex asked.

"You are welcome." The three humans exchanged bemused looks as their Vulpes expert continued to use the strange, black rod that was apparently a computer. "This craft is performing within 14% of optimal capabilities based on my design."

"It that good?"

"Good enough for short range reconnaissance."

"Coming out of FTL," Alex announced and touched the controls. The stars returned to normal, and the bluish light was replaced by a sphere of the deepest azure imaginable. Lines or striations were visible around the planet as was a swirling storm highlighted with whites. "Welcome to Neptune."

"Holy shit that's beautiful!" Alison said.

"Sure is," Alex agreed.

"Looks fake," Wade said, cocking his head.

First Scout glanced up from his computer, shrugged, and went back to work.

Alex had to admit, it was a little anticlimactic. They'd had the *Azanti II* out for eight hours, and this completed their grand tour of the solar system. In no more than what was an average workday, three humans had visited every planet in the solar system.

"What about Pluto?" Alison asked.

"Not a planet," Wade mumbled, taking a selfie.

"Says who?"

"Scientists."

"Bullshit," she retorted.

"This is the last planet in your solar system based on our established norms," First Scout said. Wade gave Alison a smug look, and she narrowed her eyes dangerously at him.

"What about another solar system?" Alex asked.

"This ship is unsuitable for such a trip," First Scout said. "As we've discussed. With these drives, it would take more than one of your years to reach the closest star, and there is nothing worth visiting there."

"You've never explained why you bothered coming to Earth," Alison said. "Our technology is so poor and, according to you, we're so warlike, why bother? What do we have?"

"Life is more precious than you realize," First Scout said. "Far more precious. The system you take for granted is nearly a garden world by galactic standards. You have one world with an excellent environment, two which could be readily adapted, and three moons that, with some work, could be made usable as well."

"So, just real estate?" Alison persisted. "Doesn't seem worth it to deal with us." Alex shot her a look. "What? I mean, look what happened."

"We saw potential in you as well."

"What do you think of our potential now?" Wade asked. He'd finished taking selfies and was playing a game on his smart phone.

"Somewhat diminished. However, even with our ship repaired, we've stayed."

"So, there is hope for us yet," Alex said with a little nod.

"I believe so." First Scout tapped his computer. "We should return the sensor data to your government."

"You recommend both Mars and Venus?" Alex asked, working the controls. It was simple and enjoyable, now that First Scout and Nikki had helped engineer new control interfaces.

"Yes. They are different, yet both offer advantages. The two worlds are also within our present technology to perform…what do you call it?"

"Terraforming," Alex offered.

"Yes, terraform. Venus will take much longer, while Mars will yield a less rich environment."

"Why do you want Europa?" Wade suddenly asked. Alison and Alex both glanced at First Scout. It was a question they hadn't asked when their alien mentor said they wished to establish a colony there. "I mean, there's only two of you here."

"More will come," First Scout said.

"When?" Alex wondered.

"At the appropriate time. Now, it is best to return to Shangri-La. Life support is down to six hours, and the trip will take 4.1 hours. I will let Nikki know we are on the way back."

Alex nodded and finished setting the course. The *Azanti II* went from a standing stop to relativistic speeds instantly without the ship's occupants feeling anything. Inside the ship, Alison and Alex looked at each other, both thinking the same thing. *What isn't First Scout telling us?*

* * *

Nikki looked up from the diagrams, the movement catching Jeremiah's attention. "Something wrong?"

"No," she said, "First Scout has said they are on the way back."

"How is the *Azanti II* performing?"

"Within acceptable parameters."

"Good," Jeremiah said. "Good. Did First Scout add any of the survey results?"

"Yes, and he agrees on Venus and Mars."

"Oh, wow," Oz said and set the tray of food he was carrying on a nearby workbench. "We have a lot of work ahead of us."

"We already knew that," Jeremiah said. He left the diagrams displayed on his bench and went to the table. He selected an egg salad sandwich and picked it up, still marveling at how perfectly normal it felt. He held the food and manipulated it, smiling.

"You like the limbs?" Nikki asked.

"Without a doubt," Jeremiah said. "Marvelous." They'd amputated his left arm just below the elbow, and his right at the elbow. He'd been despondent about getting any sort of prosthetic worth a damn, considering the condition of the world. His ship was a mess, and even though he had 3D printers, he didn't have the files.

After he recovered, he was introduced to the living Vulpes. They looked a lot like the dead one he'd found, seemingly years ago, in Texas. They'd already examined his ship, the *Azanti*, and were impressed with how he and his people had figured out rudimentary uses for the drives. They wanted him to work with them to move humanity into space, bootstrap human technology as it were, and begin building real spaceships.

When he'd said he would love to, but his lack of hands would make his contribution minimal, Nikki had fabricated a new pair of limbs using a machine called the Pandora. They were shiny silver, living metal with nanites that allowed them to move just like real arms. They reminded him of the second *Terminator* movie. They were grafted to his stumps in a quite painful procedure, but it was over in minutes, and all pain was gone. The point where the limbs joined his skin was as seamless as though they had grown there naturally. The only cosmetic difference was that they had three fingers instead of four, something Nikki had said was a regrettable error.

"The Pandora will adapt to your physiology, extending into your skeletal system as necessary, so the limbs are not a danger to you in any situation."

"Do I have to recharge them or anything?" he'd asked.

Nikki had smiled, her tiny teeth flashing. "They are self-contained, and their power source will outlive you."

Jeremiah found out how sensitive they were when a razor-sharp, metal spar slipped from the crane in the machine shop a week later and landed on his arm. It hurt, but only like being bumped hard. He'd lifted the spar off with his other hand and couldn't find so much as a scuff on the shiny metallic surface.

He'd experimented after the accident and found that his new arms gave him more strength than he'd had, but not to an extreme. Maybe 20-25% more was his guess. However, the hands and wrists never got tired. They also relayed sensations with the same feel his own hands had. There was one thing he'd yet to get up the nerve to do with his hands. Maybe someday.

When he was out and about, he wore a long sleeve shirt and gloves. The arms drew far too much attention. Word had spread, and he found himself increasingly showing them off around Shangri-La. General Rose had been asking to see them for a long time.

Jeremiah munched his sandwich and drank some water. As usual, by the time the meal was done, he'd once again forgotten they weren't his natural limbs and was surprised by the silver hand that wiped his mouth. *Shit, how long is that gonna keep happening?*

"We haven't started on the Venus colony structure yet," Oz pointed out.

"There is no need," Nikki said. "Floating installations of the type we'll use on Venus are in my databases. They have been used on many gas giant worlds. All that is required is to find the altitude where the atmospheric conditions are the most favorable, sufficient oxygen can be found, and the gravitational field generators can be constructed."

"Oh, so it's no big deal building floating cities, then?" Oz asked and laughed.

Jeremiah was glad his cousin had survived his injuries. They'd spent a lot of time together as kids. But while Jeremiah had grown up rich, the beneficiary of his father's engineering firm's success, Oz had grown up on the poor side of the family in Gary, Indiana. He'd gone into computer programming and software, while aerospace and hard engineering were Jeremiah's preferences. Still, Oz was proving to be a vital asset to the budding planetary engineering project.

Jeremiah had gotten a peek at the atmospheric processors Nikki had retrieved from her databases. She was protective about giving the humans access. Jeremiah couldn't blame her, considering how they'd been greeted by energy weapons upon their arrival at Earth.

He took his drink back to the electronic drafting table and examined their work. The *Mayflower* would be the first colonization ship and the first colony. Thanks to the Vulpes' anti-gravity and shield technology, the humans could fly the finished city to Mars, land, and begin processing the atmosphere. They'd drop a few gigatons of ice asteroids on the poles and set up alien-powered heat generators. Nikki had said they could probably reheat the planet's core to jumpstart its magnetic field, though she'd need to do some deep core work after they got there to be sure.

"Now, we just need President Bisdorf on board," Jeremiah said, admiring their handiwork. Of course, lacking deep space mining and enough ships, they'd have to build the *Mayflower* from Earth's resources. It was all lying there, waiting for them. All they needed was the manpower.

"Your president will agree, eventually," Nikki said with certainty.

"What makes you think so?" Oz asked.

"These floating cities have drawbacks, not the least of which is that explosive decompression from a failure could kill everyone on them."

Jeremiah's head came up, a horrified expression on his face. "You said it was impossible."

"Impossible, to a degree, yes. However, accidents happen, as you humans are all too aware."

"Don't I know it," Jeremiah agreed, visibly calming.

"The other reason is size," Nikki continued. "You can only grow so far before things will become difficult. I also suspect you humans will tire of staring at your lost world, so close and tantalizing. Perhaps many will think the Russians are correct and want to return home. The results would not be favorable."

"I'm sure," Jeremiah agreed. "If we did though, would you still stay and help?"

Nikki looked back, her little black eyes studying him. "I don't know."

* * *

Lisha watched the technician run the quality control test, careful to observe his use of the strain-positive test and the microscope. She noted her results on the card attached to the test article and passed it on. She moved into the next room where Weasel was hunched over a bench, working on some apparatus. He looked up when she entered.

"How are the tests?"

"Around 72%," she said.

Weasel frowned. "That low?" She nodded. He turned and stared at the equipment he was working on. "It's something about the wavelength," he said. "Not enough energy to penetrate denser flesh."

"I think you're right," Lisha agreed, walking over to stand next to him. "Let's try those three-emitter configurations."

"We haven't run enough versions on the single," he complained.

This was the main problem with transitioning Weasel from a back-room IT troubleshooter to a medical device designer/tester; he refused to accept the failure of a certain design. He kept at it like a dog licking itself. Just a few more licks, and I'll have it. The truth was more likely that the thing they were licking was long gone or there to stay. Move on.

"We're moving on to test the three-emitter design," she said. Weasel looked up at her to complain. She crossed her arms under her breasts and glared.

"Oh, okay."

"Thank you."

There was no problem with the larger Februus Devices. The issue was making a smaller, lighter, field version. General Pendleton and Colonel Sleg, the Marine Commander, were both screaming for a small version. Scaling the Februus down was proving a tough nut to crack.

Lisha came by every three days to evaluate Weasel's progress and provide gentle guidance. Well, sometimes, not such gentle guidance. She wished she still had Oz. The man understood Weasel, and their friendship helped. However, Jeremiah Osborne had taken Oz from her. She shrugged. They were cousins, after all; it was only fair.

She left the practical labs and went into her research lab. Over the last half year, the salvage teams had done a fantastic job equipping her with top notch apparatus. They'd also rescued more than a few qualified technicians and scientists. Dr. Gallatin had elected to set up his own facilities, allowing her to continue to focus on Strain Delta, or Pandora as the Vulpes called it.

The Vulpes had given her some samples of un-differentiated Pandora so she could set up side-by-side comparisons and get a better understanding of how the nanovirus worked. She'd never completely understand it. Their technology was about as advanced as hers would have been to the ancient Egyptians.

Besides using the Februus Device for purifying food and treating people before their brains were rebuilt, she was mostly concerned with how the nanovirus affected humans and other creatures. It was what had initially fascinated her enough to take a former colleague consumed by the virus and turn him into a test subject. Now that she was back in proper quarters and had her supercomputers back in operation, she'd begun resequencing work.

Strain Delta had amazing potential as a tool. HAARP's goal had always been to remove all disease and suffering from humanity. It was, after all, the reason Project Genesis had funded them. She'd often wondered where the money had come from, and she was surprised Michael hadn't known. However, Chamuel did, and she'd quietly explained it to Lisha.

"You were the second choice to be Ariel, our biologist member, but it was decided you were better off where you were."

"Why didn't Michael know about me?" she asked.

"Michael wasn't as important as he thought he was. Unfortunately, the way things shook out set up a situation where he had control.

Once I realized the probabilities, I cast him aside. The others agreed."

"How long did you manipulate the situation?" she asked.

"Manipulating is such a nasty word," Chamuel said, then winked.

Lisha checked on the results of the tests she'd left running when she went to visit Weasel, made sure nothing was out of the ordinary, then checked her watch. She should have met Leon fifteen minutes earlier. He would understand; he always did. The man was kind of clueless, but Chamuel said it was important to keep him close, so she did.

She decided she had a few more minutes and went to the rear of the lab. Like her old facility, the rear of the lab was designed for biological contaminants and specimens. Also like before, it held more than met the eye.

She flipped the light switch and the three infected howled and gnashed their teeth, beating at the armored plastic to get at her. She went over to verify that the wireless transmitters were still attached to the probes in their brains. The Februus Device had worked perfectly on them, shutting them down so she could surgically insert the sensors deep into their cerebellums. Afterwards, she'd placed a miniscule amount of contaminated flesh in their mouths. The speed with which they reactivated was, for lack of a better word, astonishing. A total of 5.2 seconds to come alive.

She'd timed the second reactivation at 4.9 seconds, and the third at 5.1 seconds. "Amazing." She decided to let Colonel Sleg know she needed more specimens. His US Navy scholarship was paid for by a Project Genesis grant. A potential future Michael.

He could only get her so many at a time. Bringing up more than a couple was obvious and a bit dangerous to his men, which was the reason she needed Weasel to concentrate on developing a portable Februus Device. Next to the three active zombies was a rack of instruments dutifully feeding data from their brains into the supercomputer. She knew it might take years to decode Pandora's internal dialogue, but she'd get it.

There were two more containment cells. One was empty, available for her next experiment. The last held a solitary figure. He was tall, muscular, and lean. He was in his fifties yet still in peak physical condition. He was naked from the waist up, only wearing dark pants and combat boots. He stood perfectly at attention, eyes looking forward, not responding to any stimulus. Like the other three, he had probes in his brain, but these fed stimuli in addition to reading EEG data.

Lisha tapped the glass in front of his face. There was no response. She nodded and picked up a tablet, making some notes and reading the results. Ninety-six hours and not a twitch. Motion sensitive cameras were watching and confirmed.

"Excellent."

She went to a table and picked up a handgun. She disliked the devices; however, she wasn't beyond using the right tool for the job. Standing as far from the case as she could get, Lisha tapped the release button, and the case opened. No response. Good. Next.

"Forward one step," she said. The figure instantly obeyed.

A smile cracked her face. "Face left." He turned in a precise military about face. "Go to the table in front of you." He did. "Pick up the gun."

A weapon identical to the one she held rested there. He scooped it up and held it at his side, finger off the trigger. She'd realized all the residual data was still in the brain shortly after beginning these rounds of experiments. At least, all the movements and motor reflexes. She'd started giving instructions and was surprised to find they worked. They could learn.

"Raise the gun and point it at me." He complied immediately. "Shoot me." The finger went to the trigger but didn't pull it. "I said shoot me." There might have been the barest twitch. She was too far away to be sure. "Shoot me!" she yelled and raised her own gun and pointed it at him. There was a twitch this time, though only a little, but the trigger didn't move.

"Put the weapon back and get in your cell." A couple of seconds later, she secured the door. Her breath was a little short as she retrieved the other gun and put the two away. The one she'd let the zombie pick up was unloaded; hers was not. She was relatively confident in the conditioning process, but not confident enough to needlessly risk her life.

"Still, not bad," she said and made some more notes. "Might be time to try another." She grinned. Imagine the prospect of an army of such workers, all laboring tirelessly for hours, days on end. Pandora had made their bodies into machines. As long as they were in fit shape before the transformation, or maybe she could take them before using the Februus Device and condition their bodies with training. She made even more notes.

Her watch beeped. She was 30 minutes late now. Time to go. She didn't want Leon mad, just annoyed, as Chamuel had said. By now, Gregory should have gotten to Leon and begun the process of getting the General to agree to defend the Heptagon. Gregory would be sure to make a good show of the trial, all the while ensuring that they didn't get more than community service. "A lifetime of helping humanity atone for their sins." Lisha liked the sound of that.

She put the tablet in its charging cradle and turned to go. The soldier was standing at attention, just as she'd found him. The scar on his chest was completely healed, thanks to Pandora. She tapped the glass. "At ease, Michael. We'll do some more work tomorrow." She turned the lights off on the way out. It had been surprisingly easy to reanimate Michael. The process held fascinating possibilities, and the behavioral conditioning was working. *Excellent.*

As she headed for the ball field, she was humming a tune. "To Everything There is a Season" by The Byrds. It had always been one of her favorite songs.

#####

## ABOUT THE AUTHOR

Living life as a full-time RV traveler with his wife Joy, Mark Wandrey is a bestselling author who has been creating new worlds since he was old enough to write. A three-time Dragon Award finalist, Mark has written dozens of books and short stories, and is working on more all the time. A prolific world builder, he created the wildly popular Four Horsemen Universe as well as the Earth Song series, and Turning Point, a zombie apocalypse series. His favorite medium is military sci-fi, but he is always up to a new challenge.

Find his books on Amazon at https://www.amazon.com/Mark-Wandrey/e/B00914T11A/

Sign up on his mailing list and get free stuff and updates! http://www.worldmaker.us/news-flash-sign-up-page/

*****

The following is an

**Excerpt from Book One of the Earth Song Cycle:**

# Overture

---

# Mark Wandrey

Now Available from Theogony Books

eBook and Paperback

**Excerpt from "Overture:"**

Dawn was still an hour away as Mindy Channely opened the roof access and stared in surprise at the crowd already assembled there. "Authorized Personnel Only" was printed in bold red letters on the door through which she and her husband, Jake, slipped onto the wide roof.

A few people standing nearby took notice of their arrival. Most had no reaction, a few nodded, and a couple waved tentatively. Mindy looked over the skyline of Portland and instinctively oriented herself before glancing to the east. The sky had an unnatural glow that had been growing steadily for hours, and as they watched, scintillating streamers of blue, white, and green radiated over the mountains like a strange, concentrated aurora borealis.

"You almost missed it," one man said. She let the door close, but saw someone had left a brick to keep it from closing completely. Mindy turned and saw the man who had spoken wore a security guard uniform. The easy access to the building made more sense.

"Ain't no one missin' this!" a drunk man slurred.

"We figured most people fled to the hills over the past week," Jake replied.

"I guess we were wrong," Mindy said.

"Might as well enjoy the show," the guard said and offered them a huge, hand-rolled cigarette that didn't smell like tobacco. She waved it off, and the two men shrugged before taking a puff.

"Here it comes!" someone yelled. Mindy looked to the east. There was a bright light coming over the Cascade Mountains, so intense it was like looking at a welder's torch. Asteroid LM-245 hit the atmosphere at over 300 miles per second. It seemed to move faster and faster, from east to west, and the people lifted their hands to shield their eyes from the blinding light. It looked like a blazing comet or a science fiction laser blast.

"Maybe it will just pass over," someone said in a voice full of hope.

Mindy shook her head. She'd studied the asteroid's track many times.

In a matter of a few seconds, it shot by and fell toward the western horizon, disappearing below the mountains between Portland and the ocean. Out of view of the city, it slammed into the ocean.

The impact was unimaginable. The air around the hypersonic projectile turned to superheated plasma, creating a shockwave that generated 10 times the energy of the largest nuclear weapon ever detonated as it hit the ocean's surface.

The kinetic energy was more than 1,000 megatons; however, the object didn't slow as it flashed through a half mile of ocean and into the sea bed, then into the mantel, and beyond.

On the surface, the blast effect appeared as a thermal flash brighter than the sun. Everyone on the rooftop watched with wide-eyed terror as the Tualatin Mountains between Portland and the Pacific Ocean were outlined in blinding light. As the light began to dissipate, the outline of the mountains blurred as a dense bank of smoke climbed from the western range.

The flash had incinerated everything on the other side.

The physical blast, travelling much faster than any normal atmospheric shockwave, hit the mountains and tore them from the bedrock, adding them to the rolling wave of destruction traveling east at several thousand miles per hour. The people on the rooftops of Portland only had two seconds before the entire city was wiped away.

Ten seconds later, the asteroid reached the core of the planet, and another dozen seconds after that, the Earth's fate was sealed.

*****

Get "Overture" now at:
https://www.amazon.com/dp/B077YMLRHM/

Find out more about Mark Wandrey and the Earth Song Cycle at:
https://chriskennedypublishing.com/

*****

The following is an

**Excerpt from Surviving the Fall:**

# Surviving the Fall

---

## Eric S. Brown

Available Now from Blood Moon Press

eBook and Paperback

**Excerpt from "Surviving the Fall:"**

Of late, the number of dead wandering up to Sheehan's gates had been steadily decreasing. Joseph liked to think the monsters were dying off. The virus that reanimated the creatures vastly slowed their normal rate of decay, but the dead still rotted. Nothing could stop nature from taking its course. She was a bitch like that. A more likely explanation was that something out there was killing the monsters off and clearing them out of the region. To him, that was a sure sign Rapier's people were coming. It was just a matter of time.

"Yo, man!" Mike snapped at him. "You paying attention or what?"

Joseph's head snapped around to glare at Nick. He wasn't keen on someone who was as much a slacker as Mike was calling him out on losing his focus for a moment—but then a moment was sometimes all it took.

Mike was pointing out along the road that led to Sheehan's gates. A man dressed in a flowing black cloak was walking down it toward the town.

"Frag me!" Joseph muttered, bringing his rifle up to brace it against his shoulder and take aim at the approaching figure. Apparently none of the other snipers on watch had noticed the man, either. He'd just come out of nowhere on the road. That struck Joseph as odd. He knew Henson was leading the watch tonight, and that guy never missed *anything.*

"Stop where you are!" Henson's voice rang out.

The man in the black cloak was almost through the main kill zone and to the gates when Henson called out. He paused, though, throwing back the hood that obscured the features of his face.

One of the spearmen nearby turned on the powerful searchlight that had been mounted atop the wall. Its beam fell over the man like a spotlight upon an actor on a stage. Joseph could swear the man was smiling despite the rifles aimed at him.

"Identify yourself!" Henson yelled.

"As you wish," the man answered. His voice didn't seem to be raised, but somehow Joseph still heard his words clear as day.

"I am called Hammer." The man grinned. "I come to you in the name of my lord, Rapier, to offer you protection from the dead and to bid you and yours to lay down your arms and allow us entrance into the community you've worked so hard to establish in this land of horrors."

"Look sharp," Mike urged Joseph. "There must be others with him."

Joseph's eyes scanned the woods at the far end of the road through the scope of his rifle, but all he could see were trees and shadows. If this Hammer had brought others with him, they were well hidden, and staying that way for the moment.

"Is that so?" Henson snapped at the man on the road. "Well, you can tell your lord Rapier that the good people of this town don't want any trouble, but we're doing just fine on our own. Thanks. Now I strongly suggest you turn around and head back to wherever you came from. Some of my boys up here have got itchy trigger fingers, if you take my meaning, Mr. Hammer. I'd hate to see anything untoward happen to you."

"I'm afraid that's not an answer I can accept." Hammer frowned. "Seeing as you've refused Lord Rapier's generous offer, you leave with me with no choice but to annex your town in order to ensure the safety of the city of Augur's southern border. I will, however, give you one more chance to open your gates so things may proceed in a peaceable manner."

"Go frag yourself!" one of the spearman yelled before Henson could reply.

"So be it." Hammer shrugged and snapped his fingers.

*****



*****

Made in the USA
Middletown, DE
09 January 2024